Best Wishes
& God Bless

Troy E. Peterson

Isaiah 40:31

PLATORO
THE SUMMER RANGE

Trouble and adventure awaited them around every bend.

★★★★★

Troy Everett Peterson

Copyright © 2020 Troy Everett Peterson.

All rights reserved. No part of this book may be reproduced, stored, or transmitted by any means—whether auditory, graphic, mechanical, or electronic—without written permission of the author, except in the case of brief excerpts used in critical articles and reviews. Unauthorized reproduction of any part of this work is illegal and is punishable by law.

ISBN: 978-1-7168-2335-0 (sc)
ISBN: 978-1-7168-2333-6 (e)

Library of Congress Control Number: 2020911531

Because of the dynamic nature of the Internet, any web addresses or links contained in this book may have changed since publication and may no longer be valid. The views expressed in this work are solely those of the author and do not necessarily reflect the views of the publisher, and the publisher hereby disclaims any responsibility for them.

Any people depicted in stock imagery provided by Getty Images are models, and such images are being used for illustrative purposes only.
Certain stock imagery © Getty Images.

Scripture taken from the King James Version of the Bible.

Lulu Publishing Services rev. date: 12/22/2020

Contents

What Others Are Saying vii
Dedication ix
Acknowledgements xi
Map xiii
Prologue xv

Canyon of the Witches 1
Chama 10
Alamosa 22
The Golden Willow at Las Mesitas 35
The New Foreman 43
The Church Picnic 56
Headed for the Summer Range 65
Making Fox Creek 71
Rockslide 78
Elk Creek 84
Silver Top 88
A Life Changing Decision 94
Flash Flood 101
Attacked 107
Making the Lake Fork 114
The Summer Range 120
Platoro 128
Red Mountain 134
Lost on Mammoth Mountain 139
Independence Day Celebration 145
Silver Top's Revenge 157

The Dangerous Toll Road	170
Ambush Along the Del Norte Trail	180
Rustler's Lair	190
Three Forks and Blue Lake	197
Tracking A Killer	206
Surrounded	221
Hot Pursuit	229
The Return of Silver Top	237
The Home Coming	247
Unexpected News	257
Steps to Salvation	265
Bibliography	267
About the Author	269

What Others Are Saying

"In the style of Louis L'Amour and Zane Grey, Troy Peterson has entered into authorship of the Western genre in a way that captivates every reader. Troy's writing style is refreshing, wholesome, and creative. With a unique style and focus, his works will rise to the top." -Del Shields, Western Music Singer/Songwriter/Cowboy Poet/Co-Host of the television show "Best of America by Horseback"

"A well-told, fast paced novel packed with excitement and tension." -Madge Harrah – Spur Award Winner (Western Writers of America)

"A real pleasure to read. The story line and characters were very well developed and believable. I couldn't put it down." -F. D. Kisor

"As an avid reader of Westerns this book ranks as one of my all-time favorites. A very refreshing read." -Dr. Fred Krusekopf

"What a wonderful and exciting story. I fell in love with the characters. The book made my soul sing! A magnificent novel." -Carolyn Gorman

"A real page turner from the first to the last word. Definitely a God-given talent displayed in a wonderful story." -S. L. Beasley

"As an avid reader and collector of Western novels, I genuinely loved this book. Thanks for taking me along to an era and place I would have loved to live in. Better than Louis L'Amour in my opinion." -Steve Benavidez

Dedication

To my parents, Bob and Dixie, for years of sacrifice and unwavering example of faith. You have been and always will be a guiding light.

Also, to Don and Miss Mary, Larry and Madge, Dan and Katherine, with fond memories.

Acknowledgements

This book is the result of two decades of prayer, much research, and countless hours of attention to content detail and plot development in order to make this story as true to life and historically accurate as possible.

Platoro, The Summer Range, was inspired by such ranches as the H. B. McNeil Ranch and the Marble Woods Ranch who were some of the very first outfits to run cattle in the high country for the summers around Platoro.

I would also like to acknowledge the Ruybalid family who were among the earliest residents of the San Luis Valley and the settlement of Las Mesitas, the setting that I chose for the Golden Willow Ranch. The Ruybalid family were instrumental in naming several of the geographic regions mentioned in this book and some even bear their name's sake.

This work could not have happened without the help of family and friends and others who stepped into my life at critical moments to provide inspiration, historical and structural criticism, and typing and editing services.

Many gave of their time including and especially my very capable editor, Mary Otero, who typed and edited every page in spite of many other responsibilities. I would also like to thank Dixie Peterson for her input and advice; Bob Peterson for running to get paper, ink, and correction tape; and Tron Peterson for helping to develop the pre-production of the book, layout, and cover before going to the publishing process.

I would also like to thank all my Platoro friends and neighbors who pointed me to various books, notes, and legends of local history.

I would also like to acknowledge the staffs at the Ghost Ranch, Palo

Duro Canyon, Fort Garland, and other historical sites who gave me access and direction at one time or another within the process.

    All glory be to God who gives me strength and inspiration. He has delivered me from a lifetime of debilitating chronic Lyme disease and fatigue, years of inability to hold down food, and many other issues of chronic illness, and He continues to deliver me. I praise Him for the burdens He has lifted from me and the ones He has yet to and will. What illness has robbed from me; God is redeeming. What life has broken in me; God is renewing. Isaiah 40:31

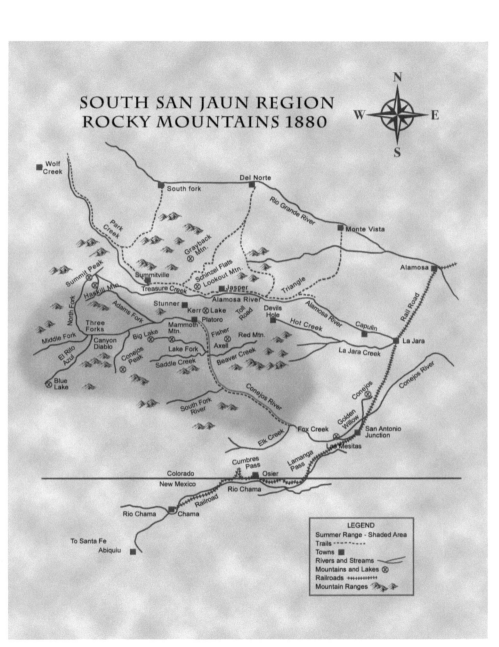

Prologue

> "WE WILL BE KNOWN FOREVER BY
> THE TRACKS WE LEAVE."
>
> -DAKOTA SIOUX

James Morris Fenamore's first murder had been surprisingly easy. He looked around then up to the heavens. No one had seen him. He quickly stuffed the stolen items into his saddlebag, mounted his horse, then rode away, confident his sins would never find him out.

The family's name had been Harden. They had been traveling alone and unarmed when he had come upon them. He had left not one of them alive to know of his deeds...or so he thought. But God did see and so did another, and although twenty years had now passed since that terrible day, neither one had forgotten.

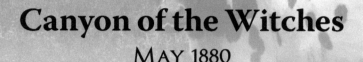

Canyon of the Witches
May 1880

"Yea, though I walk through the valley
of the shadow of death, I will fear
no evil; for thou art with me..."

PSALM 23:4

The rain pattered softly on the sod roof of Cordova's Cantina and streaked down the dusty windows in crooked trails. Inside, four gunmen sat in a dimly lit corner passing a bottle of rye whiskey. They waited anxiously as random flashes of lightning cast soft strobes of light upon the gray stucco walls and across their calloused faces.

The sharp clip-clop of iron-shod hooves drew up outside. A figure passed by the window. Soon the latch on the door lifted, and it swung open. In the doorway loomed a tall, gray-haired man with weathered face wearing a cowboy hat and a long oilskin slicker. A cattleman's carbine tilted downward in his left hand. The man shut the door against the rain and stood dripping for a moment as his eyes swept the room. His spurred boots jingled as he approached their table.

"Let's get this over with," he grumbled. His tone was steady and authoritative as that of a man used to power. The man's right hand disappeared inside his slicker for an instant then emerged holding four envelopes; one for each of them.

One of them opened his envelope and fingered through its contents. "This is a lot of money. What exactly do you want us to do?"

The man wearing the slicker pulled a metal flask from his pocket, took a drink, and wiped his mouth with the back of his hand. "I sent for you fellas because you're some of the best there is when it comes to huntin' men. There's a man named Cole Harden carrying incriminating dispatches about me. I want him stopped before he reaches Judge Parker in Alamosa."

One of the others leaned and spit on the floor. "And you figure it'll take four of us to do it?"

"I figure at least that. Harden ain't just some drifter or cattle tramp. He's a war hero and a legend to boot. Governor Lew Wallace himself hand picked him to make the trip. Now, Harden's done left sometime this morning, and he'll probably take to that ghostie country around Abiquiu called the Canyon of the Witches."

The man reached beneath his slicker once again and pulled out a paper. "You'll need this," he said, handing it to one of the men. "It's an old rustlers' map showing how to get through the canyons."

"They say that stretch of country is haunted by spirits," one of the men said, "guarded by brujos, Navajo witch doctors. Men go in there but never come out. Are you sure Harden's taken to that route?"

"I'm sure of it," the man said. "You fellas best get goin' cause time's awastin', and if any of you are thinkin' he's gonna be an easy target, then you got another thing comin'." The man turned and walked out the door. The others followed shortly after, like men with a purpose.

After leaving Santa Fe, Cole Harden held to a secret route northeast of Abiquiu with the foreboding sense he was being followed. He rode alongside a tall, red mesa known as Kitchen Mesa and past a couple of towering hoodoos that stood vigil over a dry, red-pigmented landscape that led into a desolate labyrinth of meandering fissures, twisted monoliths, and massive alcoved walls above immense stone slabs and crumbled heaps of talus. This area was known as the Canyons of the Witches; a place rumored to be littered with the bones of ancient beasts and men who had entered but had never made it out. He chose his way, carefully following a map he had been given.

Cole directed his buckskin up through a jumbled mass of boulders and twisted scrub pine until he came to the edge of a deep box canyon. At first look, it appeared to be a dead end. He turned in his saddle and observed his back trail. The sudden flight of birds, some two hundred yards behind, caught his attention. As he suspected, he was being followed. He found himself with a dilemma; he could turn back now and face his pursuers, or he could find a way forward.

He gave the canyon another look. Its colorful walls spanned over a mile in length and descended more than a hundred feet in depth. Above him a large, buttressed cliff jutted out over the edge of the rim nearly the entire length of the canyon.

Just under the overhang of the cliff, there appeared to be a narrow ledge of loose shale that stretched the length of the rim. The ledge's face was punctuated by large broken slabs and weathered ruins of cliff wall. Cole stepped from his horse and climbed up to the ledge to check it out. It looked narrow and unstable.

He slid back down the slope and took the bridle reins to steady the horse. He unfastened and pulled up the latigo, gave it a couple of hard tugs, and refastened it. He tightened the back cinch then stepped back up and sat his horse once again. Without further thought, he put the buckskin forward onto the crumbled ledge.

Having a full rein, the horse stepped one foot then the other along the sliding shelf. Each hoof sank into the loose shale displacing broken shards of rock, causing them to grate and tumble down the hillside to the canyon floor below. The buckskin lunged and scrambled to keep its footing. There was no turning back now.

"Easy, Chief," Cole coaxed. He glanced down at the depths below, and his heart beat within his chest like it wanted out. Just one misstep would surely mean a fall to their death. He gripped the horn and the cantle of his saddle and leaned into the hillside, praying all the while.

Upon passing some fifty feet of ledge, there was a strengthening of the breeze within the cliffs followed by a marmot's piercing warning from the adjacent rocks. Cole searched for the source of the animal's vexing calls. No one in their right mind would follow along such a treacherous path.

A thundering blast shattered the solitude as a bullet tore through Chief's shoulder causing him to lose his footing. Cole found himself and the horse tumbling down the side of the canyon until his body folded around the trunk of a pinon near the bottom, knocking him unconscious.

How long he was unconscious, he didn't know, but when he awoke, his body ached, and the hot New Mexico sun blazed down from a hand's width above the cliffs. Cole raised his head with a painful groan, sat up and looked about. He was bleeding from cuts to his arms, legs, and forehead. His horse lay motionless a few feet away. It's chest neither rose nor fell.

Cole crawled over and placed his hand on its body. The life that once gleamed from his clear brown eyes had already been replaced by the milky gray shadow of death. His heart flooded with sadness though there was no time now to grieve.

He opened the flap on the saddlebag and reached for the satchel containing the dispatches. To his relief, it was still there. Turning his attention to the saddle, he unfastened the cinch strap, rolled the horse over and stripped the saddle along with his bedroll, saddlebag, and scabbard, then hurried back to the cover of the pinon. As he did so, a bullet zipped by his shoulder.

Positioning his saddle in front like a shield, Cole unbuckled his scabbard and slipped out his rifle. He pointed his barrel toward the canyon rim and squinted, trying to locate the shooter. Someone was still hiding in the rimrock above, watching as a hawk watches a rabbit hoping to flush him out. He was no rabbit, though. He was not so vulnerable.

Cole checked his rifle, opening the breech with the half cock of the lever, then slid the action back in place. A shell rested in the chamber.

He lay still for some time. After a long spell, he stretched out his cramped legs. As he did so another shot shattered the silence. Instantly a bullet tore through his britches, grazing the skin of his right leg.

He pointed his rifle toward the rim again straining his tired eyes for the slightest detail that might give away the shooter's position. A brief flash of sunlight reflecting on metal winked from the heights. A moment later it happened again in the same location. A man with a rifle was hiding between the two gnarled pines.

Once again, he wiped the sweat from his eyes and aimed carefully at the base of the pine where he had seen the flash of light. He took in a half breath then slowly squeezed the trigger. At the rifle's recoil, the shooter fell backwards out of sight.

A volley of shots followed from farther along the rim, scattering sand and rock all around him. As he figured, there were others, at least two more. A long period of silence followed.

Cole waited as the sun continued to beat down on his face and cracked lips with little mercy. He tipped up his canteen and managed only a few drops. He shook the vessel and tapped it but got nothing for his efforts.

Water was scarce in this land of painted rocks and rattlesnakes. Only an experienced Army scout like himself could find it if it was to be found at all. He knew that he had come here for such reasons. It was raw looking country that appeared as though it had been clawed out and forgotten. This desolate route had been his plan though he hadn't figured on being afoot.

He was also well aware that most men were scared to come into these parts because of the stories. Fugitives and cattle rustlers had made these canyons a hideaway for stolen cattle and loot, and they often killed anyone who stumbled upon their secret. They spread stories of evil brujos, Indian witches who guarded the canyons, conjured spells, and summoned evil spirits. That is why the Spanish had named these parts Canyon de los Brujos, the Canyon of the Witches. Cole knew the brujos were a real threat, but their powers held no hold over him or his God. However, the violent history of the place did spook him a bit, considering that he had already come upon a human skull and a scattering of picked over bones not far back.

Unlike others who came here as fugitives of the law, he had been chosen by Governor Lew Wallace of New Mexico to deliver important dispatches to Judge Parker in Alamosa, Colorado at the Judge's request. Now it was obvious that someone had sent men to stop him. It was moments like this that made him glad that this would be his last mission before retiring from the military.

From where Cole lay, he had a good view of the canyon wall. The men who followed him would be foolish to try to descend it in the daylight. Instead they would wait until dark at the rising of the full moon, and so he waited, also.

As evening approached, the burning sun dropped behind the rim causing a lilac sky. Before long, darkness enfolded the canyon below. Cole watched as the sky transformed into a slate black expanse crowded with newborn stars. As he waited for his pursuers to make the first move, he ate some jerked beef and a biscuit.

The night air had already cooled significantly. He unfasted the wool blanket from his saddle and wrapped it around his shoulders. There would be no warm fire again tonight.

The first hour of darkness was eerily quiet. After a time, he heard a vague stirring in the darkness, and his mind turned to the ghostie stories of this place, and he wondered as to their truth. What if a brujo had heard the shots and was now slipping in on him? His eyes sought the darkness where shadows were appearing among the rocks, pinon, and brush. Cole moved his right hand to touch his pistol. Its presence was reassuring.

The silence was soon broken by the sound of tumbling rocks which shattered on a ledge high above. The rolling rocks could have been sent in motion by a cougar or deer, but he didn't think so. This was a dry, harsh environment that offered no sign of tracks. This time it was most likely men who caused the commotion, and they were closing in.

He grabbed his saddle and moved down the gully below him until it opened into a long sandy arroyo. He found a cut bank and crawled beneath it where he had a better view in the dim light.

Before long, Cole could hear his pursuers' horses as they clumsily made their way down. He pointed his rifle in that direction and waited for them to show themselves. The moon had risen higher into the night sky and was now spilling its light upon the base of the cut bank where he was hiding. He moved deeper into the moon's shadow. All but his boots were now hidden.

One of the men who had been coming down split off from the other and circled around to a ledge not far above Cole. As he looked around his eyes searched every shape and shadow until he finally spotted Cole's boots sticking out from beneath the cut bank. He crept closer, moving to his right until he finally reached a position just feet away from Cole. He peeked around a large boulder. Harden was still there.

He raised his gun and stepped around the boulder. A puzzled look settled upon his face. He was staring only at a pair of empty boots.

Instantly he felt the cold steel muzzle of a pistol press against his flesh behind his right ear. Like most men before him, he had underestimated Cole Harden, and in doing so he had made a deadly mistake.

"I'll take that gun," Cole said, wrenching the rifle from the man's hands. "Keep your hands up where I can see them." He took the man's pistol from its holster then proceeded to search his clothes for weapons.

Cole jerked a second pistol from inside the man's jacket. Once confident there were no more weapons, he flung all the guns into a deep crack in the rocks, then proceeded to slip on his boots.

"How'd you know I was comin'?" the man asked.

"I heard you on the rocks and could smell you on the breeze."

Cole took a closer look at the man's face but didn't recognize him. "Who are you, and why are you after me?"

The man hesitated, then finally answered. "My name's Randall Bowdry. A man named Lassiter hired us to see you don't make it to Alamosa."

Cole recognized the name, Bowdry, but not the other. "Who do you have with you?" he questioned.

This time the man didn't answer. Cole pressed the pistol against the man's flesh and thumbed back the hammer.

"My brothers, Bill and Ben. Bill's dead up top."

"Randall? Where you at?" a voice called from the dark.

"Tell him to come on over," Cole said, pressing his gun again.

"Over here," Randall hollered.

Seconds later, a man led three horses out of the crevasse and into the moonlight. Cole stepped from the shadows holding Randall Bowdry at gun point.

"Tarnation," the man said when he realized the situation. He started for his gun, but Randall stopped him.

"Don't be a fool, Ben. He'll kill me."

The man lifted his hands away from his pistol. "What now?" he said.

Cole pointed. "Take off your guns and drop them in that crack over yonder."

The man unfastened his belt and walked over to the edge. "Down there?"

"You heard me. Drop 'em," Cole said. The man did as he was told.

"I'm gonna need your horses, too."

"You can't leave us out here without our horses, we'll die." The man cursed. "And besides, we've heard stories about this place. Without our horses, we'll be easy pickins' for the Brujos. They'll catch us and blow corpse powder in our faces, and we'll get the ghost sickness. They say it's a terrible way to die."

"You should have thought of that when you came after me. I figure leavin' you afoot is better'n leavin' you dead, Brujos or not."

Cole tied the horses in a train, put his saddle on the paint horse, then climbed on.

"Don't come lookin' for me, or I'll kill you."

"Darn your hide, Harden. Without horses and water, we're as good as dead, and you know it," the other shouted.

"There's a little water back at Blind Pony Flats. I suggest you head that way before it dries up."

"That's near twenty miles back," the man said.

Cole nodded, "That's the life of an outlaw."

"Graham Lassiter ain't gonna let you get to Alamosa," Randall Bowdry spat. "There's others sides us been paid to stop you from reachin' the judge with those dispatches you're carryin'. You shouldn't have got involved in affairs that weren't your own."

Cole ignored the warning, clicked his tongue, and nudged the paint forward with the other two horses in tow. He rode all night with the moon behind him and the smell of sage in the breeze upon his face and didn't stop until the sky paled in the east and offered contrast against the Sangre De Cristos in the far distance.

When he reached a small grove of pinon he stepped from his horse and led them back inside to a sandy clearing about thirty feet wide. He untied the lot and led them each to their own space and half hitched them separately by their lead ropes where they could crop what little sprigs of grass grew around their feet.

Cole examined the contents of each saddle bag and took stock of his supplies. In the first he found a half full canteen. He drank from it just enough then portioned the rest between the three horses.

He dug around some more and found smokes, tobacco, and a box of matches that said Bulworth on the side. He stuffed the matches in his pocket and checked the second bag. There he found some dried beef, a small can of Arbuckle coffee, some dried beans, a slab of cured bacon wrapped in waxed paper, and a biscuit. In the last bag, he found a near empty bottle of whiskey and a good amount of rope as well as a box of .45 cartridges and an old cooking pan.

Cole built a small fire from a dead cholla and took some strips of bacon and wrapped them around a stick and set it to cook on the fire. When the bacon was crispy, he let it cool, then ate. Afterwards, he stretched out on the bare ground in the shade and fell asleep. When he awoke, it was noon and the sun was straight overhead and hot.

He tied the horses in a train again then sat the paint. Cole reined the horse around and proceeded northeast toward the distant mountains. An hour later they appeared no closer. He would have to find more water soon or risk severe dehydration.

Before him lay a terrain no different than the country he had just quit: a vast sea of sand dotted sparingly by desperate stands of sage, pinon, and cholla. The landscape offered little hope for water, but if it was there to be had, he would find it. By and by he came to a small waterhole bearing no tracks. He stepped down from the paint and cupped a handful of the stagnant looking liquid to his nose and smelled it. The water was alkali and would be poison to drink.

He traveled north into the late afternoon following the faint impression of old wagon tracks until they finally ended. Nearby lay four rusty wagon wheels and some old weathered boards.

Cole sat his horse a moment, the sun warm on his back. A dust devil twirled around up ahead snatching up blades of dry grass and red dust high into the air. Higher still, a buzzard rode the wind currents in broad half circles. He wondered if it could see water.

He rode to a crest looking north. There was still no sign of water. He continued in the direction of the San Juans. The air between him and the mountains shimmered quietly in the heat. By now his horses were dead beat.

Chama

Cole continued his search for water with the knowledge he had learned from his experience up on the Llano when, as a major in the 4th Cavalry, soldier's lives had depended on him for survival.

There he had found playa lakes: small indentions in the land that collected moisture. Here there were none, just rolling hills of sand and gravel with an occasional clump of sage or cholla cactus mingled with a few salt cedars.

Cole led the horses up a hill and to a crest overlooking a dry gulch. A horned toad scurried off in front of him headed in the direction of the gulch, and so he followed it. He directed the horses down a cut bank and into a gully, following it for some time until he finally came to where it forked.

He took the left fork and followed it into a dry basin until he finally came upon some willows. Willows, he knew, were a good sign that at one time or another there had been water here and so he continued onward.

After cresting another hill, he saw in the distance a green valley with a river lined with mature cottonwoods which he figured to be the Rio Chama. At the sight of it, the horses began to stamp their feet and nicker with anticipation. Upon reaching the river, he led them down to the water and unhitched their ropes. He stood his horse a moment and let it suck in the cool flow.

Cole stepped down and walked a ways upstream of the horses. He cupped his hand into the flow, passed it over his face and raised another to drink.

PLATORO THE SUMMER RANGE

The horses waded farther out into the river and drank some more, occasionally lifting their heads to cough and breath as they cleared their lungs of dust from the trail. Before they could drink themselves sick, he waded in and led them from the water where they quickly found the lush grasses which grew along the bank.

As far as he could tell he was still in northern New Mexico. His hunch was that the little village of Chama was not far. His plan was to follow the river there in the morning, get a hot bath, a comfortable bed, and a hot meal.

As evening approached, he led the horses farther back away from the river. Cole took the ropes and staked each horse separately. He then stripped their gear and rubbed them down with handfuls of grass.

Cole found a good flat spot, untied his bedroll, and spread it upon the ground. When it became dark, he built a small fire for warmth. He took up his King James Bible that had been his father's and opened it to where he kept a picture.

He took out the picture and studied it as he often did. It was a photograph of his family as they had been twenty years ago, just before they had all been murdered.

The picture brought back many treasured memories and emotions. His family had been very close. They had worked the fields around the little community of Nashville, Missouri together, with mules and plow, and fished for bull head catfish with cane poles along the banks of the Little North Fork Creek. There had also been wonderful Sunday dinners with his Ma, Rose Harden's chicken and noodles and Papa David's fiddle playin'.

Those special times had ended when someone robbed and killed his father and mother as well as his little brother, John Andrew. His sister, Lauren Rose, had been taken and no doubt, killed as well. He had never seen or heard from her again. Cole vowed that awful day that he would see the killer brought to justice, but to this day there had been no answers.

He slipped the picture back into its place and began to read from the first chapter of the book of Psalms. "Blessed is the man that walketh not in the counsel of the ungodly, nor standeth in the way of sinners, nor sitteth in the seat of the scornful. But his delight is in the law of the

Lord; and in his law doth he meditate day and night. And he shall be like a tree planted by rivers of water, that bringeth forth his fruit in his season; his leaf shall not wither; and whatsoever he doeth shall prosper."

He looked around at the ancient cottonwoods that towered above him; some so big it would take two men to reach around their girth. They were true examples of what the Psalmist had in mind.

Cole fed more wood to the fire and coaxed the flames higher to abate the chill night air. He pondered the scriptures as he read. To be without God was to be a tree with neither root nor branch. What a sadness that would be.

The firelight danced on the huge trunks. The bats were now out, darting and swooping as they fed on insects. In the distance, he could hear the gentle flow of the river and the sound of the horses cropping the grass and chewing it.

He thought about the documents he was carrying. This would be his last mission for the government. He was looking forward to retiring from the military and working for a Brand or starting his own ranch.

As Cole read some more scripture, he remembered back to the time when, as a boy, he had given his life to Jesus. It was during a revival at the little country church in Nashville, Missouri. Brother Tom Marsh baptized him in Flaker's Creek to the north of town, and his wife, Lenora, had led in the singing of the sacred hymns. Cole continued to read from his Bible until his eyelids grew drowsy, and he could no longer stay awake.

The next morning the sun broke over the hills and shone bright in his face causing him to blink as the light fell across his eyes. A lively bluebird lit in the bushes nearby. Cole watched at the quivering and swelling of its throat as it opened its beak in song.

High above, a raven flew to the west giving slow, mournful caws as it went on its way to parts unknown. Yellow dandelions spread out along the riverbanks like a tapestry. Their golden petals spread open in the sunlight, but in the shade, they had not yet opened. Four-wing saltbush and sage also added to the beauty. Cole's breath escaped in white puffs as he exhaled in the brisk air.

He rubbed his jaw and the stubble that grew from his face. Checking his pistol and his Winchester rifle, he found they were clean, loaded,

and ready. He swung his gun belt ar
third notch.

The warming of the morning su
fog to rise and settle over the river.
Arbuckle coffee from the sorrel's sad
to blow life into its seething ashes.
brought them back to life. He sat h
cooked his bacon draped over a sti
rocks. A hungry whiskey-jack flitte
hopped closer, hoping for a crumb.

After breakfast and some coffee, he bathed and cleaned his wounds. He also scrubbed his clothes as well, hanging them on the willows to dry in the breeze. When they had dried, he put them back on and headed for Chama.

Topping a hill, in the distance he saw the village of Chama. Upon reaching the bottom of the hill, he turned the horses onto the wagon road that led to the little town and followed it north until he reached its edge.

Chama appeared to be typical of small western towns in that it wasn't very old. His first impression was that it held an atmosphere of coming prosperity and seemed to bustle with a sense of urgency.

Cole noticed a large banner that spanned the main street in front of a new looking boarding house. The banner read: "Welcome, San Juan Train and Denver Rio Grande Railroad." Off to the side, two children chased each other around a wagon, screaming with laughter.

The street was rough and uneven, with deep ruts cut by wagons during the spring thaw which had now hardened under the sun. The road clopped loudly beneath his horse's feet. Down the street, a man loaded a couple of burlap sacks onto his wagon. In front of the mercantile, two men stood talking.

Cole sat tall in the saddle as he rode into town. There was a countenance about him that drew respect. His quiet confidence had been well earned as a major in the Cavalry and upon the plains as a cattleman. Now in his mid-thirties, he was said by his peers to be a man who left big tracks.

As he rode along, he tipped his hat to a pretty, dark-haired young lady in a blue dress. The woman returned a courteous smile as she

...ooden steps into the mercantile. Her son followed as Cole passed.

...ced a large barn with the words "Livery" written across ...sed the street and rode over to it. He stepped from the paint ...the string of horses around back through the big double doors, ...ing for a moment as he waited for his eyes to adjust to the darkness. ...ays of sunlight slanted down through the cracks in the plank board walls illuminating the dust that stirred and lifted in the air.

Cole shut the big door behind him and led the horses to an empty set of stalls. He stripped their gear, then brushed them down. "There you go, big fella, that feels good, doesn't it?" He talked softly to the paint as he gently brushed along the horse's neck and shoulders.

As he continued grooming, he heard footsteps coming along the side of the stables. Someone was moving outside along the west wall. He could see their shadow flickering between the sunlight and the narrowly spaced boards as they made their way around to the front door.

Cole stepped behind the paint and peered over its back toward the door. He instinctively dropped his hand down to his side and rested it on the handle of his pistol. The door opened slowly with a creak. In a second, he would find out if the visitor was friend or foe.

It was a young boy who appeared in the doorway. His hair was cut neatly, and his clothes were clean. The boy's eyes lit up when he saw Cole. "Howdy, Mister. I saw you ride into town a moment ago. That's a fine horse you got there. It looks like an Indian's horse."

"Would you like to meet him, son?"

"Yes, sir, I would. I don't believe I've seen many quite like him. What's his name?"

"Well, I haven't had him long, but I'm thinkin' of calling him Comanche. What do you think of that?"

The boy smiled. "I like the name Comanche."

"My name is Cole Harden. What's yours, Son?"

"Brian Myers," the boy answered as he gently stroked Comanche's velvety soft nose. "We have a ranch north of here in Colorado near Las Mesitas. My mother and I took the new train here from San Antonio Junction."

"That's a far piece."

The boy shrugged. "Ma's twenty-seven, and I just turned nine. She carries a derringer in her purse, and she's a fine shot. I am, too. We can take care of ourselves pretty good." The boy continued to stroke Comanche's nose and face as he chattered on.

"I see you have a way with horses. They take well to a gentle touch like that."

Just then a woman's voice called from outside. "Brian? Brian Myers? Where are you?"

Brian suddenly looked guilty. He stuck his face up to a crack in the side of the barn and hollered out. "I'm in here, Ma."

Presently, a beautiful woman entered the doorway. It was the woman he had seen on the porch of the mercantile. Her auburn hair was pinned up neatly under a white bonnet, and her face was flushed pink with worry.

"Brian, what have I told you about running off without telling me where you were going? Come along now."

"Do we have to go now? I was just talking to Cole and pettin' Comanche."

The woman acknowledged Cole with a smile.

Cole tipped his hat. "How do you do, Ma'am. My name is Cole Harden."

"How do you do, Mr. Harden. I'm Brain's mother, Abigale Myers."

The lady beckoned her son with a white gloved hand. "Come along, Brian. Mr. Harden probably has things to do."

"I'm passin' through on some business, Ma'am. After that I'd like to find some steady ranch work."

Abigale took another look at Cole. He looked honest and strong. "My father owns the Golden Willow Ranch near Las Mesitas. He's always looking for good help, and he's fair. If you're interested, you might pay him a visit."

"I would like that."

The woman smiled warmly. "Thanks for taking the time to talk with my son. It was nice of you."

A loud steam whistle blew in the distance signaling that the train would soon be boarding passengers. "We should go now if we're to catch the train. I hope you find what you're looking for, Mr. Harden," she said.

Abigale turned and aimed her son across the stable, toward the door and the sunlight of the street.

"It was a pleasure to meet you, Mrs. Myers," Cole called after them.

The boy turned his head. "It's Miss Myers. She ain't married no more."

"Brian!" Abigale scolded. "Mind your manners."

Brian waved. "Good-bye, Mr. Harden. Good-bye, Comanche."

"Good-bye, Brian. Mind your ma."

After the two had left, Cole stood staring. Abigale Myers was a lovely woman. She was refined and dignified, yet there was an approachability about her. The love that she felt for her son was also obvious. Cole went back to his task of grooming the horses, but his mind was no longer on his work.

Abigale and Brian boarded the San Juan train and took a seat near the front. Abigale sat in silence as she thought about the man they had just met. He was attractive, but more importantly, though, there was kindness and sincerity behind his eyes and in his voice.

She wondered who he was and where he came from. He looked as though he had traveled far and fast. She had very little time to form any real opinions of the man. All she knew was that when he had smiled at her she felt weak in the knees. She would probably never see him again so why did he occupy her thoughts so now.

The train's whistle blew once again and soon the steel wheels began to turn as the train lurched forward. The repetitive chug of the engine became faster as it picked up speed. Abigale gazed out the window at the passing trees and the beautiful scenery. She closed her eyes and prayed, "Father God, I know you can hear me. Please bring me a man who knows you and loves you, to be my husband. A man to fill the loneliness in my heart that has been left by Keith's death. A man to raise my son in a good way. Amen."

Cole smiled at the memory of the woman standing in the doorway and the faint smell of her rose water perfume. She was so beautiful. As he was still thinking of her, someone slipped into the far end of the livery unnoticed and moved his way. Suddenly he felt the presence of another directly behind him, two stalls down.

Cole stepped behind his horse and observed the man. It was the owner of the Appaloosa, and he hadn't seen Cole. The man led his horse from the stable and disappeared down the street.

Cole walked to the boarding house. He rang the hand bell on the counter, and a Spanish man entered the room.

"What can I do for you, Señor?" he said.

"I'd like a room for tonight if one's to be had."

"Yes, I have rooms. Very comfortable. That will be one dollar."

Cole put down one silver dollar and signed the register. "Where can a fella get cleaned up around here?"

"The bath house is just past the saloon," the man pointed.

Cole raised his finger to the brim of his hat. "Thanks."

He took a hot bath then got a shave and a haircut. When he stepped back outside, he felt like a new man. Down the street, he found a brown stucco building with a sign that said "Restaurant" and walked in. He took off his hat and found a seat and sat down at a little table near the door. A lady soon came from the back and took his order. As he waited for his food, he observed his surroundings.

At a nearby table sat a man and woman with their young son. He gave them a friendly nod. "Where you folks from?"

"New York," the gentleman answered. "We're headed for California."

"I want to see an Indian," interrupted the little boy.

"Jonathan, it's impolite to interrupt while I'm talking," the man said.

The woman's cheeks flushed with embarrassment. "All he talks about is Indians," she said.

Cole spoke to the boy. "I'm afraid there aren't many Indians left around these parts."

The little boy eyed him suspiciously. "Have you ever seen an Indian?"

"Oh, I've seen a good many Indians. Comanche, Kiowa, Apache." The boy's eyes widened, and his mouth drew up in a circle as he turned to look at his father.

The boy's father raised an eyebrow. "Jonathan, mind your manners, and eat your food before it gets cold." The boy's posture slumped, and his bottom lip protruded in a pout.

Cole's eyes met with an old cowboy who sat in his workworn clothes, dusty from the trail. The cowboy met his gaze momentarily with tired, red eyes and nodded slightly as he forked himself a piece of meat.

At the back table, a man dressed in expensive looking clothes sat with his back to the wall. It was the man he had seen in the stable earlier. His open coat revealed turquoise handled revolvers resting against each hip. His eyes were dark and penetrating. Cole figured the gentleman for a gunfighter. The man was obviously paid well for his services as his fancy clothes and custom pistols suggested.

It wasn't long before the woman reappeared with his food. He thankfully took it and gave thanks over it, then ate slowly, savoring each bite. When he had finished, he took up his hat and walked out.

The man with the turquoise handled pistols reached into his vest and pulled out a rough sketch drawing. He observed it a moment, nodded, then put it back into his vest. He got up and left soon after.

Cole stopped for a wagon to pass before crossing the street. In the distance, the blacksmith's hammer pounded in a steady rhythm. He took his horses from their stalls and examined their hooves. Each needed some work. He tied the sorrel and the chestnut on behind Comanche and led them to the blacksmith who was pounding on a wagon wheel when he arrived.

Seeing him, the blacksmith straightened up slowly. "Howdy," he said.

"The sign says you're a farrier."

"That I am. What can I do for you?"

"I've got three horses needin' shoes."

The man drew his gritty arm across his sweaty face and wiped his hands on his apron. "My name's Peter Downing, but most folks around just call me Pete."

He extended his hand, and Cole gripped it. "My name's Cole Harden. Pleased to meet you."

Pete Downing walked over and took a look at the horses. "They've throwed some shoes, have they?" He lifted each one of the horses' hooves, gently touching their forelegs and talking softly to them as he did so. Cole leaned against a wagon while Pete got his tools and went to work.

The farrier pulled one of Comanche's hooves up between his thighs and held it there. He then took a small metal pick and cleaned the frog of the hoof free of dirt and clay.

"I've shoed horses all over this country. I get to know a lot of folks, their stock, too. I've shoed this paint before. Who'd you buy him from?"

"I took him from some men who shot my horse out from under me. Brothers by the name of Bowdry."

"I know of them. They're a bad lot," Pete said, pausing in a moment of recollection. "I used to do some farrier work for a rancher named Lassiter. Rumor was that the Bowdrys were hired guns he called on from time to time to take care of *business*." Pete picked up another hoof and went to work on it.

"Tell me more about this Lassiter," Cole said. "That's the second time I've heard that name."

Pete worked a file back and forth with the ease of an experienced farrier. "Well, I'm not sure what's worth tellin'. He's a mean, foul-mouthed man. He used to own a ranch here in New Mexico along the Pecos outside of Las Vegas. He bought most of his stock from a Comanchero named Escabarda. Poor lookin', abused stock. I used to hate to do work for him."

Pete took a hoof trimmer and cut off some hoof where it had split. "Lassiter never fixed a thing himself, always hired it done. Everyone knew his men weren't real cowboys: just outlaws and hired guns with very little cattle experience."

Pete took a long metal tong and placed a shoe in the forge until it glowed red hot, then took it up and pounded on it with a big hammer, bending it over an anvil. He then dunked it in a bucket of water with a loud hiss and sizzle of bubbles.

"Last I heard, Lassiter picked up and moved to Colorado in the San Luis Valley. Word is he bought up several smaller ranches after he forced folks off their land.

I've been told he recently hired two range detectives: brothers, Jude and Shiloh Tremble. There's no tellin' how many men those two have killed."

Pete pulled nails from a loose shoe and took it off then cleaned the hoof. He pruned the hoof with clippers until it was evenly rounded. He pointed as he squatted. "Hand me that larger file in my work box if you would." Cole found the file and handed it to Pete.

"Have you ever seen these Trembles?"

Pete looked up. "No, I can't say as I have, but I've seen plenty of their kind."

"There was a man in the restaurant earlier, a tall, lean man with dark hair and wearing fancy turquoise plated pistols on both hips. Have you ever seen him around?" Cole said.

The farrier nodded. "I saw a stranger that meets that description ride into town yesterday on an Appaloosa. I put a shoe on his horse last night. He was a steely-eyed fella. Didn't say much, as I recall."

Pete took the shoe from the bucket of water and put several nails in his mouth. He held the shoe in place and drove in the nails then filed off the ends. He raised up. "You expectin' more trouble?" Cole didn't answer.

"The reason I ask is, you see that feller down the street sittin' under that porch drinkin' like there's no tomorrow? That's Kenny Blythe, the town drunk. He's been watchin' us like a hawk. I bet ol' fancy pistols paid him to keep an eye on you."

Cole nodded. "I had planned on staying the night and taking the train in the morning, but I think I'll be on my way."

"I know you're partial to the paint, but would you consider sellin' the other two? They'll just slow you down. I'll give you fifty dollars each and call it good on the work. How's that sound?"

"Sounds fair enough," Cole said.

Pete wiped his hands on his apron then pulled a wad of money from his pocket. He handed Cole a hundred dollars.

"A friend of mine has a cabin a few miles north of here. You could board up at his place for the night. He looks rough, but he's friendly. His name is Clarence Morgan, but he goes by Buffalo."

"How would I find him?"

"You'll follow the Rio Chama north about eight miles until it bends sharp left. After that, you'll come to a big meadow. The tree line comes to a point at the upper end of the meadow. There you'll find an aspen tree with a notch in it. Enter the trees there and go straight west until you come to a large dome-like rock that sticks up high above the pines.

Morgan's cabin sits about two hundred yards behind the rock along the draw. If you go that way tell him you're a friend of mine. That way he don't shoot you."

Cole took Comanche by the bridle reins and stepped up in the saddle. "Much obliged," he said. He reined the horse about and set off upriver to the north at a gallop.

Back in the saloon the man with the turquoise plated revolvers sat at the table knocking down tumblers of whiskey while he played another hand of poker. A short time later, Kenny Blythe stumbled through the doors and joined him at the table. His breath reeked of whiskey.

"I've got some information for you," he said with a smile. "That feller you had me watchin', he just left town. He ain't waitin' to take the train tomorrow like you thought he might." The gunman pushed his bottle toward the man then stood and walked out the door.

Alamosa

The Rio Chama flowed gracefully along as Cole rode beside it. He pressed the heels of his boots into the horse's flank, and the big paint waded out into the ford. He traveled in the river for a time, crossing back and forth from the river to the bank then back trailing and crossing again.

Cole put the paint into a gallop until he reached the big meadow Pete Downing had described to him. He crossed the meadow and halted the horse on the edge of the tree line at the upper end.

With a little effort he found the tree with the notch and entered the pine timber there following a faint path. From there the trail wandered in a westerly direction. Cole followed it until he came to the large dome-like rock Pete had described to him.

Behind the mound of rock was a draw which he followed until he could see the sod roof of a cabin hidden well among the pine and oak brush. He circled around, following a lightly traveled path to the cabin. As he drew close, he called out loudly. "Buffalo Morgan. My name's Cole Harden. Pete Downing sent me."

"What do you want?" The voice was gruff and came from inside.

"I'm a friend of Pete Downing. I need to talk to you."

The string latch on the door opened and out stepped a large bear of a man. He wore a buckskin shirt and pants and carried a big bore Sharps rifle in his right hand.

"Any friend of Pete Downing is welcome at my fire anytime. Come on off your horse and lite a spell." Cole swung down and extended his hand.

"Welcome, stranger," Buffalo said shaking hands. "Come on in. It's been awhile since I had company."

Cole tied up his horse, pulled his rifle, and followed the man inside. The cabin was cluttered and smelled of the musk of drying animal hides. Buffalo moved some boards with wet coyote hides stretched around them and gestured toward a sturdy chair made of aspen. "Go ahead and lite a spell." Cole placed his hat on the table and sat down. Buffalo joined him.

"What brings you here, Cole?"

"I've got trouble on my trail. I'm on my way to Alamosa on official business for the law. It appears there's been men hired to stop me. I'm needin' a place to stay for the night. I'll be leavin' before first light."

"You're welcome to stay here tonight, and if trouble should follow you here, then so be it. It's been a while since I got in a good scrap. I figure I'm due for another anyway."

Buffalo took up a coffee pot he had been heating in the fireplace. "I don't know about you, Cole, but I like my coffee to kick up in the middle and pack double."

"The same here," Cole chuckled.

Buffalo poured two steaming cups of the thick brew then handed Cole his. "You could tar a roof with this Arbuckle brand coffee," he said.

Both men sat staring into the crackling fire as if it were able to conjure up conversation for them. Buffalo took a long sip of coffee. "When should we be expectin' trouble?"

"Anytime," Cole said, placing his pistol on the table beside his rifle. "I figure after dark is more likely."

The man with the turquois-handled revolvers found Cole's tracks along the river below the big meadow. He crossed the river and dismounted. He began to lead his horse, searching carefully for more sign in the fading light.

He knelt down and stuck his hand in a divot where a piece of sod had been flipped over in a northerly direction. The soil had not had time to dry in the sun. The gunman led his horse across the meadow to the upper end. There he found a tree with a notch in it. He entered the trees there and followed a faint path to the north.

It was dark now. Buffalo lit a lantern and placed it on the table. Its flickering glow cast large shadows behind both men as they visited.

"Tell me about yourself, Cole. You strike me as a military man."

"I was a major in the Fourth Cavalry and served with Colonel Mackenzie protecting the plains settlements from Comanche and Kiowa raids. Until lately, though, I was a line rider and a trail foreman for the J. A. Ranch runnin' longhorns from Palo Duro Canyon to Dodge City."

The window shutters rattled from a gust of wind causing both men to look that way. "I don't mind trouble, but I always hate waitin' on it," Buffalo said. "My stomach's gnawin' at me to eat. How about you, Cole? You hungry?"

Cole nodded. "I could eat," he said.

Buffalo got up and took some smoked venison from a jar and a block of cheese from another. He cut off the crusty edges of the cheese, sliced it, then carved some strips from the smoked meat. He slid the meat on a pan to Cole.

"Have at some of the that, Cole. I put some red peppers in it to give it extra flavor."

Cole took a bite. "That's mighty tasty," he said.

As the two ate, they continued in conversation. "What will you do now that you're no longer with the J. A. Ranch?" Buffalo said.

"I hope to find work for a reputable brand. Eventually, I plan to buy my own spread in the San Luis Valley."

Buffalo nodded. "I thought about cowboying myself, but I can't kick the gold fever. They say there's some good ore showin', up at Platoro. I have a notion to try my luck at gold huntin' once the snow gets off the high country."

Buffalo grubbed another piece of meat from the jar with his fingers and stuffed it in his mouth. "Where do you hail from, Cole?"

"Missouri and Kansas," Cole said proudly.

"I thought maybe I recognized some accent of that part of the country in you. Hard-barked, rugged stock, them Missouri folk. I spent some time there myself on a steamer boat on the Missouri River. I also laid track for a spell for the railroads. It was pretty country, but I didn't cotton much to the heat nor the skeeters.

I had a woman there, but she ran off with a slick feller out of St. Louie. I found him, and we had it out. I had to go on the dodge for a while, and I fell into a spell of outlaw livin'. I left there about 20 years ago and joined up with a fur company out of Taos, and I've been trappin' ever since. I also did some buffalo huntin', too, for a spell, till I got tired of all that skinnin' and such in the summer heat."

Buffalo reached into his pocket and pulled something out of it and handed it to Cole. "It's a buckeye nut. My Granny Fenamore always said them was good luck. Maybe you need it worse than me."

Cole turned the brown nut around in his hand and put it in his pocket. "Thanks," he said. "I find the words of the Bible give me my comfort."

Buffalo nodded. "Granny Fenamore was always readin' the Bible to us youngin's before she died. I take it up every now and again myself."

Cole got up and opened the shutter and looked out. It was raining now as the brunt of the storm had now moved in. The wind whipped the treetops in a writhing sway and soon it came a downpour. He closed the shutter against the brisk wind and rain and sat back down.

Up on the hillside above the cabin, hidden by the trees, the gunman who had been pursuing Cole sat atop his horse in the pouring rain. He had come to kill Cole Harden but not under these circumstances. The man turned his horse and headed back to the cover of a cave he had found about a mile back. With any luck, he would catch up with Harden in the morning.

The next morning Cole left before daybreak. He arrived at the small depot at Osier not long before the train was ready to pull out. He loaded Comanche in a stable car then took his seat. The train smelled of coal soot and smoke. A short time later the train announced its departure with a long drawn out whistle then coughed a cloud of black soot and pulled forward. Ahead lay La Manga pass followed by the descent into Conejos Canyon and eventually the San Luis Valley.

The train strained against the grade as it climbed the last pass then sped up as it made its descent into the San Luis Valley. Once on the plains, they started a small herd of antelope that tried their best to outrun the train.

Cole observed the Sangre De Cristo, or "Blood of Christ" Mountains which loomed to the east like a jagged curtain. To the west were the beautiful San Juans, with their round snow-capped peaks, which snaked along the Great Divide. The two mountain ranges nearly touched at both ends of the Valley almost sealing it away from the outside world.

When the train finally pulled into San Antonio Junction, the conductor announced there would be a twenty-minute stop over before going on to Alamosa. Those who needed to stretch or use the outhouses could do so. Cole left his seat and checked on Comanche. The horse appeared to be fine.

A stack of newspapers sat on a table inside the depot, so he bought one and took it back to his seat. At the moment, he was the only person on the train and so he read the paper in solitude. The front page featured an article about the San Juan train. It explained how it was helping local business and how it had opened up travel for common folks. It also spoke of hard feelings from those who had been forced to give up their land so as not to stand in the way of progress. Farther down the page was an article on better farming practices and another on Mormon settlement.

At the bottom of the page, in the corner, was an article titled: "Sheep Men and Cattlemen Fear More Grizzly Trouble This Summer in South San Juan, Platoro Area." Cole read the article with much interest. It spoke of a troublesome bear locals called Silver Top.

On the following page was a segment titled, "Today's Scripture." Today it featured a verse from Psalm 146:5,6 KJV. He read it out loud.

"Happy is he that hath the God of Jacob for his help, whose hope is in the Lord his God: Which made heaven, and earth, the sea, and all that therein is: which keepeth truth for ever: Which executeth judgment for the oppressed: which giveth food to the hungry." He nodded in agreement.

Cole's eyes drifted over to an article titled: "Golden Willow Gets Summer Range Grazing Allotments." The segment spoke of the Golden Willow Ranch out of Las Mesitas and their plans to graze longhorns up in the San Juans this summer near Platoro. The thought of running longhorns in the high country piqued his interest. Beside the article was an ad that read: "Foreman Wanted: Golden Willow Ranch." He tore out the ad and put it in his pocket.

Cole started to read another article titled, "More Gold Found at Platoro," when a man boarded the passenger car. He was wearing a black long-tailed duster that hung down to his knees. One of his arms was tucked inside his coat and on his hip, under the duster, was the bulge of a pistol.

He walked to the back of the car and took a seat where it was fairly dark. Seconds later another man boarded the train and stood in the aisle. Cole recognized the man as the same one he had seen in the restaurant back in Chama, *Fancy Pistols*.

"Cole Harden," the man said.

Cole laid down his newspaper. As he did so he unfastened the strap of his holster. "I'm Cole Harden. What do you want with me?"

"You have documents that I need, Harden. Give them to me now, or I'll kill you."

"I can't do that."

The man's hands moved closer to his guns. "Do you know who I am?"

"It doesn't matter. I still can't let you have these documents."

"I'm Jude Tremble. I work for Lassiter."

Just then a voice threatened from the back. "Go for that gun, Tremble, and you're a dead man. I'm a Pinkerton. You're under arrest for attempted murder. Drop your guns."

A sudden blast of the train's whistle caused the lawman to glance away. Tremble went for his guns. Cole went for his, also.

Bullets flew, and guns blazed, then all was still. Two of Cole's bullets struck Tremble in the chest. The gunman convulsed, and with a shriek, he clawed at his chest then sunk to the floor. When the smoke cleared, Jude Tremble lay dead. The Pinkerton lay on the floor bleeding from Tremble's bullet. Cole rushed to his side and examined him. He was still alive. He dragged the lawman off the train onto the sidewalk where a crowd was quickly gathering.

"Someone get a doctor. This man is hurt bad."

Cole bent close to the man's face. "Can you hear me, mister?"

The man opened his eyes and began to speak in a shallow voice to those who had gathered around. "I'm a Pinkerton lawman out of Denver. It was Jude Tremble that shot me. Harden shot Tremble in self-defense." They were the last words the man ever spoke. He turned his head to the side and closed his eyes.

The deputy who had been among the crowd heard the Pinkerton's testimony. He walked past Cole and boarded the train. He examined Tremble's body for a moment then stepped back off the train.

"It's Jude Tremble all right. He's dead."

The deputy glared at Cole. "Mister, when this man's brother, Shiloh, finds out about this he'll be gunnin' for you for sure. You best be leavin' the Valley. We don't need no more killers."

Cole looked the deputy in the eye. "I have business in Alamosa with Judge Parker. After that I plan to look around and maybe settle in somewhere. You see to it that Shiloh Tremble gets the true story. If he comes lookin' for me, his blood will be on your hands."

Cole boarded the train and took his seat. He had been in the San Luis Valley only a short time and yet he had already made some dangerous enemies. Now others would come for him, and when they did, he would be ready. He feared no man.

When the train pulled into Alamosa, Cole unloaded Comanche and rode to the courthouse. His eyes searched the rooftops and shadows for anyone who might be waiting to pick him off, but he saw no one.

He tied up to the hitching rail and walked up the steps. Near the entrance to the Conejos County Courthouse were two marble slabs with the Ten Commandments engraved on them. They were similar to the granite tablets he had seen displayed at the capital buildings in Denver and Santa Fe, except a little smaller. As he paused to read them, he let his eyes drift reverently over each line.

1. Thou shalt have none other gods before me.
2. Thou shalt not make thee any graven image.
3. Thou shalt not take the name of the Lord thy God in vain.
4. Keep the Sabbath day to sanctify it.
5. Honour thy father and mother.
6. Thou shalt not kill.
7. Thou shalt not commit adultery.
8. Thou shalt not steal.
9. Thou shalt not bear false witness.
10. Thou shalt not covet.

He entered the courthouse and walked down the hall to a room with a plaque beside the door that read, "The Honorable Judge Parker." The door was open. He took off his hat and knocked on the door frame. Judge Parker, who was sitting at his desk, looked up to see Cole standing in his doorway.

"Come on in. What can I do for you?"

"I'm Cole Harden. I'm here at the request of Governor Lew Wallace. I have some dispatches for you."

The judge stood. "Mr. Harden, welcome. I've been expecting you." Cole shook hands with the judge.

"You've done the entire Valley a great service by delivering this information. I hope you didn't run into too much trouble along the way."

"Twice men tried to kill me, but the Lord showed me favor both times. This morning a gunman named Jude Tremble tried to take the dispatches. He drew on me, and I killed him in self-defense. He said a man named Lassiter sent him."

Judge Parker was shocked at the news. "You killed Jude Tremble?"

"Yes, I did," Cole nodded.

"That was a dangerous man. I put a lawman on the train to help protect you. What happened to him?"

"He and Tremble had a shootout. Tremble killed him."

The judge shook his head. "I was afraid early on that Tremble or Lassiter would try to stop you." He gestured toward a chair. "Please, Cole, take a load off. Have a seat."

Cole handed over the leather satchel containing the dispatches. The judge opened it and pulled out a large sealed envelope. He opened the envelope and began to look over the information.

The judged looked up and peered over the glasses which rested on the bridge of his nose. "I had Lew gather me all the information he had on Lassiter from New Mexico records. I've been trying to build a case on this Big Shot for over a year now. Everything from shady land deals to murder. These dispatches should give me enough to put Lassiter behind bars for good."

Judge Parker continued to look over the papers. A short time later he leaned back with a smile. "This is good stuff, Cole. I can't discuss the details, you understand, but thanks to you, I have enough information here to put Shiloh Tremble and Graham Lassiter and plenty others away for good.

Tonight, I'm going to gather a large posse and arrest those we have evidence against. According to what I see here there's a lot of 'Bar L' men with plenty to answer for."

The judge stood and extended his hand to Cole. "Cole, I've heard a lot of good things about you over the years. It was good to finally meet you. Where will you go from here?"

"I plan to find some steady work for a brand here in the San Luis Valley, maybe buy some land and run my own herd, if it works out."

"A good friend of mine is in need of a foreman, if you're interested," the judge said. "He's got a real nice spread south of here near Las Mesitas called the Golden Willow. His name is Lindle McKnight. He's an honest, God-fearin' man like you and I, and he pays top dollar. It's a first-class operation."

"I believe I'll head that way and pay McKnight a visit," Cole said.

"You do that and tell Lindle I sent you his way."

Cole nodded. "Take care, Judge. I'm glad I could be of help."

The judge walked with him to the door. "For what it's worth, McKnight has a widowed daughter who is just the classiest gal and the very definition of beauty. She would make someone a real fine wife. I thought a lot of her deceased husband, Keith, too. They made a fine family, them and their boy, Brian."

Cole smiled. "I appreciate the information."

The judge took a cigar from his vest pocket and struck a match alight in his other hand and held it to the tip of the cigar until it smoldered, then put it in his mouth. He took a draw upon it and let out a steady stream of smoke as Cole untied his horse and stepped up in the saddle.

"I'll let Governor Wallace know you arrived safely. The last time I talked to the good general he said he was working on writing a book. Did he mention that to you?"

Cole nodded. "He mentioned he had finished it and had sent it off to be published. He titled it, *Ben-Hur,* as I recall."

"Ben-Hur," the judge mused.

Cole steadied his horse by pulling back slightly on the bridle reins. "You be careful, Judge. If you need any help, send for me."

The judge raised his hand and nodded. "Keep your powder dry. Come back sometime, and we'll jaw over a fine steak dinner."

"I'd like that," Cole said, tipping his hat. "Adiós." He put his horse forward into a canter and was soon out of town.

Heading south, he soon reached the Rio Grande River on the outskirts of Alamosa and put his horse into the shallow waters lined with corrizo and cattail. He crossed over and soon came to a plowed field that smelled of fresh turned soil. Water stood like blue streaks in the furrows where the irrigation canal gate had been opened to flood the field. Water also ran through the pasture and flooded the bar ditch.

Cole observed the snowcapped mountains to the west. From the amount of snow which still clung to the peaks, it looked like there would be a steady supply of run-off for quite some time. The sight made him ponder on God's magnificent provision for watering the earth. It was brilliant how the Creator had planned for the snows to collect and store up so deep on the peaks during the winter and be preserved there until spring and summer when it was needed most. At that time, it would slowly melt, releasing its moisture little by little, following the slope of the earth as it channeled into draws, then rivers, and finally to the ocean as it nourished everything in-between.

There was so much design in everything in nature it was easy to see God's fingerprints all around. On his left Cole passed a pasture where knee high grasses hid all but the heads of a dozen resting newborn calves.

He passed a group of workers grubbing weeds with hoes and waved. They waved back and went about their work. The scene reminded him of some verses from Psalm 65:9-13:

"Thou visitest the earth, and waterest it: thou greatly enrichest it with the river of God, which is full of water: thou preparest them corn, when thou hast provided for it. Thou waterest the ridges thereof abundantly: thou settlest the furrows thereof: thou makest it soft with showers: thou blessest the springing thereof. Thou crownest the year with thy goodness; and thy paths drop fatness. They drop upon the pastures of the wilderness: and the little hills rejoice on every side. The pastures are clothed with flocks; the valleys also are covered over with corn; they shout for joy, they also sing." (KJV)

Continuing south he made the town of Conejos as the evening sun hung low in the west. He rode past the courthouse then the "Our Lady of Guadalupe" church just as the bell began to ring.

A mile west of the little town he made camp along the river in the cottonwoods. He shot a rabbit and skinned it, then gutted it and washed it clean in the river. He gathered a good amount of wood and built a fire. When the flames had died down a bit, he cut a willow stick and skewered the rabbit upon it then set it to cook above the coals. Occasionally he turned the spit until the meat was fully cooked all the way around. It smelled wonderful, and he was hungry.

Cole said a prayer then ate the delicious meat especially enjoying the backstraps. When finished, he took his bed roll and spread it outside the glow of the flames and lay with his back against a log and listened to the soft crackle of the fire. His rifle lay beside him within easy reach. Flickering shadows danced upon the trunks of trees and upon the body of Comanche as he stood quietly nearby. Not far in the distance, the Conejos River murmured as it flowed leisurely along.

Cole reached for the watch pocket of his vest and pulled out a silver locket that had belonged to his late wife, Lucy. He held it gently between his calloused fingers as his chest tightened with that old familiar pain. He sighed as he stared at the picture inside of the bride of his youth who had died so shortly after they had been wed. Cole lingered a moment longer at the memory then closed the clasp and returned it to its place next to his heart.

He bowed his head and said a prayer. "God, I am lonely. Please help me to find another woman like Lucy. Amen."

The next morning, he was awakened by the sound of a noisy flock of turkeys calling from their roost down river. He sat up, rubbed his eyes, and slipped on his boots. Blue birds and jays were calling as well, and the sky was clear and now empty of stars.

Cole took some jerky from his saddle bag and sat down on a nearby log. As he ate, a gray jay fluttered over and lit on the far end of the log. The bird hopped along closer and closer, begging for some morsel of food.

"Here you go, you camp robber," Cole said, flicking it a little piece of jerky. The peculiarly silent gray bird picked up the crumb of food in its beak and fluttered off.

When he was done eating, Cole set off for the Golden Willow Ranch as the horizon began to glow and hint of the breaking forth of the sun. Such a morning sunrise always reminded him of the verse in the Bible found in Proverbs 4:18: "But the path of the just is as the shining light, that shineth more and more unto the perfect day." (KJV)

Cole put Comanche ahead at a good pace and before long began to see wooden signs with the words "Golden Willow Ranch" painted on them. Now on the side of a distant mesa he could see the letters "G.W." done up in white stone. He sat his horse a moment, taking in the view. "So, this is the Golden Willow," he said, approvingly.

Graham Lassiter had been waiting to hear that Jude Tremble had killed Cole Harden when a foreman for the Bar L rode into Bar L headquarters with surprising news.

"It looks like Cole Harden got them documents delivered to Judge Parker after all," Lee Manter told his boss. "Somehow Harden got the jump on our boy and killed him," he nodded. "I'd hate to be him when Shiloh finds out his brother is dead." Manter struck a match alite on his gun holster and lit a cigarette as he waited for his boss to respond.

Graham Lassiter sat still at his desk in his study trying to absorb the news. It was obvious that he had underestimated Cole Harden, and now there would be consequences.

Manter drummed his fingers against his holster anxiously. "What do you want to do now, Boss?"

Lassiter stood. "The law is gonna be comin' just as soon as they can get a posse."

Lassiter grabbed his gun belt from a peg on the wall and began to formulate a plan. "Here's what we'll do. We'll split up for a few days and lay low. After things blow over a bit, we'll meet at the mine shaft on Greenie Mountain.

Me, Cordova, Gilcrest, and Bacca will go to the La Garita. We've got guns and ammunition stored there in the cabin, and it's got a good spring.

You and Shiloh and the rest of the boys hole up at the triangle in the cabin there until you get word. Take plenty of guns and ammunition. If you don't hear from me in three days, you're on your own. I suspect Shiloh will head for the mountains. He knows them well."

"What about the stock?" Manter said.

"Run them into Wild Horse Canyon. It's about a mile west of the cabin there. There's plenty of grass and water."

With that, Lee Manter left to warn Shiloh Tremble. Lassiter took his best rifle from the cabinet and a belt of cartridges and headed for the La Garita range.

The Golden Willow at Las Mesitas

The Golden Willow Ranch lay along the Conejos River mingled among large groves of ancient cottonwoods, pine, aspen, and willows. Pinon and sage grew along the lower regions. Cole sat his horse and took in the land.

A tall rocky mesa rose high above to the west off in the distance. At the moment, it was all aglow from the reflection of the rising sun, making it appear a brilliant rust-red. The ranch house sat on the hill near the river bottoms in a grove of sprawling cottonwoods. To the side lay several sod bunkhouses and beyond that a large pole corral. He put Comanche forward along the river.

When he arrived at the headquarters, the cowboys were finishing up breakfast. He dismounted and stood, holding Comanche by the bridle reins.

A tall, lanky, tan-skinned man with silver hair and dark eyes was walking toward him. "Welcome, mister. My name's Lindle McKnight. What can I do for you?" McKnight extended his hand in a gesture of goodwill, and Cole took it firmly; a clasp shared by two calloused hands.

"Pleased to meet you, sir. My name is Cole Harden. Roy Parker sent me this way. He said you might have need of a foreman." Cole's voice was loud and commanding and held a tone of confidence.

"The position is open. Do you know Judge Parker?"

Cole nodded. "Well enough to know he's an honorable man."

"He is that." McKnight rubbed his chin and smiled. "I figure if he sent you this way then I ought to give you a moment of my precious time."

The older man drew him aside. "I take it you have experience with longhorns?"

"Yes, sir, with longhorns and with men both. I was a range foreman in the Palo Duro Canyon for the J.A. the last several years, and I have ramrodded many drives, taking big herds of longhorns through the Pecos country and to Dodge City over the Comanche lands. Before that I spent a year in south Texas gatherin' wild cattle along the Nueces. I learned a lot living amongst them like that."

The rancher studied Cole for a moment then smiled. "I'm bettin' you're the same Harden that was with Colonial Mackenzie. Am I correct?"

"Yes, sir. I was a major in the Fourth Cavalry protecting the plains settlements against Comanche, mainly in Texas."

"I sold some beef to the cavalry some years back, and it was Mackenzie that brokered the deal. If I remember correctly, you picked up the herd at Trinidad."

Cole nodded. "In a windstorm, I recall."

"Do you plan on sinking roots around here, Cole? I'm needin' somebody for the long haul, not just the summer."

"I intend to settle down here in the Valley. The Palo Duro is some of God's finest work, but it's no place to raise youngin's or keep a wife. I figure the Valley to be more suitable."

"Do you have a family, Cole?"

"No, I don't, but I'm at a time in my life that I would like to, if the Lord sees fit."

"I sense you're a man of faith and ambition."

Cole nodded. "Yes, sir. I believe in God, Jesus, and the Holy Spirit, and the Bible is my guide for everything I do."

Lindle liked what he heard. He had always had a way of reading men. This one was a leader of men and carried himself with confidence and authority.

"Cole, I'm not one to leap quickly into any decision. I don't do any hiring without consulting my brother-in-law and cattle partner, Bob

London, first. I don't believe in making decisions on an empty stomach either. What do you say we get some breakfast in our bellies, and then we'll go from there? Sound good to you?"

"Sounds good to me."

Lindle and Cole helped themselves to some bacon and biscuits and gravy. Cole filled his plate with only a modest portion of chow. He knew better than to take advantage of a man's hospitality when he had not yet earned it. He shoveled the hot food to his mouth with grateful appreciation.

Several of the cowboys were still finishing their breakfast while others worked in the corral, cutting out and sorting cattle. Some appeared young and full of vigor while others looked experienced and work hardened.

A short, stout man came over and sat down. "Howdy. My name's Stump Patterson. I'm responsible for the vittles around here."

Cole nodded, "Howdy. The food's real good."

Lindle gave Cole a wink. "Wait till you've had it awhile. You may change your mind," he joked.

Stump pretended to be indignant. "So, you're gonna rib me, Boss, after I give you the biggest piece of bacon. See what I have to put up with?"

Cole smiled and then observed the good number of cattle that ranged upon the mogote hillsides. "How many cattle do you run here?" he said.

"All together a little less than 3,000 head during the summer. We couldn't run that many if it weren't for an agreement we have for grazing rights up in the high country all summer. We're fixin' to take a herd up to the San Juans real soon. I'm just waitin' for the grass up there to get a little more growth."

McKnight chewed another piece of bacon. "We're taking mostly longhorn steers, a few cows and calves, a few bulls, and some lead oxen. We'll leave the sickly and the older ones here as well as those that will be ready to sell soon."

Stump held out a pan offering Cole the last piece of bacon. "You best eat it because the boss sure ain't gettin' any."

"Thanks just the same, but I'm as full as a tick on a Texas hereford."

"Suite yourself. I'll eat it then." The cookie stuffed the bacon in his mouth.

Cole turned back to McKnight. "There's still a good amount of snow left in the passes yet."

McKnight nodded. "Judging from the snow on the peaks, I'd say you're right. We may run into some drifts up high. The Willow gets the Conejos Canyon all the way to the divide. There's talk the Bar L plans to run their cattle up the Alamosa Canyon this summer. That canyon sets over to the north, but it wouldn't surprise me one bit if they let their cattle help themselves to our grass, too."

"Who is the Bar L?"

"The Bar L is Graham Lassiter's spread. He hasn't been in the San Luis Valley long, but he's already staking a big claim to it."

While McKnight was talking, a gentleman over by the corrals motioned him to come over. "Pardon me, Cole. I better go see what my business partner wants." McKnight ambled over and began to visit with the other man.

"That feller over yonder talking with the boss is Bob London," Stump said. "He's the boss' brother-in-law and as good a fella as you'll ever know. They was some of the first to run longhorns here in the Valley."

Soon McKnight came back over with Bob London and some of the men. He whistled loudly and gestured for everyone to gather around. When they all had gathered, he began to speak.

"Men, we'll be movin' the herd up the Conejos Canyon in two weeks. That day will be here before you know it. That means we have a lot of work to do before we pull out."

"I need a ditch dug from the north spring to run toward the east pasture. We also need to build a water flow regulator box for the new ditch and get it in place. There's lumber in the wagon you can use to build it. There's plenty of fence needs mendin', too."

McKnight turned to London. "Bob, would you like to add anything?"

Bob London addressed the men. "There's about two dozen head missing somewhere. I suspect they are over in the west pinon draw next to the Bar L where the herd of elk took out the fence last week. We better get to them before Lassiter slaps on his brand."

"We need to cut some poles for that section and rig up a way we can lay the fence up or down, so the elk don't keep takin' it out as they move up through there. I need a couple of you young bucks to get on that."

When Bob had finished, McKnight motioned to Cole. "Gentlemen, I'd like to introduce you to Cole Harden. He rode in this morning lookin' for a job. Mr. Harden and I will ride fence. The rest of you know what to do. If there ain't no questions, then let's get to work. The day's slippin' away from us."

Lindle turned to Cole, "We'll need an axe and some wire for splicin'." Cole fetched an axe from a stump by the woodpile and tied it onto his saddle. He grabbed some wire as well.

A man could tell a lot about another by the way he took to work. He himself enjoyed hard work, and he wanted to be sure McKnight knew he was serious about the job.

McKnight saddled his roan and slipped a Spanish bit in its mouth then gingerly stepped up into the saddle, his bridle reins in hand. Cole put his paint horse forward and followed McKnight along the river until they came to the fence.

"There's a cottonwood down on the fence up ahead. After we get it taken care of, I want to show you around the place," Lindle said.

When they came to the fallen tree, Cole took up his axe and made short work of it. He stretched the fence wire tight and tied it secure.

Lindle nodded with approval then swung his arm wide. "This spread runs both sides of the Conejos all the way on top of that far hillside to the south. It goes east and west between the two mesas clear on top then over to the north about five miles to the wagon road." Cole took in the boundaries that lay within his sight as they rode along.

"Across the river about two miles, where you see that big white letter "S" on the hill is the Sandoval Ranch. The Sandovals settled here before most. They are hard workers and good neighbors. To the north of them is the McEntire Ranch. They are good neighbors, too."

"A man is blessed that has good neighbors," Cole said.

"I wish that were the case all the way around, but we are bordered on the west by the Bar L, Graham Lassiter's spread. Us neighbors have always helped each other out especially come round-up or branding time but not Lassiter. He's as stickery as a prickly pear cactus."

"It sounds like Lassiter needs some reckoning. I'm surprised someone hasn't called his bluff a long time ago," Cole said.

"I'm afraid he's not bluffing. He means business. Most of us are just hard-working family men tryin' to make an honest living. We're not lookin' for trouble."

"I've had my experience with men like Lassiter. A strong hand is all they understand," Cole said. "If they aren't stopped, more lives will be lost, and more family ranches will be torn apart."

Lindle nodded. "Maybe so. I believe the Lord will take vengeance on Lassiter and his hired guns soon enough."

"Maybe he's already started his vengeance," Cole said.

Lindle stopped his horse. "What do you mean?"

Cole looked Lindle in the eye. "I had to kill Jude Tremble yesterday morning in self-defense. Lassiter hired him to kill me."

"A fella's past is his own business, but Jude Tremble is a pretty big enemy to have gunnin' for you, Cole."

"I was commissioned by the Governor of New Mexico to deliver important dispatches to Judge Parker. I didn't know it at the time, but those dispatches held incriminating evidence against Lassiter. Tremble drew down on both me and a Pinkerton man at the rail station in San Antonio Junction."

"You did the right thing, Cole. A man does what he needs to do to defend himself. It may bring trouble our way if you hire on, but it was bound to happen sooner or later. I didn't figure anyone could get the jump on Jude Tremble, but you did it. That's to your credit. With the tensions the way they are, it just may be the spark that lights the haystack."

"Sometimes it takes a fire to burn out the weeds and let what's good take its place."

"Yes, I suppose you're right," Lindle nodded.

The two men came to where another tree had fallen upon the fence and went to work on it. After they had removed the tree, Cole chopped down two aspen trees for poles and set them in the ground then stretched the wires tight and secured them.

"I envy your vigor, Cole. I wish I still had that kind of giddy-up. I used to be quite a worker before my ticker seized up on me a couple years back. I ain't been the same since. It's left me with very little strength."

"Yes, sir," Cole said. "I'm sorry to hear that."

Lindle examined the fence. "Splendid work. That ought to hold till the Lord comes back."

McKnight appeared to be winded, and his skin complexion was very pale. "Are you okay?" Cole asked.

"I'm fine. I'm just having one of my sinkin' spells. Don't tell my wife, Charlotte, or she'll have me sittin' in a rocker shellin' peas," he said with a laugh.

Cole and McKnight rode the fence upward to the west. McKnight pointed to a cross on the mesa. "That cross up yonder is where my daughter Abby's late husband, Keith, is buried. He was up there lookin' for stray cattle when lightning got him. We figured it an appropriate place to bury him. Abby says it's sorta like he's still up there watchin' over us."

Lindle looked at Cole from under the brim of his hat. "Keith knew better than to be up there during a storm, but he was determined to find them strays." McKnight looked back up at the cross. "He was like a son to me."

Cole nodded. "I buried my wife a year after we was married. You never fully get over it."

"No, you don't."

Lindle turned his horse west. "Let's ride on up there. I want to show you the view." He put his horse forward, and Cole followed. When they reached a ledge about a hundred feet below the top, McKnight stopped his horse. He wiped his brow and took a drink from his canteen then took a couple of deep breaths.

"You sure you're all right?" Cole asked again.

"Yeah, I'll be fine. I'm just havin' one of my dizzy spells is all. They come and go. I'll be fine after I rest a spell."

Cole helped McKnight down from his horse and took his arm as he made his way to a large slab of rock and sat down. McKnight dabbed some sweat from the back of his neck with his bandana, then took a drink after Cole fetched his canteen.

Lindle pointed off to the west. "Yonder lies the San Juans. Ain't they a beautiful sight?"

"Some of God's finest work, I reckon," Cole said.

Lindle let out a long sigh. "It reminds me of one of my favorite scriptures. 'I will lift up mine eyes unto the hills, from whence cometh my help. My help cometh from the Lord, which made heaven and earth.'"

Cole nodded. "It's fittin' for the view."

"Have you ever driven cattle in rugged mountains like them up there, Cole?"

"No, sir. I've ran herds in the Delaware Mountains but never in country as rugged as the San Juans. It sounds like quite an adventure takin' so many cattle to the high country for the summer."

"It surely does, doesn't it? Unfortunately, I won't be going this time, and it irritates me somethin' awful. I would love to see the Conejos Canyon and that Platoro country again, but my heart just won't take the thin air up there no more. I've got family to think about, and there's plenty needs done here at the ranch, I guess," Lindle sighed.

"I used to take Charlotte and Abigale way up the Conejos Canyon to what's now Platoro, to see the wildflowers every July. We'd all spend a week or so in that cool mountain air, sleepin' under the stars and fishing or watching the elk. Abby and Charlotte would paint."

McKnight continued to reminisce of earlier days spent with family in the beloved Platoro area. He picked up a pinecone and tossed it playfully at a chipmunk.

"Yes, sir, Cole, I love those mountains." McKnight stood up. "I believe I can lite atop my horse now without fallin' off." He climbed back in the saddle. Cole did the same.

"If you think this view is good, I got one better. Follow me."

The New Foreman

Cole followed McKnight up through a series of switchbacks through more pinon and yellow rock. There the trail topped out in a flat plain of pinon, rock and short pine. From there they followed a boulder strewn path to a magnificent overlook.

They sat atop their horses and took in the view. The land fell away to the west, then heaved upward in umber colored saddle ridges of pinon and of a lighter green where aspen mixed with pine rose upward to purple mountains of blue spruce timber until finally reaching the gray snowcapped peaks.

"All that high country you're lookin' at is what we call the summer range. Up there it's suitable for summer livin' only. The heavy snows push everything down except the snowshoe rabbit, the grouse and those that den up."

"The winter up there gets awful quiet, I imagine," Cole mused.

McKnight nodded. "It gets so still you can hear the snow settle. Now if that ain't peace and solitude, I don't know what is." He leaned over the side of his horse and took hold of a coil from a broken strand of barbed wire that was sticking up along the path and began to roll it up. "Soon the whole Valley will be fenced in, but not up there. Up there it's still open land, untamed and wild. The lushest meadows you ever rode in, the clearest streams you ever drank from, and the bluest skies you ever laid eyes on. And of a night, the stars are so bright you feel like you are right among them."

"How far you reckon that round peak is on the far left?" Cole wondered.

"That there is Conejos Peak. I'd say it's thirty miles as the crow flies, a good bit more by horse." McKnight stared off as if reliving some pleasant memory.

Cole held his impatient horse in check. "I had the pleasure of meeting your daughter and grandson in Chama the other day," he said.

"Yes, I recall her and Brian mentioning they had met someone there."

"Brian seems like a well-mannered kid. I admire anyone who raises a child by themselves."

"Well, it was always a joint effort between Keith and Abby. Abby's not alone, though. She's got me and Charlotte to help her. Brian's our only grandson so we favor him like he was our own."

Lindle looked toward a draw far below. "I thought maybe our missing cattle would be down there, but I don't see 'em nowhere."

The two rode to another ledge which faced to the east. It too was a magnificent view. "Charlotte and I talked of building a cabin here once because of the view it affords of the ranch," McKnight said.

Cole took in the sight. Below them lay the ranch and the lower Conejos River which gave verdure to the dry rocky landscape. He could also see the ranch house and the bunkhouses and the brown circular patch of earth where the corrals were nestled among the cottonwoods. The cattle below appeared as small as ants, while some of the cowboys' horses kicked up tiny dust trails as they went about their duties.

"It's a good view of the ranch," Cole said.

"Maybe a little too good," McKnight mused. "A few years back we had a man and his gang come up here and spy us out. His name was William Coe. He and his men swiped a number of our cattle, and we never got them back."

"I had a few run-ins with Coe myself along the Santa Fe Cut Off route," Cole said. "I saw to it that he was hanged over in Pueblo."

"You know, Cole, the more I mull it over, the more I feel we could really use a man with your experience at leadin' men and drivin' longhorns."

"Charlotte and I have been praying for a foreman with your qualities. A man with your intimate knowledge and understanding of the breed is hard to find. I'll have a talk with Bob London, my partner, before we make it official, but for my mind, I feel the foreman job is yours if it would suit you."

"I would like to join up with this outfit," Cole said.

"Come on. I want to take a gander at one more place. I have a hunch where our missing cattle might be."

As they continued along the rim, they jumped a couple of hen grouse. The birds ran a ways and paused to crane their necks at them. Lindle halted his horse. "How's your aim, Cole? It's been a while since I had a mess of grouse." Cole drew his pistol and took a quick sight on the birds. He fired twice and rode over to where the two grouse lay dead.

"That was mighty fine shootin'," Lindle said.

Cole picked up the birds. They were warm and downy soft in his hands and smelled of sage, and their heads lolled over the side of his hands as he held them. "These are some plump birds. They should make for some mighty fine eatin'."

"My, they are, aren't they," McKnight said, admiring them. "I'll see if Charlotte will cook them for supper. I'd like for you to join us and meet the family. My wife sets a fine table. What do you say?"

"I'd like that." Cole tied a rope peel to the birds' legs and hung them over the saddle horn.

Lindle rode over to the edge of the rim and shielded the sun from his eyes and smiled. "Well, would you lookie over there." He pointed to a draw below. "I knew them rusties couldn't hide from us up here."

Cole looked down where several cattle fed busily in a shadowed drainage. "I count two dozen of them," he said.

"I believe that's all of them. Let's go fetch 'em and bring 'em on home."

Cole followed McKnight down a series of switchbacks. Fifteen minutes later they reached the cattle. Cole put Comanche into the bunch and maneuvered the cattle with the artistry of a seasoned cattleman. In short fashion, all the strays were trotting in a line for the ranch except one, a stubborn steer named Ol' Rebel.

When they reached the main pasture, a cowboy who introduced himself as Paulie held the gate open as the cattle trotted in. McKnight watched with appreciation as Cole heeled up the bunch and closed the gate behind the last one. He liked what he saw in the strong cowboy whom it seemed more and more like God had brought their way.

"Well done, Cole," McKnight said. "They led in like they were followin' a feed bucket. All except for Ol' Rebel. He likes to go his own way. He's always wanderin' off into trouble. I thought about selling him, but I just keep wantin' to give him another chance. Ol' Rebel is a fine-looking longhorn. He's strong and sturdy, but because he's stubborn, he fought the lasso one day and ran himself hard into a pine tree. He's been blind in his one eye ever since."

Cole smiled. "I've dealt with many a rebel in my life. Some come around, some don't. I'll go see if I can fetch him and bring him through the gate."

"Good luck," McKnight said, with a smile.

A short time later Cole was back, with the steer stubbornly in tow behind. Lindle opened the gate and tipped his hat to Cole with a chuckle.

That evening the men of the Golden Willow trickled in one by one, tired from a good day's work and hungry for supper. McKnight spoke with Bob London for a time before addressing the men.

"Gentlemen, please gather around and listen up. I have an announcement to make before you get your supper. I know you're hungry, so I'll keep it short. Bob and I have talked it over, and we've hired a new foreman today. His name is Cole Harden. I assure you that he has the experience to do the job, and then some. You can trust our judgment. I'll let him say a few words. Cole, the floor is yours."

Cole stepped forward with confidence. He stood tall and straight. "Good evening, men. I came here today lookin' for a job doin' what I've done all my life and that's leading men and driving longhorns. Mr. McKnight and Mr. London graciously offered me the job of foreman, and I accepted.

I know longhorns. I was a range foreman for the J.A. Ranch for Mr. Charlie Goodnight. I made my living trailing big herds of longhorns across the Comanche occupied lands between the Llano and Dodge City.

I know men, too. I was a major in the Fourth Cavalry. I believe in respect, and I won't tolerate dishonesty, laziness, or profanity, especially using the Lord's name in vain. We are better men than that."

Cole looked over each face. "Our first President, General George Washington said, 'We can have little hope for the blessings of Heaven if we insult God with our speech.'

Washington was a man of great faith. I am a man of faith, too. I look forward to working with each of you. If you're as hungry as I am, then I guess I'll quit talkin' so we can eat."

"Thanks, Cole," McKnight said, stepping forward.

The men sensed a genuine confidence in their new foreman that could only have been earned through experience. What's more is they trusted Mr. McKnight and Mr. London's judgment. One could be sure that the decision to hire Cole Harden had not been taken lightly. It would have only been made with everyone's best interest in mind.

McKnight directed the men's attention once again. "Gentlemen, what do you say we eat now."

"I say amen to that. I'm hungrier than a starvin' ol' grizzly bear," one of the young men barked. The cowboy's words drew laughter from his peers.

"That's fine, Garth," McKnight nodded.

The rancher removed his hat. "Gentlemen, let's give thanks to our Lord for the chow we are about to eat, shall we?" Everyone removed their hats and bowed their heads as McKnight began to pray.

"Our Father in heaven, we thank thee for the blessings of the day and for the safety we had as we went about our tasks. We thank thee for the nice weather we were blessed with today as well as thy hand of mercy and favor upon us. We thank thee for another day's food and water. Forgive us our sins and shortcomings as we look to thee for guidance. We thank thee for sending us Mr. Harden to help lead our trip to the summer range. In the name of Jesus, we pray. Amen."

Two cowboys approached Cole and introduced themselves. "My name's Lightning Wells, and this is my brother, Rusty. Welcome to the Golden Willow."

"Welcome to the Willow," Rusty echoed. Others soon followed their lead.

"What's for supper, Cookie?" said a sturdy Mexican with a scar down the right side of his face.

"Stew and biscuits, with potato puddin' for dessert. There's also some of yesterday's cookies in the wagon."

The Mexican held out his plate. "Ladle me up some grub. I'm hungry."

Stump Patterson filled each man's plate with two piles of steaming stew over biscuits. Everyone ate while Cole and Bob London visited over by the wagon. London cut off a willow branch and began to whittle as he enjoyed the cool of the evening.

"We've got a good group of men. F. D. Hurly, Gilbert Mackey, and Jack Moore are over at Capulin picking up a couple of bulls. They are top rate hands.

The Wells brothers, Lightning and Rusty, drifted in last spring. They were mainly following the grub line west when they ended up here. They're good hands, too.

Griz Montoya over there was a tracker for the Seventh Cavalry. He learned from the Pawnee. He also spent time trapping in the Sangre De Cristos and the San Juans both. He even survived a grizzly attack."

"I reckon that's how he got the name Griz," Cole said.

"Yes, his given name is Fabian."

"You've already met Stump Patterson, our cook. Best camp cook as ever there was."

Bob London motioned toward a tall, skinny, middle aged fella getting himself some food. "That feller there is Paulie McPhee. He's another top hand. He does anything and everything without being told or complaining. McKnight and I even considered him for the foreman position before you came along."

London peeled a long strip of skin from the willow branch. "Lee Hansen is the big blond-haired fella standing next to Paulie. He's a very good hand as well. A good blacksmith and farrier, too. If it's broke, he can fix it.

Now take those fellers leanin' against the wagon talkin' and laughin' together. They're all good cowboys, but sometimes, because they're younger, they need someone to direct their attention in a more productive manner. The one on the left is Kent Severs, the next is Seth Callahan then Luke Parnell, Titus Martin, and Carlos Sanchez," he said, pointing each of them out. "Far as I can tell, ain't none of 'em on the dodge, but you don't always know where they drifted in from or what their real story is.

The feller that's tendin' to his horse is Garth Benoit. His daddy was a French fur trader who moved to the Valley from the Northwest Territories a few years back.

All the men will be going to the summer range except Hurley, Mackey, and Moore. Oh, and I almost forgot Wilkins."

"Which one is Wilkins?" Cole said.

"He's the one yonder ridin' out through the gate. I sent him for supplies. McKnight filled him in on your run-in with Tremble before he left. He warned him to be careful because some of the Bar L boys may try to get revenge on us."

Cole nodded. "I reckon I better go get cleaned up. The McKnights invited me to supper tonight."

Bob London tossed his stick and put his knife away. "I suppose I better skedaddle, too. I'll see you up at the house shortly."

Inside the ranch house, the mood was happy and festive as the McKnights made preparations for their supper guests. Having a new guest for fresh conversation would be a nice change.

Abigale covered the table with a new tablecloth and dressed it with family china reserved only for special occasions such as this. She went outside and returned with a bouquet of wildflowers which she cut and placed in a vase as the centerpiece.

Miss Charlotte took up the roasted grouse and brought it over for her husband to carve. "Lin, tell me about the new foreman you hired. I'd like to know a little about him before I meet him."

"Well, he's a very likable fellow. He's a man of faith, too. He has a lifetime of experience working with longhorns, and he was a major in the Cavalry. He's also a very hard worker and has a fine horse under him," Lindle said, as he cut up the tender meat.

"Is he married?" she asked, with a hopeful smile.

"No, he's not."

"Good. Is he handsome?"

Lindle shrugged. "I suppose so. He's a sizable fellow, and he carries himself well. I'd say he can handle a gun pretty well, too, because he killed Jude Tremble yesterday morning in self-defense."

Miss Charlotte gasped and raised her hand to her chest while her eyes pleaded for an explanation. "Oh, my word, Lin," she kept her hand resting on her chest.

"I know what you're thinking, Charlotte, but he came here lookin' for the foreman job, and I figure with all the problems around we could use a man with his experience. He's a man of principle and faith who just happens to have a real fast gun and a good aim, that's all. It comes with the territory sometimes. Trust me, once you meet him, you'll really like him."

"If you say so, that's good enough for me." Charlotte checked the potatoes on the stove. "We've been praying for the right man to help ramrod the drive up Conejos Canyon, and now, maybe God's answered our prayers. I'm going to trust so," she said.

Abigale had been listening to the conversation with interest. "What's his name, Daddy?"

"His name is Cole Harden."

Brian put down the book he was reading and looked over at his ma. "That's the man we met in Chama the other day. Remember, I talked to him and petted his horse, Comanche. He was nice."

"Yes, I remember, Brian. He was nice."

Abigale glanced out the window and soon had a smile on her face. Her heart began to beat faster. "Here he comes. And yes, he is handsome."

Cole opened the gate in the picket fence and walked across the yard. He had cleaned up and put on his best clothes. When he reached the house, he knocked on the door. It opened, and he was pleasantly surprised to see McKnight's lovely daughter, Abigale, standing there.

"Hello, won't you come in?" she said with a smile.

"Yes, ma'am. Thank you," he said, kicking the dust from his boots.

Once inside he was greeted graciously by Lindle and Miss Charlotte. "Welcome, Cole. I'd like to introduce you to my wife, Charlotte."

"How do you do, ma'am. It's my pleasure."

"Welcome, Mr. Harden. I hope you'll feel at home," Charlotte greeted.

"You have a beautiful place here, ma'am. I appreciate the invitation for supper."

"We have grouse to eat thanks to your fine shooting," Charlotte said with a smile.

Cole grinned. "Well, ma'am, I have to admit they made it easy for me." Everyone laughed.

"Supper is nearly ready. Perhaps you and Lin would like to visit in the parlor until the table is filled."

"Yes, ma'am," Cole said.

"I can take your hat and your overcoat to the parlor for you," Abby said.

"Thank you." He took off his coat and Stetson hat and handed them to Abby.

He admired the furniture and beautiful paintings as he followed Lindle into the parlor. A red longhorn hide stretched across the west wall, and above the fireplace, a long Comanche spear spanned two elk hoof pegs.

Along the north wall was a large collection of books and a roll top desk as well as a gun cabinet filled with beautiful guns. No doubt these were the guns that had fed and protected family and helped in the opening up of the American West.

Cole admired the horns of a magnificent seven by seven point bull elk fastened to a thick cross beam overhead. "Where did you get him?" he said.

"I got that big brute up on Conejos peak four years ago, near Tobacco Lake. He had just finished watering with his cows and was headin' back to the spruce to bed," Lindle said.

Just then Bob London and his wife, Beth, entered the room. "Hope we're not too late," Bob said.

"Right on time, Bob," Miss Charlotte hollered from the dining room. "Supper's ready."

Lindle gestured toward the dining room. "After you, Cole. Be our guest."

When everyone had found their seats, they joined hands while Lindle said the prayer. When he had finished, Charlotte looked up and handed Cole a basket which contained some freshly baked rolls. "There's plenty of food, Cole, so help yourself."

After eating his fill of supper, Cole took up his napkin and wiped his mouth. "Miss Charlotte, Abigale, thank you for the fine meal. I didn't know grouse could taste so good."

Lindle got up and gave his wife a kiss on the cheek. "Thanks, dear, for the fine meal."

After the table was cleared away, everyone moved to the parlor for conversation. Charlotte sat down next to Lindle. "Where are you from, Cole?" she asked.

"I'm a Missourian by birth. I was born near a little town called Nashville. Later we moved to Kansas along the Spring River."

"Do you have any family back there?"

"No, ma'am, my family was killed when I was still a boy."

"Oh, dear, was it Indians?"

"No, ma'am, it was thieves."

"Did they ever catch who did it?"

"No, they never did."

The conversation grew quiet until Lindle broke the silence. "After the war, Cole came west to help out with the Comanche situation. After that he worked for Ol' Charlie Goodnight down on the Palo Duro."

"I've heard that's a real nice place," Charlotte said, nodding.

"It's a magnificent country, but it's no place to raise a family," Cole said.

His eyes admired a couple of paintings that hung on the north wall. "Those are beautiful paintings," he said. "Where did you get them?"

"Abby painted those. She and Charlotte are the artists in the family," Lindle said.

"Did you paint the others, too, Abby?" Cole said.

"Some of them. Mother and Daddy painted some as well."

Cole admired a grand painting of a herd of longhorns and another of a remuda of running horses. "They all look like they belong in a fancy art gallery in San Francisco or somewhere. They're better'n any I've seen."

"Thank you," Abby said.

As the conversations continued, Abigale took notice of the things Cole spoke of, the way he laughed and joked, and how he interacted with Brian and her parents. Some of his mannerisms even reminded her of her late husband, Keith.

Cole took notice of Abby as well. She was articulate and talented and exuded dignity and grace. When it came time for him to leave, he said good night and retired to his bunkhouse.

That night he could not sleep for thoughts of Abigale and her family. He had enjoyed the conversation and delicious food, and as he closed his eyes, he relived the memories of the evening.

On his first day as foreman, Cole arose in the starlight and bridled and saddled Comanche as Stump Patterson built a fire for coffee and breakfast. The cook shuffled around pots and pans, banging them loudly, making no effort to be quiet. It wasn't long before lanterns began to glow within the windows of the bunkhouses as the men got ready for breakfast. The horizon was red to the east as the last of the stars dissolved into the sky. It would be a clear start to the day.

While the men took their breakfast, Cole met with London and McKnight to discuss the day's plans. Afterwards he addressed the men of their duties then dismissed them. He himself went to work digging a channel for the new irrigation ditch. The first day on the job went well without any problems.

It was noon the day following when Jake Wilkins finally came riding in, bloody and beat up with a message for Cole. "A couple of Lassiter's men jumped me and beat me. They said they wanted me to give a message to Cole Harden that he would get it worse for killin' Jude Tremble." Lee Hanson and Lightning Wells helped Wilkins off his horse and into the house where Miss Abigale and Miss Charlotte tended to his wounds.

"Me and one of the boys will ride into town and make a formal complaint with the sheriff," Bob London said to McKnight. "He's a good, fair man. He'll do something about it."

"I agree. I don't want the men to retaliate. Let's see what the law will do first," McKnight said.

Some of the men came to McKnight with their concerns. "Is it true that Cole killed Jude Tremble?"

"Yes, it's true. He told me the details before I hired him. His actions were in self-defense with plenty of witnesses."

Garth Benoit's jaw dropped. "So, it's true? Cole out drawed Jude

Tremble? I didn't think anyone could get the jump on a Tremble, but Cole, he…"

"Garth, my good friend, I reckon you fellas have work to do, don't you?"

"Yes, sir."

Garth looked at his cohorts. "Come on fellas. Let's get back to work."

As the men were leaving, a rider rode through the gate and into the yard. It was Ezra McEntire, a neighbor who owned the ranch to the northeast. He stayed his horse and took off his hat and wiped his brow with the back of his hand. "Howdy, Lindle."

"Howdy, Ezra," McKnight greeted. "What brings you this way in such a hurry?"

"I have some news that should interest you. Judge Parker and the sheriff got a posse together and arrested Graham Lassiter and several of his men last night. They're in the Alamosa jail."

"I reckon they didn't go easy."

"No. Eddie Baker and Simon La Trude were killed. Shiloh Tremble was wounded. Him and Manter and a couple others got away."

Ezra stepped down from his horse and ladled up some water from the well bucket and took a long drink. "It appears that maybe a half dozen more of Lassiter's men might be arrested by tomorrow morning if all goes well."

"You say Shiloh got away, Ezra?"

"Yes, sir. J.D. Meadows was part of the posse, and he said that rascal got to the mountains before they could catch him. There's men lookin' for him right now, but I don't reckon they'll find him up there in the high country with all them places he's got to hide.

Shiloh's uncle knew the mountains well and rumor is that he had a cabin or two tucked away somewheres he used for huntin' and trappin'. Shiloh used to go with him some. He knows that country, too." Ezra climbed back up on his horse.

"Tell that new man of yours to watch hisself. I'm afraid Lassiter's men, Shiloh especially, will have their sights aimed on him from now on."

"I'll give him the information."

"Well, I best be gettin' back to the ranch. I'm puttin' a new roof on the house."

"Thanks for the information, Ezra. If you need any help on that roof, holler. I'll send some of the boys over."

"Thanks, but no need. The Sandovals are comin' over to help." Mr. McEntire turned his horse to the east and touched boot to hide.

"See you Sunday, Lindle."

Lindle raised his hand in the air. "See you Sunday." McKnight pondered on his neighbor's welcomed news long after the sound of his horse's footfalls deadened and died away.

Over the next few days, the men worked hard to prepare for the trip to the summer range. Cole, though he usually ate with the men during the day, joined the McKnights each evening for supper. Afterwards, he enjoyed spending time with Abby and playing with young Brian in the parlor. He felt a strong attraction to Abigale, and to his delight, she seemed to be taking quite an interest in him as well.

It was invigorating to enjoy the company of a woman again. To watch her laugh, to smell the faint fragrance of her long hair. To enjoy her beauty and share stimulating conversations and laughter with her. Those were things he had missed, though he didn't know just how much until now.

The Church Picnic

Early Sunday morning Cole posted a paper on the door of the main bunkhouse for all to read. It was a code of conduct he lived by called "The Cowboy's Creed." As the men got ready for church, they took their turn reading it. Lightning read it out loud as he slipped on his boots.

"Be loyal to the boss and the brand. Demand square dealings. Be proud of your occupation. Lay down your life, if necessary, for the brand. Grant assistance to friends and strangers in need. Never tolerate cowards. Be cheerful and never complain. Don't make excuses. Try to be better than the other fellow. Share what you own with a fellow worker. Be generous to others. Treat all women like ladies. Never quit. A handshake binds agreements, bargains, and friendships tighter than any legal document. A cowboy's word is a sacred bond."

"That's all right," Lee Hanson said as he stepped outside.

On Sundays, the men did only the work that had to be done, and no more. Sunday was to be set aside as the Lord's day; a day of rest and reflection as God had commanded in the Bible.

The church, nestled among a grove of ancient cottonwood, was situated along the Conejos River about a mile downstream from the headquarters of the Golden Willow.

Today was Basket Lunch Sunday, an occasion that happened on the second Sunday of each summer month. The tradition called for each lady to prepare a basket lunch for her family, or if single, the woman's basket would be chosen up among the single men for a chance to enjoy the woman's company and food. It was the eighth of June and the second Sunday of the month. The weather was perfect for such an event, and the air was fragrant with the aroma of spring flowers.

The McKnights all rode to church in their buckboard wagon, while some of the wranglers rode to pick up their girls. Though very few of the men had dress clothes, they cleaned up well and offered their best appearance anyway.

Cole rode Comanche to church. Whether in a town or on the cattle trail, he had always made it a priority to attend church and spend time in God's Word when it was possible to do so. He carried his King James Bible in his left hand as he walked into the church yard which was already lined with horses, wagons, and buggies. Children played outside while a few adults visited with one another.

A boy Brian's age, in black nickers and a white collared shirt with black vest, began to pull up and down on the rope that hung from the belfry. The iron bell began to sway and chime as it tipped back and forth, signaling that the service was soon to begin. Cole removed his hat and walked up the steps of the church. Inside, the structure was made of rough-cut spruce logs patched between with white plaster chinking.

Today the church was packed with folks eager to worship. He found a place along the back wall next to Luke Parnell and Kent Severs. When he noticed that the young men each had a jaw full of tobacco, he made them step outside and spit it out.

At the moment, the church was filled with the hum of boisterous chatter as people greeted one another. Abigale played the organ softly as everyone found their seats. The sanctuary smelled pleasantly of all manner of food from the basket lunches which set on a table along the back wall. As the organ music began to fade, the Reverend walked down the aisle to the front and stood behind his pulpit. The hum of voices subsided, and the congregation grew quiet.

"I am Reverend Paul Isabel for those of you visiting. I want to welcome all of you this morning. What a wonderful day it is to worship our Lord. Amen." His voice was strong and comforting.

"Would everyone please stand for the reciting of 'The Lord's Prayer'?" There was the sudden clamber of rising bodies and scuffling feet as everyone stood.

"For those of you who don't know this prayer by heart, you can find it in the gospel of Matthew, chapter 6 verses 9-13." Reverend Isabel began to recite the prayer as the congregation joined him in one voice.

"Our Father which art in heaven, Hallowed be thy name. Thy kingdom come. Thy will be done in earth, as it is in heaven. Give us this day our daily bread. And forgive us our debts, as we forgive our debtors. And lead us not into temptation, but deliver us from evil: For thine is the kingdom, and the power, and the glory forever. Amen."

"Everyone please take up your hymnals and remain standing as we sing the great hymn, 'What A Friend We Have in Jesus'."

Abigale began to play the song's melody as Cole shared a hymnal with Luke and Kent. Everyone joined along as the Reverend led the first stanza in his baritone voice.

"What a friend we have in Je-sus, all our sins and griefs to bear! What a priv-i-lege to car-ry, Ev-ery-thing to God in prayer! Oh, what peace we of-ten for-feit, Oh, what need-less pain we bear, All be-cause we do not car-ry, Ev-ery-thing to God in prayer!" …. When the song finished, everyone was seated.

"Today's sermon is titled, 'He Hangeth The World Upon Nothing.' You can follow along in your Bibles by turning to Job chapter twenty-six."

Cole opened his Bible to Job and listened intently as Reverend Isabel spoke with passion and conviction as he told of how God didn't need ready resources to provide for His people since He created everything from nothing. How much more then could He provide for the needs of His people even when provisions didn't seem to be available.

When the sermon was finished, the congregation stood to sing the closing chorus of "Amazing Grace." Afterward, the Reverend proceeded with the announcements.

"I would like to remind everyone to stay for the fellowship and picnic directly after the service, as if the wonderful smells haven't reminded you already. I also want to wish the men of the Golden Willow safe travel as they take their cattle up to the high country around Platoro at the end of the week. As we know from our knowledge of the Spanish language, Platoro means silver and gold. I wish I was going along myself, but Don Burrell and I are planning a trip to Ruybalid Lake for brook trout. We like to be the first ones to wet a line up there if the snow will let us in.

I also want to welcome a new guest with us today. His name is Cole Harden, and he is the new foreman for the Golden Willow. Cole, we welcome you to the community and hope that you will feel this your church home from now on."

Cole nodded. "Thank you."

"Well, then, if there are no further announcements, everyone is dismissed. I'll see you at the picnic."

As everyone filed out of the church, people began to visit on the grounds. Cole visited with the Reverend a moment before finding Abby.

"Hello, Abby," he smiled.

"Hello, Cole. Will you be staying for the picnic?"

"I plan to. I thought I might bid on the basket with the green checkered cloth. The food in that one smells real good."

Abby's eyes twinkled. "That's mine."

"I know," Cole admitted.

"Why, Mr. Harden. You're just going to have to wait and bid, like everyone else."

She thought for a moment. "Are you bidding on my basket solely for the food, or is it for the privilege of my company?"

"Both."

"Good answer."

There were several other men who held interest in Abby and her basket of food, but it was Cole who won the friendly competition for her company. Cole picked up the basket, and he and Abby made their way to a flat carpet of grass under the shade of a large cottonwood tree along the riverbank.

Abby spread a quilt on the ground, then Cole placed the basket on it before sitting down beside her. "My parents offered to watch Brian so we could enjoy some time alone together. I hope you don't mind."

"No, not at all. I would enjoy time alone with you."

Cole placed his hat to the side, then poured a couple of glasses of sweet tea from a mason jar. He handed Abigale hers. "Thank you, kind sir," Abigale said, taking the glass and setting it beside her. "I made this blanket from pieces of Grandmother's old quilts. Some of the patterns are my own design. What do you think of it?"

"It looks real nice, Abby. I'm sure it was a lot of work."

"More of a joy than work, really. I enjoy sewing and cooking."

Cole looked at Abby and smiled. "Let's give thanks for this wonderful food, shall we?"

The two bowed their heads as he prayed a simple prayer. When finished, they filled their plates with the delicious smelling food while they continued to visit.

Cole watched Abby, sitting across from him, as he bit off a tender piece of chicken. She sat with her legs bent and tucked modestly to her side. Her long beige colored dress was adorned in tiny white flowers. Her long hair tossed a little in the light breeze. He wanted to reach out and hold her in his arms, but that would have to wait.

"What do you think of my cooking, Cole? I want your honest opinion."

"It's delicious."

Abby watched him curiously. "What are you thinking about?" she smiled.

"I was thinking how when you smile your eyes shimmer like the sun on a dew drop."

Abby laughed. "You know all the right things to say to a lady," she said, smiling.

"When you're finished with my chicken and potato salad, there's strawberry short cake for dessert."

Cole smiled. "I can hardly wait."

He took the last piece of chicken from the basket and tipped it up. "I reckon an empty basket says as much as words do. You know Stump is a mighty fine cook, but I'm sure we won't be eating like this up in the high country."

Abby smiled, then looked away. "My father would love to go with you to the high country this summer. He used to take us up there every July when I was a girl. He loves the mountains. I love them, too."

"The mountains are still wild and majestic. That's part of their beauty. I see that kind of beauty in you, Abby."

"Are you saying you think I'm beautiful?"

"Yes, you are very beautiful."

Abigale took a deep breath. A swell of emotion caused her to look away.

"What is it?" Cole asked.

Abby looked at him, her eyes contemplative. "Sometimes I wonder if I should say out loud the things that are in my heart. There is so much I want to say, but I wonder if it should wait."

"I've learned what's worth sayin' is better said outright."

Abby bit her lip. "Cole, do you ever think about settling down and getting married and having a family?"

"I think about it. I'm ready for it, too," Cole said. "After Lucy died, I didn't think I'd ever love anyone again.

Lucy and I grew up about a mile apart. I just assumed we'd always be together. I used to push her in the rope swing that hung from the big oak tree in the front yard when we were kids." Cole smiled at the pleasant memory. "She was my best friend, and we married at 18. We had plans for a home along the Spring River, children, and a farm with corn and lots of cattle. We hadn't been married a year when she caught diphtheria and died a short time later."

"I'm sorry, Cole, about your wife, and that you've had to endure such loss, but I do believe that God is a redeemer of things that are lost."

The two sat in silence for a while enjoying the strawberry shortcake.

"If you could plan your future, Cole, what would it look like?"

Cole thought for a moment. "I would like to have a sizable spread here in the Valley. Have a nice house with a big fireplace. I'd like for it to have big windows looking off to some majestic view. I'd like a covered porch where I could sit and watch the sunset after a long day out with the herd. A place to visit with neighbors."

"Does that home include a wife and children?"

"Sure it does. My wife and children would be beside me, on our own land. We'd have lots of cattle and horses."

"And you see that happening here in the Valley?"

"Yes. I feel like the Lord led me here to get a fresh start."

"I'm glad you don't mind sharing your thoughts with me, Cole. I like that."

Abby watched a couple of boys playing and began to grin. "Boys are so fun to watch. Tell me something about when you were a boy, Cole. What's your favorite memory?"

Cole leaned back against the tree and stretched out his long legs. "I would say my favorite memory was when we lived outside of Nashville, Missouri. Ma and Pa and Grandpa and Grandma gave me a .22 rifle for my tenth birthday. That mornin' Ma packed me some food in a burlap sack and me and my dog, Samson, went explorin' all day. That night I camped in the river bottoms west of Nashville with the Osage Indians that lived there. I brought them a squirrel that I shot, and we cooked it up for supper. The next mornin' I went home."

"Were the Osage friendly?"

"Yes, they were very friendly."

"That must have been some adventure."

"It was. I have many fond memories of the home place in the Nashville woods and Grandpa and Grandma and Lars while they were still with us."

He and Abby talked and laughed for the remainder of the picnic. After putting away the basket, he took Abby's hand and helped her to her feet. "Thank you, Abby."

"Thank you, Cole. I haven't had such a peaceful time with a man since my husband's passing. I miss it."

"The day doesn't have to end yet. I thought I might gather a couple of willow poles and take Brian fishing if you wouldn't mind. I'd like for you to come, too."

"I'd like that. I know Brian would as well. I'll see if I can find him."

"Well then, I'll go fetch a couple of poles and meet you and Brian down river in a bit."

A short time later he returned with two willow poles, some grub worms and some night crawlers. Abby was reading a book, and Brian was sitting along the riverbank watching a mayfly hatch.

Brian pointed. "I just saw a big fish rise over by that log. He looked like a good one."

Several mayflies hovered in the air. Cole caught one and took a moment to observe it. "Is that what they're eating, Cole?"

"Yes. They're called mayflies, and they hatch from the river when the sun's out bright. The fish love them."

He handed Brian a pole and some bait. Brian watched a fish take a mayfly off the surface of the water. "Wow, did you see that, Cole? That was a big one."

"Look," Abby said, pointing to where another fish had broken the surface then darted back down into the deep.

"God is feeding the fish," the boy said.

Brian baited his hook with a juicy grub worm and tossed the line at a swirl with a flip of his pole. The worm sank and drifted downstream until the line was tight.

"That was a good toss, Brian. Let the bait sit there in the current a bit then give it another toss."

Brian repeated the process several times with no luck. "They don't seem to like it," he said.

"I've got an idea," Cole said.

He walked over to Comanche and plucked a couple of hairs from his mane. He then took a stick about a half inch long and fastened it to the small hook. After this he tied a piece of a feather to it with the horsehair, weaving it carefully together.

"What on earth are you doing, Cole?" Abby said.

"A friend of mine, Larry Ancell, taught me how to tie up a false bug like this. It's supposed to be a mayfly."

"Will it work?"

"I've caught a good many fish this way. The trick is making it look enough like whatever they're feeding on at the time."

Abby laid down her book and watched with fascination as Cole secured the fake mayfly to the end of his line then motioned for Brian to come over.

"Take this and give it a toss over toward that rock. I've got a feelin' there's a big trout waiting in that calm pool just behind it."

Brian took Cole's pole and carefully tossed the offering onto the water and watched it drift with the current until it was sucked around the boulder and into the calm pool. Suddenly, a big trout took the lure in its mouth and dove for the bottom.

"Hurry and give it a yank, Brian," Cole encouraged. Brian pulled as the fish began to fight against the line.

"That a boy. Keep the line tight," Cole said.

Abby stood and began to cheer on her son. Brian battled the darting fish until it finally grew tired. He pulled it from the water onto the bank where it thrashed about for a moment.

"Grab it, Brian. Don't let it get back to the water," Abby said. The boy pounced on the trout, trapping it with his body. Cole helped him get the fish into a pail of water.

"That fish is so big we'll have to find a bigger pan to cook him in," Cole laughed.

"He sure liked the bug you made, Cole. Could you teach me how to make one?"

"I'd be glad to."

Abby watched Cole take time to patiently teach her son. The more time she spent with this man, the more she believed that God had brought him here for more than just the foreman position of her father's ranch.

Headed for the Summer Range

By the end of the week, Cole and the men of the Golden Willow had finished branding and sorting all the cattle and tallied them in the Stockman's Mark and Brand book. Cole, Bob, Stump, and Paulie gathered enough supplies for the trip to the high country to sustain fourteen men for about four months. The supplies would be equally distributed between two wagons; one being the chuck wagon. Paulie and Stump would be the drivers.

The contents of the wagons were to include: 300 lbs. of flour, 150 lbs. of dried beans, 300 lbs. of cured bacon, 100 lbs. of dried fruit, 25 lbs. of coffee, 30 lbs. of sugar, 20 lbs. of salt, pepper and varied spices as well as molasses, yeast powder, and cider vinegar.

Other provisions included were: five extra Winchester rifles capable of holding 18 rounds each, 300 rounds of extra ammunition in addition to what the men carried on their person, numerous skillets, pots, pans, Dutch ovens, a large tarp, a dozen wool blankets, 9 fifty-foot picket ropes, an axe, a felling saw, a bucking saw, extra horseshoes, horseshoe nails, file, clippers, two dozen hobbling clasps, extra bridles, bits, liniment, salve, and a doctoring bag containing various necessities as well as 50 lbs. of stock salt. Under each wagon was tied a rolled-up rawhide cooney to be used for carrying wood and numerous other tasks. Counting the drivers, each wagon weighed in at under 2000 lbs. They would be heavy loads, but the big Missouri mules that McKnight had recently purchased were plenty strong for the task.

The evening before they were to make the trip, Cole and Abby took one last ride across the sage in front of the house. The full moon hung high in the night sky bathing the land in a wash of soft light. Far behind them, the lamp-lit windows of the ranch house glowed from within.

The two rode in silence until they reached the river where it bent and shoaled and lay still in the side water. "This is the place I wanted to show you," Abigale said, bringing her horse to a stop. "It's where I come of a morning to have my prayer time with God. There's something peaceful about it even at night. I've always loved the sound of water."

Cole got down and led Comanche over to the two large boulders which lay along the edge of the riverbank. Abby followed, leading her horse by the bridle reins. They sat in silence for a while listening to the murmur of the water as it passed by. It would be their last time together like this before the trip to the summer range.

Cole reached down and tossed a rock at the reflection of the moon in the water. The reflection scattered, then slowly gathered and righted itself, then lay as it had before. Abby moved closer and slid her arm in his.

"Cole, I know we have only known each other for a short time, but the past two weeks spending evenings sitting in the parlor with you makes it seem as though we've known each other for a lifetime. Now I won't see you for the entire summer."

Abby leaned her head on his shoulder. "I'll miss you."

"I'll miss you, too, Abby."

Abby grew quiet as if troubled by something. "What is it, Abby?" Cole asked. "What's on your heart?"

"I had a dream about you last night, Cole. I dreamed you were up in the mountains, and something dangerous was in the shadows stalking you. Just when I was about to see what it was, I woke up."

"Well, I wouldn't let a silly dream trouble you, Abby. I'll be fine."

"Sometimes my dreams have a way of coming true. I dreamed about Keith's death before it happened, and it came true just the way I dreamed it."

Cole looked into Abby's brown eyes and answered her concern with calm assurance. "Don't worry. The Lord has always taken care of me. I'll be fine. Once we get up to Platoro, I'll write you when I can."

"I know. It's just that it will be such a long time to not see each other."

He put his arm around her shoulder and felt her relax against his side. "Every night we can share the same sky, and during the day, if you ride up to the mesa, you can see the mountains I'll be in. And when I'm up there, I'll be able to see the San Luis Valley and the ranch."

Abby leaned closer to his side. "It hasn't been long since I buried Keith, and father's heart isn't well. I don't want that terrible feeling of losing someone again."

She lifted her hand to his cheek. "You will be careful in the mountains, won't you?"

Cole placed his hands on Abby's shoulders and held her gently as he looked into her eyes. "I'll be careful. I promise." He stroked Abby's hair tenderly, then leaned over and kissed her on the forehead.

"Nothing can keep me from coming back for you, Abby. I promise."

The two sat quietly on the large rock listening to the bubbling of the river. The horses grazed nearby, dragging their bridle reins as they cropped at one clump of grass and then another.

"Cole, the other night in the parlor you mentioned that you believed your sister to be dead, but you said you never found her. Do you think she could still be alive somewhere?"

"No. I've accepted the fact that Lauren Rose is dead. It's been twenty years since the murders. I never found her alive or heard from her since.

I found parts of her torn dress and her blood on the bushes. A year later I heard that someone had found the scattered bones of a child just two miles from where my family was killed. I went and got the bones and buried them in the family plot with the others just in case they were Lauren's."

Cole shook his head. "I know she's dead, Abby. If she was alive, she would have contacted me by now. I'll see her and the rest of my family someday in heaven but not here on this earth."

Abby put her hand on Cole's arm. "I'm sorry. I can't imagine having gone through that. Would it help you to talk about it?"

Cole looked up from her thoughtful gaze. "I've never really talked to anyone about it much." He paused, took a deep breath, then let it out with a troubled sigh. "I was only fifteen at the time. We were traveling back home from Missouri, and I took our only rifle out into the brush to hunt us up a rabbit for supper. I was only gone a little while when I heard shootin'. I hurried back just as fast as I could, but I was too late in gettin' there." Cole looked at the ground.

"In my mind, I can still see my parents and my brother, John Andrew, laying there dead." Cole tossed a stick into the water and watched it float a moment. "I searched and hollered for Lauren Rose until my voice gave out. I've never cried like that since. Sometimes I wonder if I hadn't taken off with the rifle, maybe they'd all still be alive."

Abby wiped a tear from her eye. "No, Cole, you couldn't have known. You didn't do anything wrong. Never think that," she said, shaking her head.

"The killer left a buckeye nut in each of their pockets after he killed them. I never could understand that. Someday I'll find him and see that he gets justice."

Eager for a change of subject, he plucked a heart-shaped leaf from an aspen and gave it to Abby. "Each time you see an aspen leaf, think of me. When the leaves turn golden, high on the mountainsides and begin to fall, it won't be long until we see each other again."

He sat with his arm around her shoulder as she leaned against his side. He felt her sigh as though something still weighed heavily on her mind. "Is everything alright?" he asked.

"I overheard father telling Uncle Bob that lately some men have been watching the ranch from up on the mesa."

"One of the men was on a gray, and the other was riding a black. He thinks they may be waiting for you to leave with the herd."

"I know. He spoke to me about it this morning. It's getting late. I reckon we should head on back to the house to join your folks and Brian."

"Yes, I suppose you're right. They will worry about us if we stay much longer."

As the two rode for home, Cole glanced toward the rim of the mesa. Even in the moonlight he could see the distant silhouettes of two men sitting on horseback watching them. Abby looked that way, too, but if she saw the men, she said nothing.

By the time the sun began to rise the following morning, the wagons were loaded, and the teams were hitched and ready to go. The cattle bellowed with anticipation for the change they sensed was coming. Altogether, fourteen men would make the trip to the summer range and four would stay behind to help the McKnights.

The first wagon would be driven by Paulie McPhee. Stump Patterson would be at the helm of the chuck wagon. They would precede the cattle, if all went well.

Each man checked his riggings and gear to make sure it was sufficient and ready to go. From every man's saddle horn hung a full canteen. Each saddle bag contained strips of dried beef, biscuits, ammunition, and any personal items one wanted. Tied to every cantle was a bedroll with two wool blankets wrapped in a rain slicker. Each man carried upon his person a pistol or a knife. Those who had rifles carried them in a scabbard or kept them in the wagon.

Cole, Bob London, and Griz Montoya would ride point while Lee Hansen, Seth Callahan, Garth Benoit, Carlos Sanchez, Luke Parnell, and Kent Severs would take the flanks. Titus Martin and the brothers, Lightning and Rusty Wells, would ride drag.

The morning was clear and made for the start of a great traveling day. A cross-breeze would carry away the dust from the moving herd making travel more pleasant.

The men were filled with excitement and anticipation for the trip. The summer was an adventure waiting to unfold, and Cole felt a renewed stirring in his soul. This was what God had created him to do; trailing cattle through new territories each with their own unique beauty and challenges.

Altogether they would drive nine-hundred and fifty-two head of cattle to the summer range. This number would include nine-hundred longhorn steers, two bulls, a mix of fifty longhorn and durham cows, a few of which were with their calves who were still not quite of weaning age.

Lindle McKnight stood by the corral with Charlotte, Abby, and Brian. There was a sense of longing in his voice as he addressed the men.

"Gentlemen, you are about to embark on a wonderful adventure for the summer. Our cattle will fatten on some of the best grasses on God's green earth. Come fall, they will have plenty of flesh on their bones.

I feel that the Golden Willow has been blessed with some of the best cowboys in all the Valley. It gives me real peace of mind to know my cattle are in good hands. Enjoy yourselves, men, but always be vigilant. Be on your guard against rustlers and thieves. For those of you worried about Ute Indians, there's plenty of room up there for everyone. Leave them alone, and they'll leave you alone.

Don't be careless. The mountains can be unforgiving. Watch out for rockslides and the ever-likely stampede. Listen to Cole's advice like it was my own. He has more experience driving longhorns than all of us put together.

And one last thing. Gold camps always seem to breed trouble, and Platoro is no exception. Look out for one another, and I'll see you all back here when the snows start to fly."

Lindle walked over to Cole and shook his hand. "Take care of yourself and bring them all back safe," he said.

"Yes, sir. I will."

Cole turned to Brian. "Be good, and mind your mother, Brian. Work hard."

"Yes, sir. I will."

Cole turned to Abby. "Abby, I know we've already said our good-byes, but take care of yourself."

"Good-bye, Cole. You take care of yourself, too. I'll miss you."

Cole tipped his hat to Abby, then after a moment of pause, he sat his horse and addressed the men.

"Gentlemen, let's start this trip off with a prayer and then be on our way."

Cole removed his hat and began to pray. "Father, we ask Thee for Thy hand of protection and Thy graces upon us and the cattle as we travel. Help us to make good time with few troubles. In Jesus' name, amen." When finished, he raised his hat high above his head and hollered with enthusiasm. "Let's take 'em on up to the summer range, men."

The group whistled and hollered as they waved their hats over their heads and began to prod the herd onward. Soon the cattle were spread out in a long, moving line. The herd was loud, fresh and cooperative. A bony, speckled-faced lot of colorful rawhide in a sea of dust. Many were black, others red and some a mixture of colors with patches of white. The trip to the summer range had begun.

Making Fox Creek

The wagons rolled onward ahead of the herd. Not far behind the last wagon was a small cavvieyard of five horses followed by a lead steer named Moses, who plodded steadily along near the front. He had sweeping horns that hooked wide. His hide was red, and his rump was dappled with dark splotches over gray blots. Moses' running partner, Samson, also a red lineback, trotted along beside him.

Right behind Samson was Trail Boss, a long-legged brindle cow who also loved to lead the herd. At her heels trotted her sturdy calf, a little dun heifer that Brian had named Peaches.

"Let 'em string out," Cole hollered. "Let 'em take their places and stretch out like they want, as long as they keep movin' along steady."

By noon the noisy herd had traveled past the rocky mesa and far out of site of the ranch. Cole rode back towards the flank to see how the men were doing.

"How's it going back here, men?"

"The cattle are working well. It's almost as though they can already smell the summer range with all that grass," Garth Benoit said.

"It wouldn't surprise me if they can smell good grass, with the breeze blowing off the mountains like it is," Cole said. "Nothing has a nose like a longhorn."

Carlos Sanchez rode up with a message. "The bigger of the two bulls keeps laggin' behind for the last mile. I think a rattler might've bit him back there in the rocks."

"Is he swollen bad in the ankle or the shank?"

"Yes, he's swolled up pretty good, Boss."

"Well, keep an eye on him. Let me know if he gets any worse."

"Yes, sir."

Cole rode over and helped Kent Severs bring down six steers who had wandered onto a bench above the wagon road. "From now on, Kent, keep the cattle on the trail and out of the rocks above us. If they get up there and cause some rocks to tumble down on the rest of us, somebody could get hurt bad."

Cole eventually made his way back to the drag where several of the mamma cows bellowed to their calves to catch up. "Rusty, you and Lightning help keep them calves moving along with their mammas, and keep an eye on Ol' Rebel, too, the steer with the blind eye. I've a bad feelin' about him. He could be trouble."

"Yes, sir. He's been a mite skittish all day. He keeps tryin' to wander off and do his own thing,"

"I hope I don't regret bringin' him along," Cole said.

Titus Martin, who had been listening to the conversation, rode up. "I've been singin' 'Good-bye, Old Paint' to him. He seems to like it."

Cole chuckled, "I would have taken Ol' Rebel for a 'Utah Carol' type."

The young cowboy grinned, "Well, I don't know all the words to 'Utah Carol' like I know 'em to 'Good-bye Old Paint'."

Cole rode back up to the front. The trail ahead was dry and bumpy making the wagons rock and pitch from side to side. The big iron wheels rolled over deep ruts and small rocks with measured progress.

By mid-afternoon the men had pushed the herd more than six miles, and by evening they reached the Fox Creek meadows, a big open area of sage and pinon that was bordered by mesas on two sides, with the Conejos River running to the east.

Cole rode over to Bob London. "We can bed the cattle up against the hillside tonight. The ground there is solid underneath and not so hollow sounding like it is down along the river," he suggested.

"I think you're right. The ground up there should be firm and out of the wind. Should be less spooky for the cattle."

Cole nodded. "We pret'near got the first day under our belt. If we can keep 'em here overnight and get an early start tomorrow, we may get to the mouth of Conejos Canyon by night fall."

PLATORO THE SUMMER RANGE

Bob London tipped his hat down to shield the evening sun from his eyes. "I'll tell the men we're here."

"Whoa, hold up now mules," Paulie said as he pulled up.

Cole rode over to the wagon. "How'd the mules do, Paulie?"

"They really done good. They didn't struggle much with the load at all. Even when the trail steepened, they just kept pluggin' along."

Paulie stepped down from the wagon and slapped the dust from his clothes. "A feller can sure take a beatin' on that road, though, if you can call it that. I think half my teeth have been jarred loose."

Stump pulled up next to Paulie. "Looks like the loads held together fine. I'll get to warmin' us up some supper."

"What ya got planned?" Cole said.

"Miss Charlotte sent us off with a big pot of chicken dumplins. She sent some of her sugar cookies, too." Cole nodded with approval then he, Bob, and Griz rode back to help bring in the remainder of the herd.

The men got the cattle settled just before dark. By now Paulie and Stump had a fine supper warming over the flames. One by one the men came in to the fire, hungry and tired.

"Well, Cole, we did it. The cattle are blowed off and calm as a hoss trough," London said.

At dark, the stars came out and soon crowded the night sky. In the background, the cattle lowed softly as Cole led the men in the Lord's Prayer before eating.

After everyone had gotten their grub, Cole took a plate of hot dumplings and a cup of coffee and stood near Bob London as he ate. "There ain't a sweeter sound than a pasture full of contented cattle," he mused.

"Yeah, a change of pasture sure makes for a happy calf. Course, change can make 'em a might more skittish, too. We'll see," Bob said.

"There's plenty more dumplins, gentlemen," Stump Patterson said. "Better help yourselves cause we won't be havin' fresh chicken dumplins for a long time unless you count mountain grouse as chicken."

When everyone had finished eating, the men squatted or stood around staring into the flicker of the fire while they drank their coffee. Up in the night sky, the Big Dipper shone brightly. Tonight, it tilted in such a way that it appeared to be pouring its contents upon the earth.

"Looks like the Big Dipper and the North Star are out bright tonight," Cole pointed. "We'll use their position in the sky to tell us when to change the night watch."

Seth Callahan looked up from his cup. "How do you know about the stars?"

"I learned about them while I was in the cavalry. If you look with a thoughtful eye, you'll see they have plenty to say."

"Like what?" Luke Parnell asked.

"Well, it's not by chance the good Lord flung them so far and placed them where He did. The stars and the moon tell you when's best to plant crops or wean cattle or how to navigate the plains. Many a night I used the stars to point me across that open country up on the Llano in Texas."

"The study of the stars is called astronomy," London said. "Drovers have used the stars for years to point the way after dark. You just aim the tongue of the wagon toward the North Star, and if it's cloudy the next mornin', at least you're started off in the right direction."

"I know the mountains is upriver and ranch is down river," Seth Callahan said. "I know that much."

Kent Severs sat down on a log next to Cole. "When we get up there in the mountains, I'm gonna get me some of that Platoro gold."

"I ain't never been way up in the mountains before," Titus admitted. "I suppose it's one thing to look at them at a distance and another to be up in among the clouds and the storms and the snows."

"I'd like to see a grizzly or a mountain lion just once," Garth said. "My pop used to tell me stories about them from when he trapped up north."

Garth locked eyes with Griz Montoya. "What do you think, Griz? Is there any grizzlies left up in the San Juans?"

Griz Montoya stood across the fire peering with ponderous eyes into it as the smoke curled upward around him. When he finally spoke, his voice held a grave tone. "The higher we go, the better chance we will have to see them. Most are up along the divide. The largest and meanest live in two sacred canyons: The Navajo Canyon and Diablo Canyon. I've seen them there."

As Griz continued to speak, his eyes held a look of uneasiness. "At the head of the Navajo Canyon lies a lake called the Azul, or to you gringos, Blue Lake. Some say its dirt banks still hold the tracks of a very large grizzly, a man eater.

Two rivers run from Blue Lake. One drops into the Navajo Canyon. The other flows north to join the Conejos River at a place called Three Forks. The Spanish and the Ute say that Three Forks is, 'where the devil dances at night'. They say this because of how the lightning dances there during a storm. The Spanish believe you can see the devil dancing within the lightning. I'm of the same notion." Griz's coal black eyes met with the curious glances of the cowboys as he nervously stroked his necklace of grizzly bear claws.

"I'm warning you, compadres, don't go near Three Forks, Diablo Canyon, or Navajo Canyon. Those places are dangerous. Some believe they are cursed." Griz paused. "I believe this." The Mexican seemed genuinely afraid of what the trip to the high country might bring. He was a man steeped in superstition and lore, and he, too, held secrets.

Griz began to growl from deep in his throat to tease the younger cowboys. Just then the fire popped loudly, and several of the men jumped at the sudden noise.

Griz chuckled. "You'd be wise to sleep with one eye open from now on, amigos," he teased. "In the mountains, there are many things that can find you and eat you."

Lee Hansen tossed the remainder of his coffee into the fire with a hiss and stood up. "That's enough grizzly stories for me. I'm gonna turn in. See you gents in the mornin'."

The blacksmith pulled his bedroll and pitched it just outside the glow of the fire. He tried to sleep, but Griz's stories had him spooked. He lay uneasy on his side.

After a quiet spell, Carlos Sanchez broke the silence. "I wonder if Shiloh is waitin' for us up in them mountains?"

Cole looked beyond his cup toward the dark outline of the distant peaks and remembered Abby's disturbing dream. Abby had dreamed that she had seen someone or something stalking him in the darkness.

The voice of Rusty Wells interrupted Cole's thoughts. "Creed Thomas saw Shiloh shoot Ned Walker at the Palace Saloon. He said Shiloh shucked his gun and fired before Ned could even grip his pistol."

"Every cattle drive has its share of trouble. I'm sure this one will be no different," Cole finally answered. "The San Juans are still an untamed wilderness with their own perils, but at least they don't have the likes of the Kwahadi Comanche to deal with. I survived the war and the Comanche. Shiloh or whatever trouble lies ahead doesn't worry me so much."

The cattle began to grow restless as a pack of coyotes began to yap excitedly at the rising moon. "I'm going to go check on the cattle and ride nighthawk for a while," Cole said, standing. "The coyotes have them stirred up. I'll see if I can't settl'em down a bit."

Cole had seen many a coyote spook longhorn cattle in the night. Some nights it seemed anything could get them going: thunder and lightning, a rain slicker flappin' in the wind, a group of ducks exploding in flight from the river. Almost any noise or movement could trigger a stampede.

He rode amidst the herd, softly singing the hymn, "Nearer, My God, to Thee," until the cattle finally settled and began to lay back down.

One by one the men left the fire and went to bed. Those whose turn it was to ride watch took their places around the perimeter of the cattle.

Lee Hansen still lay awake listening to the night. He could hear something walking directly behind him. Suddenly a pinecone snapped under the weight of something heavy. Lee's heart began to race. Whatever was there seemed to be creeping closer.

Suddenly something grabbed his leg causing him to scream out in bloody terror. "Help! Help!"

"Ha, ha, I got ya good, ya big lug," Garth laughed. "You thought a grizzly bear had you, didn't ya?"

"Dawg-gone ya, Garth, ya ornery cuss. You always gotta be pullin' a joke on someone when they're tryin' to get some sleep."

"Just admit it, Lee. You thought a grizzer had ya, didn't ya?" Garth taunted.

"I knew it weren't no grizzly. Now leave me alone, ya pesky pup."

"Why'd ya scream like a little girl then, Lee?"

Lee turned away from his tormentor and pulled his blanket around his chin, closing his eyes once again. "I'll get you back, Garth, wait and see."

Garth made his bed and laid there awhile with a big grin, laughing on occasion at the thought of Lee's high-pitched screams. He loved razzing Lee and getting him riled. He himself wasn't afraid of no grizzly or anything else, except maybe the dark. He peered up at the stars which shone brightly in the far reaches of the vast vault and noticed how they paled as they drew closer to the glory of the three-quarter moon.

Rockslide

The next morning Cole let the cattle start grazing upriver on their own until they fell in place behind the leads. The men took their places with the herd and began to prod them steadily onward. With each mile, the canyon narrowed, and the rugged gray cliffs rose higher. Soon the mountains, which towered above, threatened to close them in. On both sides of the trail, ancient ponderosa pines rose more than a hundred feet tall.

Cole noticed up ahead several gray rocks protruding from the cliffs, leaning precariously as they frowned down upon the canyon below. He turned Comanche about and went to warn the men to keep the cattle shy of the rock.

He rode back along the flank of the herd where he noticed several cattle wandering unattended in the rocks above, a sight that experience told him boded trouble.

"Kent, it's your job to keep the cattle down out of them rocks," he hollered above the chaos. "Keep 'em down below on the trail like I told you earlier. Go fetch them now before they cause a rockslide. You hear me?"

The young cowboy nodded, then watched Cole ride out of sight. In spite of Cole's warning, he made no effort to retrieve the stubborn steers. It wasn't long before the cattle's clumsy clamorings caused a number of large rocks to dislodge and fling themselves down the mountain, at a dangerous tumult, toward the men and the herd.

"Rockslide! Watch out!" Kent began to holler over the growing rumble.

PLATORO THE SUMMER RANGE

The herd panicked as more and more rocks began to bound downhill toward the men and cattle below. A large rock slammed hard into Seth Callahan's head. Another hit him in the side with a sickening thud, knocking him from his horse. Other rocks bounced hard off trees and cattle as they continued pell-mell down the hill on their way to the river.

Cole, upon hearing the commotion, turned his horse about, then rode with urgency to the scene of the rockslide. "Anybody been hurt?" he hollered out.

"Seth's been hurt bad," Kent hollered back. "A rock hit him in the head."

When Cole reached the young man's side, Seth lay on his back in great agony, gasping for air. A good amount of blood trickled from an open wound on his scalp and ran down his face and neck. Cole pulled his bandana from around his neck and mopped the blood from the boy's eyes and face then applied pressure to the head wound.

"Just lie still, Seth. You're gonna be okay."

He took ahold of the cowboy's hand as others arrived and gathered around. "Seth, if you can hear me, squeeze my hand." The young cowboy did not respond. Cole asked a second time but still no response.

"Is he gonna die, Cole?" Kent said, his voice frantic with worry.

"I don't know." Cole put his arm out to the side. "If you wanna help, you all can move back and give me some room and start prayin'."

Cole opened Seth's blood-soaked shirt and examined him further as the others looked on with solemn concern. "He's got some broken ribs, too. Garth, hurry and fetch clean rags from the wagon. Toss me your canteen first."

Cole spoke to the men with grave urgency as he worked on Seth. "Drivin' cattle up here in the mountains, men, is a far sight more dangerous than pushin' cows around on flatland. A careless attitude up here will get a man killed faster'n anything. It may already have."

Kent dropped to his knees and ran his fingers through his hair as he bowed his head in regret. "I should've done what you told me, Cole. I'm sorry, Seth," he repeated over and over.

Garth arrived back with the linen, and Cole worked fast, as only a man with a great deal of experience in such things could. "There's not much more we can do for him here," Cole said. "Kent, you and Luke take Seth down the mountain and get him to a doctor as fast as you can. You best get goin' now. This is serious. Get goin'."

Within minutes, the three were out of sight. "Anybody else hurt?" Cole said, looking around. The men shook their heads. "Good. Best we check on the cattle then."

Cole and Bob examined the cattle that had been near the slide. Some had cuts from the rocks, but miraculously, none had broken legs or serious injuries.

"This is a terrible start to the trip," Cole said, slapping his hat against his leg in frustration.

By evening, the men had pushed the cattle to the mouth of the Conejos Canyon. Cole sat his horse on a narrow point which commanded a sweeping view of the river valley. The Conejos River glistened while it flowed majestically between wide bends of slow water, finally losing itself among the cottonwoods and pines that flanked its shallow banks.

It was here the trail split, with the left fork progressing over LaManga Pass and on to Chama, while the right fork followed the Conejos River up the canyon. "Keep 'em to the right," Cole hollered. The men pushed the cattle along the river trail to where the canyon widened and gave way to lush green meadows. As they arrived within the Conejos Canyon, the entire herd began to spread out and graze upon the emerald green grass. "Hah! ... Hah! ..." The cowboys hollered and whistled as they brought the cattle into the meadows.

Bob London motioned towards the trees. "Appears there's some good flat ground above the river just before the Elk Creek that would make a fine place to camp for the night."

Cole motioned back to Paulie and Stump to head their wagons toward a flat glade of aspen. Paulie pointed his mules in that direction and put them on their way.

Cole continued to ride along the Conejos River which meandered like a snake trail through the broad canyon. They had now made passage into the beginning of the summer range and all in good time.

That evening, he and the men made camp on the lee side of the canyon, up away from the river, as the sun sank behind the mountains. A short time later, darkness enfolded the canyon.

Not long after nightfall, a spike bull elk and several cows made their way down the Elk Creek drainage to the river to get a drink. They were nervous of the cattle and hurried to quench their thirst at the riffles.

Before the shifty bunch could finish drinking, a sentinel cow began calling a warning to the rest of the herd. A second later, the small group of elk turned and ran back to the safety of the trees. The popping of branches and the pounding of their hooves caused quite a commotion as they hurried up the steep mountainside. Because of the chaos, the cattle began to stand and lift their noses into the air with snorts of discontent. Even Moses, the gentle, neck ox, was nervous and on edge.

"The cattle are just a stick break away from headin' back to the ranch," Cole warned the men. "If they stampede, turn the leads back into the drag and get them to mill to the right. I don't want no shootin'." The men held their breath, knowing the cattle might stampede at any moment.

Cole and Bob slowly weaved their horses through the herd, singing softly to calm them. The serenade seemed to work, for in a few minutes, the unruly beasts, one by one, had begun to lay back down and blow off once again. The cattle were worn down and a tired steer was less of a threat to stampede than one that was fresh-legged.

"Bob, I think it would be a good idea if we keep the cattle here one more day," Cole suggested. "We could put some of them into the first meadow of Elk Creek tomorrow so they could spread out a bit."

"I agree. We should let the cattle and the horses tarry here awhile before pushing onward. I'll tell the men."

In a jail cell in Alamosa, Graham Lassiter sat contemplating his situation. Collin Bean and Clay Rayburn, two of Lassiter's right-hand men, sat in the cell across from him.

When Mrs. Lassiter stopped by in the afternoon to visit her husband, she handed him a note. It was from Saul Bardello, another of his men.

The note read: "I was with Shiloh and Manter when the posse came. They tracked us as far as Cat Creek where we holed up for the night in the sheepherder's cabin. They winged Shiloh, but he escaped and lit out for the mountains. We split up. Shiloh's headed for Grayback, and I am headed for Spruce Hole. Shiloh needs Lee Manter to bring some supplies to the lake on Grayback mountain and leave them. Manter is holed up in the triangle at the old Wiescamp cabin."

Graham Lassiter tore up the note into tiny pieces and handed it back to his wife. He borrowed a pencil and paper from her and quickly scribbled out a note of his own. He folded it a couple of times and handed it to her.

"Martha, see that this note gets to Lee Manter. He's hid out at the old Wiescamp cabin over on the Alamosa River. He'll know what to do. See that you're not followed."

Mrs. Lassiter took the note and pinned it to the inside of her bonnet. "How are you, Graham? You don't look well," she said.

"They've set my bail at $100,000, and I'm scheduled to stand trial next week. They plan to charge me with twenty counts of murder, cattle theft, and who knows what all. Good gracious, Martha. How do you think I'm doing?"

Mrs. Lassiter looked down at the floor while her husband paced in his cell. She had only been trying to make conversation.

Graham Lassiter leaned against the bars and gripped them with both hands. "I'm innocent, Martha. I didn't do what they say."

"Have you found a lawyer?" Mrs. Lassiter asked.

"I've hired the best lawyer money can buy. A man named Neil Travers out of Trinidad."

Lassiter reached out and put his hand on his wife's wrist and squeezed it tightly. "Martha, I want you to hear me good. You are not to read the note I gave you. The less you know, the better. The note is for Lee Manter only, understand?"

Mrs. Lassiter nodded and jerked her wrist away from his tightening grip. "I understand."

"Very good. You best go now before the guards get suspicious."

Martha Lassiter drove her horse and buggy into the night finding Lee Manter hiding out in the cabin along Alamosa Creek where her husband had said he would be. She delivered the note and left abruptly as if in a hurry to get home.

Lee Manter opened the paper and read it. It said: "Load two pack horses with food and supplies and take them up to the little lake on Grayback for Shiloh." There were further instructions that disturbed him, but who was he to question the orders of Graham Lassiter.

As Mrs. Lassiter hurried home along the steep and very narrow mountain road, someone stepped from the darkness onto the path in front of her and purposely frightened her horse. It was someone she recognized.

In an instant, the startled horse reared then veered off the road. Mrs. Lassiter screamed as she and the buggy began to tumble down the steep cliff to the bottom, a hundred feet below.

"I'm sorry, Mrs. Lassiter," the man said quietly as he stared down into the darkness. "Your husband's note had instructions for me to see that you didn't come back. We couldn't take a chance on you knowin' our plans." Lee Manter turned his horse west and rode toward the safety of the dark canyons.

Elk Creek

The next morning, Cole and Griz decided to ride up the Conejos Canyon past Elk Creek to scout things out. They rode upriver another two miles to where the meadows spread out wide between the cliffs when Cole began to smell smoke.

Across the river to the east he noticed a wisp of smoke curling up through the pines that grew along the cliffs. He and Griz rode that way to check out the situation.

When they entered the trees, they could see four horses tied farther up the hillside in front of what appeared to be a cave. A sorrel, a roan, a bay, and a big black stood tethered to a cross-picket line out front. By the looks of the trampled soil and piles of manure, the horses had been tied there for several days. Cole moved his eyes from the horses to the cave itself. There appeared to be a good amount of ore tailings piled up outside the entrance.

"This is someone's claim, Griz."

Griz nodded and pointed to a weathered board with words written on it. The board read: "Kep off Ore Git Shot." In spite of the misspelled words, the message was clear. Visitors were not welcome.

The sound of an iron pick striking rock inside the claim suddenly stopped, and a big man with a dirt stained face and wild, flowing hair came out of the entrance holding a double- barreled, side by side shotgun. The man wore an old black felt hat and tattered bib overalls that were soiled from wear.

"Howdy," Cole hollered. "We saw the smoke from your fire and thought we'd say hello."

The man pointed the shotgun at Cole's chest and bared his teeth. His throat clicked in a dry, raspy growl. He motioned to the sign. "Can't ya read? This here claim is ourn' and ain't no claim jumpers gonna take it." He leaned forward and spit a glob of black goo upon the ground then glanced over at Griz who had his hand on the end of his rifle but hadn't pulled it yet.

"You better not shuck that gun, Mex. I got a barrel here for you, too." The man took his thumb and pulled back the hammers on both barrels until they clicked back in place.

"She's ready to talk now. She throws a bloody swath, too. If you ain't left by the time I count to five, I'll turn her loose." Three more men came out of the claim, dirty and holding rifles. The man spit another glob of tobacco at the ground then began to count.

"One…"

"Hold it right there, mister," Cole said. "We're not lookin' to take your claim. We're the Golden Willow Ranch out of Las Mesitas. We're out scoutin' the canyon before we move a big herd of cattle up through tomorrow."

The man was not deterred. "Two," he continued to count.

Cole turned his horse to leave. "Let's go, Griz. There's no talkin' with this one."

The man hollered after them as they left. "Keep your cattle away from our claim, or I'll kill 'em and eat 'em."

Cole whipped his horse around and faced the man once again, pointing his finger this time. "Mister, killin' cattle is still a hangin' offense. You lay a hand on any of our herd, and I'll hang you myself."

He pointed at the others. "That goes for all of you." Cole was madder than a run-over snake, but still he turned his horse around to leave.

"Come on, Griz. We best give these vermin a wide berth. If we don't, I may have to kill that fella."

That afternoon, when they returned to camp, they told Bob London of the encounter with the man at the gold claim. London was very concerned. "I ran into a man a few weeks back at the Palace Saloon I believe is the same man you're describin'. He had to spend the night in the jail for fighting and pulling a knife on a miner. Sheriff Simcox told me his name is Mordecai Lundy."

Cole shook his head. "This fella is gonna be trouble, Bob. I can feel it down to my boots. It sure makes you wonder what he's doing up here in the mountains. I bet he's got his sights set on robbin' the gold coming out of Platoro."

Bob nodded. "We better swing wide of him with the cattle tomorrow. I don't want to lose any more men."

That evening feathery clouds resembling mares' tails drifted randomly in the blue sky above. "Looks like it may rain," Cole said, pointing up. "Mare's tail clouds are a pretty good sign. We better tarp the wagons and get some kindlin' piled, just in case."

Cole had some of the younger men gather firewood. Carlos and Rusty showed up with an armload of sticks. "Where do you want this kindlin', Cole?"

"Put it under the wagon so it will be dry, come a rain."

"Yes, sir," they said.

Later that night, a steady drizzle settled into the canyon covering it with a thick veil of mist. The air was aromatic with the pleasing fragrance of wet spruce intermingled with that of the rain.

Soon brilliant bolts of lightning splintered the night sky in jagged lines followed by loud claps and peels of thunder which echoed and rolled in seemingly endless reverberations.

"Just listen to that thunder roll," Paulie said. "That's a wondrous sound. A body can't hear long rumbles like that on the flatland, only in the mountains."

"The lightning will become more fierce the higher we go," London said. "I've heard folks say it don't strike twice in the same place, but anyone who believes that nonsense ain't never been in the high country."

Cole kept an eye to the troubled sky. "What do you think, Bob? You think this one's gonna turn into a toad strangler?"

"Naw, my bones has a way of lettin' me know when a toad strangler's comin', and so far, they ain't talkin' much."

"I hope you're right. The cattle sure are restless, though. I believe I'll keep a close watch on them tonight. I'll take Griz along with me."

Bob nodded. "Me and some of the younger bucks will relieve you later."

The storm broke sometime in the night, and come morning, the sun rose into a clear blue sky. The canyon was soundless and still, the air fresh, and the bushes dripped with moisture. The cattle grazed calmly.

As the morning progressed, Cole and some of the other men rode six abreast loose herding nearly a thousand head of longhorns. Cole rode Comanche in high elegance, his heart swollen in his chest. He loved trailin' cattle.

Spotting a handful of wayward steers that were laid up in a willow thicket, he put his horse into the mix and brought them out. One of them was Ol' Rebel who was reluctant to come.

Cole pushed the steers to the south side of the river away from the miners they had trouble with the day before. After some effort, he got Ol' Rebel to cross and join the others.

Across the river, up among the trees, Mordecai Lundy watched and listened to the commotion of the cattle bawling and the cries and whistles and the crack of the bull whips in the air as the large herd passed by.

Lundy's empty stomach gnawed at him for a taste of fresh beef. He turned and walked back into the cave. Seconds later he emerged with his rifle in hand, determined to do no good.

Silver Top

Cole galloped up to the front of the herd where Bob London was riding point. "We've done got most of the cattle up past that miner we had trouble with yesterday," he informed him. Cole removed his hat and wiped his brow with the back of his hand. "I was worried we'd catch some grief from that fella."

"The day ain't over yet," Bob reminded.

Cole and Bob rode on opposite sides of the Conejos River searching for strays among the willows. About a mile in the distance, Cole noticed a dozen or so buzzards swinging in slow, lazy circles against the deep blue sky. The tightening of their carousel suggested they had found something below that interested them. The buzzards' presence piqued his curiosity, so he rode in that direction to see what had gotten their attention.

Cole worked his faithful paint horse in and out of the willows on his way upriver occasionally finding an ornery steer hiding there. Suddenly, Comanche alerted to something ahead and stopped. His ears swiveled forward on his head, and the bores of his nose flared in and out.

Cole stood in his stirrups and looked ahead. He couldn't see a thing for the tall brush. The slow carrousel of buzzards gliding overhead and the sight of magpies resting on yonder willows suggested that whatever was dead was close.

There was a strengthening of the breeze and a change of direction with it. Cole caught his first whiff of a carcass and recognized the awful stench of death. He looked around for Bob but didn't see him for the tall willows that grew about, so he rode up to a knoll overlooking the river to observe the land below.

Just beyond the magpies, he spotted movement among the willows. At first glance, it appeared to be a durham cow with a steer at her side, but on second look, he realized it was a large mamma grizzly with a big two-year-old cub. They appeared to be on a kill of some sort.

Cole looked over and saw Bob riding right upon them. "Look out, Bob!" he hollered, waving his hands above his head. "It's a sow grizzly and her cub. Get out of there quick!"

Just then the mamma grizzly raised and stood on her hind legs, her large head and broad shoulders clearly visible above the willows as she peered over them at Bob. When the bear saw him approaching, she let out a threatening roar, dropped back down on all fours, and charged.

Cole swung up his rifle as the she bear closed in on Bob. Looking down the barrel, he could see willows parting and hear water splashing as the sow came on full bore ahead.

He fired a couple of shots then another as Bob lost control of his frantic horse. Buck reared high, throwing Bob to the ground onto his back, then bolted away with an empty saddle and stirrups flopping against his flanks.

The nearly grown cub let out a moan and plunged into the river. The sow grizzly turned also and followed the cub. Seconds later, both bears ran up the hillside into the cover of the trees. As they did, Cole continued to shoot. One of his bullets appeared to have hit the adult cub, though he wasn't sure how badly.

Cole put Comanche into a gallop, soon arriving at Bob's side. "Bob, are you alright? Are you hurt?"

"I ain't hurt 'cept my tail-bone and my pride." Bob sat up. "Are the bears gone?"

"They ran off into them trees up yonder," Cole said, pointing across the river.

"Good enough. I would have been gut grease, though, if you hadn't shot when you did." He picked up his hat and held out his hand. "Here, heft me up. I ain't as young as I once was."

Cole gripped Bob's hand and helped him to his feet. "Are you sure you're alright, Bob?"

"I believe so. I think my heart is back to beatin' again. Do what you need to do. I'll be along shortly soon as I catch my horse."

"I'm gonna go take a look at what them bears were feeding on," Cole said. He maneuvered Comanche through a maze of well-defined trails until he came to a small clearing within the willows. The grass inside was flattened down and tinted red with blood. In the center of the blood-soaked circle was a body.

"Bob, you should come see this." Cole got down and examined the body. The corpse was mangled, but he could tell it was a man. The awful stench made him cough and gag. He pulled his bandana over his nose, but it did little good.

Bob dismounted and pushed through the willows until he came to Cole's side. "Goodness, gracious," he gasped, when he saw the mauled body. He pulled his bandana over his nose and moved closer to the mangled corpse.

"I think I recognize this fella, Cole. I believe he's the miner that was fightin' with that Lundy fella in the Palace Saloon."

"Are you sure, Bob?"

"I can't be certain sure because his face is so swolled up, but I'm pretty sure."

"You don't suppose Lundy could've murdered this fella, do you, Bob?"

Bob looked at him from under the brim of his hat. "I'd say it's sure enough possible, but there's no way to be certain. I know one thing. This man's been dead for a good while."

Cole put his foot in the stirrup and swung back up in the saddle. "I don't know what's worse; having a killer grizzly around or having a cold-blooded murderer on the loose lurking about. We got us one or the other. Either way, we better warn the boys to keep the cattle away from this mess. Them steers get a whiff of it, they'll stampede for sure."

Griz Montoya came riding up. "What was all that shootin' I heard? What happened?"

"Bob rode up on a sow grizzly and her cub. They were on a carcass when he surprised them."

"Cole turned her charge with his shots, or she would have had me," Bob said.

"Is she dead?"

Cole shook his head. "No, I believe I hit the big cub, but the sow never acted shot. They both lit a shuck up the hillside over yonder."

"What were they eatin' on?" Griz questioned.

"They were eatin' on a dead man. Bob thinks it's the same miner he saw fighting with that Lundy fella back in town."

Griz shook his head. "Now that she's tasted human blood, she could be very dangerous. She could be bad news for the cattle, too."

Cole nodded. "Could be a trouble-bear folks call Silver Top. I read somethin' about it in the paper. Griz, have the boys swing the cattle up away from the river so they don't get wind of the bear or the body and stampede."

"I'll bury the man and mark the grave in case we find out who he belongs to. He deserves a proper burial and some scripture read over him."

Later that day, as the herd moved steadily along, the wind began to change. Some of the steers began to lift their noses. It didn't take long for their fearful body language to stir up the entire herd. In a split second, they all bolted.

"Stampede!" Lee Hansen hollered.

The ground began to rumble with the sound of pounding hooves as the entire herd was now on the move. The cattle continued to run upriver until they eventually tired in the meadows a mile or so below where the South Fork flowed into the Conejos River. When everyone was accounted for, they took a tally of the livestock. All the cattle were accounted for as well.

With all the herd now gathered in the large meadows below the confluence of the two rivers, the men decided to make camp there in a dale between two saddle ridges. Once the herd had settled in, the men built a fire and trickled in for supper.

That night Cole and Bob decided to let the men unwind before giving them the details about the dead body they had found. As the men gathered around the fire, there was a loud whoop and a holler from down the trail. It was Kent Severs and Luke Parnell. They had returned safely back after taking Seth down the mountain the week before.

"I'm glad you two made it back safe," Cole said. "How is Seth?"

"He's alive, but he can't talk just yet because his brain's been hurt. The doc says he's gonna live, but he's not sure if he'll ever be *okay*," Kent said glumly.

"The doc doesn't think Seth will be able to join us again this summer," Luke added.

"It sounds like we need to keep prayin' for Seth," Cole said. "There's plenty of vittles left. Go get you some while it's hot. Welcome back."

"Yes, sir. It's good to be back. Oh, I almost forgot. Judge Parker stopped by the ranch while we was back. He left a book for you. He said the Governor of New Mexico wrote it and wanted you to have the first copy. It's in my poke," Luke said. "I'll fetch it."

Luke dug the book from his saddle bag and handed it to Cole. "It's a bit dusty from ridin' in my poke."

Cole read the book's cover. *Ben-Hur* by Lew Wallace. He opened the book, and it cracked with newness. Inside the cover was written some words:

My friend, Cole. I found it only fitting that you should have the first copy of my book. After the grievous loss at Shiloh some years back, I felt the need to purvey an assessment of my faith and to that end, have found my faith anew, and that in Christ.

The result of my searching has brought about this book. I only hope its message can bring a healing to our nation as the writing of it has done for me in my own soul.

To God be all glory, Lew Wallace

Cole closed the book and put it away. Later, when everyone had gathered around the fire, Cole decided it was time to make an announcement.

"Listen up, everyone. I've got a couple of things I want to address. By now I'm sure you all know about the grizzly Bob encountered back down river. What you may not know is that it was a man those bears were eatin' on."

The men looked surprised. "We may have a man-eating grizzly around camp. Could be a trouble-bear folks around call Silver Top, so we need to be vigilant and keep a well-lit fire every night. And with the greed for gold up in these parts, we can't rule out that it was a murder either. So, whether we got us a mad grizzly or a cold-blooded killer around, we better keep our guns close and sleep light until we get this sorted out."

A Life Changing Decision

"Cole, I was wonderin' if you'd ride with me tomorrow? I'd be glad for the company," Bob said.

"Sure, Bob, I'd be glad to."

The following day, Cole and Bob rode the perimeter of the herd together. As they worked, Cole noticed that Bob seemed to be taking labored breaths.

"The air is already a lot thinner up here. I can feel it," Bob said. "I take a deep breath, but I get less air. Today I feel a tightness in my chest and a numbness in my arm." He rubbed his arm and straightened it.

He looked over at Cole with a grin. "I may get winded easier then I used to, but at least my horns ain't sawed off yet."

Cole leaned over the side of Comanche and pulled up a stem of grass and stuck it between his teeth. He chewed lightly on the tender shoot as he rode along, with his hat tipped down to shade his eyes. At the moment, most of the cattle were moving well on their own, eager to enter their new surroundings.

Cole pulled something from his vest pocket and smiled. He smelled it a moment and smiled again. Between his thumb and forefinger, he held one of Abby's hair ribbons she had given him.

"You're real sweet on that niece of mine, aren't you, Cole."

"Yes, sir. A woman like her is hard to find," he said.

London nodded. "She's a special one. My wife and I couldn't have children, so we favor her like she is our own."

The two rode in silence for some time before London spoke again.

"You know, Cole, time in the saddle gives a man pause to ponder on things, especially up here in the mountains with its beauty and its perils."

"I could have been killed by that sow grizzly just the same as not, and we've already had us a scare with young Seth. One moment you're here and the next you're gone. Death can happen to any of us before a body knows it."

Cole noticed a melancholy tone in Bob's voice he hadn't heard before. "Is somethin' troublin' you, Bob?"

Bob chewed on his thoughts a while before answering. "The past few months I've just had this feeling like my life is drawin' short. Something tells me I might not be goin' back home this time."

He fidgeted uncomfortably with the bridle reins that lay folded in his hands. "Lately, I've been wrestlin' with what happens to a feller after he dies? You have a lot of knowledge about the Bible. I figure being a man of faith, you might could help me out?"

"I'd be glad to," Cole nodded. "It's a fair enough question. I know if I died today, I'd be with the Lord in Heaven, and that's a comfort."

"I suppose it is a real comfort to know where a fella stands with the Lord before he dies," Bob said.

"It is," Cole nodded again.

"How did you know you were squared up with the Lord, Cole?"

Cole thought a second. "I settled it in my heart one day that I needed to know the God of the Bible my parents knew.

One Sunday we had a revival, and after the minister preached on God's love and mercy and forgiveness, he gave the call to accept Jesus and repent and be baptized in accordance with scripture. I realized I was a sinner, and my sin hadn't been covered yet because I had never repented and asked Jesus into my heart. I was still separated from God. That day I asked Jesus to forgive my sin and come into my heart, and I was baptized in a little creek up the road from our church."

"Can a fella really know God?" London said. "I mean know Him like one knows a kin folk or somethin'?"

"Sure, they can. We can learn about God by what He's created. Also, by readin' and studyin' on His Word and spending time with Him in prayer. And we can know God by knowin' God's son, Jesus. Jesus said he and the Father are one. 'If you have seen me, you have seen the Father'."

Cole rode over closer to Bob. "I kept my pa's Bible after he died. I remember one of the passages he had marked was in Romans chapter one. It says that God reveals Himself to us through what He created."

Bob looked at Cole and nodded. "His fingerprints is all around, ain't they."

"The Bible also says that God desires to know us and forgive our sins, but he can't unless we repent and ask for forgiveness for our sins."

"What does repent mean?" Bob asked.

"To repent means to turn away from your sins and feel remorse for them and confess them to God and ask His forgiveness then be buried with Him in baptism. That's what's called bein' 'born again'. The Bible says that our sin separates us from God and keeps us from truly knowing Him. It also says that there is no one righteous; that all have sinned."

"If we all sin, what can a body do to get right with God?" Bob said.

"We can't ever get right with God on our own, Bob. We can't make ourselves clean. Only the blood of Jesus can do that. Jesus said that, 'Unless a man be born again, he cannot see the kingdom of God.'

Sin exacts a debt we can't ever pay on our own. The Bible says, 'the wages of sin is death, but the gift of God is eternal life through Jesus His son.' Only Jesus Himself could pay that debt for us. And if that payment is enough for God, we know it covers all sin.

Just think about this, Bob. The very God that made us and the mountains and the stars cared enough about you and me to leave Heaven's glory and come as a babe and willingly die on the cross to pay the debt for our sins. That means our lives aren't just our own to live for ourselves. We were bought at a price with the precious blood of Jesus.

He took our sin with Him to the cross and nailed it there. After three days, He rose from the dead, and He promises that we can be with Him in Heaven forever, if we accept His gift of salvation. He did the hard part. Our part's simple."

Bob London chewed on Cole's words as he rode along. He respected Cole for his genuine faith. "Let me ask you another question then, Cole. I have loved only one woman, and I've stayed faithful to her all these years. I've always been kind and generous to folks, too. Are you sayin' that ain't enough to get me to Heaven? I still need to be born again?"

Cole nodded. "Yes, that's what the Bible is sayin', Bob. I heard a preacher say once that a good person can't get themselves into Heaven any more than a good steer can get into a corral by themselves unless there is a gate, and someone opens that gate and lets them in. Even then that steer still has to choose to enter through the gate before he can get into the fold.

Some are stubborn about it, too, rebellious, like Ol' Rebel. They don't want to go through the gate. God gives us a free will to choose His son or go our own way. Jesus is the gate. The gospel of John tells us that no one can enter Heaven except through the gate, which is Jesus. Jesus also said, 'I am the way, the truth and the life. No one comes to the Father except through me.'

So, you see, Bob, you can't just know about the gate and know that it's open. You have to enter through it to get into the pen. You have to choose Jesus as your Savior."

Bob London nodded. "I'm hearin' you, Cole. Keep on talkin'."

Cole continued to speak from his heart. "One of the first things I learned as a scout for the Cavalry is that everything leaves a track, and a pattern of tracks leaves a trail. The trail a person is on tells us not only where a body's been, but where he's goin'. Every one of us is on one of two trails, Bob. One trail leads to Heaven, and the other leads to Hell. You can't stay on the one trail and get to the end of the other. It don't work that way. The Bible says, 'There is a path that seems right to a man, but in the end, it leads only to death.' That's the trail of our sinful nature.

The Gospel of Matthew says that, 'Narrow is the path that leads to Heaven and only a few find it.' It's not because it's so hard to find, it's because only a few choose to look for it. You need to choose in your own heart what trail you want to be on, Bob, yours or God's."

Bob London nodded and sighed. "You're sayin' a lost sinner is like an ol' ornery steer, always wanting to go his own way."

"That's exactly right, Bob, and God is like a rancher that cares for His cattle. You can trust Him when He says, 'Don't go that way. There's no water that way.' or, 'The water is too swift and too deep to cross there, you'll drown. Don't go that way. Come this way. This is the right way. I created you. I know you.'"

Bob looked at Cole from under the brim of his hat and smiled.

"Sometimes we must really seem like a stubborn ol' steer to God, I reckon, like Ol' Rebel."

"I reckon so," Cole said with a chuckle. "Just like Ol' Rebel."

"I'd like to have the same assurance about my future that you have, Cole. A body never knows when he might take a horn, or get hit by lightning, or end up in the gut of a grizzly bear. By then I reckon it would be too late."

"Yes, I reckon so," Cole said.

"I figure it was for a reason the Lord spared me from that bear back yonder. It could've killed me, and I'd be in the eternal flames of Hell right now, but I ain't."

Bob halted his horse. "I ain't gonna fight it no longer. At my age, I got nothin' to lose and everything to gain. I'm ready now. I feel peaceful about it, too. I want to receive Jesus into my heart."

Bob removed his hat and bowed his head. Cole did the same. Bob prayed a sincere prayer of repentance as Cole listened.

"God, I know I've sinned against you. I'm heart broke about it, and I'm wantin' to repent and change. I ask for your forgiveness. I don't want to be separated from you no more cause of my sin. I want to be in your pasture and drink from your springs. I believe you sent your son, Jesus, to die on the cross and shed his blood to pay the price for my sin, and I accept that. I want you, Jesus, to be my Lord and Savior. Amen."

When he had finished, Bob London gave a big sigh of relief and put his hat back on. His face now held a peaceful countenance that had not been there before.

"I done it," he smiled.

"You're in His hands now, Bob," Cole said.

"I wish now I'd done it years ago. Thanks, Cole. It's not easy for a man my age to let go of old ways. I want to gather the boys tonight and let them know ol' Bob London's done got saved. I want to be baptized like the Bible says, and I want you to baptize me, Cole, there in the river."

"I'd be happy to, Bob. I'll tell the boys tonight."

That night after supper Cole made an announcement. "Bob's got some good news, but I'll let him tell you."

Bob stood in front of the men. "Today I got saved. I asked the Lord into my heart. It weren't hard neither. Cole helped me with it. Tonight, he's gonna baptize me in the river, and I want all of you to be a part of it."

Later that night, Cole and Bob made their way down to the riverbank where a fire was burning brightly. When everyone had gathered around, Cole held his Bible and stood next to Bob. "I want to read some scripture first before I baptize you, Bob."

Cole opened his Bible and began to read from Acts 2:38. "Repent and be baptized, every one of you in the name of Jesus Christ for the remission of sins, and ye shall receive the gift of the Holy Ghost."

He flipped over a page and continued reading. "Acts 3:19 says, 'Repent ye therefore, and be converted, that your sins may be blotted out, when the times of refreshing shall come from the presence of the Lord.'"

He flipped over again several more pages in his Bible and read II Corinthians 5:17,18. "Therefore, if any man be in Christ, he is a new creature: old things are passed away; behold, all things are become new. And all things are of God, who hath reconciled us to himself through Jesus Christ...."

After singing "Shall We Gather at the River," Cole and Bob continued to stand together on the bank within the warmth of the crackling fire. The men stood around with their hats removed in reverence as Cole spoke.

"Today Bob made the confession of faith and repentance. He asked Jesus into his heart. He acknowledged before God and man that he was a sinner. You see Bob didn't want his sin to stand between him and God no longer. Sin separates us from God and truly knowing Him, but Jesus made a way for us to be brought back to fellowship with God so we don't have to go to everlasting Hell.

What Bob is fixin' to do now is called baptism. Baptism is an outward symbol of the covenant a person makes with God. It symbolizes the death and burial of our old self by going under the water and then rising to walk anew with God. It symbolizes us being born again.

King David once said, 'Blessed is he whose transgression is forgiven, whose sin is covered.' Today Bob's sin debt has been covered. Today Bob asked for forgiveness for his sins, and God forgave him.

The Bible tells us that when God forgives, He forgives completely. The 103rd Psalm says that, 'As far as the east is from the west, so far hath he removed our transgressions from us.' That's God's way of saying forever, gentlemen." With that, Cole handed his Bible to Lightning, then he and Bob waded waist deep into the river, gasping at the cold touch of the water.

"Bob, I want to ask you, do you believe that God's son, Jesus, died for your sins and rose from the dead so that you also can have eternal life through Him?"

"Yes, I do."

"Bob, in the sight of these witnesses, do you accept Jesus as your Lord and Savior to live for Him from this day forward?"

"I surely do."

"Because of the covenant you made today, Bob, to accept Jesus as your Savior, I now baptize you in the name of the Trinity, that is, the Father, the Son, and the Holy Ghost, in accordance with scripture."

As the two men stood in the river, Cole laid Bob under the flow then raised him up from the water sputtering and dripping wet. "Woo, wee," Bob hollered.

Cole looked around. "Does anyone else want to get right with God tonight? There's no better time than right now. If you can't accept God's gift of salvation now among friends, here in God's creation, then when will you ever? If you died tonight would you go to Heaven? Jesus is reaching out His hand right now. Will you take it?"

Lightning and Rusty Wells stepped forward, followed by Carlos Sanchez. After they made the confession of faith and were baptized, they walked from the river and soon stood with blankets draped around their shoulders, shivering within the warmth of the fire.

In closing, Cole led the men in singing the first verse of "Near the Cross." "Jesus keep me near the cross; There a precious fountain. Free to all, a healing stream, Flows from Calvary's mountain..."

"Whoever wrote them words must have stood right here along the Conejos River," Bob said with a grin.

One by one the men began to go to bed except those whose turn it was to ride the watch. The day had been a long but very good day, and for some, it was the best day of their lives.

Flash Flood

Down river, Mordecai Lundy and his men were growing restless. "I think it's time we move upriver. There's not much gold here," Mordecai grumbled. "Maybe a hundred dollars' worth when it's all said and done."

"Don't forget we have to split it four ways," Hiram Leech reminded. "That's only twenty-five dollars apiece."

"I can cipher," Lundy scolded. "I do all the work around here, and I'm supposed to split the gold with you lazy buffoons. What if I don't wanna?" The three men were uncomfortable with the question and didn't answer.

Mordecai rubbed his beard then grinned. "If there weren't so many of us, we wouldn't have to split the gold so many ways. Maybe that's the problem; too many fingers in the pot. I got me an idea what can remedy that, though."

Lundy leaned and spit a glob of tobacco. "For instance, Hiram, you could kill Bones and Fritz tonight in their sleep, then we could split the money just two ways. Or maybe Bones and Fritz might knife you in your sleep tonight, Hiram, and leave you to the buzzards and magpies."

"Don't listen to him, boys," Hiram said. "He's just tryin' to get into our heads and confuse us like he always does."

Hiram looked at Mordecai and the others with a sheepish grin. "I guess there's another option you ain't thought about Mordecai…"

Lundy's eyes shaded. "And what might that be?"

A fearful tingle tracked up Hiram's spine causing him to swallow hard. "Well, I guess the three of us could…"

"Could what?" Lundy began to laugh. "The three of you can't kill me. I ain't killable. Even if you did kill me, still I'd come back as a ghost and carve your livers."

Lundy began to boast of his terrible deeds. "Remember when we robbed the bank back in Lamar, Missouri, how the law put three bullets in me, and still I lived?

Remember when I boarded with old lady Tabor, and she poisoned me because she was afraid of me? That didn't work either. Now she's takin' a dirt nap with the worms and the maggots. Even Frank and Jessie James were fearful of me, and rightly so."

Fear crept over all three men though they tried not to let on so. "You ought not to have killed the fella that had this here claim," Fritz said. "Sooner or later all this killin' is gonna get us caught or worse yet, get us hung. We'll be lucky if them cowboys ain't already found the body you hid upriver."

Lundy's eyes began to flash with anger. He drew his big knife from its sheath and held it up. "There you go again, Fritz, sassin' me just like the Hansen brothers did."

Fritz remembered how Lundy had brutally killed the Hansen brothers in their sleep for back talkin' him, and his face flushed hot. He got up and walked outside to get some air. He knew firsthand what Lundy was capable of.

Lundy sheathed his knife then took a long drink from the crock of whiskey. He wiped his mouth with the back of his hand. "I'm done with this here claim. The real gold is upriver at the gold camp, Platoro. We'll be leavin' at first light in the mornin'."

Five miles away to the north, over on Lookout Mountain, Shiloh Tremble found the supplies Lee Manter had left for him on Grayback Mountain and packed them to an abandoned cabin on the edge of Schinzel Flats near Elwood Pass. The cabin was quaint and smelled of age and neglect, but it would serve him just fine. There he spent only one night before leaving the morning following, for the lee of Lookout Mountain.

With the morning sun, warm on his face, Shiloh sat on the flat windswept crest with his back against a large gray boulder, observing all that lay within his sight. The anvil shaped peak offered a magnificent view of the wilderness below and far beyond.

To the southwest rose the gray faced peaks of the divide and to the south, Conejos Peak and Banded Peak. Far to the northeast rose the Sangre De Cristos some 100 miles distant.

Directly below him, Lookout Mountain had crumbled away with time and the elements, leaving an exposed scar of red, yellow, and white colored earth. Below that was a vast sea of spruce timber, dark in the shadows and brighter green where the sun touched it.

To the left, Alum Creek cut a deep gorge shortly after it flowed from the rocks nearby. It ran muddy with a sick ocher color at first, then cleared somewhat as it reached the Alamosa River far below.

Along the river, the canyon road wound its way upward through silent shaded glades of aspen rising in a spiral of switchbacks until it lost itself among the spruce on Stunner Pass.

Shiloh watched the road all day until darkness enfolded the lower reaches of the canyon and crept its way toward him. He repeated the process of keeping watch for the next five days.

On the sixth day, he left to restock his supplies. After leaving the old cabin, he noticed five riders, more than a mile off, crossing Schinzel Flats, headed his way. He knew these mountains better than most. He turned his horse and headed down Alum Creek. An hour's descent brought him to the river. He crossed it, then was quickly absorbed into the spruce and gone.

By the fifteenth of June the cattle were grazing contentedly above the South Fork in the lush meadows there. The heat of summer was causing the snow on the peaks to melt rapidly in the afternoon, thus swelling the river. By late afternoon, dark clouds had moved into Conejos Canyon.

The men made quick shelter among the spruce by running ridge poles over the wagons between two trees and throwing a couple of large tarps over it. The wind kicked up and soon the rain began to pour, blowing slant ways in heavy sheets.

"We got us a toad strangler now," London hollered over the noise of the storm.

Gullies and drainages that had been dry, quickly turned into raging torrents of flood water that merged one into the other, finally spilling into the already swollen Conejos River. The rising water soon trapped part of the herd.

"We have to get the cattle up to higher ground," Cole hollered. His words were all but swallowed by the roar of the pounding rain.

By the time the men could get to the cattle, many were surrounded by knee deep water which was rising steadily. The stranded cows bellowed and bawled as they realized their eminent peril. Each man put his horse into the rising flood waters. Once on the other side, the men surrounded the stranded cattle and drove them to the river.

The cattle were reluctant to cross, but with a great deal of prodding, they plunged into the water, headed for higher ground. Their sides heaved, and their bodies bobbed like plank boards as they made steady progress and began to emerge on to the higher ground.

The stronger cattle began to gain their footing and scramble up the far bank amidst the lightning and driving rain while some of the older and weaker cattle, as well as the young, began to be swept by the current downstream.

Cole and some of the men rode down river looking for floaters. "Come on, ol' girl," Cole hollered to an older cow that was struggling to keep her footing. "Come on, fight it, girl," he repeated. Suddenly the mamma cow slipped, and the current rolled her over a couple of times. He swung his lariat at the sinking cow, catching her around the neck. Comanche pulled against the tremendous drag of the current which pushed against the cow until the rope was tight. He drug the exhausted cow over to the bank to safety and set her loose. She lay there a moment before finally gaining her feet.

Titus Martin and Carlos Sanchez both lassoed drowning calves. The horses began to pull the calves to safety. When he reached the river's edge, Titus jumped from his horse and cradled his calf in his arms. He stumbled up the slippery bank and sent the calf sprawling onto the wet ground. The calf quickly recovered its footing and ran to the side of its waiting mother who smelled of it, gave a maternal bellow, then took it in. Eventually the cattle were safe on higher ground with the rest of the herd.

"I think we got 'em all," Bob said.

"We don't have Ol' Rebel," Rusty hollered. "He's still over across the river. I tried to fetch him over, but he wouldn't come." A flash of lightning revealed Ol' Rebel stranded on a small rise across the river. The steer bellowed nervously as the water, which surrounded him, continued to rise.

"It's too dangerous to go after him now," Cole hollered. "He chose his fate. Let's look after them that's with us."

The men were exhausted and soaked to the bone. They stayed up under the cover of the trees until the storm broke. When it finally abated, they built a fire with dry kindlin' from under the wagon and began to dry off. Cole gathered blankets from a chest on the wagon and handed them out.

"It looks like we just got another taste of the perils of the high country," Bob said.

A large pot of coffee soon finished brewing against the fire. The men filled their cups and drank in its steaming warmth. Cole held out his cup in a toast. "Men, you risked your lives for the brand. Bob and I won't forget it and neither will Mr. McKnight."

As he finished his coffee and waited for his clothes to dry, he thought of Abby. He wondered how she was doing and if she missed him as much as he missed her. Although he had known her for only a few short weeks, he felt as though he had known her for a lifetime.

Cole knew the character of the family from which Abby had been raised and the values of work and faith that defined her. Together they could build a ranch and a love that would last.

That evening after supper, while sitting around the fire, Cole brought out his new book, *Ben-Hur*; the one his friend, General Lew Wallace, had written. Cole began to read it as the men listened quietly with no other sounds but the distant flow of the river, the light rustle of the breeze among the spruce, and the crackle of the fire.

"Book First, Chapter 1," he began. "The Jebeles Zubleh is a mountain fifty miles and more in length, and so narrow that its tracery on the map gives it a likeness to a caterpillar crawling from the south to the north. Standing on its red-and-white cliffs, and looking off under the path of the rising sun, one sees only the Desert of Arabia…"

Cole read on for nearly an hour before marking the page and closing the book. He followed with a prayer and bid the men goodnight.

"Maybe you could read to us more from that book this summer, Cole," Paulie said. "It's a comfort to hear words read out loud. I'm afraid I never learned."

"I ain't ever learned to read either," Stump admitted as well. "Not like you can read, Cole. Goodnight to yah."

By morning, the sky was once again a deep blue except for where white clouds of mist clung to the mountain tops. Along the river, dew-laden bushes sparkled in the morning sunlight. Far to the southwest, a brilliant double rainbow spanned the breadth of the sky in vivid colors.

The river, still swollen, carried a large pine tree which tumbled over and over as it was swept along by the angry current. There was no sign of Ol' Rebel.

When the clouds finally drifted away, they revealed a white dusting of snow upon the peaks. Because of the soft ground and washed out trails, Cole decided it best to stay the herd another two days. They would use the time to dry out and repair the trails for the passage of the wagons. When ready, they would push the cattle on to the Saddle Creek and Lake Fork meadows below Platoro.

Cole rode downstream searching for Ol' Rebel. He found him, one mile downriver, trapped in a tangle of trees and brush, his body partially penned below the water. Only his head and right front leg were visible. When Cole approached, the steer turned his head. Ol' Rebel was still alive! With a little work, he was able to free the stubborn longhorn from the river's angry grip and pull him to safety.

Attacked

The next day Cole took Luke Parnell along with him to clear the trail up ahead so the wagons could pass without obstruction. They hadn't gone far when they came upon a place where the rain had washed out the wagon road, leaving it covered with rocks, logs, and brush. Cole climbed down from Comanche and went to work clearing the trail.

Together the two men cleared the path and repaired the road by filling in the gaps with rocks and logs. Farther up the trail they found a similar wash out and went to work on it. When they had finished, they stopped a moment to rest.

"You're a good worker, Luke. Keep up that attitude toward workin', and you'll go far in life."

"Yes, sir." He took a drink from his canteen. "I'm just doin' my best to keep up with you."

Cole noticed that the young man's complexion had turned very pale. "Are you okay, Luke?"

The boy nodded. "The air seems thinner up here. I try to get a good breath but can't. How high do you reckon we are, Cole?"

"I'd say we're over nine thousand feet, for sure. I suspect we'll find the air a lot thinner when we climb another thousand feet. That's where we'll eventually run the cattle for the summer. We may even run some higher than that."

"Why don't you rest a spell, Luke. We'll go ahead and eat a bite."

Luke dug through his saddle bag looking for food but found none. "Mr. McKnight told me that Platoro sits at ten thousand feet elevation," he said.

Cole nodded. "I reckon so." He rummaged through his saddle bag and pulled out some jerked beef. "I'm hungry. Let's eat." He bowed his head and prayed, then looked up. "You gonna eat, Luke?"

"I forgot to grab some grub from the wagon," Luke admitted. "All I got is water and whiskey."

"Well, that won't do, workin' in this high country. Here, take some of this jerky. I got plenty."

Luke took the meat and tore off a bite between his teeth and leaned back against a log. "Mr. McKnight says a body has to drink more water up here in the mountains and needs to keep some food in their gut or else they could get the mountain sickness."

Cole nodded. "It's good advice. You can die from the mountain sickness. Even cattle have to be watched over, in the high country. They get what's called *the brisket*. They get to coughing in their lungs and such, then can't breathe and die."

Luke tore off another bite of meat and chewed it awhile. "I'd like to know the Bible like you do, Cole, but I can't read so good. I just know a few words. When I hear you read it out loud, it's comfortin'." Cole nodded and chewed on his beef.

"I've heard you say that God loves us all, but I don't reckon He could love me," Luke said.

"Sure He does, Luke. He loved you enough to die for you. Always remember that. There ain't no greater love than to give your life for another. Have you ever heard John 3:16?"

"No, sir. Can't say as I ever have."

"It says, 'For God so loved the world that he gave his one and only Son, that whosoever believeth in him should not perish but have everlasting life.' My ma taught me that verse when I was just a spud. You'd do well to memorize it, too," Cole said.

"I never knew my ma or pa. They both died in a Blackfoot raid when I was two," Luke said. "The soldiers found me. I lived in an orphanage up in Bozeman till I was sixteen."

"I'm sorry to hear that, Luke. That must have been hard."

"It was." Luke picked up a pinecone and tossed it. "I'd always felt kinda lost till I joined up with the Willow. The Willow's my family now."

PLATORO THE SUMMER RANGE

"You know, Luke, the Lord says in the 68th Psalm that He will be a father to the fatherless and that He setteth the orphan in families."

Luke lifted his eyes to meet Cole's. "Honest? The good Book says that?"

Cole nodded, "Sure does."

"Could you show me, since I can't read so well?"

Cole fetched his worn Bible from his saddle bag and brought it over. He showed Luke the passage and read it out loud to him.

Luke smiled at the thought. "I swear," he said. "I wonder what else it says?"

Cole carefully turned the pages until he found the book of Matthew, then chapter 18 verses 12 and 13.

"This is the parable of the lost sheep, and it's Jesus Himself talking to us, Luke. It says: 'How think ye? If a man have a hundred sheep, and one of them be gone astray, doth he not leave the ninety and nine, and goeth into the mountains, and seeketh that which is gone astray? And if so be that he find it, verily I say unto you, he rejoiceth more of that sheep, than of the ninety and nine which went not astray.'" Cole kept his finger in the page and closed the Bible. "Jesus is the shepherd, and we are the sheep in the story."

"Sheep?" Luke said. "I ain't no dumb sheep."

"I don't know, Luke. When you think about it, we often go our own way and get into trouble like a sheep does. The book of Isaiah says, 'We all like sheep have gone astray.' That's why Jesus came; to show us the way. He cares about those souls that's lost. Even way up here in the mountains. He cares about you just the same as He does me. He won't give up on you either."

"Kinda reminds me of you and Ol' Rebel," Luke mused. "You never give up on Ol' Rebel no matter how much he deserves it." Cole nodded with a smile. The two ate in silence for a time listening to the persistent chatter of a squirrel somewhere up the trail.

"Did you know your pa, Cole?"

"Yes, I did. He was a good man. I learned a lot from him."

"Like what?"

"Well, he taught me how to love a woman by watchin' him treat Ma with dignity and respect. He always put her needs before his own. He taught me how to work hard and never give up on a task until I finished it; how to plow and plant crops; how to hunt and shoot a rifle; how to defend myself. He also taught me never to kill a man unless you or another are in danger." Cole said.

"Is your pa still alive, Cole?"

"My pa and ma and my brother and sister were all murdered by some drifter when I was fifteen."

"I swear," Luke said, looking down. "I didn't know."

After a time of silence, Luke spoke again. "What was your ma like?"

"My ma's name was Rachel. She was a God-fearin' woman. She loved Pa and us kids. She clothed us and fed us and prayed for us every day. I remember she wasn't afraid to take a willow stick to our backsides if we misbehaved. Her and Pa taught us right."

Luke nodded. "It sounds like she was a good woman."

"Yes, she was." Cole smiled at the memory of her. He stood up and stretched. "We best be getting back to work, Luke. We've got a lot of trail to cover yet."

"Yes, sir. I feel much better now."

Cole and Luke filled in more washed-out gullies along the trail with rocks and logs. By late afternoon they had cleared and repaired the wagon road in a stretch of about four miles. They were just about to head back to camp when both horses began to alert to something up the trail.

"Wait here, Luke, while I go see what's troubling the horses."

"Be careful, Cole. It could be a grizzly."

Cole drew his rifle and proceeded with caution. Luke stayed behind and watched from a safe distance.

Comanche flared the bores of his nose. With the wind blowing from the north, he could smell something. Cole smelled it, too.

Suddenly, Luke caught a flash of movement closing in from the rocks above. It was a mountain lion. "Cole, watch out!" he hollered.

Cole began to swing his gun just as the figure leaped and knocked him from his horse. The big cat sunk his teeth through his flesh, into his shoulder bone, and held on tight. Luke tried to shoot the lion but had no clear shot. He fired in the air in an attempt to scare the animal away, but it didn't work.

Cole struggled to get to his rifle, which had slid a dozen feet down the hill. As he fought off the cougar, he remembered his pistol and pulled it from its holster. Thrusting the colt .45 into the big cat's side, he fired until the animal let go. It ran only a few feet before collapsing.

Cole could feel blood trickling down his arm and the back of his shoulder where some of his flesh lay open and bleeding. He was losing a lot of blood. Luke now stood at his side.

"I'm sorry, Cole. I wanted to shoot it, but I was afraid I'd hit you instead."

Cole shook his head. "First a grizzly tries to kill Bob, and now a cougar tries to kill me. It's been quite a week."

Luke tore off some of his shirt sleeve and tied it around Cole's forearm to try to stop the bleeding. "Take your bandana, Luke, and tie it together with mine to make a long bandage." Luke tied more cloth around Cole's shoulder where it was bleeding, also.

"Luke, I've got a couple of clean bandanas in my saddle bag. Fetch them for me along with my canteen." Luke fetched Cole's bandanas and a canteen, then took a half empty bottle of whiskey from his own saddle bag. He knelt at Cole's side. "Here you go. Tell me what to do, and I'll do it."

"Run some water over your hands and clean them a bit, then wet these bandanas. We've got to wipe the wounds clean, then pour some of that whiskey over them." After cleaning the wounds, Luke tied the bandanas tightly into place. "That should get me back to camp until it can be done proper," Cole said.

He stood up and looked around for his horse. Comanche stood off to the side, his nostrils flaring as he stared nervously at the dead beast.

"Fetch my horse for me, Luke." Luke caught Comanche and brought him over, handing Cole the bridle reins.

"Easy boy, shh, shh…It can't hurt us no more," Cole reassured the paint.

With Luke's help, he raised his leg with a wince of pain and thrust his boot into the stirrup. He swung his other leg up and over the horse's back. The loss of blood was causing him to feel faint. "Let's get back and get these wounds doctored proper," he said with urgency in his voice. A short time later, the two arrived back at camp.

"We need some help," Luke hollered. "Cole's been attacked by a cougar. He's gonna need the doctorin' bag in a hurry." Bob London grabbed the bag from the wagon and hurried over as Cole rode in.

"You look like you tangled with a cougar alright," Bob said. "Let's get you down off that horse."

"I'll be fine, boys," Cole said. "It looks worse than it is."

"You're losing a lot of blood," Bob said. "Tell us what we need to do."

"I'll need some whiskey, carbolic acid, hot water, iodine, a needle and thread, and fresh bandages from the wagon. You'll need to boil water to sterilize the bandages."

The men did as Cole said. Bob and Paulie put water on to heat and gathered up some strips of linen while Lightning and Rusty Wells fetched the ointments and medicines.

When the water was hot, Paulie brought over the pail and a bottle of whiskey and went to work cleaning Cole's wounds. "I'd say that cat sure got close to skinin' you," Paulie said, as he poured hot water over the wounds. He then began to doctor them with the whiskey. Cole winced a little with each sting of the whiskey but never made a sound.

After the wounds were flushed well, Paulie and Bob applied the carbolic acid and iodine. When they had finished applying the ointments, they sterilized a needle and thread and began to stitch up the wounds. After the wounds were sufficiently stitched, they wrapped them with clean bandages.

"Your right leg looks awfully red," London said. "You better keep an eye on it."

Cole pointed at a lifetime of scars. "I've been shot six times, arrowed twice, horned, and snake bit, but I ain't never been cougar bit till now. I guess I can add that to my list," he said with a good-natured chuckle.

"I'll leave that experience to you, Cole. That would be a feelin' I could live without. The only cougar I want to see is a dead one," Bob said.

"That lion is laying about a half hour gallop up the trail." Cole reminded. "Luke, you and Carlos go skin it out and put the meat in a burlap sack. Cougar is good eatin'. Bring the claws and the hide back, too. I want to keep them."

PLATORO THE SUMMER RANGE

"Yes, sir. We'll get goin' now," Luke said.

Griz Montoya rode up to the wagon. "I heard a cougar got to you, boss. I'm glad you're okay. I bet it don't feel no better than being grizzly bit, though. Neither one feels too good."

After he was bandaged and dressed, Cole ate a bowl of venison and potato stew while he sat by the fire.

"Here's some coffee, Cole," Stump said. "Hot and black, just like you like it."

"Thanks, Stump."

Bob London came over and sat down next to him. "The good Lord was watching out for us again," he said. "Either one of us could have been killed by now."

Cole nodded. Bob was right. They both could easily be dead, and so early in the trip, too.

"Me and Griz will take your shift tonight, Cole. You should get some rest. You're gonna need all the strength you can muster to fight off any infection."

Bob reached into his vest pocket and pulled out a small amber colored bottle. "Here, you're gonna need this laudanum for the pain. I'll see you in the morning, Cole. Get yourself some sleep. We all need ya."

"I'll be fine, Bob. It's really not so bad."

Making the Lake Fork

The next morning, after fresh bandages and breakfast, Cole felt much better and decided to ride Comanche upriver. That day the men drove the cattle up to where the Saddle Creek and Lake Fork Creek joined about five miles below the gold camp of Platoro.

When evening came, the men gathered around a crackling fire and ate their supper. After they had finished eating, Paulie pulled out his harmonica and began to play a new song he had heard called "Home on The Range." Before long, everyone joined in. Cole sang "Swanee River" in his deep baritone voice, to everyone's delight.

The big longhorn steer, Moses, hung around camp looking for handouts of potato peels or hard biscuits. He had been named "Moses" by Lindle McKnight because when he led the large herd of cattle, he resembled the great leader of Israel, Moses, leading God's chosen people, the Israelites, out of Egypt.

Moses' running partner, Samson, had been named by the McKnights after the Samson of the Old Testament, because he was very large and strong, like the Bible character. Moses and Samson had both been bottle-fed from birth and acted as though they preferred human company over that of their own kind, and so they were tolerated around the camp like pets.

Carlos reached into a burlap sack and pulled out a handful of dried sweet peppers and fed them to the big brutes. He took the sack and led them away from the fire where they had become a nuisance.

PLATORO THE SUMMER RANGE

Luke Parnell suggested the next song. "How about, 'The Old Chisolm Trail'." It was one of everyone's favorites. Kent Severs requested, "Sweet Betsy From Pike."

Other songs that filled the air this night were: "Nearer My God to Thee," "Jesus, Lover of My Soul," and "Good-Bye Old Paint." There was a pause as the men thought on what the next song would be.

"What was that song I heard you singing the other day, Cole?" Paulie asked. "I remember something about a dream or something."

"It's called, 'Cowboy's Dream.'"

"Let's hear you sing it," Garth Benoit suggested. "I'm always lookin' to learn a new song."

Cole stood up with his thumbs hooked into his pockets. He stood tall and straight with his shoulders back and his chest slightly forward. "Here goes," he said. "It plays to the tune of a song you may know called, 'My Bonnie.' The newspaper I learned it from didn't say who wrote it." Paulie knew the tune of "My Bonnie" and began to play the melody as Cole sang:

"Last night as I lay on the prairie and looked at the stars in the sky. I wondered if ever a cowboy, would drift to the sweet by and by. Roll on, roll on, roll on little doggies, roll on, roll on. Roll on, roll on, roll on little doggies, roll on.

They say there will be a great roundup, and cowboys, like doggies, will stand, To be marked by the riders of judgment, who are posted and know every brand.

And I'm scared that I'll be a stray yearling, a maverick unbranded on high, And get cut in the bunch with the rusties, when the Boss of the riders goes by.

For they tell of another big owner, who's never overstocked, so they say, But who always makes room for the sinner, who drifts from the straight, narrow way.

They say he will never forget you, that he knows every action and look, So for safety, you better get branded, And have your name in the great tally book.

Roll on, roll on, roll on little doggies roll on..."

"That was a good song," Paulie said. "I liked the words especially. They make you think about things." The men continued to sit around the fire. When the songs finally ran out, they began to tell stories.

"How'd you get the name Griz?" Carlos asked.

Griz measured his words for a time as he whittled on a willow stick. "I was running a trap line here in the San Juans up by Blue Lake when I came across a couple of sprung traps with grizzly tracks all around them. I followed the tracks and found the bear working on a beaver I had caught.

I tried to scare it off, but it charged me and attacked me. I drew my knife and fought with it. I stabbed it in the throat and in the chest. That was the last I remembered. When I woke up later, I found the bear dead, off in the willows, with my knife still stuck in his chest." Griz touched the bear claw necklace that hung around his neck. "I made this necklace from his claws. It brings me protection."

Lightning Wells leaned over and examined the necklace a moment, then turned toward Cole. "What about you, Cole? I bet you've got a passel of stories from fightin' the Comanche and all. Would you tell us some?"

Cole took a sip of coffee. "I've got a few." His words held a hint of indifference. "One time, I was on a scouting expedition up on the Llano in west Texas with my friend and fellow officer, Angus McCord. We were leading a regiment from the Fourth Cavalry back to our supply camp on the Washita to restock on food, ammunition, and water when a good number of Comanche attacked our flank.

We took cover in a dry buffalo waller and dug in. The Comanche tried to wait us out, hoping we'd die of thirst. The sun was blazing hot with no cover overhead. After two days of no water or food, we were down to just a handful of bullets apiece.

Colonel McKenzie's reinforcements finally showed up and engaged the Indians. We took on water and ammunition and chased them all the way to their camp on the headwaters of the Brazos."

"I ain't never had excitement like that," Kent Severs said.

"Be glad of it," Cole retorted. "The Comanche were fierce fighters. I lost a lot of my men out there on the plains." The men were silent a moment as they searched the recesses of their memories for the most interesting and daring parts of their lives.

Bob London spoke next. "I talked to an old Spanish drover who said he had seen what he called 'St. Elmo's Fire' crawling all over a herd of longhorns. They were trailing through that grease-wood country of west Texas.

The drover said he had stopped to water along the Pecos when a lightning storm came up. The cattle were all bunched up tight tryin' to drink when lightning struck one of the cows then spread through the entire herd. He said it looked like balls of light sparking between their horns and all over their bodies. Now that would be a spooky sight."

"Not as spooky as a grizzly or a pack of wolves starin' eye to eye with you," Griz said.

Cole watched Griz staring off into the darkness as if he sensed something ominous there. Whatever it was that had the Mexican spooked about the country ahead, it held no power over him.

"You reckon you could read to us some more out of that book of yorn?" Bob said.

Cole had been reading aloud out of the Bible nearly every night as well as reading from the book *Ben-Hur* by Lew Wallace. He decided to oblige everyone again, and so he fetched the book and read from it as the men sat around listening. As Cole read, the men were soon immersed within its pages once again. A half hour later, Cole marked the page then closed the book. He looked at Bob. "Well, it's gettin' late. I believe I'll turn in."

"I believe I will, too," Bob said.

Cole grabbed his bed roll and spread it out near the fire. It wasn't long before the others went to bed as well.

He tried to sleep but couldn't because the pain from his wounds kept him awake. He got up and fetched an ink quill and paper from a small chest on the wagon and gently laid back against his saddle so as not to disturb his bandages. He began to write a letter to Abby:

Dear Abigale,

The men and I are fine and the cattle content on this night. We've had no real trouble with stampedes as of yet. The views as we travel are a true testament to our Creator's hand, and they change upon every rounding of the bend of the river.

Our endeavor is a cherished freedom and promises already to hold all the adventure that a man could want. There is some trouble about, but I rest secure in the God that watches over me. I fear no man or unknown trouble.

The men have proven to be real cowboys and true friends. The mountains, the waterfalls, and the abundant critters call loudly to me but not so loudly as my heart calls for you tonight.

As I lay staring up into these bright stars, I'd like to think that I'm sharing the same view with you, though the miles separate us.

I miss you and Brian and your dear folks. I believe God brought me to the Willow for you and Brian, and He knew how much I needed the two of you. I love you, Abby, and when the men and I return, I aim to continue to prove the love I have for you.

Soon we will reach Platoro and the country beyond. For now, the cattle have plenty of grass and water and seem quite content. Comanche is proving to be quite the mountain horse and a very capable night horse as well. I am honored to be charged with the care of your father's cattle. I assure you; they are in good hands. I will write again soon.

Love, Cole

Cole folded the letter and put it away. By now the fire had burned low, so he got up and added several logs before laying back down.

Bob London removed his hat from covering his face and looked over at Cole. "She's a good woman, Cole. Don't let her get away. She deserves a good man like you."

Cole stretched back out on the ground then pulled his blanket up to his neck to keep out the cool night air. As he lay awake, he thought of Abby until he fell asleep.

From an overlook on the side of Cornwall Mountain, Shiloh Tremble watched the cowboys' camp from the back of his horse. Soon he would make his move on Cole Harden, and when he did, he would show no mercy. He turned his horse about and rode toward his hideout. For the time being, he had been keeping to a cabin along Treasure Creek in a big meadow near the base of Stunner Pass. It had been a hunting cabin of his uncle's, and he kept some supplies in it. He knew the whereabouts of other cabins as well where he could find shelter and hide out as long as he needed.

Shiloh had been at the Treasure Creek cabin for more than a week now, and it was time he moved on. He gathered his things and made his way up the winding switchback and game trails that led him to Stunner. From there, he followed a game trail to an old trapper's cabin. The door was open and held a drift of snow against it. On the shaded side of the cabin, the snow clung halfway up the logs. Inside, it smelled of age and disuse; still it would serve him well for what he had planned.

The Summer Range

The morning following, just before sunrise, the men arose and filled their bellies and got an early start with the cattle. By mid-morning, they had pushed the herd to the meadows just below the gold camp of Platoro where Bob London and Cole gathered and addressed the men.

"We are not far from Platoro," Bob said. "Look around, gentlemen. This is the heart of the summer range. From here all the way up to the deep blue sky belongs to no one but God and the men and cattle of the Golden Willow. Our grazing rights do have boundaries, however.

We have rights to everything on both sides of the Conejos River all the way up to the divide. Directly around Platoro, we have Red Mountain and Willow Mountain to the east, Mammoth Mountain to the southeast, and Cornwall Mountain to the north," he said, pointing.

"To the west of Platoro is Klondike Mountain. Up near the divide, we have the Blue Lake region, the North Fork, Gold Creek, and the Adams Fork all the way up to Summit Peak.

We don't have the next canyon over on the north side of Cornwall. That's the Alamosa Canyon. That grass is allotted to Graham Lassiter and his hooligans this year. I don't expect they'll bring any cattle up this summer bein's most of them are probably in jail. There's no need for us to be over on their range anyway. We have all the grass a herd could ever want within our own allotment.

We'll keep the cattle spread out here along the river until after we've scouted out good stock driveways for each range. Remember, there's likely to be every sort of individual up here in these mountains near Platoro and Stunner, so don't let the beauty fool you into believin' our worries are over. We need to stay vigilant and keep our guns loaded. Where there's gold, there's greed, and where there's greed, there's trouble. I want you to stay shy of the saloon and those places in town where trouble is likely to abide."

London pulled out his handkerchief, blew his nose, then stuffed it back in his pocket. "Don't forget, there's still some Ute up here as well. Griz says they can be unpredictable. We'll leave them alone, and they'll leave us alone. Let's not forget about that prickly character Cole and Griz ran into the other day down river near the Elk Creek: Mordecai Lundy. My gut tells me we ain't seen the last of him. Let's not forget, either, that Shiloh Tremble could be hid out up here in these parts and gunnin' for Cole. So be alert."

Bob looked over at Cole. "I have a feelin' that if he tangles with Cole, he'll wish he hadn't."

Griz nodded, "I say amen to that."

Bob looked again at the eager faced young cowboys. "I'm guessing you young bucks are itchin' to check out Platoro to see who's there," he grinned. "There'll be plenty of time for girl chasin' later on. Right now, let's concentrate on the task at hand, and that's scouting the new range for the summer."

"Cole, do you have anything to add?"

Cole stepped forward. "I'm gonna ride up and scout the grass above Platoro along the Conejos River today. I'll be lookin' to find a good stock driveway to move the cattle up through to higher ground.

Griz is going over to Red Mountain to scout the grass situation and find good stock driveways to get the cattle up top. The rest of you stick around here and ride watch over the cattle. Does anyone have any questions? If not, then let's get to work."

Cole rode on up the river in the direction of Platoro. After traveling about a mile, he noticed that scattered up and down the hillsides were several digging piles where small mining claims had been excavated and abandoned.

Around the bend was yet another claim. Two haggard-looking miners stood near-by fingering through a pile of ore. The men wore tattered coats and long beards, their hands and faces stained with dirt. Cole gave a wave and hollered to them, "Howdy!"

The miners snatched up their rifles and looked his way. They kept their eyes fixed suspiciously on him until he rode out of sight.

Continuing on, he followed a gully up through a mix of spruce and aspen to another meadow. Ahead, a porcupine gnawed on the wet bark of an aspen tree. When it saw him, it dropped to the ground and waddled off into the willows.

Near the far side, Comanche's hooves began to sink deep into a mossy bog where a seep had soaked into the ground there. The sudden suction of the soil gripped at Comanche's feet causing the horse to panic. It lunged several times to free itself until it finally regained a solid footing. Cole continued along the meadow on the high side now, more careful to avoid any more seeps.

He passed into another clearing that was full of dandelion, Indian paintbrush, arnica, and blue-flag iris. At the lower end was a water pool hidden among a growth of reeds. Bog sedge and skunk cabbage grew all about. Yellow marigold blooms floated on lily pads which lay on top of the amber-colored water. The air was filled with the odor of skunk cabbage which was now at the stage of growth where it gave off a similar fragrance to that for which it was named.

Cole guided Comanche up to higher ground into an open aspen glade. The dull thud of an axe ringing on the air aroused his curiosity. Straight ahead, he noticed a white ribbon of smoke curling upward through the trees. As he rode closer, he was surprised to see a neat log cabin which lay tucked into the hillside. It appeared to be new and well built.

Behind the cabin was a corral that currently held three mules and a dun-colored horse. In front was a small, lonely grave with a stick cross in the center of it. A large pile of stove wood was stacked neatly against the uphill side of the cabin.

Cole noticed a man, toting an axe, walking toward him through the trees. The man wore a clean shirt and denim pants with brown suspenders. He was clean-shaven and walked with confidence as he approached.

Cole raised his hand. "Howdy. Fine day, ain't it."

The man continued closer. "Can I help you, mister?" His eyes held no clue of resolve or emotion.

"Name's Cole Harden. I saw the smoke from your chimney and thought I'd say hello. I'm with the Golden Willow Ranch out of Las Mesitas. We're running our cattle up here in the high country for the summer. I'm out scouting the grass situation."

The man's eyes softened. "Welcome, Mr. Harden. My name's Otto Kulman. My wife, Heidi, and I live here."

"It's a pleasure to meet you, Otto. Have you lived here long?"

"This is our second summer. We find it a beautiful country in summer but very harsh in winter."

Cole pointed down river. "We're camped in the meadow just down river a ways. We plan to spread the cattle out along the meadows here and eventually above Platoro."

Just then the cabin door opened, and he turned his attention that way. A lovely, sunny-haired woman in a long brown dress stood in the doorway. She was pleasant of feature, and her face held an expression of calm curiosity. She wiped her hands on her apron and lifted one hand to shield her eyes from the sun.

"Who is our guest, Otto?" she said.

"His name is Cole Harden. He's with a cattle ranch from down in the San Luis Valley. They are running cattle here in the high country this summer."

Cole tipped his hat. "Nice to meet you, ma'am."

The woman's eyes rested softly on him. "It's a pleasure to meet you, Mr. Harden." Like her husband, the woman spoke with a German accent. "We don't get many visitors. Will you please stay and visit for a spell?"

Cole looked up at the sun to gage the time. "I would enjoy that ma'am, but I have a full day of ridin' ahead of me. I should be on my way."

The woman and her husband looked disappointed. "I have fresh baked bread, and there is plenty. We haven't heard any news from down below in quite a while. Please, won't you stay and join us?"

Cole fidgeted with his horse's reins. "I reckon it wouldn't hurt to tarry for a short spell. I'd like that, too." He dismounted and half hitched

Comanche to the hitchin' post then followed Otto to the door, removing his hat before stepping inside.

The cabin was neat and clean and smelled pleasantly of baked bread and mint tea. He looked around. Nearly hidden behind the fireplace was a small loft with a wooden staircase, hand hewn of small, peeled aspen. Over in the corner was a bed covered with a colorful quilt, checkered with squares of red, blue, and green. Along the back wall, a few portraits hung above a cedar chest.

Otto placed his rifle horizontally on two pegs above the fireplace, then sat down at the table while his wife stood by the stove. "Please, won't you sit down, Mr. Harden, while I get you and Otto some bread and tea. The tea is of dandelion and mint leaves."

Cole smiled and took a seat next to Otto, placing his hat on the floor beside his chair. "There's no lack of dandelions this year," he said.

The table and chairs were sturdy and made of aspen and held his large frame without flexing. A vase of fresh picked wildflowers sat in the center of the table, their fragrance filling the room.

"I like your cabin. It's real comfortable."

"Thank you."

Heidi took up the warm bread and placed it on the table. After pouring tea for everyone, she sat down.

Otto folded his hands. "Let's take this time to pray to our Heavenly Father, shall we?" he said. Otto took Heidi's hand in his as everyone bowed their heads.

"Heavenly Father, we thank Thee for this food we are about to eat. May we bring Thee honor with the nourishment it provides. We thank Thee for our new friend, Mr. Cole Harden. Bless him and protect him as he goes about his work. It is in Thy precious name, Jesus, we pray, amen."

Cole looked up. "Thank you."

"Are you a Christian, Mr. Harden?" Heidi asked. Her beseeching eyes rested warmly on him.

"Yes, ma'am, I am."

Heidi smiled. "I thought you might be. You have a presence about you that causes one to sense it."

Otto was curious about Cole's bandages. "If you don't mind me asking, Cole, what has happened that you are bandaged so?"

"I was attacked by a cougar a few days back. It got ahold of me pretty good."

Heidi gave Otto a concerned look. "Oh, dear, a vicious cougar, around here?"

"It won't be botherin' anyone no more, ma'am. I saw to it."

"Is there anything we can do for you to make you more comfortable?" she asked.

"No, thanks, ma'am. I'm fine."

Otto took a sip on his tea. "Have you any family, Cole?"

"No, sir. My wife died years ago. We had no children."

Otto pulled a tobacco pouch, a pipe, and a match from a drawer behind him. He struck the match alight and touched it to a wad of tobacco he had stuffed in the barrel end of the pipe, then shook out the match. Soon the entire room was filled with the sweet aroma of tobacco as a series of wreaths expanded from Otto's mouth. "Could I offer you a pipe of tobacco, Cole?"

"No, thank you. I never took it up. I will have some of this bread, though. It smells delicious." He took a slice and troweled some butter on it. "Umm, that's tasty," he said, after taking a bite.

"It's German bread. My mother's recipe," Heidi said.

Otto sucked slowly at the pipe stem then blew another wreath of smoke into the air. "Heidi and I moved from Germany to Ohio ten years ago. We were farmers. One year we had a fearsome drought and lost everything.

There was an outbreak of cholera, so we decided to come west with a caravan of Amish to the San Luis Valley. We put what little money we had on this here claim. We call it the Golden Egg."

Heidi looked out the window and rested her eyes on the little grave. "Living here has been harder than we thought it would be."

Otto removed his pipe and took a sip of tea. "Last spring, we started the cabin. We didn't get it finished until late in the fall. It wasn't so bad at first, but then the big snows came one after another. Soon the drifts were as high as the roof."

Heidi looked at Cole, her eyes welling up with moisture. "The winter was terrible long and lonesome."

Otto reached over and gently placed his hand on hers. "Heidi gave birth to a baby boy, but we lost him during the winter. He was just a month old when the lung fever took his life."

"That's little Uriah's grave outside," Heidi said. She dabbed at her eyes with the sleeve of her dress as she talked.

"Otto tried to go for a doctor, but he had to turn back because of the deep snow."

Otto's eyes flicked quickly and repeatedly as he held back his own tears. He clasped Heidi's hand firmly for support. "It still hurts to speak of it."

"I'm sorry," Cole said. He understood their pain deeply. He took another bite of his bread and drank some tea. Everyone was quiet for some time.

"The bread is real good, ma'am, and so is the tea. Thank you kindly."

Heidi smiled. "You're welcome. I'm glad you like it."

"How many cattle did you bring with you?" Otto said.

"A good bunch, near a thousand."

"I imagine it takes a number of men to keep watch on that many?"

"Yes, sir. There's twelve of us in the grub line plus the cook. One of our wranglers took to misfortune in a rockslide awhile back and had to go home."

"The mountains and the folks and critters that inhabit them can be a harsh lot," Otto said. "Especially when gold is around to be had."

Cole nodded. "I should warn you folks about some rough characters we ran into at a claim down river. There's four of them, and they're no good. I'm afraid they could be real trouble, so keep your guns loaded and ready."

"We'll do that," Otto said.

"There's something else, too. We found a dead body not far from those fellers' claim. We believe a grizzly done it, but we're not sure. It could also be it was a murder. Either way, I'd keep my eyes open for that bear and those four fellas, too." Cole picked up his hat from the floor and placed it on his knee. "If you folks have any problems, come get me and the boys."

Otto's eyes shaded. "I believe we may have seen those four fellas yesterday in Plataro. I had went inside the mercantile while Heidi waited in the wagon. When I came back outside some men were standing in front of the saloon whistlin' and sayin' vulgar things to her. We left right away, and they followed us. Last night we saw one of them peerin' through the window." Heidi glanced downward; her face flushed with embarrassment.

The news disturbed Cole. "If you ever see them again, you let me know, okay?"

"We will. Thank you, Cole," Otto said. "It's a comfort to know you'll be looking out for us."

Cole nodded and stood up to leave. "I best be goin' now. The day is slipping away from me. I'll stop by again some time when I can tarry a might longer." The Kulmans followed him outside.

"I saw one of your cowboys this morning," Otto said. "He had one arm in a sling and rode a grulla horse. It's the second time we've seen him around."

"What did he look like?"

"I never got a real good look at him. The sun was in my eyes. I remember the grulla horse, though."

"No one in our outfit rides a grulla. Whoever he is, he's not with us. If you see him again, let me know. I'd like to find out what he's up to."

Cole stepped into the saddle and tipped his hat. "I'll stop by and say hello when I can," he said. Otto and Heidi waved after him as he rode away in the direction of Platoro.

Platoro

Cole followed the flower-skirted riverbank looking for good crossings and flat places to water the herd. As he rounded the next bend, he saw Platoro not far in the distance. It was sited on a level plain between the mountainside and the Conejos River. He put his horse to cross at a ford and entered from the east along a meadow of yellow dandelions.

About a dozen buildings lay spread out on both sides of a single street with a sign nailed to a post that read "Conejos Avenue."

Cole rode west. A hand full of log cabins and canvas tents lay scattered in front of him in no particular order. The first structure he came to was a livery stable made of long spruce logs. A small pack train of three mules stood loaded with picks, shovels, and screens.

He passed a blacksmith shop where a big man in a dirty black apron was visiting with two miners. They were looking at a broken wagon wheel. Beyond the blacksmith shop, on the same side of the street, was another livery stable, and across the street was a boarding house. Beyond the livery was the saloon and dance hall followed by a long narrow log building with a sign on the front that read "Weiss Mercantile Company - Adam, Julius and Augustus Weiss, Proprietors." The American flag waved in front of a building at the far end of the street, and Cole could make out the words "Post Office."

The little mining town seemed strangely empty, at the moment, except for a couple of horses tied up outside the saloon. He eyed them with a rider's eye, taking in their finer points. One of the horses, a black, he recognized. The other, a gray colored horse, he did not.

PLATORO THE SUMMER RANGE

The black horse he recognized as belonging to Mordecai Lundy. It was long and lanky with a white spot on its left side. The gray horse or grulla, as some called the color, was a rare sight. It was a mousey gray where the sunlight hit it, with darker stripes along its lower neck, back, and shoulders. It had a black tail and mane with black bars on the lower leg. The shaded side of the horse held an almost bluish tint. Cole remembered that Otto and Heidi had mentioned seeing a rider on a grulla horse.

Cole decided he would mail his letter to Abby first, then ride over to the saloon and meet the man who owned the grulla. He was studying the grulla when a big fella showed in the doorway of the saloon. It was Mordecai Lundy. He clutched a bottle in one hand and held a sunny-haired dance hall girl with the other. The girl studied him and gave a flirtatious smile. The big man offered Cole an icy stare, and Cole obliged the same back. After a moment of tension, Lundy gave a sly wink, then he and the girl walked back into the saloon.

Cole rode on and tied up in front of the post office. "Can I help you, sir?" A voice came from within the post office tent. Cole turned and stepped inside. A man, with red hair and a scruffy red beard, sat in a chair behind a plank board table.

"Howdy," Cole said.

"Yes, sir. My name is Claud Mix. How can I help you?"

Cole pulled a letter from his vest. "I need to mail this here letter."

"You're just in time. The mail goes down every other Friday. That means it's goin' down termorrer."

Cole handed the postman the letter. The man stamped it, then pushed it through the narrow slit in the locked chest. "Sending a letter to your sweetheart, are ya?" The man's whimsical words disconcerted Cole, and he offered no answer.

"Who would I report to about finding a dead body?" he said.

The man shrugged his shoulders. "There ain't no law up here. Closest would be back down the mountain at San Antonio Junction. That's better'n fifty miles."

Cole nodded. "That's what I figured."

"What did this dead feller look like? Could be I might know him," the man said.

"He was an older fellow, tall and skinny. He had gray hair and a tuft of white on his beard. He was wearing tan britches and a black coat."

The postman nodded. "That fits the description of a miner named Jake Hollister that comes up here to Platoro every weekend to drink and gamble. He had a claim down somewheres around the Elk Creek, as I recall. I ain't seen him around lately."

"Did Hollister have any kin?"

"Don't know of any. He kept a house somewhere down in the Valley, but I ain't sure where. He never received any mail as I recall."

Cole nodded and thanked the man, then stepped back outside into the sunlight. The grulla and the black that had been tied up in front of the saloon were now gone. He mounted Comanche and rode up Sawmill Gulch. From an overlook, he watched a posse of five men ride into Platoro and go into the saloon. A short time later, they came back out, mounted their horses, and tore out in a hurry. They splashed through the river and crossed a clearing below him where they disappeared among the trees, headed west.

Cole continued up Sawmill Gulch through a pleasant aspen glade. He traveled a couple of switchbacks and crossed a secluded dale dotted with white daisies and pale-blue flowers. On his left, Sawmill Brook trickled down through the willows as he passed through another series of small woodland meadows. Eventually the trail topped out in a long narrow meadow with lush green grass and a gradual slope. Sawmill Gulch would make a fine stock driveway for the cattle to get onto Cornwall Mountain because of its gradual incline and abundant supply of grass and water.

Having learned what he needed to know, Cole turned back, riding until he reached Platoro again. From there he headed west up Boiler Canyon, nooning at a spring in a glade of aspen. He ate some jerky and soda biscuits. When finished, he turned his horse up along the edge of the woods.

Cole maneuvered Comanche through clusters of willow, skunk cabbage, and cinquefoil as he made his way up country. A swish of the west wind touched the willows, launching white puffs of cotton-like tufts to drift upon the air.

Hoping to find a sufficient route for a stock driveway onto Klondike

Mountain, he followed a drainage up the side of Stunner Pass. As he rode farther into the deeply shadowed forest, Cole noticed a dim trail leading upward along a gradual drainage. He followed it under towering ancient spruce from which hung long strings of brown, horsehair lichen.

Cole enjoyed the quiet shaded glens as the mystery of the forest unfolded before him. The intense blue of the vault above him was soon lost to the overstory and now only occasionally peeked through the dense growth, and when it did, it cast beams of sunlight down through narrow portals in the treetops. He rode along with joy in his heart, his eyes and ears appreciative to the sights and sounds and smells that alerted his senses. "Thank you, Lord, for creating all this," he said out loud as though speaking to a friend, and indeed, he was.

To his left, over the edge, he could hear the murmur of running water and in the trees, the songs of the forest creatures. He followed the trail around a large deadfall, rotten with age, covered in moss. On the other side, he saw where the hoof prints of a single horse entered the trail. The tracks fell at a deliberate gate and appeared fresh. A hundred paces up the trail another set of tracks entered the path; those of a large bear.

Cole dismounted and squatted to examine the prints. The pads were larger than his hand and belonged to a grizzly, not a black bear. He stood and looked around with the sudden feeling he was being watched.

He stepped back up into the saddle and rode on with caution, suddenly aware that a melancholy hush had fallen over the forest. An intruder had entered the woods, and so he pulled his rifle from its scabbard and placed it across his lap. His eyes swept the country before him then dropped to his horse, relying on its keen alertness. The tracks of the grizzly lay within the trail for a time then disappeared over the edge into the drainage.

Some movement up ahead caught Cole's eye and aroused his curiosity. A mule deer doe stepped from behind a moss-covered boulder and stood in a patch of sunlight, unaware of his presence.

The doe looked back over her shoulder at something behind the boulder and wiggled her short, stringy tail. She gave a bleat and was soon joined by a wobbly legged fawn that eagerly found her swollen teats and began to nurse. The fawn looked to be not more than a day old.

Cole continued onward up the trail, following the tracks of the horse and rider. When the doe saw him, she swiveled her large mule-like ears and bounded off without her fawn who instantly flattened out on the ground and was absorbed beneath the foliage. The doe, unwilling to leave the area, stood snorting and stomping her feet as Cole passed by.

He kept his eyes open for any sign of the grizzly. A mile or so later, the trail again topped out in a broad, beautiful meadow with an island of aspen at its center. It held plenty of grass to hold cattle. He had found a passable route up the side of Klondike Mountain that would serve as a fine stock driveway.

Comanche stopped and swiveled his ears toward the island of trees. Looking in that direction, Cole noticed a log cabin back in the shadows. The grulla he had seen in front of the saloon stood tied up outside.

Experience with Comanche Indians had taught him to always be cautious. Who was this rider of the grulla horse? He had to find out. Instead of approaching the cabin, Cole turned Comanche into a cut in the trees and followed it up to an overlook where he could watch and wait. He was about to dismount when he heard a shot. He leapt from his horse and crawled to the edge as a second shot rang out.

A short time later he caught a glimpse of a man on the grulla riding away in a hurry. Not far behind were the five riders he had seen earlier that morning. Shortly after they disappeared, there was another volley of shots followed by silence. Cole was unsure of what to make of it all. He had come up this way to scout for a sufficient stock driveway not get mixed up in someone else's fight.

When he felt it safe to move on, he continued south. A half hour's ride brought him to the Adam's Fork of the Conejos River. From there, he followed the stream down to where it entered the Conejos in the valley. There he found a wide flat above the flood plain which held an abandoned Ute camp.

Chert piles of obsidian and flint lay scattered about. There were several lodge rings where their dwellings once stood. Smaller campfire rings were also evident. Looking around, it was easy to see why the Ute had chosen this spot. The old camp was situated well, with a great view of the surroundings and was near steady water.

To the south, Cole observed the majestic Conejos Peak and the juniper choked drainages which tracked like scars down its north face. At the moment, nearly a hundred elk were feeding high above the timberline. Their tan bodies glowed orange in the sunlight and disappeared when in shadow.

Cole left the old camp and continued upriver. As he gained elevation, the grass became more stunted and browner in its color. To the left, a ribbon-like waterfall leapt over a cliff where it thinned and fell some two hundred feet until it lost itself in the spruce below.

He crossed two more small streams before coming to Three Forks; the place Griz had warned him about on more than one occasion. Ahead, three glacial rivers plunged down deep gorges to merge as one in the gentle meadows. Up among the spruce, piles of dirty looking snow clung to the shaded areas where it had been sprinkled by falling pine needles. He nudged Comanche forward, crossing the river, then rode a short way up the middle fork but stopped short when the high drifts cut him off. This area would need more time before the grass would be ready for the cattle.

As he sat his horse, he began to get the feeling he was being watched. He turned in the direction of a squirrel which chided and scolded at something, its tail flicking wildly. Tick-tick-tick-tick...tick-tick-tick came a rapid flurry of distressed calls which burst in rhythm with the flicking of its tail and continued on with urgency. The black-eared critter fussed, not at him, but at something beyond him, higher up the mountain. Something moved among the shadows of the dark timber amidst the moss-covered deadfalls.

A pinecone crunched. Someone or something was there, watching him, though he knew not whom or what. Comanche was also aware of it and flared the bores of his nostrils as he danced nervously against his taut bridle reins.

Red Mountain

The Ute brave watched the cowboy down below with curiosity and caution. He had been watching him for a good while, and even now, as the cowboy sat his paint horse. He wondered what the white man was doing so high in the mountains. Was he here to trap and hunt? Or did he have other purposes that were less noble? The cowboy was the first white man he had seen since the year before.

Every year there were more. He knew the threat the newcomers posed to his people, and he didn't like it. They had tried to avoid the white man by moving to the most remote reaches of the forest. First had come the Spanish sheep men, followed by those with the steel traps. Now those with the big hats had come more and more. Some friendly, some not. The brave watched the cowboy leave, following him at a distance, careful to stay behind the cover of the trees. He had learned to step softly, as subtle as the falling of a leaf.

When he was sure the threat was gone, the Ute checked a deadfall trap. The other traps had been empty. If this one was empty, too, his family would go without meat again tonight.

Thankfully the trap had worked, and underneath lay a fat snow-shoe rabbit. It would take every portion of it to nourish the family he must feed. He took the rabbit from the trap and reset it by propping up the rock with a stick. With his provision in hand, he left for his camp up the Middle Fork above the waterfall.

When Cole topped out at Stunner Pass on his way back to camp, it was dark, for the moon had not yet risen. Far below, he could see the lanterns glowing outside the Platoro Saloon and beyond that, the welcome flicker of the Golden Willow's campfire.

When Cole rode into camp, he was greeted by the lonesome sound of Lee Hansen's harmonica and the delicious aroma of fresh cooked stew. "What's for supper, Stump? It smells real good," he said.

"I call it Wilderness Stew. It's venison, mountain lion, tators, wild onion, mushrooms, and a surprise, secret ingredient."

Stump ladled Cole a steaming bowl of the stew. "Here ya go, Cole. Everyone's done et 'cept you and Griz and Kent and Titus."

"Griz isn't back yet? Where are Kent and Titus?"

"The boys went up to scout Mammoth Mountain this morning."

Cole was surprised that the young cowboys had not yet returned. He wasn't so worried about Griz. Griz could take care of himself, but Kent Severs and Titus Martin were green to the ways of the mountains.

He took his supper and his coffee and sat beside London, next to the fire. After a prayer, he commenced to eating. "This is real tasty. Did you get plenty, Bob?"

"Sure did. How'd your scoutin' trip go?"

"The grass is good all the way to the mouth of the Adam's Fork. It needs a couple of weeks' growth before it's ready above that."

"How far did you ride?"

"I turned back at Three Forks Park. There's a good amount of snow left in the spruce up there, but it looks to be melting fast."

"I figure we have plenty of grass around here for a while, if need be," Bob said. "What did you find in the way of drive-ways for the cattle?"

"I found a good one through Boiler Canyon onto Klondike. There's also good grass and a good drive-way up Sawmill Gulch onto Cornwall."

London nodded with approval. "If Griz found a proper stock driveway to the top of Red, we may put a portion of the cattle up there, too. I'd like to put some on Mammoth as well."

Cole finished supper, then went out to keep watch over the herd. As he rode the perimeter, he worried about what had become of Titus and Kent.

Earlier in the day, Griz Montoya had ridden up the Beaver Lake drainage as he scouted for a good stock driveway onto Red Mountain. He had found two small lakes which had been formed from where beavers had dammed up Beaver Creek. The Beaver Lake drainage was steep, willow-choked, and not favorable for driving cattle but would work if he did not find better.

Near the top of Red Mountain, he had come upon a long meadow with dozens of cow elk and their newborn calves; a traditional calving ground to be sure. It was a sight to behold.

That evening, on his way back to camp, Griz led his horse down along a narrow, willow-choked stream known as Fisher Gulch. As he came to a small crossing in the willows, he noticed a boot track, visible in the mud.

Griz knelt and inspected the footprint. It was long, wide and deep, made by a large man. There was a hunk missing from the sole of the boot which left a distinctive print in the mud. The water around the track had not yet cleared. It was fresh. A twig snapped somewhere above him. It was dark now and hard to see.

He led his horse down through the willow drainage along the brook to a secluded meadow and let the bridle reins drop. He then circled around a ledge on foot, climbing higher as he went. He was the hunter now.

Griz moved as a cougar does, silent and slow, until he reached another ledge more than a hundred feet above the brook. He heard his horse whinny nervously once.

The night was still and dark with only an occasional gust of wind. Below, he could hear only the brook. He crouched, stone still, with his knife drawn.

After a long spell of seeing or hearing nothing more, he was about to move when a pebble rolled down to him from up above. Perhaps it was an Indian. A Ute or a Navajo, maybe? There were still a few around. In time, he sensed someone close. Someone or something.

The moon broke from a bank of dark clouds just long enough to cast its silver light on the form of a man crouching beside a tree directly above him. The man had not seen him and now crept slowly away and uphill.

Griz stayed motionless for some time until he was sure the man had left then he turned and moved silently toward his horse, choosing to circle upwind of it rather than going directly to it. Before long the horse caught drift of his scent and came to him. This was an old Indian trick that served him well tonight.

The Mexican mounted up and reined his horse about, putting it forward along the edge of the trees until he hit upon Fisher Gulch. He followed Fisher until he hit upon the Conejos River a half mile below camp.

When Cole saw Griz arrive back at camp, he rode over to him. "How was your trip to Red, Griz?"

"Bueno. I found good grass and a good drive-way all the way to the top."

"Did you run into any trouble?"

Griz nodded. "Someone tried to ambush me along Fisher. I found his fresh track in the mud. Part of the sole was missing from his left boot. I tracked him up the hill a ways and saw him crouching by a tree. I believe he was a Gringo. I drew my knife and waited for him, but he left up the hill."

Griz sniffed the air. "The grub smells bueno. I hope there is some left."

"Everyone's done ate 'cept Kent and Titus."

Griz looked concerned. "Them tenderfoot pups ain't back yet?"

"I'm guessin' they're lost," Cole said. "If they don't get back by midnight, we'll need to go look for them."

Griz shook his head. "Them two are about as useful as a knot in a stake rope. They don't have no mountain sense."

Griz made his way to the fire and ladled up some stew. He scooped a spoonful to his mouth. "Bueno, mountain lion," he said.

Rising above the rustle of the spruce in the wind was the distant bay of a wolf, followed by another, then the lonesome cries of an entire pack. The eerie notes rose and fell in melancholy tones as Cole listened.

"The wolves are active tonight on Mammoth Mountain," he said.

Griz nodded. "It's the full moon," he said. "The wolves are making the cattle uneasy."

Cole looked off toward the dark mass that was Mammoth Mountain and thought of the boys. He said a prayer in his heart for their safety and safe return as he watched the big moon rising behind the treetops.

Lost on Mammoth Mountain

"Kent, you hear them wolves?" Titus said. "There must be a half dozen of 'em. We never shoulda' went off lookin' for Big Lake."

"We found it, didn't we? You're the one that had to stop back yonder and carve 1880 in that aspen tree so's someone a hundred years from now can see we been here."

"Yeah, but now it's dark, and we're lost. Things is different in the dark." The horses whimpered softly and jerked their heads at the continued baying of the wolves.

"Let's follow this stream down. It's bound to run into the Conejos somewhere."

Kent led the way down the Lake Fork Branch. As the night thickened, he gathered dry stalks of miner's candle. Cole had said the plant would burn well, and when he struck a match to it, it flared up and cast a good deal of light for the horses.

"Be careful not to get that light in the horses' eyes. It'll blind 'em."

"What's that over there? I think I see somethin'," Titus pointed.

Kent held his torch out and put his horse forward, stopping against a rock ledge. "It's a crack in the rocks that looks like a cross."

"Give me that torch," Titus said.

"What for?"

"I want to check it out. It looks like it would be a good place to hide somethin'." Titus slid off his horse and walked up to the crack. He reached inside.

"You ain't gonna find nothin' but maybe a lizard or a snake," Kent said.

Titus felt around until his hand brushed against something. "There's somethin' here," he said, closing his hands around it.

"What is it?"

"Feels like a pouch."

"A pouch, my foot. You're joshin'."

Titus pulled out his hand and held it up to the light. "It's a woman's money pouch, and it's got words stitched on it. Someone's name."

"Someone's name? Well, what does it say?"

Titus sounded it out. "It says, Eva Thurman."

"Eva Thurman. Who's that?"

"I don't know, and I don't care." Titus dumped some of the contents into the palm of his hand. "It's gold coins. Must be fifty of 'em."

"Naw, it ain't neither," Kent scoffed. He rode closer to where he could see better.

"I ain't joshin'. Take a look." Titus held out his hand.

Kent stared at the coins in disbelief. "You better put it back. It ain't ours to take."

"It's finders keepers the way I see it. Besides, this pouch looks like it's been here a while. Could be whoever put it here forgot about it or might be dead and ain't ever comin' back for it."

"Put it back," Kent warned. "Cole would frown on us takin' somethin' that wasn't ours to take."

There was a rustling sound behind them. "What was that?" Titus said.

"I heard it, too. Maybe it's them that hid it."

"Well, I ain't waitin' to find out." Titus stuffed the money pouch in his coat and swung up on his horse. "Come on. Let's get out of here." He headed his horse straight up the mountain.

"Where you goin'?" Kent hollered after him.

"I think I recognize this drainage. We can take it up to the top and drop down the other side. Come on."

The two cowboys hung on tight to their saddle horns as their horses lunged up the mountain in powerful jerking movements. When they finally reached the top, they rode through a narrow strip of spruce, then broke out into a higher meadow that ran long and to the right. To the left, not fifty yards, was a lake. "I bet this is Mammoth Lake," Titus said. "We should spend the night here and ride out in the morning."

"You're forgetin' that you just stole someone's money stash, and they could be after us. Besides, Cole and Mr. London will worry if we ain't back tonight," Kent said.

The pack of wolves began to howl once again. "Those wolves are gettin' closer. I say we take a short cut back. It'll save us some time," Titus said. Kent sat his horse and looked unsure. He shook his head. "Cole says never to take shortcuts."

Titus waited impatiently. "Well, if we're goin', let's get goin'."

Kent sighed and shrugged his shoulders. "Okay, let's go then."

The two bailed off the mountain at the lower end of the meadow. Soon the slope became too steep to ride. They dismounted and led their horses amidst a large number of deadfalls. The intense slope made it hard to keep their footing.

"The trees are so thick I can't see the moon no more," Kent said. At one point, Titus stopped.

"What's wrong?"

"I can't see nothin' at all." He felt around at his heel and found a rock. He tossed it in front of him, and it fell and never seemed to hit bottom. Titus lit another stalk of miner's candle and watched it flare up.

When it blazed up, he was terrified to find he was standing on the precipice of a cliff, on the edge of a deep gorge, that dropped several hundred feet. One more step, and he would have fallen to his death. Titus led his horse around to a slide.

The two cowboys carefully picked their way, falling and sliding, holding bridle reins with one hand, and clutching and clinging to small spruce saplings with the other to slow their descent. It would be a long, dangerous night getting off the mountain as they still had hundreds of feet to descend with reluctant horses in tow.

Back at camp, Cole was getting worried. Three hours had passed and still no signs of Kent and Titus. Cole, Griz and Paulie gathered lanterns and rope and began to head out when they heard a shout from down river. It was the lost cowboys. Their horses were lathered up, rode down, and bleeding from cuts on their cannons. The two young cowboys were cut up, too.

"What happened to you fellas?" Cole said. "We were fixin' to come look for you."

Kent looked from under the drooped brim of his hat. "It was gettin' late, so we took a shortcut instead of goin' plumb back around the way we came up."

Cole observed the tattered leg of Kent's britches and the cuts on the horse's legs. "That was some shortcut you was on."

Griz scoffed, "Shortcut, my foot."

Kent wiped his forehead of sweat with the back of his hand. "We started out right, but then the drainage we was followin' down cut back to the east, I guess. It was so dark we couldn't see nothin'. We ended up down by the Lake Fork."

Cole saw this as an opportunity to teach the young men a lesson. "There's no such thing as a shortcut in country you're not familiar with, especially after dark. Next time come out with plenty of daylight and always leave the same way you came. That's one of the first rules of the mountains. You're lucky one of you didn't ride right off a cliff or break a horse's leg."

"Yes, sir," Kent said. "It won't happen again." Titus agreed.

Kent looked longingly at the fire. "Is there any grub left?"

"Stump's been keepin' it warm for you. You fellas can get some after you tend to your horses." Cole said.

"Yes, sir." The young men glanced knowingly at one another but made no mention of the gold coins they had found.

When Mordecai Lundy arrived at his camp on the top of Red Mountain, it was the middle of the night, and his partners were sleeping. Bones raised up and rubbed his eyes. "Where you been, Mordecai? It's the middle of the night." He wished now he had kept his mouth shut. "I'm just sayin'," he said.

"I been out tryin' to knife that Mex that rides with that cattle outfit. I almost got him, too."

Lundy kicked a smoldering stick back into the fire. "I'm thirsty. Where's my whiskey?"

Hiram rolled onto his side and tossed over a half empty bottle. "I thought you were watchin' that German woman," he said, with a yawn.

Lundy put the bottle to his lips and drained it dry. He wiped his mouth with the back of his hand. "I was headed to see the woman when I ran into the Mexican."

Mordecai lifted the lid to the cookpot. "I'm hungry. What's for supper?"

"Rabbit," Fritz said. "We saved you a shank." Lundy grabbed the meat with his grubby hand and tore off a piece with his teeth. He ate quickly, then made his bed near the fire.

The next morning, as the first rays of sun caressed the peaks, Lundy and his partners made plans to ambush gold shipments. Mordecai studied his map and pointed. "This here is the toll road, and here is where we are, Red Mountain," he said, sliding his index finger across the paper. "From up here, we have the best view of the gold route. We'll learn when the shipments is comin' through, and then we'll make our move."

Unbeknownst to Cole, Buffalo Morgan had been in the mountains around Platoro since the second week of June, and after a couple of weeks of prospecting, had staked a claim he named the "Valley Queen." The claim was located in a narrow canyon hidden between Forest King and Forest Queen Mountains, a mile southwest of Platoro.

The Valley Queen held its own spring and an abandoned cabin that sufficed as a suitable shelter. The claim was closed in narrowly by the two mountainsides which nearly touched and rose straight up through hundreds of feet of tall spruce and sedimentary rock cliffs.

The canyon floor saw very little sunlight and lay in shadow most of the day. Drifts of dirty snow clung to the hillside and lay against the tree trunks and lower logs of the cabin. Unidentifiable critter tracks of varied size and age indented the snow and mounds of shredded pinecones which squirrels and chipmunks had piled about.

Buffalo kept to himself, fixing up the cabin and digging in a natural cave that recessed some ten feet back inside the mountain. He filled another bucket with ore and carried it outside to the light of day to sort through. To his surprise, several of the rocks held nuggets of gold. After admiring them a moment, he took them over to his horse and placed them in the saddle bag for safe keeping, then went back to digging.

As always, it grew dark quickly in the narrow canyon, causing the temperature to drop like a rock. As darkness enfolded, he went to bed, but not to sleep. Now that he had found gold, he was worried that some greedy soul might try to kill him for it.

Buffalo Morgan lay under his buffalo hide blanket with his rifle at his side, listening. He could see the stars shining brightly against the dark sky as he peered up through a hole in the roof.

The canyon was sealed off to outside sound by the close flanking mountains, giving it an eerie silence, broken only by the whisperings of the wind blowing high in the cliffs. Inside the cabin, the persistent gnawing of a mouse inside one of the logs kept him awake. Outside, he could hear the hollow thuds of the chestnut's hooves upon the hard ground as it walked about nervously at the end of its picket rope.

Buffalo suddenly felt uneasy as though he was being watched. He reached inside his pocket and closed his hand around a buckeye nut he kept there for good luck. It stood to reason that a man might kill another in such a place as this, and the report of his rifle would go unheard. Such a death would remain a mystery, and a body might not be found before the deep winter snows encased it like a tomb.

As the night lingered on, Buffalo's trepidations were finally overcome by drowsiness, and he drifted off to sleep. The chestnut kept vigil and on occasion stamped at the ground and whimpered nervously at something above them. Something only it perceived.

Above the claim, the sow grizzly, locals knew as Silver Top, sat on her haunches, lifting her nose as she tested the night air. She smelled something that caught her interest, so she made her way quietly in that direction.

Independence Day Celebration

For the cowboys of the Golden Willow, the month of June ended without incident. On the morning of July 4th, the much anticipated Platoro Independence Day celebration got under way with much fanfare. The younger men were excited and ready to let off some steam. The town, which had been nearly empty, was now alive with wagonloads of people arriving by the hour.

Lightning and Rusty Wells, Lee Hansen, Titus Martin, and Carlos Sanchez left early for the fun and festivities while Cole and the others stayed back with the herd for the time being. The men of the Golden Willow tied their horses to a long hitchin' rail in front of the saloon.

"That's a big chestnut," Titus said, admiring the horse tied up on the end.

Lightning spotted a horse he really admired. "Ya'll, look at that grulla over yonder. Now that's a fine horse. You don't see many gray colored horses like that."

Carlos Sanchez eyed a big bay horse with a Cheyenne rig with silver conches on the saddle skirt. "That's too fancy a rig for a workin' man's horse. I'm bettin' that's a gambler's horse," he said.

The men walked up to a big poster board which described the weekend's events. A long list of festivities was scheduled to run throughout the day and well into the night.

"Look here, "Lee said. "This says there will be a church service tomorrow outside under the hill with the three crosses. It says the sermon will be brought by the Reverend Lemuel Phillips and special music will be performed by Jerry and Ann Ellis."

Lee looked at the others. "I bet Cole and Bob would like to go to the service."

"I know me and Rusty and Carlos are goin'," Lightning said.

Lee Hansen continued to read down the list. "Team pullin'; one half mile foot race; horseshoe pitchin'; lumber jack skills; three-legged race; tug-of-war; arm wrestlin'; boxin'; pie eatin' and shootin' contest; Faro, Pike Monte, and Poker matches at the saloon all day; Drinks half price; Meet Poker Alice." Lee stopped reading and turned to Titus. "Who's Poker Alice?"

Titus shrugged his shoulders. "How would I know? I guess she's supposed to be somebody famous."

"I'm gonna enter the shootin' contest," Lightning said.

"I think I'll enter the shootin' contest, too. You might be fast, but I'm a better shot," Rusty said, with the jab of his elbow.

"I believe I'll enter the pie eatin' contest," Lee said with a lick of his lips. "It says here, featurin' Miss Mary's famous pies."

Rusty pointed to the time of the contest. "Look here, Lee. The pie eatin' contest is done over. You done missed it."

Lee looked disappointed. "Boy, I bet them pies were good. Maybe there's still some crumbs left over."

"Maybe we could pay this Miss Mary to make us a pie for ourselves," Carlos said.

"I think I'll enter the lumber jack, the arm wrestlin', and the horseshoe pitchin' contests," Lee said.

He turned to the fellas with a cheesy grin on his face. "Do you reckon the shoes will still be attached to the horse's hooves?"

Titus laughed. "Lee actually made a funny joke." He playfully slapped the big man on the back. "See, Lee, it's not so hard to laugh a little bit, every once in a while, instead of bein' a grumpy ol' gripe most of the time."

"Well, it is a holiday," Lee grinned.

Titus turned to Carlos. "Carlos, that leaves you and me. I guess we'll take the boxin' then. Someone's got to stick up for the brand and show folks that the men of the Golden Willow are tough as they come."

"You go ahead and get yourself killed if you want to, but not me,"

Carlos laughed. "I'm more of a runner. I think I'll enter the half mile foot race."

Titus playfully slapped Carlos on the back just as he had done to Lee. "Ah, come on, Carlos. You'll change your mind after a few drinks. What do you say we go get us some whiskey?"

As the cowboys stepped inside the saloon, they saw men and women of all sorts, but most looked rougher than corn cobs and tougher than barb wire. Several games of faro and poker were already underway.

Titus sat down, and the others joined him at the table. He raised his hand and called for a bottle of whiskey, and a pretty young lady brought one over.

"Here's your whiskey, cowboy," the woman said, handing Titus a bottle.

"Thank you, ma'am. The drinks are on me, fellas," Titus said, rather loudly. He pulled a gold coin out of his pocket and handed it to the woman. "Here you are, lovely lady."

Lightning looked with surprise at Titus. "Hey, that was a gold coin. Where'd you get that?"

"None of your bees wax," Titus answered. He looked up and smiled at the woman. "What's your name, sweetheart?"

"My name's Eva." The woman's lips were stained a bright red and her lashes were long and dark. "Eva Thurman, but you can just call me Little Eva like everyone else does."

Just then a man in a suit came over and began to demand the young lady's attention. "I best be goin' now, fellas. Bye, bye," she said with a smile. The men tipped their hats to her as she walked away.

Titus pondered on the money pouch he had found with the name Eva Thurman stitched on it. He resolved that the Eva he had just met was the same person who had hid the gold up the Lake Fork in the cross-shaped crack in the rocks. Now that he knew who the gold belonged to, he had a decision to make about how to return it properly.

Titus took a drink of whiskey and passed the bottle to Lightning. "Here you go. Drink up."

"Thanks just the same, but I ain't drinkin'. Cole says alcohol impairs good judgment, and I aim to stay sober."

Titus frowned. "I ain't askin' you to get drunk, just imbibe a little.

It's Independence Day, ain't it? Let's celebrate." Rusty and Carlos decided to refrain as well.

Titus shook his head. "Horse feathers. You're all a bunch of saps."

Lightning stood and put on his hat. "I think I'll go outside and visit with the ladies."

"There's plenty of ladies in here," Titus said.

"Not my kind of ladies. I'm lookin' for a lady like Miss Abigale."

Titus took another drink. "Go right ahead then. Who needs you? The ladies are already comin' to me like flies on honey."

"I don't know about the ladies, but the flies sure like you," Lightning said, with a grin.

The cowboy walked outside and leaned against a pole to observe his options. Soon a pretty girl his age came walking by. She looked smart, dignified, and modestly dressed. His kind of woman. He tipped his hat to the young lady and flashed her a charming smile. "Howdy, miss."

The young woman turned her head and smiled back. "Hello," she said, her blue eyes meeting with his briefly.

Lightning stepped from the porch and followed her. "I didn't catch your name, miss. Mine is Lightning. I'm the head honcho of our cattle outfit." He stood straight and tall with his thumbs hooked in his front pockets.

The lady smiled once again but didn't give her name. To his dismay, he watched as she soon joined up with a fella who had been waiting for her. The man gave him a threatening look then walked off with his woman in arm.

Disappointed, but not defeated, Lightning's eyes soon met with another young lady who stood alone. Once again, he mustered his courage and went over to introduce himself.

By noon more than two hundred people had gathered for the festivities and more were arriving by the minute. There were cowboys, miners, loggers, gamblers, mountain men, farmers, and others of various professions, many recognizable by their attire.

People came from the San Luis Valley, Creede, Summitville,

Stunner and places in-between. It was rumored that Poker Alice had arrived in town to gamble.

The first event of the hour was the foot race which started in front of the saloon. The route was to continue down Conejos avenue to the single log bridge, across the river, then back down the wagon road, across the wooden bridge, then back to the saloon. Carlos entered the foot race, along with two dozen others. After the sound of the pistol, he took off and was the second person to reach the one-log bridge and the first to arrive back at the saloon, to much applause.

The second contest to take place was the arm-wrestling event. The winners of the first match faced one another. Although Lee Hansen did better than most, the final competition came down to two men; a strong mountain man by the name of Pat Williams and a miner named Clarence Morgan. Williams won the hard-fought match.

The next event to take place was the log pulling contest in which teams of mules pulled heavy spruce logs to see which could pull the farthest. Paulie McPhee, behind McKnight's four big mules, won out right, taking first place.

When it was time for the log sawing contest, Lee Hansen paired up with a logger from Southfork by the name of Enos Cook. When the official shouted, "Go!" the six teams of men began to saw with all their might. The serrated teeth of the saws bit deep, and with each pass a flurry of sawdust piled on the ground below. When the first log fell, it was at the feet of Lee Hansen. He caught his breath and shook the hand of his partner.

A man began to shout from the steps of the saloon, "Listen up, folks! The boxing matches will start in fifteen minutes. Those of you interested need to gather in the big tent behind the livery stables." He pressed a button on his pocket watch, then walked back inside. Titus and Carlos made their way to the big tent where a large crowd had already gathered. The excitement was about to begin.

Soon the announcer climbed into the ring and motioned for everyone to grow quiet. "Ladies and gentlemen, it's time to see who the bull of the woods is. The first man who can last two rounds against the champion, Sebastian O'Flannery, will win a cash prize of fifty dollars."

"Sebastian O'Flannery has traveled the West, boxing in cow towns and mining towns all over, including Denver. To this day, he is still undefeated. He stands six feet seven inches and weighs two hundred and forty pounds."

"Is there anyone here man enough to face this giant?" challenged the announcer.

A large man in the back raised his hand and pushed forward through the crowd. "I will fight. I have boxed back East in Kansas City and have never lost a fight." The man appeared to be a lumber jack.

The two men met in the middle of the ring, shook hands, and went back to their corners until the official rang a rusty old cowbell to start the match. At the clanking of the bell, each man came out of his corner circling and rolling his fist, waiting for just the right opportunity to deal the first blow.

The two contenders soon collided in a flurry of fists. The challenger fared well at the beginning, but Sebastian O'Flannery's pounding blows soon took their toll. Another hard-right cross and a sweeping uppercut from O'Flannery left the challenger unconscious on his back causing a loud collective gasp from the crowd. The champ dusted off two more challengers in quick fashion before Titus mustered the courage to enter the ring.

"I think I can take him now, Carlos. He's got to be gettin' tired," Titus said.

"You're crazier than a cross-eyed June bug if you get in the ring with that giant."

"I'll be fine. Don't worry. I'm tougher than I look."

Titus took off his shirt and gave it to Carlos to hold. He walked up and ducked under the ropes, entering the ring. Holding his hat high, he waved to the crowd with a confident smile. "Put your money on me if you want to make a fortune."

He noticed a pretty young lady in the front row and gave her a big smile. "Hey, pretty lady, would you look after my hat for me till I'm finished here? Afterwards I'll buy you a drink," he said, with a wink. The young lady smiled and held out her hands in order to catch the hat.

"Be real careful with it now, ma'am. It's the only one I got." Titus leaned over the ropes and tossed her his hat. As she caught it, the dust made her wrinkle her nose and turn her head to cough.

Titus gave the young lady another smile. "I'll be right back. Then we'll have us that drink."

The young lady rolled her eyes. The young man was foolish and brash, but a part of her admired his confidence and spunk. She decided she would root for him in spite of his arrogance.

Titus and the giant of a man met in the center of the ring and shook hands. The man's strong grip made Titus feel as though his hand was being crushed between a rock and a wagon wheel.

When the official clanked the cowbell to start the first round, Titus began to dance around and weave in and out like he had seen the others doing.

He managed to duck a hard right from O'Flannery that resembled the swipe of an angry grizzly bear. O'Flannery's second punch, however, caught him under the chin and lifted him over the ropes. He landed at the young lady's feet who was holding his hat. She leaned over him, concerned. "Are you okay?"

"No. I ain't. The room is spinnin'."

The official began to count to ten, slowly. "One…, two…, three…,"

"I better be goin'," Titus moaned. He raised to his knees and tried to stand.

"Four…, five…," the counting continued.

"Don't go. He'll hurt you bad," the young woman pleaded.

"Six…, seven…,"

With Carlos' help, Titus climbed back through the ropes and nodded to the official that he was okay. He took a deep breath, cleared his head, and raised his hands into position.

Titus began to move around on wobbly legs and managed to duck a series of punches. He landed two quick blows that bounced off O'Flannery's rock-hard belly. Titus jumped back and began to run around, avoiding the champ's advances. He ducked right instead of left and ran right into the champ's next jab. The blow to his chest caught him by surprise and made him gasp for air. Presently, he blocked a hard left with his arm causing it to go numb.

Titus moved in and wrapped his arms around the big man and held on for dear life. O'Flannery reached down and clasped him in a crushing embrace that forced the air from his lungs. The crowd let out a collective groan as if they could feel his pain. The official rushed over and forced the two men apart. Before O'Flannery could land another punch, the bell clanked to end the first round.

Titus was still bleeding from his chin when the second round started. At the clank of the bell, he danced around for a bit, then suddenly came in swinging with all his might, catching the big man by surprise.

He landed four more quick blows to O'Flannery's body and face. Titus ducked a punch and blocked another then struck the big man a glancing blow to the chin. Sebastian O'Flannery staggered backward, his hand to his cheek. He had now begun to bleed.

Titus danced around some more, ducking a couple of punches, then moved in once again with a flurry of solid blows. Sebastian stumbled backward a step, then wiped a trickle of blood from his upper lip. "I'm through playin' with you now," he said.

The big man rushed at Titus, trapping him near the corner ropes. He landed a hard punch to the cowboy's exposed ribs. There was a loud crack as the big man's fist slammed repeatedly into the young man's side. Titus doubled over in pain. O'Flannery's next swing was an uppercut that lifted Titus off his feet and onto his back. The champion had knocked him out cold.

The official counted to ten. When Titus didn't move, he made his announcement. "The winner by knockout is Sebastian O'Flannery!" The official held up one of the champion's thick arms which closely resembled a tree trunk.

The girl who had been holding Titus' hat followed Carlos into the ring and rushed to his side. Carlos leaned down to see if his friend was breathing. "Titus, are you okay? Can you hear me?" The girl also pleaded with him. "Titus, if you open your eyes, I'll have that drink with you." There was no response.

Carlos became worried. "Somebody get a bucket of water. Someone go for a doctor, too. Hurry. My friend is hurt."

Minutes later a man entered the tent with a bucket of cold water from the river. "Here's your water. My wife went for the doctor. He's on his way."

Carlos took the pail in both hands. "If this don't wake him up, nothin' will." He bent over and dumped the water into Titus' face. The cowboy gasped and sputtered as he came to. "Am I dead?" he groaned.

Carlos was happy to see his friend was still alive. "Just lay still, Titus, a doctor is on his way."

In a short time, a doctor arrived at the scene. "It looks like you got yourself mauled by a grizzly bear," the doctor said. The doc placed his bag down at his side and began to carefully examine Titus. He pushed around on his stomach and side. Titus gasped with each bit of pressure.

"How bad is the pain, son?"

"Bad."

"Let me see you move your arms and legs." Titus groaned as he moved one arm then the other. He did the same with his legs.

The doctor shook his head. "Mm, Mm, Mm, that's not good. You have at least two broken ribs. I'm gonna wrap them now, and it's gonna hurt." The doctor motioned to Carlos," I need you to gently help your friend up to a sitting position so I can wrap him." As the doctor carefully wrapped Titus' ribs, the pain was unbearable, but the young cowboy did not holler out. He only gasped and grimaced until the torture was over.

"Can I still ride a horse, Doc?"

"No siree, Bob! I don't want you even getting near a horse until after the end of the month. Broken ribs are a serious matter, son. You play around and get the sharp end of one of those ribs to puncture a lung, and it could kill you. You're going to have to take it easy. That's doctor's orders."

"The boss sure ain't gonna be happy about this."

"No, I suspect not, but that's still my orders. I know you cowboys. You'll get right back up on your horse the first time you take a notion to. I'm warning you, though, you better not."

The doctor picked up his bag and shook his head with disapproval. "All this for a chance at fifty dollars. I hope it was worth it."

He turned to Carlos. "You see that your friend here keeps some ice on those ribs, and make sure his bandages stay tight. The more moving he does the more his bandages is going to loosen and that will hinder his ribs from settin' back together like they should. If he needs me, I'll be in the saloon all day. After that, he's on his own."

"What do I owe you, Doc?" Titus asked.

"Nothin' today. It's Independence Day, and I'm feelin' generous. Take care, son. God be with you."

The young lady was still kneeling at Titus' side, holding his hat. "You fought very well, Titus," she said.

"Thank you. What's your name?"

"Callie Dawn Grigsby."

"Pleased to know you, Callie."

Titus grimaced as he tried to move. "Carlos, help me up. Me and Miss Grigsby are gonna have us that drink I promised her."

The sound of a gunshot rang out from the steps of the saloon. A man in a black bowler hat holstered his pistol and began to speak to the crowd. "Listen up, everyone. The shooting contest is about to start over by the river. Anyone who is interested should head on that way."

Rusty and Lightning walked over to the river and joined up with ten other men who were just as anxious to show off their speed and accuracy. Many looked like very hard men. Some had likely even killed before.

The Wells brothers tried to size up the competition. It was hard to gage a man's shooting skills by their appearance or the size of the guns resting on their hips. Many a man had misjudged another and paid for it with their lives.

The twelve contestants were divided into two groups of six. First one group would spread out along a line and shoot and then the other.

During the first challenge, contestants had to shoot a bottle off a log from thirty feet away. In the first group, just half of the men hit the bottle. Lightning and Rusty hit theirs on their first shot.

The second challenge was shooting at a burning candle from ten paces. Though shooting the candle proved to be more difficult, Rusty and Lightning hit their candles on their first attempt.

Next was the swinging bottle challenge. After hitting the swinging bottle, Lightning began to stand out. At the end of all challenges, there was a tie between Lightning and a man with his arm bound in a sling who had shot with the other group.

PLATORO THE SUMMER RANGE

For the tie breaker, a can was tossed in the air. The man with his arm in a sling hit his can, and Lightning hit his as well. The judge walked over and examined the cans. While he was busy tallying up the scores for first, second, and third place, the man with his arm in a sling approached Lightning. As he did so, his left hand rested on the butt of his pistol, and his eyes flashed with a sudden anger.

"How good are you, Harden, when you're shootin' at somethin' that can shoot back?"

Lightning was confused. "I'm not Cole Harden."

"I say you are," the man said.

Just then the contest judge made the announcement. "The winner of the shooting contest is Mr. Lightning Wells. Second place goes to Mr. Johnny Diablo and third to Mr. Rusty Wells.

The man with his arm in a sling looked puzzled. "I was told you were Cole Harden."

"Well, you were told wrong, but if I was Cole, you'd be shuttin' up about now."

The man stared at Lightning a moment. "You're pretty good with that gun. Is that why they call you Lightning, because you're so fast?"

"My pa named me that cause I was born with a pistol in my right hand. I shot a whiskey bottle out of the doc's hand before he could slap my bottom."

The man was not amused. "Can you shuck a pistol faster than Cole Harden?"

"No, Cole is faster. He's the fastest I ever seen."

The man pondered on Lightning's words. "You know you didn't beat me fair," the man said.

"How's that?"

The man touched his sling. "I got a bum arm. I ain't my true self till it heals up."

"How about I tie one arm behind my back, and we go at them targets again?" Lightning said.

The man's eyes were cold and calculating. "I generally prefer to shoot targets that bleed," he said.

Lightning was disturbed at the man's calloused nature. "Just who are you, mister?"

"I go by Johnny Diablo. I work for Lassiter. You Golden Willow boys ain't seen the last of me either. That goes especially for Cole Harden."

Lightning leaned in close to Johnny Diablo. The two men now stood toe to toe. "Any problem you have with one of us, you have with all of us."

Rusty tugged at his brother's shoulder. "Let's go, Lightning. He's not worth it."

Lightning turned to leave. As he did, he heard Johnny Diablo's taunting words.

"Hey, Lightning-Bug, there's one more thing you should know before you go."

Lightning stopped and turned around. "What's that?"

"If we'd a squared off just now, you'd been drawin' an empty gun. You haven't reloaded. A real gunman would have thought of that."

Lightning's face flushed hot. The man was right. He was carrying an empty gun.

"Tell Harden to be ready cause Shiloh Tremble's comin' for him."

"You better tell Shiloh to leave Cole alone," Lightning warned.

"Well, I got a feelin' ol' Shiloh ain't too scared."

"Is Shiloh around here close?" Rusty asked.

"Closer than you think," the man said. He turned and walked off into the crowd.

There was something about this Johnny Diablo that made the Wells brothers very uneasy; the way he moved, the way he carried himself. It all added up to only one thing; an experienced gunfighter and a cold-blooded killer; maybe one of Lassiter's best; maybe even better than Shiloh Tremble. Lightning was fast and accurate with his gun, but he had never turned it on a man before, not even in self-defense. Suddenly his legs became weak, and he felt sick to his stomach.

"We better tell Cole about this Johnny Diablo fella and warn him about Shiloh, too." Rusty said. "He'll know what to do."

Lightning and Rusty mounted their horses and left to warn Cole. In their haste, they failed to notice that the grulla horse they had been admiring earlier was gone, as was the big chestnut and the bay with the Cheyenne rig with the silver conches on the saddle skirt.

Silver Top's Revenge

In a corner of the saloon, Hiram, Bones, and Fritz played a game of poker with a well-dressed stranger; a gambler from Creede. All four of the men were in the company of dance hall women.

Fritz looked around the room. "Where's Mordecai? I thought he was gonna join us?"

Bones shrugged his shoulders as he studied his cards. "He mentioned somethin' about somethin' to do with the German lady. I believe he's taken a fancy to her."

Hiram peered over the top of his cards, barely able to hide his excitement. "Everyone lay down your hand. Let's see what you got." Bones revealed a pair of tens while Fritz had three sevens.

"I've got four nines and a queen," Hiram crowed. "How do you like them apples?"

The nicely dressed stranger smiled. "I've got four of a kind, too, only mine are all aces," he said, laying them down for all to see.

"Thanks a lot, gentlemen." He thrust out his arms and raked all the money into a pile next to his belly. Suddenly he seemed to be in a hurry to leave. He scooped his winnings into his hat then stood to leave. "I've got to be going now, gentlemen. It's been a real pleasure playing with you gents. A real pleasure." He bowed his head to them and turned to leave.

Hiram, who never took well to losing, stood up. "Hold it, mister. I think you been cheatin' us." Hiram was about to draw iron when Bones leaned over and took hold of his arm.

Bones shook his head. "Not here." Hiram jerked his arm away and sat back down. The gambler, realizing he was off the hook, turned and left in a hurry.

Hiram, who had already had three bottles of whiskey and was soon too drunk to play anymore, invited a woman to join him over at another table where the two of them could sit and drink alone.

Hiram handed the woman a bottle. "What's your name?"

"Eva Thurman," she said as she played with her hair. "Most folks call me little Eva." She tipped up the bottle and took a drink.

"Are you from around here, Eva?"

"I used to be a dance hall girl over to Creede, but lately I been here in Platoro dancin', among other things," she said with a smile. "They pay me in gold. That's better than paper money."

The young woman took the cigarette from Hiram's mouth and put it between her red-stained lips. She took a long draw on it then exhaled a steady stream of smoke into his face. "You know, you ain't paid me yet. You gotta pay me if you're looking for some more affection."

Hiram shrugged his shoulders and handed her two gold coins. Eva smiled and took the money. "I hide my gold in a place I call the cross cause it looks like a cross in the rocks. I'm savin' up so my little brother can go see a doctor back East."

Hiram leaned in and tried to steal a kiss. Eva pulled away with a giggle. "You should know I got a beau who is sweet on me. He gets awful jealous, too, when anyone pays attention to me. He killed the last fella that tried to show me affection."

Hiram looked around. "Is he here?"

"No, he's over to Creede. I don't expect him back for another two days, though." Eva playfully batted her long eyelashes and exhaled another cloud of smoke in Hiram's direction.

Hiram smiled back and reached out and took her hand. "Well, Eva, it looks like we have a couple of days to celebrate." He held up his bottle of whiskey in a toast. "To love," he said, tapping his bottle against hers. "To love," she giggled.

PLATORO THE SUMMER RANGE

While there was still a little light left that same evening, Luke Parnell found Cole riding herd in the meadows below Platoro. "Howdy, Cole. Some folks from the Valley who came here for the Independence Day celebration asked me to give you this letter."

Luke handed Cole the letter. "It's from Miss Abigale."

Cole opened the seal, then looked up at Luke. "Thanks, Luke."

Luke nodded. "You goin' into town tonight, boss?"

"No, I believe I better keep watch on the herd."

"Yes, sir. I guess I'll be gettin' back to town then."

"Keep a watch out for that sow grizzly. I cut her fresh tracks a while ago," Cole warned. "After the stars come out tonight, you boys keep an eye on the Big Dipper. When it gets right up there, I want several of you to switch with the others and ride nighthawk."

"Yes, sir, I'll tell the boys." Luke clucked his tongue and nudged his horse forward with the heel of his boot. He turned it about and headed back to Platoro.

Cole opened the letter from Abby and began to read it. It was dated July 2, 1880, two days ago:

Dearest Cole,

I hope this letter finds you safe and well. We are fine here. We had all planned to come up and surprise you, but it wasn't meant to be. We came as far as Elk Creek when Daddy's heart began to trouble him. I thought about coming on to see you by myself, but we had heard rumors of trouble up there. Sadly, I have resolved that Daddy needs me here with him for now to help run operations at the ranch until he recovers.

We all miss you, I especially, but Brian misses you as well. He wanted me to tell you hello and let you know that he caught a really big trout the other day with a homemade bug that he tied the way you had taught him. You never saw a prouder boy. I believe by the time you see him again he'll be quite noticeably taller.

I did receive your letters. What a joy they were to read. I've read them several times as it comforts me to do so. I look forward to your next one.

I should probably let you know that Graham Lassiter and several of his men have been found guilty and sent on to Denver to the prison there. Judge Parker had the Bar L's summer range grazing permits revoked. That's an answer to prayer, also.

Some of the boys have had some run-ins with a couple of Lassiter's men in town, but they were of little consequence. Gilbert Mackey and F. D. Hurly caught a couple of fellows up on the mesa watching the ranch about a week after you left for the high country. It turned out the men had been paid by Lassiter to spy on us.

Please take care of yourself, Cole. Take care of the men, too. Daddy says they set store by you for your faith and experience.

We have heard rumors of a murder and grizzly trouble up there. We heard that Roman Romero lost a half dozen sheep up on Cornwall. He said he saw the bear that killed them and thinks it was the same big female that killed some of his sheep and two McNeil Diamond F cattle last year up the Adams Fork. They call her Silver Top.

Daddy also heard that Shiloh Tremble was recently sighted up by Platoro by a gambler that recognized him. So please be careful. I know I should rest in knowing that our God is with you no matter where you are and not worry so much, but it's hard not to.

We were filled with joy to hear that Uncle Bob made the decision to follow Jesus as his Savior. Father and Mother cried. I did, too. We had been afraid that Bob would stay eternally lost. Now we will all spend eternity together, thanks to you.

It is getting very dry here, so we are praying for the July monsoon rains to come soon. I imagine the wildflowers up there will soon be in full bloom, if not already. I can imagine the columbine, the lupine, the bluebells, the monkshood, and the red Indian paintbrush are beautiful.

Mother and I have been canning beets and making pickles as well as baking rhubarb pies. Tomorrow we plan to make a batch of strawberry and rose hip jam.

We had to go into town the other day to get some more canning wax and some jars and we saw Sarah McEntire. She and Ezra are expecting another grandchild from Rupert and Shelly.

Mother and I have started another quilt. Grace McNeil and Ruby Wiescamp have been coming over and working on it with us. It is coming along beautifully.

I can't wait to see you as the summer seems longer without you. Remember you have my love and my prayers. Mother and Father and the men send their regards as well. I hope to hear from you again soon but will have to assume that no news is good news for now.

I almost forgot to mention that Seth Callahan is doing much better and is talking some now. The doctor doesn't know if he will ever be like he was but feels he's making progress in his recovery. Bye for now. I miss you.

Love always, Abigale.

Cole carefully folded the letter and placed it in the pocket of his vest. The letter gave him comfort. He would read it again back at camp.

It was now dark. He rode the perimeter of the herd. As he rode along, he sang softly to the cattle to keep them calm.

Uphill, among the Aspen, he could barely make out the cabin that belonged to Otto and Heidi Kulman. The light from a lantern shown through the window suggesting they were still awake.

In the distance, at Platoro, fireworks began to light the night sky in brilliant displays of color. Loud pops and booms accompanied each display. As the fireworks continued, the cattle grew increasingly nervous. Cole rode slowly among the herd, calming them by singing the night herding song. Some of the other men were spread out, also keeping watch.

As the night progressed, a silent visitor stalked along the river near the perimeter of the herd. It was the sow grizzly, known as Silver Top, that had rushed Bob London down river, and it was heading in the direction of Platoro, enticed by the smell of food that carried on the breeze.

The grizzly walked along with its nose into the wind. She could smell fresh meat. Up ahead, she could see a log cabin. It was the cabin of Otto and Heidi Kulman. The big bear stood on her hind legs a moment then dropped back down to all fours with a grunt. A long string of drool hung from her mouth as she headed that way.

Silver Top could smell meat. She came around to the back of the Kulman's cabin and found a meat pole. From it hung a quarter of venison. Raising up on her hind legs, she reached as high as she could, then leaned her weight against the pole. She locked her jaws around the leg bone and tore the quarter from its place with little effort. The bear carried the hunk of meat off into the brush and began to tear the flesh away from the bone as she gripped it firmly with her claws.

Later that evening, Mordecai Lundy waited along the river below the Kulman's cabin hoping to catch a glimpse of Heidi Kulman coming for her evening bath. As he hunkered among the cinquefoil bushes, he heard movement behind him. He turned to look but saw nothing. It was probably one of the cattle from the cowboy outfit coming to water. "Darn cattle," he muttered. "Always leaving green mushy cow pies everywhere." He was squatting in a pile of it now. A short time later, he heard something slogging through the seam water as it crossed to the other side, just around the bend.

For a time, there was no other sound above that of the reassuring flow of the river. It wasn't long before he could hear a female voice singing directly across the way. The German woman was coming!

Lundy craned his neck and peered over the bushes. Presently, he saw a woman and a man and cursed under his breath. It wasn't the German woman at all but instead, the dance hall girl, little Eva, and Hiram. They were walking along the opposite bank, headed down river. Both were singing and laughing loudly.

Behind them, Lundy caught movement among the willows. He thought it to be a cow at first, but when the animal walked through a clearing, it showed itself to be a grizzly. The big beast appeared to be stalking Hiram and Eva. Lundy wanted nothing to do with the bear, so he left to find his horse. Hiram and Eva were on their own.

The bear continued to stalk along the river. After traveling around a bend, she stopped and raised in the air. She stood high on her back legs and peered over the bushes, working her nose into the wind and grunting. She could smell humans and hear singing and laughter not far ahead.

Hiram Leech began to sing at the top of his lungs as he stumbled along in a drunken stupor, his new woman at his side. "Camp town lady sing your song, Doo Dah, Doo Dah." He stopped and tried to kiss Eva.

"Keep your hands off of me," Little Eva giggled. She ran from him playfully and tripped and fell. She continued to laugh as he helped her up.

"Come on. All I want is a little kiss," Hiram pleaded.

Little Eva raised her finger to her lips. "Shh, I heard somethin'."

Hiram looked around. "I didn't hear anything." He reached for her again, and she slapped at him.

"Stop. Don't you hear that? It sounds like growlin', and it's coming from over there," she pointed.

Suddenly, she could see the female grizzly rushing in their direction. She screamed in terror as the bear came upon them. There was no time to run or escape. There was only a flurry of teeth and claws, screams of pain, then nothing but silence.

In the distance at Platoro, the celebrations continued with loud explosions and brilliant displays of light. The revelers continued to sing and dance, unaware of the horrors taking place not far away in the night.

The following morning, the community of Platoro gathered for church services under the hill with the three crosses. Of those in attendance, nine were men from the Golden Willow.

It was a beautiful day. The sky was a deep blue, the air clean and crisp, and the land shimmered under a bold sun. The congregation sat on the ground or stood, while others sat on horseback.

The attendees included folks from all over the San Luis Valley and mountain settlements, many of which were attending church for the first time. Cole looked around. He counted seventy-nine people in all.

The Reverend Lemuel Phillips preached a thought-provoking sermon on Jesus' parable of the Prodigal Son from Luke 15:11 and following. After the sermon, the Reverend introduced the Ellis family who sang "The Old Rugged Cross" and several other hymns.

Cole sang the song "Cowboy's Dream" and was joined by Lee and Bob in a trio performance. When finished, they sat back down on the front row along with Lightning, Rusty, Paulie, Luke, Stump, and Carlos.

During a testimonial time, a woman named Mary Burrell spoke of an answered prayer concerning the health of her friend she called Sweet Dixie. When she had finished and sat down, Cole stood up and volunteered to read some scripture from the 91st Psalm. He then spoke of how Jesus had saved him as a young man and how Jesus had always been with him throughout life's dangers and hardships. The service was considered a wonderful success, and everyone talked as though they should do it again the following year.

Directly after the service, a rider rode up with the news that, overnight, a gambler had been found dead upriver from Platoro in Boiler Canyon. While Cole and the man were talking, Garth Benoit came riding up in a hurry. "I need to talk to you, Cole," he said, short of breath.

Cole took Garth aside. "What is it, Garth? You look like you've seen a ghost."

"Worse," he gasped. "Me and Griz found two people dead, downriver in the meadows, just a while ago. A man and a woman. They were mangled and tore up bad. There was grizzly tracks all around them. The girl was one of the dance hall girls I seen in the saloon yesterday."

The man Cole had been visiting with, a moment before, came over.

"Pardon me, but I couldn't help but overhear the young man just now. Could you describe the man and woman you found?" he asked Garth. Garth described the two in detail.

The man listened and nodded. "I remember them. They sat at the table in front of me at the saloon all last evening a drinkin' and a carryin' on. Before they left, I heard them say they were headed to Axell." The man paused in thought. "Are you sure it were a grizzer what kilt 'em?"

Garth looked at the ground. "Yes, sir. Sure as I can be. Ain't no man could've done what was done to them two."

The man rubbed his jaw. "I bet it was that grizzer they call Silver Top."

Cole turned back to the man. "Who were they?"

"The woman was one of the dance hall girls who went by the name of little Eva. The man that was with her, I believe, said his name was Hiram. He was real smitten with her, like an old tomcat."

Cole nodded. "And the gambler they found dead in Boiler Canyon. What do you know about him?"

"Well, near as I recall, he played several games of poker with that Hiram fella and his friends. The gentleman won and took a good bit of money with him. That didn't set too well with them fellas he was playin' with. The gentleman left in a hurry, and that's the last I seen of him."

"Did anyone see or hear anything in the area of Boiler Canyon?" Cole asked.

The man rubbed his jaw. "Word is that a chestnut, a grulla, and a black had all been seen in the area. The man who found him dead, Lloyd Betts, said he saw a man standing over the body, and when he hollered out, the man mounted up on a chestnut and lit a shuck out of there. He said the gambler's pockets had been turned inside out, and there weren't no money on him. The only thing left in his pocket was a buckeye nut."

"A buckeye nut?" Cole said.

"Yes, sir. Nearest I can figure, either the killer put it there, or the gambler had been totin' it around for good luck."

Cole remembered the buckeyes he had found at the scene of his family's massacre back in Missouri. Could the murders be related? It was unlikely, but could the man who murdered his family 20 years ago in Missouri be hiding out up here somewhere in these very mountains? Cole also remembered the buckeye that Buffalo Morgan had given him for good luck, and the fact that Morgan had admitted he had been in Missouri 20 years ago at the same time as his family's murders. The thought of this troubled him.

A good number of folks had travelled through Boiler Canyon overnight on their way home from celebrations, and any one of them could have been guilty of the murder. Whoever the murderer was, odds were that he was still around, camped somewhere near Platoro, watching and plotting for his next victim.

As Cole rode back to camp, he was troubled by the tragic events that had unfolded in the night. When he got back, he met up with Griz.

"That bear has to be killed," Griz said. "Me and Garth covered the bodies and put them in the wagon. I'll show you where it happened."

Together, Cole and Griz rode to the bloody site where the attack had occurred. Griz squatted there, taking in what knowledge he could. The stout Mexican spread his hand out wide and placed it over the print of the bear's front foot pad. The print was wider than his hand and the claw impressions, long and deep.

"That's a big bear," Griz said. "I think it's a female. For sure, a grizzly."

"She's likely the same bear that rushed Bob," Cole said. "Silver Top."

Griz stood up. "It appears she's following the river down canyon. I'm going after her soon as I gather my Hawkin."

"You be careful, Griz. Why don't you take my Winchester? The weather's fixin' to turn bad."

"My Hawkin has never failed me yet," Griz said. Griz rode back to camp and gathered his leather parfleche, lead balls, his powder horn, and other possibles he needed, as well as, his rifle and pistol and headed out.

By late afternoon, he had tracked the bear down the Conejos and halfway up Saddle Creek. It had been a steady drizzle all afternoon, and now a white mist hung like thick smoke over the mountains. It continued to rain lightly.

The Saddle Creek, which was normally a lucent little brook, barely two feet deep, with gentle rills and quiet pools, now rushed noisily through the bottom of the meadow. Dwarf willow grew thick along both sides of the brook.

The narrow vallecito or little valley in which he rode was flanked on the south by a sharply rising slope of blue spruce capped with stark sedimentary cliffs. Upon the sheer face of the cliff, not far below the top, was an eagle's nest. Just below it, the rock face was stained with excrement from generations of use.

Griz continued to track the bear along Saddle Creek as he kept a watchful eye to his surroundings. Eventually, he topped out into the bottom of a wide, glacial bowl that resembled a v-shaped notch, widest at the top and tapering down to him. He reined up his horse and took in the land. At the top of the glacial bowl was a steeply sloped gravel field with a noticeable game trail crossing it. Below that was a grove of trees, a copse mixture of stunted spruce, and engleman fir.

The bowl was flanked on both sides by steep stands of blue spruce, and the carved-out valley between was lush and green, choked with cinquefoil bush, dwarf willow, and stunted stands of juniper. The landscape sloped downward in a series of descending benches, and through the center slipped the infant start of Saddle Creek. Griz continued to survey the bowl. Though it appeared to be open, the undergrowth was taller than it looked and could easily hide a grizzly that didn't want to be seen.

He urged his horse forward toward something that caught his attention. On a gentle slope grew large patches of alpine bistort, cow parsnips, sweet cicely, bear root, and other plants known to be favorite foods of grizzlies. Stair-stepping down the slope was a large area of clawed out earth and heaped over dirt about a foot deep. It was a grizzly dig, and Griz had seen plenty of them before. Beside the fresh dig was a large pile of bear dung. It was black, moist, segmented, and tubular in shape.

Griz dismounted and took a stick and poked at the dung revealing pieces of roots, bone, seeds, and grass. Its pungent odor suggested its freshness.

The horse whimpered and nervously jerked its head against the reins. Not far away stood a spruce tree with deep, furrowed claw marks reaching to more than seven feet above the ground. Beyond that was another similar marker.

Griz nervously stroked his bear claw necklace as he began to replay in his mind that awful day years before when he had been attacked and nearly killed by a grizzly up by Blue Lake. The bear had slashed a deep gash across his face and bit into the back of his neck, picked him up, and shook him so violently that he felt he would snap in two. The grizzly had raked its claws deep through the flesh of his shoulders and rolled him over on his back. When she began to attack his left leg, he had thrown up his hands, and pulling his knife, had stabbed the bear in the neck twice before he blacked out.

The horrifying memory was interrupted by the sound of a steer bellering somewhere distant within the bowl. It sounded like Ol' Rebel. Griz rode up to a high bench clearing where he could see the area below much better.

Rumblings of thunder had grown louder and now cold, fat drops of rain began to rattle upon the ground. Soon it was raining harder. A loud clap of thunder shook the bench.

Water ran over the brim of his hat as his eyes searched across the ravine for the source of what sounded like bones snapping. He had heard the sound before, and it brought a chill to his flesh.

The crunching noise was coming directly across from him. He could see the bear now. She was climbing up a scree slope, dragging a four-hundred-pound yearling steer, a red lineback he recognized as Ol' Rebel's running partner. The bear stopped on a flat bench and began to feed on the fresh kill once again.

Griz got a good look at her for the first time. The animal's forelegs folded into massive shoulders, and above that was the silver hump that identified her as a grizzly. It was Silver Top, the bear he was after.

The big sow grizzly had both of her front paws on the steer's body, and her jaws locked on the dead animal's thigh. With one powerful shove of her forelegs and a backward jerk of her head, she ripped the hind quarter from the steer's body and began to once again snap bones with her powerful jaws.

Silver Top looked his way with the bloody hunk of meat clamped between her red stained teeth. If the bear decided to rush him now, she could be on him in an instant.

Griz drew up his Hawkin rifle and aimed down the barrel at the bear's massive head. The rain continued to run down over the brim of his hat as he brought the hammer to full cock. He took in a breath, steadied himself, then dropped the hammer. The powder hesitated in the damp air, finally flared, then responded with a fizzled bang and a cloud of gray smoke. The Hawkin had misfired. The rain must have doused the powder in the pan and caused it to cake up. A clean miss. When the smoke cleared, the bear was nowhere to be seen.

Griz remembered his Hawkin pistol he kept under his slicker. Its powder would still be dry. Even so, he would only have one shot if needed.

He went to find the lost steer, and when he finally located him, it was indeed Ol' Rebel. Griz began to push 'Ol Rebel back toward the rest of the herd. He kept his eyes open for the sow grizzly, but she never showed herself again. Still, he had that strong feeling that he was being watched and maybe even followed. He hurried to get out of the canyon before dark. He would send some of the boys back to retrieve what meat they could salvage from the dead steer.

The Dangerous Toll Road

On the sixth of July, Bob London was by himself, packing salt into the meadows above Platoro to concentrate the cattle there, when he noticed a grulla horse grazing in an aspen glade a short distance up the Rito Gato Creek. He decided to leave the steers unattended and went to check out the situation.

When he reached the meadow, he saw a man sitting in the shade, leaning back against an aspen tree not far from the grulla. The man's head drooped in slumber; his hat tipped down over his eyes.

"Good afternoon to you," Bob called out in a friendly voice. The man looked his way but said nothing. "I say, howdy, feller," Bob greeted, a second time. "Looks like you found a good place to noon a spell." Bob noticed the man's arm was bound in a sling. "What's a matter with your arm? Did your horse throw you?"

"Somethin' like that," the man answered. His eyes were piercing. It was obvious he was not a friendly sort.

London took careful measure of the stranger before him. The cowboy appeared to be in his late twenties, and there was an arrogance about him that was unnecessary.

The man noticed the "GW" brand on Bob's horse and rested his eyes there. "You with the Golden Willow outfit, mister?"

London nodded. "Yes, I am. We've got permits to graze the high country this year."

At Bob's words, the man's countenance stiffened, and his eyes shaded. "You wouldn't be Cole Harden, would ya?"

"No, I'm Bob London. I own the cattle. Cole is my foreman. What do you want with Cole?"

"I work for Lassiter. My name's Johnny Diablo."

Bob remembered that the Wells brothers had mentioned they had met a man named Johnny Diablo and that he had threatened Cole once before. He assumed the man was a fugitive of the law. The fact that the stranger worked for Lassiter made him a bad seed.

"I understand Lassiter's grazing permits for the high country have been revoked. Makes me wonder what you're doin' up here. You should find another brand to work for."

The man stood to his feet and rested the palm of his hand on the butt of his pistol. "You should mind your own business, you old rooster."

"I see no one ever taught you to respect your elders," Bob said.

The man shrugged. "Well, my pa tried, but it didn't take."

Bob was growing uncomfortable with the direction of the conversation. "Some of my men have seen a rider on a grulla horse watching our herd. I guess that would be you?"

"Maybe, maybe not," the man answered. "I bought Bronco here as a colt from Hank Wiescamp down in the San Luis Valley. He had a mare that foaled twin grulla colts. I don't know who rides the other grulla, but I seen it tied up in front of the saloon the other day."

Bob was more confused than ever. "What do you want with Cole?" he said.

"You ask too many questions, old rooster."

Bob furrowed his brow. "You're a mighty mysterious fella, Mister Johnny Diablo. I don't know what you're up to, but if you're figurin' on cutting our herd or coming after Cole, you better think again."

The man grinned. "We'll see about that."

Bob looked back in the direction he had come from to see how far it was to the cover of the trees, in case he had to make a run for it. His plan was to leave calmly and then go get Cole, Griz, and Lightening to come back with him to find out more about what this man was doing watching them and the herd.

"Well, I best be gettin' back to the cattle. Yearlin' steers have a mind of their own. If they're not tended to, they'll wander off into mischief."

Bob London clicked his tongue and turned his horse toward the cattle. Before he could ride away, he heard the hammer click back on the man's pistol.

"Stop right there, mister. I didn't say you could leave."

When Bob didn't return back to camp, Cole and some of the men went to search for him, but a monsoon shower slowed them down and erased what little tracks there were to follow. After a week of searching turned up no sign of Bob London or his horse, the men feared the worst.

The following week, Garth Benoit saw a lone rider on a grulla horse riding up an un-named creek. When he rode over to question him, the man rode away in a hurry before Garth could get a good look at him.

Cole and Griz had picked up the grulla's tracks, but they lost the trail in the Rito Gato Creek drainage when they became mingled with the tracks of five other riders.

It seemed that Mr. London may have become the first casualty of the mountains for the Golden Willow outfit, and the men took it hard. The decision was made to send word down the mountain to the McKnights and Mrs. London for prayer and for the prayers of the church at Las Mesitas.

By the twentieth of July, the herd was spread out all around and above Platoro, as well as, on Red and Mammoth Mountains. Most of the snow had melted along the divide, and the grass was belly deep in places above Platoro. The gold claims of Forest King, Silver Queen, Klondike, the Mammoth Load, and the Parole Mine were already producing good amounts of gold.

Heavily guarded pack trains of mules were making weekly runs with gold and silver through the Robinson Gulch road on their way to Del Norte. Some of the miners paid a toll in gold for the protection of armed guards to escort them safely along the forty-six mile stretch to Del Norte.

The Robinson Gulch road or Toll road, as some were now calling it, was little more than a one-track mule trail and still unsuitable for wagons.

Most gold shipments were accompanied by three or more heavily armed men. Few souls had been careless enough to make the trip alone ever since a miner by the name of O. E. LeDue had been murdered and robbed the year before. The killer was caught and hung from a large tree along the trail that folks now referred to as "The Hanging Tree." The body was left to swing in the wind for months to serve as a reminder of what would happen to anyone who tried to rob and murder a miner along the route. So far, it had worked to discourage would be villains until recently when another miner had been found dead, robbed of his cash money, on his way back to Platoro.

At their Golden Egg Claim, Otto and Heidi Kulman filled their tenth bag with gold. "Heidi," Otto said, "gold makes men greedy. I'm worried that sooner or later these lazy summer days might soon reveal that unfortunate truth."

Heidi paused from her work. "If anyone finds out we have struck a good vein of gold, they may try to take our claim or harm us. I don't know what I would do if something happened to you, Otto."

Otto finished tying off the last bag of gold. "Maybe it's time we make a deposit."

Heidi nodded. "You should pay a toll for a guard or take someone with you. It's much too dangerous to go by yourself. Why don't you take Cole Harden with you?"

"I trust Cole, but he is busy with the cattle. I don't want to trouble him. I will be fine. There is a full moon out tonight. I will travel during the night and rest during the day. It will be safer that way."

Heidi reached over and placed her hand on his arm. "At least tell Cole when and where you are going and when you plan to be back."

"Don't worry, my love," Otto said, placing his hand affectionately to her cheek. "I will go tell Cole that I will be leaving just after dark tonight. Soon we will have enough money from the gold to have our farm in the Valley, and you will be able to buy all that you want."

"I will pack some food for your trip while you go speak to Cole," Heidi said. "I don't want you to starve to death trying to get our gold to town. I want you to be healthy and strong for your journey." She smiled and pondered on the love she felt for this man and all they had been through together.

Later that day, Otto found Cole moving cattle up Sawmill Gulch and told him of his plans to go to Del Norte with the gold. "If something should happen to me, Cole, could you and your men take my wife down to the Valley with you before the heavy snows come. I couldn't bear to think of her staying another winter up here by herself, all alone."

"Me and the boys will see that Heidi is taken care of," Cole assured him.

"I would be obliged if you could look in on Heidi while I'm gone. There has been signs of a man lurking around our cabin. I also had a bear take a hind quarter of deer from my meat pole the other night."

"I will keep an eye on your place for you, Otto, while you're gone. Don't worry about a thing. Just get your gold deposited safely."

"I'll be seein' you, Cole," Otto waved. "If I ain't back in a week, I didn't make it."

"You'll make it, Otto. God be with you."

Otto returned to his claim and prepared for his trip. The Golden Egg Claim was hidden beneath a large out-cropping of rocks, entered by a deep crevasse about six feet wide. After descending some twenty feet, he lit his lantern and went in. When he had brought out most of the bagged gold, he loaded the mules' paniers evenly to balance the weight, then sat his horse. Heidi joined him at his side holding a knapsack full of food.

"I left a bag behind. If anything should happen, we will still have a little to help with our needs," he told Heidi.

"Remember to keep the axe by the bed and carry it with you at all times if you go outside, especially after dark."

"I will."

Heidi handed the knapsack with the food to her husband. "This should last you for four days. Keep it wrapped tight when you travel so it will stay fresh. There's bread and cheese and some cured venison and bacon. I filled your canteen with water from the spring." Her eyes rested on him.

Otto took the food. His rifle he tucked in his scabbard within easy reach. His bed roll was tied securely on the cantle of his saddle.

"Take this wool coat with you, please, Otto. The nights will be cold without a fire."

Otto took the coat. "You're always thinking of me," he said.

He leaned in and kissed Heidi goodbye. "I'll be back soon with a new pair of shoes and plenty of material for dresses for you, my lovely bride."

Heidi's eyes sparkled above a warm, yet worried smile. "You be careful. I love you." She held her husband's hand until his leaving pulled them apart.

Otto rode on with the intention of making a good distance before daylight. His horse led the small pack train of two mules in the dim light. The mountains to the north stood in contrast against the violet sky and now the random swelling of the breeze caused the horse to jump on occasion as dark clouds brushed across the face of the moon.

Otto reined his horse along Fisher Gulch and headed up the willow choked game trail that followed the stream there. He took the drainage until it met up with the Robinson Gulch Toll Road. The willows that lined the gulch swayed back and forth in the wind, pawing at him and raking his skin like the bony fingers of a ghost as he passed by.

There was the murmur of Fisher Gulch to his right and the constant sound of the willows scraping against the mules' canvas paniers. The mixture of sounds seemed unusually loud as he tried his best to travel in secret, ever mindful of the dangers ahead.

The toll road wound around in a serpentine fashion through mountain swells and valleys and saddle ridges. Though it was dark, he could still see the distinctive outline of Red Mountain off to the right, looming darker against the night sky.

The bright beams of the full moon illuminated his path as he came to a large boulder known as thief rock. Just beyond that was "The Hanging Tree." Otto's imagination threatened to get the better of him, but he told himself to stay calm as he circled around it.

The wind caused the moon shadows to move in strange ways. As he passed by the hanging tree, he saw a sight that caused him to gasp from fright. There, up in the tree, swinging from a rope, appeared to be the body of a man. As he rode closer, he was relieved to see that it was not a body after all but only a broken branch that dangled and swayed in the wind. For comfort, Otto quoted the twenty-third Psalm.

As he traveled onward, he crossed little streams following rocky switchbacks up and down steep spruce-covered mountainsides. By the time the night sky began to hint of morning, he found himself crossing above a deep gorge called California Gulch. There he filled his canteen and continued a way farther to a flat aspen glade.

Otto followed a game trail back through a stand of white-barked quakies to a small secluded meadow a good way off the toll road. He decided he would rest there for the day as daybreak was upon him.

At the edge of the meadow, a small seep trickled down into a deep cut in the moss then gathered in a calm pool beneath a cluster of wood ferns. The hidden meadow offered water and ample cover. He would spend the day sleeping right here and when the shadows lengthened, he would be on his way. Otto dug a hole, then buried the gold, covering it with pine needles.

After picketing his horse and mules on twenty-foot leads tied to a cross picket line, he took his bed roll and spread it on a flat, thick bed of moss and pine needles under the boughs of a bristle cone pine.

Otto laid his rifle and pouch of shells at his side then settled in for an all-day nap. He ate a hunk of cheese and some bread. Through a gap in the trees, he could see Red Mountain looming high in the distance, its shear rock face still in shadow. Hopefully the mountain would keep his secret until nightfall.

The morning sun streaming down through the aspen and pine caused him to grow sleepy. The taste of cheese lingered pleasantly on his palate as he closed his eyes and listened to the rustle of aspen leaves quaking in the breeze.

PLATORO THE SUMMER RANGE

Later that morning, from their camp on Red Mountain, Mordecai Lundy and Bones Rainey had just finished eating breakfast. Lundy tossed a sip of coffee into the fire causing the coals to hiss and give forth a puff of smoke. "I got me a hunch one of them cowboys came into some gold. I'm gonna do some snoopin' around and see what I can find out."

Bones nodded with approval. "Speakin' of gold, ain't we been here long enough? We already know when the gold shipments are comin' through."

"We'll make our move on the next miner that comes through," Mordecai promised.

Bones pinched off an extra big plug of tobacco and stuffed it into his mouth. "I can't believe Hiram's dead. Of all the ways to die, I never thought it would be a grizzly that kilt him. I always figured the law would get him."

"Give me that tobacco," Lundy scolded, snatching the pouch from Bones' hand. "I swear, you better have left me some. You ain't got the sense God gave a dead mule."

Mordecai pulled a leather parfleche from his pocket and dumped a wad of cash money on the ground. He scooped it up and held it for Bones to see.

"I did that gambler over in Boiler Canyon a big favor a few weeks back. It was dangerous for him to be carryin' around all this money. Somebody might have kilt him for it."

Bones began to laugh. "Mordecai, you're one sick scoundrel." His eyes shaded a bit. "Some of that money, though, is rightfully mine and Fritz's. It was our money that gambler took, remember?"

Lundy spit a glob of tobacco juice. "So what."

Bones' eyes lost any last hint of humor and now showed fear. "I'm just sayin' some of it ought to belong to us."

Lundy glared at Bones. "Hiram's dead and you and Fritz are gonna be, too, if you keep givin' me grief. That money is mine. That gambler took it from you, and I took it from him. That's the end of it."

Lundy pointed his rifle toward the toll road. "The next miner that comes down that road by himself we'll swoop down off this mountain, take the gold, and make a run for it. I even have a hideout lined up."

"How do you figure?" Bones asked.

"I met a miner in Platoro the other day, name of Jack Dill, that has a claim way up on the other side of the divide. Soon I'll pay Dill a visit and take his claim, too."

Bones was still in a pout about the money. "I suppose you're gonna want to keep all the gold to yourself, too."

Lundy looked agitated. "I've got a hunch you ain't gonna have to worry about what I do or don't do if you keep on sassin' me." Lundy unsheathed his large knife and pointed it at Bones. "You watch yourself, Bones."

Bones got up and stomped over to the rim of Red Mountain and began to watch the gold route through his spy glass. Several minutes later he motioned to Lundy.

"Mordecai, come take a look. You ain't gonna believe it." Mordecai hurried over and leaned down as Bones pointed at a spot far to the north. "Look way down yonder in that little meadow that lays all by itself in them quakies. There's two pack mules with empty pack saddles, and to the right of them there's a man sleepin' under a tree with a horse tied up next to him. I believe he's alone."

Lundy took a look. "Well, I'll be. That's that German feller's horse. That's the German that has the pretty wife. He must've came through during the night."

"He's a sneaky fella, ain't he," Bones laughed.

"Yeah, but not sneaky enough."

The two watched as a buzzard glided upon the wind to the north. "Sometimes I wish I was a bird like that," Bones mused. "Free to go anywhere I pleased. If I had a choice that's what I'd be, a buzzard. What about you? What would you be if you could choose to be an animal?"

"A grizzly," Lundy answered. "A real mean one."

The sound of a whippoorwill came from behind them. Lundy turned his head away from the spy glass and echoed the call. It was Fritz McConnell returning from his trip, and he had something flung over the back of his saddle.

"I got us some tender beef, courtesy of that cattle outfit down there. It was easy as takin' candy from a baby." Fritz cut the rope holding the calf causing it to slide to the ground with a thud at his horse's feet.

"Are you sure you weren't followed?" Mordecai said.

"I'm sure of it. Even the mama didn't know I done took her calf till after I was gone."

Lundy shook his head. "Of all the cattle runnin' around these mountains, you go and pluck out an unweaned calf. The mama is gonna be lookin' for her baby and bellerin' louder than a coon hound on a track. She'll follow its scent all the way up here and lead them cowboys right to us. You've really gone and mussed things up, Fritz."

Lundy ran his fingers through his hair in frustration. "Well, we might as well go ahead and eat our fill of tenderloin so we can have plenty of strength to ambush that miner we been watchin' down there."

"You been watchin' us a miner?" Fritz said.

"Yup, me and Mordecai seen him through the spy glass. He's asleep down there without a care in the world."

Bones and Fritz looked at each other and began to laugh. In no time, they had the meat cookin' over the fire. When it was done, they tore into the tender flesh.

"There's nothin' like the taste of stolen beef," Fritz said with a grin.

A half hour later, the group mounted up and made their way toward Otto as he slept unsuspectingly in the meadow below. It would take them several hours to get down the mountain and across Devil's Hole Canyon. From there they would circle around past the miner to an ambush point across the Alamosa River along Lieutenant Creek where the trail choked down to a narrow gap. With that in mind, they began to close in.

Ambush Along the Del Norte Trail

Cole was packing salt for a lick up Fisher Gulch when he heard a mamma cow bellowing frantically for her missing calf. He unloaded the salt and went to see what he could do.

The cow was Trail Boss. She was smelling the ground and appeared to be trailing her calf's scent up the mountain. He followed close behind the distraught mother. "Keep goin', ol' girl. Let's see if we can find Peaches for you."

The mamma cow led him up through meadow after meadow, higher and higher, until she reached the long meadow below the peak of Red Mountain. Her sides heaved for air, and her voice was hoarse from bellowing the entire way. Her tongue now drooped from her mouth as she continued on through the long meadow.

Finally, Trail Boss turned to the left and climbed up through a copse of twisted limber pines until she reached the end of the trail. There she thrust her head forward and let out a loud, mournful bawl. She had, at last, found her calf.

As he rode up beside the cow, Cole noticed an abandoned camp site littered with empty tin cans and other trash. A fire smoldered from a rock-lined pit where a few low flames still seethed among the coals. The remains of Trail Boss' discarded calf lay beside it. Cole leaned and spat. He had suspected rustlers, but this confirmed it.

After looking around some more, he realized why these men had made this place their camp. From here, a person could see Platoro and the distant meadows where the cattle of the Golden Willow grazed to the south. More importantly, it offered a clear view of the toll road where the gold shipments were going out.

Cole walked over to the north rim of the lookout where he could see more meadows sprinkled within a sea of spruce and aspen timber rolling with saddle ridges. Below his feet he noticed where the grass had been smashed down flat along the edge as if someone had spent a good deal of time lying there watching. It was apparent that whoever these rustlers were, they had been up here scheming for several days.

He lifted his field glasses to his eyes and began to observe the vast landscape below. It wasn't long before he spotted a man lying on his back in a meadow with some mules standing nearby. He recognized the mules. They belonged to Otto Kulman. Could it be that the rustlers had also spotted them? If so, it seemed likely that they were moving in on Otto this instant to take his gold.

Cole began to search until his eyes eventually fell upon a rider on a black horse moving north directly in Otto's direction. He recognized him instantly as Mordecai Lundy. At the moment, Lundy was still a long way from Otto but closing in, none the less.

Cole knew he had to somehow get Otto's attention. He pulled his pistol and fired twice in the air as a warning. To his surprise it appeared that Otto had heard the shots. Mordecai Lundy had heard the shots as well and soon vanished into the cover of the trees.

Cole looked at Trail Boss, who was still mourning for her calf. He knew from experience that the mamma cow would have no trouble finding her way back down to the herd when she was good and ready. She had plenty of grass and water nearby and would be fine, in spite of her grief. Cole mounted Comanche and headed down the mountain in hopes of getting to Otto in time.

Hearing the shots, Otto sat up from his sleep. He wasn't sure where they had come from, but it was time for him to be moving on. He felt for his rifle. It was right beside him like a trusted friend. He got up and splashed some cold water on his face to wake himself.

After securing the empty paniers over the cross-buck saddles, he then loaded the bags of gold evenly on the mules' backs. Otto slid his rifle down inside his scabbard, mounted up, then nudged his horse forward with the mules in tow, headed for the Alamosa River. On his way, darkness overtook him, and a bright moon hung high above.

When he reached the bank of the Alamosa River, he halted his horse and stepped down, letting drop of the reins. He squatted by the river and reached a hand into the water and passed it over his face. He reached again and cupped another to his mouth and drank.

Otto checked his riggings by first pulling up the latigo on his horse's saddle, gave a few tugs on the cinches, then fastened them back. He checked the lead ropes and cinches of the mules as well.

He sat his horse once again and put him forward into the ford and across the silver-lined riffles. Once on the other side, he found the trail which led down the mountain to Del Norte and turned his horse and mules onto it.

As he rode northeast, the land fell away quickly. The road lay bounded by Range Creek and Lieutenant Creek and on both sides by stone ramparts that directed the canyon and the river northward. Ahead lay Del Norte, some several more hours away.

Otto traveled on down the trail aided by the light of the moon. His horse's hooves clopped flatly on the rocky ground as he moved onward.

As the canyon narrowed, Otto became more and more anxious and uneasy. He began to pray the 23rd Psalm: "The Lord is my Shepherd; I shall not want. He maketh me to lie down in green pastures; he leadeth me beside still waters. He...."

When he entered the place where the trail narrowed, his horse stopped abruptly and cocked its ears forward. It whimpered lightly, sensing that something wasn't right. Its ears swiveled around then back forward again. Otto's heart began to beat faster. He pulled his rifle from the scabbard and listened to the darkness. A man chuckled somewhere beyond in the night.

"If you're after my gold, you won't get it. Thievery is a deadly game," Otto said. More chuckling came from the darkness. Otto put his horse forward once again. His gun resting across his lap, at the ready.

"Leave the mules and the gold and go on back home," called a voice. "We just want the gold."

"You can't have it. I worked hard for it. I need my mules, too."

"Leave the gold, and we'll let you live," came the same voice.

"My answer's still no," Otto said. He put his horse forward on down the trail.

Bones fired a warning shot, and Otto shot back at the flash of light as fast as he could shuck the lever of his rifle. His first bullet shattered Bones Rainey's right knee and another hit his chest. His third bullet ricocheted off a boulder and hit Fritz in the belly.

As Otto fired from his horse at the threat ahead, Mordecai Lundy rode up from behind and shot him in the back with his scatter gun. Otto fell from his horse with a groan and rolled down the hill until he landed in a tangle of willow bushes, unconscious.

"Hold your fire, boys, it's me," Lundy hollered. "I just shot the German in the back. He's dead."

Lundy got off his horse and walked over to where Otto had tumbled over the edge. The hillside was very steep and not worth the trouble to go down and check on the man for proof of death. Mordecai cocked his pistol and sighted it at Otto's lifeless body for a couple of seconds then reholstered it, not wanting to waste a bullet.

He turned and called out to his partners. "Bones? Fritz? Where you at?"

"Over here," Fritz answered. "I been gut shot. I think Bones is dead."

Lundy swung his horse around. "I'm gonna fetch the mules and the gold." A short time later he returned. "I've got the gold," he said.

"How much is there?" Fritz groaned in agony.

"Enough for me," Lundy said, stepping down from his horse. He opened the breach of his gun, loaded two shells and breached it back. "Where you at, Fritz?"

Fritz could hear Lundy's footsteps getting closer. He pinched a bullet between his shaking fingers and tried to feed it into the chamber of his pistol. Before he could seat the bullet, he dropped it into the darkness.

His hands slapped at the ground as he searched for it. Suddenly, he sensed Lundy standing over him. "There you are, Fritz."

"You can keep the gold, Mordecai. I don't want it." Fritz's voice was shaky and weak. "Please just take it and go and leave me alone," he groaned, as his fingers closed on the lost bullet.

The dying man finally managed to get the bullet into the chamber of his pistol. He aimed it at Lundy, but his hands were shaking so badly that he could not hold the gun steady. Using both hands, he pointed the pistol and tried to thumb back the hammer.

Lundy kicked the gun from his hands with the point of his boot. Fritz rolled over on his side in defeat as Lundy stood over him. "I told you before, Fritz, I ain't killable."

A pack of wolves began to bay in the distance. Lundy grinned. "I think I'll leave you to the wolves rather than waste a bullet on you."

"Shoot me now," Fritz begged.

Lundy turned and listened. Someone was coming down the trail behind him. He grabbed the bridle reins of the black and swung up into the saddle. He sunk his boot heels into the horse's flanks and left in a hurry, with Otto's mules and the gold in tow.

The baying of the wolves grew louder. Fritz realized the beasts were getting closer. Maybe his life would have ended differently if he had only made better choices. He closed his eyes and breathed his last.

Cole had been riding hard when he had heard the volley of gunshots maybe a mile farther ahead. He figured Otto was in grave danger, if not already dead.

When he arrived at the sight of the ambush, he noticed Bones' lifeless body laying draped over a log. Otto's horse stood off to the side among the willows.

"Otto?" he called. There was no answer. He remained alert assuming that Lundy or his partners could still be around. He continued to call out for Otto as he looked about.

Cole found Fritz McConnel's body behind a boulder, recognizing him as one of Lundy's men, also. So where was Lundy? Where was Otto?

He walked over to the edge of the trail and peered down the hillside. "Otto?" he called loudly. "Otto? It's me, Cole."

"Down here," uttered a weak voice. "I've been shot."

Cole took his lariat from his saddle and dropped the loop down the mountain. He paid out some twenty feet of rope to where Otto lay. The German took hold of the lariat and slid the loop over his arm and shoulders.

"Hang on, Otto. I'm gonna pull you up." Cole dallied his end of the lariat to the saddle horn and led Comanche away until Otto was safely up the hill. He then removed the rope and helped his friend to his feet. "Do you think you can ride?"

"I believe I can hang on to the saddle and keep my feet in the stirrups."

"That's good enough." He removed Otto's bloody coat and took some long strips of material from his saddle bag and used them to help stop as much of Otto's bleeding as he could. He fetched his canteen and gave Otto a drink.

After catching Otto's horse, Cole helped his friend into the saddle and placed the coat over his shoulders and tucked it in around him snug to help keep him warm.

"He took my gold and my mules, Cole. I lost it all," Otto said.

"I know, Otto. We'll get it back. The important thing now is that you stay alive for Heidi. Hold on now. It's still a far piece to Del Norte."

Cole tied Otto's horse on behind Comanche and swung up in the saddle. He pressed his heels to hide, and the horse stepped out at a good pace. Even at this rate it would be morning before they reached town. Crossing Blowout Pass west of Sheep Mountain, they followed Bennett Creek in the darkness.

Just before daybreak, Cole and Otto reached Del Norte and found the home of the doctor. Otto was conscious and still alive. Cole pounded on the front door with urgency and a middle-aged man soon opened the door. A look of concern was etched upon his face. "What's the matter?"

"My friend's been shot. He's lost a lot of blood."

The doctor stepped out. "Let's get him inside. I'll see what I can do."

The doc took Otto by the other arm and helped him to a bed. He carefully removed his bloody coat and had Otto lay on his stomach. At that time, Otto lost consciousness.

"Your friend doesn't look good, but I've seen much worse. This heavy coat he was wearing stopped a lot of the blast and probably saved his life. I won't know the extent of his injuries until I examine him more thoroughly."

The doctor's wife came down the stairs in her night gown. When she noticed Otto lying on the bed, she hurried to help her husband. "I'll get some water boiling," she said.

The doctor washed his hands, then fetched his bag. He began to set out instruments from it, placing them in a row on a nearby table.

"What is your name, sir, and the name of your friend?"

"My name is Cole Harden. I'm the foreman for the Golden Willow Ranch, and this is Otto Kulman, a friend of mine."

"Pleased to meet you, Mr. Harden. My name is Doctor James Rawlings, and my wife, who assists me, is Nicole Rawlings. You've done all you can for your friend. There's a cot in the other room. Why don't you get some rest? We'll let you know if there are any changes in his well-being."

"I thank you, doctor. I believe I will get some rest." Cole found the cot and stretched out on it. In no time, he was asleep.

It was late in the afternoon when he awoke to the sound of a soft tapping on his door. The door opened slowly. It was Mrs. Rawlings.

"I hope I didn't disturb you, Mr. Harden. I wanted to let you know your friend, Otto, is stabilized and resting." The woman's voice was calm and reassuring. "My husband and I have removed the lead from his back and cleaned the wounds.

I gave him some laudanum to ease his pain. We have done all we can do for him at the moment. The best thing now is just to pray for him and let him rest. I recommend that he be inclined to stay for at least another day. You are welcome to stay here or come back in a few days, whatever suits you."

"Thank you, ma'am. I believe I'll make a visit to the sheriff and file a report on what has been my friend's misfortune. After that I plan to find a room at the boarding house," Cole said.

"I'm afraid the boarding house burned down this spring, but you are welcome to stay here. We have plenty of room and plenty of food. Please, won't you stay?"

"I'd be glad to board here and pay you for your trouble."

The woman folded her hands together at her waist. "We would love for you to join us for supper this evening. James would like to discuss cattle with you. He's thinking of buying some seed stock for a small herd."

"I'd like that, ma'am." Cole stood until she had left the room, then put on his hat and went to speak with the sheriff. That evening he enjoyed a fine meal and conversation with the Rawlings.

The next morning, when he checked on Otto, his friend was sitting up in bed, sipping warm chicken soup and drinking some rose hip and willow bark tea. There was a touch of color in his cheeks.

"How are you feeling, Otto?" Cole said.

"My back is awful sore, but they tell me I'm gonna live, thanks to you."

"I wish I could have gotten to you sooner and stopped them from takin' your gold."

Otto gave a slight wave of his hand. "Ah, don't fret it. The gold I can replace. I'm just glad I'm alive for Heidi."

"It was Mordecai Lundy that shot you and took your gold. He and his gang were watching the gold shipments from on top of Red Mountain. They must have saw you in the meadow from up there."

Otto's eyes conveyed a sense of apprehension. "Heidi will be worried. I've got to get back to her. She'll be disappointed we won't be able to buy us a farm in the Valley or get her the new dress material or the shoes she wanted."

"Don't be frettin' that way, Otto. Save your strength. I talked to

Doc Rawlings, and he said we should be able to light out by tomorrow mornin'."

"Good, we'll leave at first light then."

The next morning, after a good breakfast, a thorough examination, and a fresh change of salve and bandages, the doctor gave Otto permission to leave.

"I want to thank you and your wife for all you have done for me. I'll pay you just as soon as I can," Otto said. "I'm good for it."

"Whenever you can," the doc nodded. "I'm sending some paregoric with you to take when the pain gets too severe. My wife packed you some food for your trip home as well. You'll need your strength. Be careful to keep the wounds clean until they fully heal."

The doc turned to Cole. "And Cole, I'll be stopping by the Golden Willow to see Mr. McKnight next week about buying a few durham heifers." The doctor held out his hand. "It's been a pleasure meeting the both of you."

Cole reached out and clasped the doc's hand firmly. "I thank you folks for everything. It was a pleasure to make your acquaintance."

The two rode for Platoro making camp, for the night, in a grove of aspen just below the small mining settlement of Jasper. Cole built a crackling fire for warmth and het up the food that Mrs. Rawlings had packed for them, along with some water for coffee. They enjoyed the warm steak, buttered bread, and potato fritters along with their coffee as they listened to the seam water roll over the rocks in the nearby river. The following morning, they got an early start, and upon reaching Fisher Gulch, they saw three riders approaching from the south. Cole recognized them at a distance. It was Lightning, Rusty, and Luke.

"It's Cole," one of them hollered.

Lightning reined up his horse first. "Howdy, Cole. Boy are we glad to see you. We thought somethin' had happened to you like what happened to Mr. London."

"I'm fine. Otto was ambushed on his way to Del Norte. They took his gold and left him for dead. We've been at the doc's in Del Norte." Otto nodded to the men, and the men nodded back.

"How's the herd?" Cole said.

"We're without a dozen head. They went missin' from up Sawmill Gulch by the lily pond," Lightning said. "Griz thinks that rustlers took them. We tried to find 'em but haven't had any luck so far. We've seen that fella that rides the grulla, two separate times, watchin' the herd. We chased after him, but he gave us the slip again."

"I imagine he's the one behind our missin' cattle," Cole said. "I'll look into it when we get back." He put Comanche forward in the direction of camp. The others followed.

When Otto returned home, Heidi was relieved to see him. "What has happened?" she said, noticing the missing mules as well as Otto's bandages.

"I was ambushed on the way to Del Norte, but Cole found me and took me to the doctor there. He saved my life."

Heidi threw her hands to her lips and began to cry. "Oh, Otto, are you okay?"

"I'll be fine. The doc says the coat I was wearin' stopped enough of the shot that it saved my hide. They took our gold, though."

Heidi wiped her wet cheeks with her hand. "I'm glad you're home, and the Lord was with you. I would rather lose the gold than you. Let's get you inside and into a bath, and I'll change your bandages."

"That sounds fine," Otto smiled. "As long as I have you by my side, I am a rich man."

Rustler's Lair

When Cole arrived back at camp, the men were relieved to see him alive and well. "Glad you're back, Cole," Carlos welcomed. "We was all sorta adrift without you and Mr. London around." The others nodded in agreement.

On the Saturday of the twenty-fifth of July, Cole, Lightning, Rusty, Griz, and Luke packed salt up Sawmill Gulch to an enormous meadow along Cornwall Mountain. At the far end lay Kerr Lake. After placing a lick at the lower end of the meadow, the group split up to look for the missing cattle.

Cole rode alone through the dark timber that lined the meadow on the upper side and continued north in the direction of Kerr Lake. He kicked up a handful of cow elk from their beds in a blow down thicket. Farther along, he kicked up a black bear from a tangle of tree roots and watched it streak out across the long meadow where it quickly lost itself among the spruce on the opposite side.

Near Kerr Lake, Cole came upon some fresh cow manure. He followed the tracks to a slide that led down onto a series of shaded benches. Here was good grass and water.

Following a drainage downward, Cole came to another bench. From there the tracks followed the drainage farther down the north face to another flat bench a hundred paces wide. The narrow strip held belly deep grass, and within the low places, it held water. The uphill side was bounded by a rock wall of broken cliff that rose about one hundred feet. On the downhill side, the land fell away steeply. This hidden place held the makings for a rustler's lair and could easily hide a hundred head of stolen cattle at a time.

Cole followed cattle tracks and the shod prints of at least two horses around a large pile of broken slab rock that jutted out into the meadow. Above, a marmot gave a single piercing warning chirp from among the rocks. The curious rodent kept its nose out of its hole a moment longer, then turned and ducked back inside the safety of its den.

Cole pulled his rifle and lay it across his lap between his waist and the saddle horn. He halted Comanche in a grove of quakies and raised his field glasses at something that attracted his attention. Up ahead, through the trees, tucked back in the shadows behind a spruce and aspen covered knoll, was a cabin.

He stepped from his horse and half hitched the bridle reins to the limb of a spruce and snuck closer. As he approached the cabin, he noticed a corral in back. Two horses stood in the shade flicking their tails. One of the horses was the grulla, the other was Bob London's bay. Both were saddled and bridled. The bay was gnawing on the bark of the corral post when its head came up to look toward the cabin.

Presently, the door opened, and a man showed in the doorway. He turned and latched the door behind him and was soon obscured by the trees as he walked downhill. In his right hand, he had appeared to be carrying a pail and was probably on his way to fetch some water.

Cole hurried to the cabin, gun in hand for trouble, and unlatched the door. The inside was dark except for the light that poured in as he entered. He waited a moment for his eyes to adjust. When they did, he was taken aback to see Bob London gagged and tied up but alive. His old friend appeared ragged and thin and held a month's worth of beard, but he was alive, just the same.

Cole unsheathed his knife and cut the ropes from Bob's wrists and removed the blindfold and the rag that gagged his mouth. Bob blinked at the light that fell across his eyes and took in a deep breath. "Cole, thank God, it's you. I didn't think anyone was ever gonna find me."

"Hurry, Bob, we don't have much time." He lifted London to his feet. "Can you sit a horse?"

"Yes. I'm weak as a child, but I believe I can ride."

Cole put an arm around London and helped him to his horse. He gave him a drink from his canteen. "Who rides the grulla?" he asked.

Bob drank until he had to come up for air. "He goes by Johnny Diablo. He works for Lassiter. Him and some others have a number of our cattle penned up not far from here in a canyon somewhere down below. They can't be too far off cause I could hear 'em bellerin' earlier. They rode me in here blindfolded. I ain't even sure where I'm at."

"I'm gonna stay here and look around and see if I can't find the cattle. Do you reckon you can get back to camp?"

"If'n you tell me how to find my way out of here."

"Follow this draw up to the next bench. When you get up there, ride west till you get to a big burnt tree that leans against the cliff. Go past the burnt tree and past the large pile of slab rock. Follow the drainage up, then east, and you'll top out at Kerr Lake."

"I know how to get back from Kerr Lake," Bob said, nodding.

"You better go, Bob, before they get back. Here, take my rifle along with you. I'll go fetch the cows and bring them home safe."

Cole helped Bob into the saddle and watched him ride out of sight. When he turned around, he saw a man with a pistol aimed at him. "What did you do with my hostage, mister?" the man said, dryly. Cole raised his hands away from his guns. He sure enough recognized the man before him.

"What's a matter, Harden? You look like you've seen a ghost." The man smiled. "I didn't figure you'd recognize me, but I can tell you do. People say my brother and I look a lot alike." The man's smile turned down in a scowl. "Except he's dead now, thanks to you."

"You go by Johnny Diablo, but I reckon you'd be Shiloh Tremble," Cole said. "The one that rides the grulla horse we been seein' around."

Shiloh nodded and spit between his clinched teeth. "You got lucky when you killed Jude. You won't be so lucky with me."

"If you wanted to kill me, why didn't you come for me earlier?" Cole said. "I've been here all summer."

"I was wounded by a posse early on. They've been five of 'em on my track ever since. I had to lay low until my arm healed, and I finally throwed them off my track."

"Why'd you take Mr. London?"

"The old man rode up on me while I was nappin'. I sensed he might've figured out my true identity, so I couldn't let him leave." The gunman's eyes studied Cole with a look of puzzlement. "I can tell you're not afraid of me, Harden. Why is that?"

"Because I know myself," Cole answered. "I know what I'm capable of. I know a fraud when I see one, too. You're one of them that grew your fame by shootin' down inexperienced drifters and drunken trail hands."

"Are you willing to bet your life on it?"

"Sure as I'm standin' here," Cole answered calmly.

"I'm gonna give you a chance to find out what kind of gunslinger I am," Shiloh said, holstering his gun. The gunman rested the palm of his hand on the butt of his pistol.

Cole let his hand drift slowly toward his gun as he spoke. "I ain't like all those other men you killed, Shiloh. I've bested many an outlaw and gunfighter and faced down many a Comanche. You may be a gunfighter, Shiloh, but I'm a warrior. Have been all my life. There's a big difference. What's more is, I ain't afraid of dyin', and I believe you are."

"Ain't no one not afraid of dyin'," Shiloh said.

"Not me. I know where I'm goin' when I die, and it's a far sight better place than here, because there ain't no sin or strife there. When I go, I'll get to see my late wife and my family I lost as a young boy, because they were all believers, and I'll get to see my Savior. It's going to be quit a joyous reunion." Cole felt sorry for the gunman. The young man had no idea who he was up against nor did he have any good purpose in his life.

"Shiloh, if you like, I'll see to it you're buried next to your brother and read over proper. That's the best I can offer if you don't come with me now."

Shiloh sneered, "You talk as though I'm already dead."

"You're a wanted man, Shiloh. If you drop your gun and go with me now, you'll get a trial."

Shiloh shook his head. "I can't live in no prison like some caged animal. I'd rather take my chances with you out here, where I'm free."

"Shiloh, livin' the rest of your life on the run ain't no way to live either. Unhitch your gun belt and come with me."

"It's too late," Shiloh answered.

The two men stood squared to each other, every muscle tense, their bodies coiled like rattlers ready to strike at the slightest flinch.

"I'll take no pleasure in killin' you, Shiloh, just as I took no pleasure in killin' your brother."

Suddenly Shiloh's breathing stopped, and his shoulders pinched downward. Cole noticed the telling sign of a draw and drew before Shiloh could move.

Shiloh stood stone still, a look of dismay upon his face. He slowly raised his hands away from his gun. "I ain't never seen anything like that before," he said.

Cole kept his Colt pointed at Shiloh as he walked forward and took the man's pistol.

Shiloh looked into Cole's determined eyes. "You could have killed me, Harden. Why didn't you?"

"I don't kill unless I have to. You're goin' to jail, Shiloh. While you're there, you better think about savin' your soul. You have another chance now to get your life squared away with the Lord. The odds are high you won't get another. I suppose you'll hang, but that's for the law to decide."

Cole took some rope peels from his saddle bag and tied Shiloh up good and tight with his hands in front of him. As he was about to haul Tremble back, Griz, Rusty, and Lightning came riding up.

"We ran into Bob London up at Kerr. He told us where to find you. Carlos is with him now."

Griz observed Shiloh tied on the ground and the grulla horse standing in the corral. "The one who rides the grulla," he said.

"That's Johnny Diablo," Lightning said with a nod of acknowledgement. "I told you Cole was as fast on the draw as they come."

"Fellas, this here is actually Shiloh Tremble," Cole corrected.

Lightning and Rusty looked at one another in complete puzzlement. "Shiloh Tremble?" they said.

"We'll be takin' him back to Platoro until the law can come get him," Cole said.

"Bueno," Griz chuckled. "I knew you would catch this pistalero." Shiloh glared silently, though his eyes said plenty.

"Where's our cattle?" Cole asked.

"You find 'em yourself," Shiloh hollered.

Griz pulled his knife and held it to Shiloh's throat. "The boss just asked you where's our cattle."

Shiloh looked up at Cole. "You ain't gonna let him kill me are you, Harden?"

Cole squatted and looked Shiloh in the eyes. "You've got some decisions to make, Tremble," he said. "I suggest you answer the man carefully."

"The cattle's down that way," Shiloh said, pointing with the thrust of his chin. He kicked the ground with his boot in disgust as Griz sheathed his knife.

Griz looked at Cole. "What do you want to do now, Boss?"

Cole lifted Shiloh from the ground to his feet. "Lightning, you and Rusty take Shiloh back to camp and wait till I get back. Griz and I are gonna fetch the cattle." Lightning and Rusty put Shiloh on his horse and had him to lead the way back while they kept their rifles trained on him.

Cole mounted Comanche and reined him about to the east. He touched the heel of his boot against the horses' flank and directed him to follow along a trail of muddy tracks and tipped over grass. Griz rode beside him, keeping watch of their surroundings. Cole focused on the tracks and manure piles until they came to a drainage flanked tightly on both sides by tall rock cliffs that rose more than fifty feet above.

The narrow corridor made a sharp left turn where it ran another hundred yards, then opened into a flat, grassy canyon with a spring. The canyon was enclosed on all sides by rock cliffs and hidden well from the outside world. The sign was fresh and, indeed, there before them were the missing cattle.

"I don't believe I've came across too many places more suited for hidin' cattle," Cole said. "Let's get them out of here."

A volley of shots rang out from the rocks above. Cole swung up his pistol and fired two quick shots. Griz took aim and shot as well. Two men fell from the cliff and landed among the milling cattle where they were trampled underfoot. A third man leapt from the rocks and took Cole off his horse.

Cole struggled to free himself and soon overpowered the man. He landed several fists to the man's body and face, finally knocking him unconscious. He drug him over to the side and tied him against a tree.

In no time, Cole and Griz had the cattle moving out of the canyon and through the narrow alley that ran between the cliff walls. They continued to drive them upward from one bench to the next until they reached the tranquil waters of Kerr Lake.

Cole put Comanche belly deep into the lake and leaned down and cupped his hands a couple of times to drink. He stood his horse a moment longer in the cool water with the sun warm on his shoulders. The lake was clear and cold and had been as still as glass before the cattle broke its surface to drink.

Cole turned Comanche about and rode him up out of the water. "We'll leave the cattle here in the big meadow for now and go back and get that fella I tied to the tree, then we'll head for Platoro," he told Griz.

Later, when they arrived back at camp, they found Shiloh sitting tied with his back to a tree and Bob London resting in the shade with his rifle trained on the sulking gunslinger.

"Here's another one for you, Bob," Cole said, leading the other rustler over. "See how he likes being held captive."

The news that Cole had captured Shiloh Tremble spread quickly and within a week he had been transported to jail in Alamosa.

Three Forks and Blue Lake

"WHICH OF ALL THESE DOES NOT KNOW THAT
THE HAND OF THE LORD HAS DONE THIS"

JOB 12:9

For Cole, the summer days finally became routine once again. Each day met with cool mornings and deep blue skies. Nearly every afternoon, clouds would quickly billow up and then drape like a thick curtain and thunder would roll and grumble and when the clouds were fully burdened with moisture, they would burst with the heavy monsoon rains of August.

Oh, how he enjoyed riding the cattle range, watching the herd flesh out on the rich mountain grasses, often spending many an afternoon patrolling the high lake regions through windswept alpine meadows along the very backbone of the divide. Cole marked the high mountain lakes and alpine trails with carums by gathering and stacking rocks in tall piles where they could be seen as a landmark from miles away.

The view from Conejos Peak was his favorite, where, on a clear day, he could see all the way to the San Luis Valley and the plain where the Golden Willow lay and where Abby waited for him. At the moment, he enjoyed a piece of cold steak as he rested there.

Looking much closer and to the southeast, he could see Bonito Canyon, Hansen Creek, and Rincon Canyon, as well as, Timber and Twin Lakes. Looking to the southwest, he could see down into Diablo Canyon where a large herd of elk grazed along a high slope in the mountain shadows. Beyond the canyon lay Glacier Lake and Laguna Ruybal, its location visible only at a distance by the large rock carum that, in the far sight, resembled a grizzly bear standing on its hind legs.

Much farther to the southwest, he could see Blue Lake at the head of the Azul and Navajo Canyon behind it, and to the northwest, Gun Sight Pass and the bowl below it that cradled Lake Ann which fed the headwaters of the Conejos River.

He felt so close to God up here above the clouds, and he often found himself in prayer, deeply moved by the majesty of creation and the care with which God had so thoughtfully and lovingly crafted all things. It was peaceful on the heights, but he knew he would always have to go down and face the dangers below, and so he did.

The cattle were now spread out on Mammoth, Red, Cornwall, and the upper drainages of the Conejos River. On the eighth day of August, Cole and Griz packed salt up the Conejos River to concentrate the cattle there. The grass above Platoro had grown lush and the meadows were now adorned with every sort of wildflower of every color and design.

Cole rode in front, hunch-shouldered and loose in the saddle, his upper body swaying with the rhythm of his horse's steady walk. Comanche slogged through a couple of tiny brooks that trickled across the trail and on through alternating fingers of tall spruce and grassy meadows.

Among the stringy clumps of mountain grasses grew tall shoots of miner's candle, mountain yucca, and skunk cabbage with its broad, ribbed leaves which had now turned a yellowish-brown in color. Violets, mountain lupine, blue bells, purple monk's head, Indian paint brush, blue columbine, and red columbine were sprinkled by the hand of the Creator like a tapestry. Cinquefoil and golden banner added splashes of yellow to the landscape.

An occasional white puffball mushroom grew in the open meadows, while farther up the sides, in the dark timber, king boletes, chanterelle, and coral mushrooms grew in the damp, shaded areas that saw little sun. Of all the edible mushrooms, Cole found the tastiest to be the king boletes with their thick white stems and large brownish-red hoods and yellowish under belly. While on the trail to Three Forks, Cole picked a bolete mushroom larger than his hand and put it in his saddle bag to eat later. He also picked a cluster of coral mushrooms and put them in as well.

As he and Griz rode up canyon, they crossed the Conejos River at a ford. There they stood their horses in the riffles a moment to let them drink before continuing southwest.

When they came to the stream that ran out of Diablo Canyon, they noticed a confusion of tracks in the moist, muddy soil. Mingled among the many hoof prints was a large set of tracks that made Griz stop abruptly and swing down from his horse. He squatted to examine them.

"Look here, Cole, fresh grizzly tracks. Muy grande, the biggest I've ever seen."

Cole got down from Comanche and examined the prints himself. "These prints were left by a very large male and were made today, Griz, not long ago. This bear is still here somewhere close by, and it's much bigger than Silver Top. Looks like it lit out that a-way."

Griz nodded. "He's probably headed for that broken country up yonder," he said, pointing to the range that lay to the southwest toward Blue Lake.

Both men pulled their rifles and rode on with an eye to their surroundings. To their left, a tall ribbon shaped waterfall leapt over a cliff and cascaded several hundred feet before losing itself in the trees. Along the trail, a boulder the size of a stagecoach lay among the willows where it had finally come to rest after rolling down from the high cliffs.

"How'd you like to see one of those rascals bounding down the mountain at you, Griz? It would be a sight, wouldn't it?"

Griz looked at the large boulder as he rode by, then looked up at the mountainside above with a thoughtful gaze. "After a hard rain, I figure," Griz said. "Maybe a mud slide brings them down. Ain't never seen it happen, though."

As they approached Three Forks, Griz became increasingly apprehensive. "Yonder is Three Forks," he said pointing. "The river to the left is the Azul, the one in the middle is the Middle Fork, and to the right lies the North Fork."

Cole looked up ahead to where the three rivers merged into one. About halfway, he noticed something moving through the willows. At first, he thought it might be one of the bulls, but since he didn't get a good look, he decided he would ride up to where he could get a bird's eye view of the meadow.

"I saw somethin' in them willows up yonder, Griz," Cole said. "Let's ride up to that crest where we can see better."

From the high ground, Cole could see the willows parting across the river. Suddenly, a large grizzly emerged. Its size, long shoveled nose and big hump on its back defined it in a way that left an impression on Cole. By the enormous size of it, there was little doubt this was the same bear that had made the tracks they had seen earlier and a different bear than the sow they had run into before.

"That is a giant of a bear," Griz said.

The big bear stopped for a moment and lifted its nose in short bobbing movements, as it tested the air, downwind of the cattle. The big boar grizzly raised on its hind legs and began to observe its surroundings. A few seconds later, it dropped back down and lumbered over to a feeder creek where it disappeared into the willows once again.

Cole waited for the bear to emerge directly on the other side, but it never did. Several minutes later, he saw it climb out of the gully much farther to the south and head up into the cover of the spruce trees near Three Forks.

He contemplated shooting in the air to run off the bear, but since it had shown no interest in the cattle, he decided not to fire a shot as it would likely frighten the herd. Hopefully the bear was gone and had moved on.

"I don't like it," Griz said. "That bear is some sort of sign. We should leave now."

"No, Griz, we should stay and make a tally of what cattle are here."

Cole and Griz rode watch over the cattle for the remainder of the day until the long shadows stretched all the way across the valley, and the swallows began to circle and flare low along the river as they hunted for mosquitos.

Cole sat his horse a moment and looked around. "Griz, I think we should make camp over yonder tonight up in them short spruce so we can scout the Middle Fork in the morning right off, come sunup."

Griz shook his head. "No, I ain't stayin' at Three Forks. It's where the devil dances at night. It's a place of strange dreams," he said, stroking his bear claw necklace.

"Well, suit yourself, Griz. I'm gonna find a good flat place to make camp over yonder in them stunted spruce."

"I wish you well, amigo. I will pray for you and look for you tomorrow then." Griz turned his horse about and rode off.

Cole crossed the river at a ford along a gravel bar where a narrow channel split around it. Upon making the trees, he tied up Comanche in a small clearing back among the short spruce, then found a flat spot to pitch his bed roll and build a fire, out of the wind.

He picked a couple of miner's candles and gathered up what sticks and dead limbs he could find, then removed an empty flask from his saddle bag and took a match from it and struck it alight on the side of his holster. When it flared up, he held the flame to the miner's candle, and when it flared up again, he added some dry grass. Cole coaxed the flame up slowly by feeding it one twig and stick at a time until it held its own and began to burn.

Spying a rabbit hiding beneath a spruce, he took up a rock and threw it. His first attempt sailed high, but his second struck the rabbit between the eyes, killing it instantly. Now it lay limp in his hand with its head lolled over the side where it neither breathed nor felt any pain. It would make a fine meal.

Cole skinned the rabbit and lay the meat on a log, then took his knife and fashioned a spit from a willow branch. After skewering the meat on the stick, he set it to cook in the edge of the fire. He turned the rabbit slowly on the spit. When it had cooked somewhat, he took a pan from his saddle bag and added in the mushrooms he had picked earlier along with some beef tallow and onions. He peeled his only potato and put it in with the rest as well. The aroma rising from the skillet, as the food cooked, was pleasant indeed. While his supper cooked, he unfastened the latigo and the back cinch of his saddle. Taking hold of the cantle and the horn, he slid it from his horse and laid it at the head of his bedroll.

When the rabbit was tender, and the potatoes and mushrooms had cooked down, he filled his tin plate and rested against the saddle with his legs outstretched before him. He bowed and prayed, then ate his supper. When he had finished, he put some coffee on to heat and soon sipped a hot cup under the stars.

Cole read his Bible for a time as the firelight danced on the pages and strobed upon the woods beyond. He also read *Ben-Hur* until he fell asleep.

Sometime in the night, he startled awake. He sat up in his bed and took up his rifle. His stomach felt painful and uneasy while his head ached a good deal. The position of the stars above told him he had only been asleep a couple of hours. He figured it was not yet midnight.

Before long, Cole found himself sweating profusely in spite of the chill in the night air. His stomach churned, and his thoughts seemed vague and panicked. Everything around him appeared to move. In between the throbbing that pounded in his head, he was reminded of Griz Montoya's warning. "Three Fork's Park is dangerous. It's where the devil dances at night," he had said.

Cole felt jumpy, and his heart beat rapidly in his chest as though it wanted out. His mouth was dry and had a bitter taste, and the pain inside his stomach was becoming much worse.

He laid back down and tried to sleep. What sleep he did get was fitful and filled with vivid, wild dreams of Indians rushing him with knives. "No, no!" he hollered, his eyes still jumping wildly beneath closed lids. He raised up and put his hand to his forehead. It was hot to the touch and was beaded with perspiration. His shirt also was drenched with sweat. Cole was seeing things, hallucinating from a fever, and beginning to chill in the cold mountain air. He splashed some water from his canteen upon his face.

When he looked up again, beyond the fire, in the clearing, he noticed a giant grizzly standing there. He rubbed his eyes some more and opened them wide. Now he could see only a small spruce that swayed in the breeze. Cole remembered that the coral mushrooms he had eaten had looked different than the coral mushrooms Stump had often cooked. These had been much darker in color. They must have been poisonous and hallucinogenic like the peyote mushroom.

He crawled over a ways and began to retch violently until his stomach was fully rid of its contents. After vomiting, he felt much better and clearer of thought. He washed his face with water from his canteen then laid back down and fell asleep.

When he awoke, it was morning. He felt much better now, even hungry. Cole made some coffee and ate some bacon. When it grew light enough to see well, he searched around for tracks. What he found surprised him. In the dirt around his camp, he saw very large grizzly tracks on all sides of where he had been sleeping.

He put out the fire then rolled up his bed roll and tied it onto the back of his saddle. He rode Comanche along the perimeter of the cattle looking for signs of where there may have been trouble in the night but found none. All was well.

Cole rode up the middle fork, skirting a burial ground, then another three miles without seeing any stray cattle. He was about to turn around when he heard something that piqued his curiosity.

As he rounded the next bend in the hillside, he could hear the roar of water plunging down from great heights. There in front of him was a spectacular waterfall; the one that Lindle McKnight had referred to as Conejos Falls.

The magnificent sight was green where it leapt over black, pitted volcanic rock, then lighter where it thinned, plunging a hundred feet into a churning spray of mist and foam. He admired the waterfall on foot, examining the deep pool below it. Cole passed a handful of water over his face then lifted more to drink.

After filling his canteen, he tarried there a moment in the spray of cool mist. As he sat enjoying some jerky, he noticed a wooden carving of a bear floating along the edge of the water amid the foam. He reached down and picked it up. Probably a toy that a Ute child had left there. After studying it a moment, he put it back where he found it.

He noticed that three Ute Indian children watched him from the trees up hill. It was they who often came to the waterfall to draw water and play. "Bith Ahatini," they said amongst each other, pointing at Cole. The children went back to their camp to tell the others of the cowboy they had seen.

Cole decided to ride on up the trail to seek out Blue Lake and the

Navajo Canyon; two places Griz had spoken of with great reverence and caution: the land of the last grizzlies.

Leaving the Middle Fork, he crossed over a glacial gravel field and topped out above timber line on a wind-swept hogback that offered a breathtaking view. He sat his horse a spell, letting him catch his breath. The air was thin and crisp and the sky, a deep blue.

Proceeding on, he followed the tundra covered ridge line, crossing over the faint start of the Navajo River where it emerged from a glacial snowbank and grew in muster as it slipped through the bottom of the Navajo Canyon below.

Cole passed by a shallow tarn about three feet deep, its water clear as glass. Nearby, the charred remains of an old fire lay within a ring of stones. This was a magnificent country indeed, overlooking a most beautiful canyon.

In the Navajo basin below, he could see two large black bears digging for roots in a patch of green grass. Across the basin, high in a finger strip of engleman spruce, he could see a dozen or more elk browsing. One was a great bull still in velvet antler. As if on cue, it lifted its splendorous crown and gave a throaty bugle that reverberated through the canyon, finally loosing itself to the vastness beyond.

Up ahead in the distance, he could see a lake as blue as the sky itself and determined it to be Blue Lake. He rode toward it through patches of alpine bistort and cow parsnip, and under the shaded coolness of the trees grew sweet cicely and whortle-berry which also were favorite foods of bears and noticeably fragrant this time of year. Round about lay random piles of fresh bear scatt, dark and tubular and matted with grass, roots, and berries. A blizzard of large, green-headed flies hummed with excitement over each one.

When he reached Blue Lake, he watered there and lingered in prayer a while, and as he did so, he noticed a single, large bear track in the mud. He wondered if maybe this very site at which he knelt could have been where Griz had been attacked by the grizzly that nearly killed him several years ago.

Cole had the feeling of being watched that often accompanies those who ride the lonely lands that lay above the timber. At the moment, though, the feeling was stronger than usual. His eyes sought the shadows of a copse of trees that fringed the far end of the lake. It was time to ride on.

On his way back, he followed the El Rito Azul downward through a deeply notched drainage flanked by tall spruce-covered slopes which rose up sharply on either side and was heavily timbered all the way to its narrow bottom where it joined the Middle and North Forks in the open meadow below.

While at Three Forks, Cole did another quick check on the herd. There was no more sign of the giant grizzly. The cattle were fine for now, but the presence of another grizzly in the area was indeed troubling.

Tracking A Killer

Buffalo Morgan received an unexpected visit by a U.S Marshal and his deputies one evening. "We know Buffalo Morgan isn't your real name," the marshal insisted. "We also know you was in Missouri twenty years ago at the time of the Harden murders," he said, pounding his fist on the table.

Buffalo bowed his head and sighed, "What do you want to know?" After two more hours of intense questioning, the marshal and the deputies left in a hurry.

Buffalo knew it was no longer safe to stay in Platoro. Under the cover of darkness, he loaded his mules and tied them behind his chestnut and left his claim behind.

He made his way down canyon, following the river. After a time, he began to hear the footfalls of another horse walking parallel to him just out of sight among the trees. He pulled his pistol.

"Clarence Eugene Fenamore, it's been a long time. I hear you been talking to the law about me," said a voice from the darkness.

Buffalo recognized the voice, and his heart was filled with fear.

"You've been trying to pin them Harden murders on me. You know that kind of talk is bound to get you killed."

The familiar voice sent chills up Buffalo's spine. "Let me be," he said.

"I can't do that." The man rode out of the shadows holding a double-barreled shotgun in his right hand. It was pointed right at Buffalo's chest.

"You wouldn't shoot your own brother, would you, James?" Buffalo said.

The man gave a rabid dog grin. "You know me better'n that, Clarence." He thumbed back both hammers, then fired. Buffalo Morgan took both barrels in the chest and fell from his horse, dead.

The man spit a glob of tobacco. "Tell the law on me, will ya'." He got down from his horse and walked over and squatted next to Buffalo's lifeless body. He pulled a buckeye nut from his pocket and put it in Buffalo's open mouth. He muttered something under his breath and got back onto his mount. He turned his horse up the trail and melted into the night.

It was a visit in late August by a U.S. marshal and his deputies that broke the peaceful day to day routine for Cole and the men of the Golden Willow outfit. The marshal had three men with him, and he was asking for Major Cole Harden.

"He's with the cattle up near Three Forks Park," Bob London told them. "I'll take you to him."

Cole was packing salt to refresh a salt lick in the meadow below Three Forks when Bob, the marshal, and his three deputies found him. "Howdy, Cole," Bob greeted. "I brought you some company."

"Cole Harden, it's good to see you again," the marshal said, holding out his hand.

Cole immediately recognized his old friend, Bret Lindsey and shook his hand. "It's good to see you, Bret. What brings you this way?"

"I'm a U.S. marshal now. These are my deputies: Dirk Ross, Dick Ross, and Scott Venters. There was five of us, but one of my deputies had to go back to tend to the needs of his family." Cole nodded to the deputies, "How do you do." The three deputies nodded back cordially.

"I'd heard from Angus McCord that you were a marshal now, Bret." Cole said.

"Yes, sir, about two years now. Speaking of Angus, I had supper with him and Jenny not long back."

"How is his family?"

"Just fine. Jenny's girls are growing into young women and doing well. Cade is tall and strong like his pa. I believe he is seventeen now. Emma is sixteen and pret'near all grown up. She's got a beau, too, that comes a courtin'. Angus was fixin' to deliver a herd to Dodge City, and Jenny was expecting another little one, as I recall."

"That's good to hear."

"I suppose you're wonderin' why I came to see you."

Cole nodded. "I know by the guns and ammunition you're totein' you didn't come up to herd cattle."

The marshal chuckled. "No, not this time. This visit is of a more serious nature. What I got to say concerns you. It seems Judge Parker found some connection to the documents you delivered to him and a certain fella that was a part of your past. The law's been on the track of that same fella for several years now. We believe he's been hiding up in these parts here lately."

Marshal Lindsey pulled out a wanted poster from his shirt pocket and handed it to Cole. "This might answer your questions." As Cole examined the poster, his eyes burned with emotion. He studied the picture for a spell. By this time Griz had ridden up and joined the group. He dismounted and stood next to Bob London.

"What is it, Cole?" Bob asked.

"It's a wanted poster for a James Morris Fenamore. Also known by some as Mordecai 'Buckeye' Lundy."

Bob looked at the picture. "You're sayin' Lundy is really Fenamore?"

Cole nodded. "One and the same. Says here he's wanted for bank robbery, cattle rustlin', and countless murders. It also says here that he's wanted for killin' an entire family twenty years ago in Missouri along the Black Dog trail….my family," Cole said. A fire began to burn in his eyes as he stared at an old picture of his family. It was the same picture of them he carried in his Bible.

He shook his head. "To think that all this time Lundy was up here in these mountains, and I didn't even know who he really was. James

Morris Fenamore. If I had known what I know now, Lundy would already be reapin' what he's sowed."

The marshal took the paper and put it back in his pocket. "It seems that Fenamore likes to leave a buckeye with his victims after he murders them. It has something to do with a superstition he has. That's how we've been able to piece together some of his past. He's got a brother, too, Clarence Fenamore. Goes by the name of Buffalo Morgan now. Far as we can tell, Morgan wasn't a part of his brother's crimes. In fact, Morgan was real helpful until last week when he disappeared. We found him dead, shot in the chest with a scatter gun. We found a buckeye nut in his mouth. We figure Lundy did it."

Cole remembered the buckeye that he had found that awful day twenty years before. It had always puzzled him, and now he had lost a man he considered his friend, and it saddened him. He never figured Morgan to be a kin to such a man as Lundy.

"What do you say, Cole? I could sure use your help to catch this fella. I couldn't think of a better man I'd want to have along to go after a killer like this than you."

Cole looked at Bob. "Bob?"

"You go ahead, Cole. This is somethin' you've got to do not just for yourself but for every other life Lundy has destroyed."

"I need to stop Lundy before he kills again," Cole said.

Bob nodded. "The cattle will be just fine. Gilbert Mackey rode into camp last night with two men McKnight just hired on. Their names are Ben Miller and Jake King. They've worked for McNeil out of Monte Vista. They'll be here for a week helping out."

Cole turned to Marshal Lindsey. "Well, I'll be goin' with you then, Bret. Let's go get Fenamore."

"Glad to hear you say so, Cole. It'll be just like old times."

Cole nodded. "Like old times."

"Well then, before we go, I guess I better swear you in as an official lawman in front of these witnesses." The marshal pulled a badge and a Bible from his saddle bag and swore Cole in.

Cole lifted his hand from the Bible and took the badge. He pinned it on his chest. "Do you have any leads as to Lundy's whereabouts?"

"Marshal Reeves believes Lundy was spotted near South Fork about a week ago. I don't know that country well. I thought you might know it better."

"I've been through there a couple of time," Cole said. "I figure we can take the trail to Summitville, then follow Park Creek on to South Fork. If we ride until dark, we could make camp along Park Creek and make South Fork sometime by the middle of the mornin' tomorrow. There's a mercantile there. It might be a good place to get some answers."

"Well, we best get goin' then," the marshal said. "We've got us a killer to catch and a cold trail to follow as it is. You lead the way, Cole."

Cole led the posse on their way across Hillman Park, then up Gold Creek where they crossed above Treasure Creek at Horsethief Park. From there, the trail topped out into a beautiful, sprawling alpine meadow high above Crater Lake at a place called Schinzel Flats. There they stopped and ate a bite. An hour later they hit upon Elwood Pass and by sunset made camp along Park Creek.

Daybreak was an hour away when they made for South Fork, arriving at the small village around noon. Their horses were plumb beat. Cole and the others tied their mounts to the hitching rail in front of the mercantile and went inside. The sound of their boots striking on the wooden floor was loud and purposeful. A short, balding man entered from a backroom and stepped behind the counter.

"Good day, gentlemen. My name is Herb Benedict. You're welcome to look around…sure as you're aimin' to buy somethin'. I ain't got patience for lollygaggers."

"How do you do. I'm U.S. Marshal Bret Lindsay, and this is Cole Harden, former major in the U.S. Calvary."

"I don't care if you're the King of England hisself. You come in here, you buy somethin', or you're wastin' my time." The man proceeded to wipe the counter with a rag.

Cole leaned over and placed his hand on the man's arm and tightened his grip. "Mister, we're lookin' for a very dangerous fugitive, and we don't have much time. Now, we have some questions needs answered. Do we understand each other?" Cole's eyes shaded a bit.

The storekeeper swallowed hard. "Yes, sir. I'm listenin'."

"The fella we're after goes by the name of Mordecai Lundy. The marshal has a sketch of his likeness. His real name is James Morris Fenamore."

The marshal held up the sketch drawing of Lundy. "Ever seen this man before? We believe he's in the area."

The man leaned in and took a closer look at the sketch. "Yes, I've seen him. He was with a fellow by the name of Jack Dill. Looked like they was partners. They stopped by here maybe five days ago to get some supplies. He was ridin' a big black horse and had a couple of pack mules with him. He bought a new pick and some tobacco from me. He was a scary sort. I didn't cotton to him."

"Were those pack mules empty or loaded down?" Cole asked.

"They were empty, as I recall."

"How did he pay you?"

"He paid in gold."

Cole shook his head. "That's what I figured. He stole two mule loads of gold from a friend of mine. He must have hid it before he got here."

"Have you noticed anything else that might help us, Mr. Benedict?" the marshal asked.

"Maybe..., that miner, Dill, told me there's been some good color showin' at his claim lately. Said he made a strike a week before Independence Day. He likes to get boozed up, and the more he drinks, the more loose he gets with his tongue. Could be he told this here Fenamore fella about his gold strike."

Cole turned to the marshal. "I'm thinkin' that Lundy must have found out about Dill's gold strike and is plannin' on jumpin' his claim."

The marshal turned to the store keep. "Where might we find Jack Dill's claim?"

"Rumor is it's somewheres up Grouse Creek, but I ain't rightly sure."

Cole placed a couple of coins on the counter. "Thanks for your time. If you think of anything else, let us know."

The man reached for the money. "The saloon Dill goes to is about four miles due west of here. Locals call it the Cave. There's some mighty rough characters goes in there. Could be this fella you're after did, too. Maybe somebody saw him there."

The marshal nodded. "We'll check it out. I don't suppose you'd mind if I nail this wanted poster up by the door?"

"Naw, help yourself," the man said with a wave of indifference.

"You got any cured meat?" Cole asked.

"Sure do. I got some salt pork and some smoked sowbelly hanging in the ice cellar."

"Cut me off a pound of each and wrap it for me. I'll take a couple cans of peaches and some of them lime pickles you have on the shelf there. Put it all in a nap sack, if you got one. Oh, and a block of cheese, too."

The store keep fetched the food items and wrapped the meat in brown paper and handed it to Cole. "That'll be a dollar and ten cents," he said.

Cole placed the money on the counter and left. The others followed. There was the sound of heavy boots clunking on the wooden porch and jingle of spurs as they made their way to their horses.

"What do you suggest we do now, Cole?" the marshal said with an eye to the sky.

"I think we should split up. We'd be able to cover more ground that way. Someone should check out that Cave Saloon and see what the word is on Dill and Lundy. I'll head on up Grouse Creek and see if I can't find the Dill claim. If I can find it, I believe I'll find Fenamore." Cole stepped into the saddle. "I'd feel better if you'd loan me one of your deputies."

"Venters, you go with Cole. You could learn a thing or two from him. The rest of us are gonna visit the Cave Saloon and see what we can find out about Fenamore, then we'll join up with you at the top of Grouse Creek in two days."

"That sounds agreeable. Good luck then," Cole said.

"Be careful, Cole. Venters, you, too."

Cole and Venters nooned at a spring in a grove of shin oak and ate some salt pork and biscuits. When finished eating they made their way through a thicket of oak brush and ponderosa pine. The dry oak leaves and pine needles crunched beneath the horses' feet and gave off a pleasant aroma as they baked in the warm sunlight.

It was dry here along the western slope, much drier than around Platoro. From the looks of things, it hadn't rained on this side of the San Juans in months. The brittle scrub brush made the danger of a forest fire quite high. They would have to be careful if they built a fire for warmth tonight.

Cole led Venters up a game trail towards Grouse Creek. As their tired horses trudged upward, they kicked out a black bear from an oak thicket. It ran down the mountain away from them and was quickly swallowed by the brush. From there, the trail led out of the oak brush and up the side of a drainage into the quakies where the forest came alive with the whispering of crisp aspen leaves and the singing of the wind through the pines.

Tall ponderosa pine soon gave way to white-barked aspen and clusters of wood fern which were tinted in shades of green and yellow. As they climbed higher, the mountainside grew steeper and held more and more spruce and white pine which continued until they finally hit upon Grouse Creek. With the steeper slopes, Grouse Creek began to flow with more urgency as it tumbled and splashed noisily to their left.

The game trail they followed switched back and forth between lichen-covered boulders and around the decaying corpses of moss-laden deadfalls. Here, on top of a thick ground layer of decomposing pine needles, the earth sounded hollow beneath the horses' feet as they plodded onward.

Reddish brown horse-hair lichen hung in long draping clusters from tall blue spruce while golden beams of sunlight slanted down through open portals in the treetops giving the forest a primeval appearance. From there, the forest thickened, and they soon lost the sky to the dense overstory.

As Comanche climbed onto a wide bench, Cole halted him for a spell to admire the view and enjoy the sounds of the forest. Straight ahead, a black-eared squirrel chattered from its perch on a log. Above, beyond the spruce, he could hear the slow, lonesome call of a raven and the rustle of the breeze in the treetops. Below, he could hear the plunging of water as it rushed through the narrow gorge.

Cole and the deputy lingered a moment longer to drink from their canteens and give the horses time to catch their breath. An hour later they reached the upper arm of Grouse Creek.

It was some time in the afternoon before he and the deputy came to a clearing high on the mountainside. The air held a cool tang to it now, though the sun still shone brightly. A melancholy quiet hung over the high mountains. It was a lonely solitude, deep and unbroken. A few thunderheads had formed to the northwest where heat lightning strobed silently in the distance.

Cole stepped down from his horse and began to lead Comanche by the bridle reins so he could look for ground sign. It wasn't long before he came across a horseshoe print. It was the first sign he had seen that a rider had been this way.

"I found a print," he said, kneeling. Venters knelt as well.

"You reckon it's Fenamore?"

"Hard to say."

"How old you reckon it is, Cole?" the deputy said, still squatting.

"I'd say no more than four days."

Venters studied the track with a new appreciation. "Where'd you learn to age tracks?"

"Tonkawa and Lipan Apache, some Delaware and Seminole.... from trackin' wild cattle, too, in South Texas in that country along the Nueces River." Cole led his horse a ways farther, then paused and knelt, putting his hand to the ground. He motioned Venters over to his side again. "I found another track. This one's from the right hind foot. It's not very old. Probably made yesterday or the day before by the same horse."

"How you figure? The age, I mean."

"It has no leaves or pine needles in it, and it's not fully dried. You have to account for how much sunlight it gets, too. Tracks and sign that get a lot of sun dry out faster and appear older, where a track that don't see much sun may look new when it ain't."

They moved slowly on until Cole noticed a broken branch that had sapped up but not yet hardened. He checked it for hair and found a long black one. He pulled it out and held it between his fingers. "You know what this is?"

"Black bear. Maybe a black wolf?" Venters said, leaning closer.

"It's from a horse. A black like the one Lundy rides."

"That means it's Lundy for sure," the deputy nodded.

"We can't be sure, but I'd say it's a good bet."

Up ahead, Cole found where a cluster of big green-headed flies swarmed above a pile of loose dirt and pine needles. He kicked at the ground until he uncovered where someone had buried horse manure in an effort to hide it. He was still on the right track.

"That's a sign of a man that don't want to be followed," Cole said. Venters nodded in agreement.

There was a rumble of thunder, muted and far off. A gust of wind suddenly shook the treetops. "It's getting colder," Cole said. "And it ain't just the altitude." He stopped and put on his coat then rode on. An hour later, dark clouds had drifted in front of the sun, and a stiff northerly breeze had kicked up in front of the system.

"There's snow in them clouds, Venters. We better find us a place to make shelter and a fire."

Soon fine sleet began to fall slantways upon them and spit against their faces. Small pellets began to collect upon the ground, covering it with an icy glaze.

"How much farther do you reckon is Dill's cabin?" the deputy said, pulling his coat up tight to his neck.

"Not far. If it's up this creek, I'm guessin' it will be just below the timberline. We best start looking for a place to get out of the weather and make camp."

Cole marked the trail indiscreetly then rode Comanche along a bench and followed it more than a half mile to where it dropped off into a deep pit about two hundred feet across and half as deep. The tiny canyon was surrounded by short pine and rocky ledges. It would be a place out of the wind and well hidden.

"Down there in that canyon is where we'll make camp tonight," Cole said. He and the deputy led their horses by the bridle reins down the steep, narrow slope. When they reached the bottom, they found a small spring and enough grass to sustain the horses for several days.

Cole led Comanche to a large slab of rock which leaned out at an angle from the ground nearly seven feet. A couple of pine trees had fallen against it like a natural lean-to. Another had fallen directly in front of the point of the rock.

"We'll make our shelter here tonight," he said.

The temperature had plunged and was continuing to drop. It was beginning to snow now. Cole observed the angry sky as he blew a breath of warm air into his cupped hands and rubbed them together. "We better get busy on a shelter and get a fire goin' soon, or we could freeze," he told the young deputy.

Cole and Venters picketed their horses and went to work building a fire. By now a significant amount of snow was falling. Cole took his large knife and hacked off some pitch splinters from a burnt pine while Venters gathered kindling.

Cole collected what dry twigs and pinecones he could find and added the pitch splinters. His breath smoked from his nose and mouth as he breathed. He cupped his hands again and blew warm air over them then took his steel and flint, and along with the blade of his knife, dropped a flurry of sparks on it. He repeated this process until the twigs began to glow and smolder. Coaxing the fragile flame with his breath, he watched it take hold and flare up, all the while screening it with his body.

He fed more twigs and kindling then added more wood until they had a steady fire. He and the deputy hunkered next to it, warming their feet, hands, and body. After they had warmed up a bit, Cole positioned several stones in the coals of the fire to heat while Venters went to gather more wood.

As Cole waited for the stones to heat, he began to build the framework for a lean-to. After finding a dozen suitable poles, he leaned them against the slanting rock slab making a support that was just four feet off the ground at its highest point. The large slab of rock served as the ridgepole, roof, and the back side of the lean-to wall.

Taking his knife, he proceeded to cut green spruce and pine boughs, placing them in a large pile near the fire to dry. Next, he scraped away the debris and pine needles from the ground beneath the natural lean-to leaving a depression about five inches deep, seven feet long, and five feet wide.

Cole gathered the loose dirt into a pile for when he would need it again later. After the stones were sufficiently hot, he used a stick to maneuver them over into the cleared-out depression. Once the heated rocks were in place in the bed, he covered them with dirt and let the rising heat bake the moisture from the soil.

After this, he placed a thick layer of pine boughs for a roof over the top of the shelter. It would not only repel rain and snow but would serve as insulation to abate the cold and trap the heat within. When the roof was finished, Cole placed a thick layer of pine boughs, with the bent side upward, on the floor of the shelter to serve as a bough bed.

The big boulder and the deadfall that lay nearby blocked the wind and reflected the heat from the fire back toward the shelter. As suspected, the large slanting rock that served as the back wall and part of the roof did well to deter the cold and reflect the heat inward as well. It was a fine shelter.

By the time the structure was completed it was dark, and the sky had cleared. It would be a very cold night. The deputy crawled inside first, then Cole followed. He placed the remaining spruce boughs over the doorway behind him to block the outside cold and trap the heat.

"This bough bed is as comfortable as a feather bed," Venters said. "And the ground is warm cause of them rocks."

Cole lay down. "I stoked the fire and added plenty of wood. The warmth from the stones beneath us should last all night, too." Cole lay with his back against the fragrant boughs. He pulled his blanket up to his chin. "Let the snow fly, Venters. It can't touch us here."

Sufficiently tired, both men soon drifted into slumber in the warmth of the shelter. Outside, in the cover of the short pine, the horses stood within the heat and the slow, heavy smoke of the damp fire.

Well before sun-up, the morning following, Cole woke the deputy and emerged from the shelter. The ground was covered with a hard frost and a light dusting of snow. The stars above were as bright as he had ever seen, and the frigid air, as he took it in, stung his nostrils and lungs. The fire had burned down and only a seething ember or two remained.

As he and the deputy stood outside, their breaths condensed like puffs of smoke from a gentleman's pipe. The bores of the horses' noses also smoked against the cold.

After some salt pork and coffee, they left the canyon and made their way back to Grouse Creek. They followed the drainage upward another half mile to a depression about twenty feet deep that held plenty of lush grass and was screened on all sides by juniper bushes. While it was still dark, they put out picket lines and picketed their horses there.

Cole climbed up to a ledge overlook and cleared a spot to sit and watch. He placed his canteen and his food at his side then propped his rifle, facing forward, and made himself comfortable as he settled in for what would likely be a long wait. Deputy Venters got situated a few feet to his right.

When the sun broke softly over the ridge line, they took their field glasses and looked down over the landscape below, still cloaked in shadow. A sea of spruce timber stretched for miles. Grouse Creek sat below where it flowed from a ground spring among a jumble of rock in a ravine. Across the way was a large slide of crumbled rock, and to the west of it was a massive granite knob that jutted out from above the trees. If Jack Dill had a claim up Grouse Creek, it had to be nearby.

Cole continued to observe the landscape below through his field glasses. A long way down the hill was a little clearing cloaked in shadow. At the back end of it he thought he could see the outline of a structure tucked back in the trees.

When the sun finally spilled its light upon the shadows, his hopes were confirmed. It was a cabin. He had found the Jack Dill claim. From where he lay, he could see only the door and the window. If anyone was down there, he should be able to see them when they came out but only for a brief moment.

The time passed slowly. Around noon, he ate some salted sowbelly and canned peaches. After stabbing the last peach with his knife and swallowing it whole, he drank the remaining syrup.

The raspy caw of a raven echoed lonesomely in the canyon, then came again and died away. A yellow finch landed on a nearby juniper limb and began to sing. He watched the swelling and quivering of the bird's throat as it chirped its joyful melody. The finch was answered by a similar call from its mate, and it flew off in that direction.

The midday sun upon Cole's shoulders and back helped to chase away the chill and soothe his stiff muscles as he waited for some sign of Lundy. Two more hours passed and still there was no sign of anyone. He was beginning to wonder if he was wasting his time. After all, it had only been a hunch that Lundy might even be here. For all he knew, the outlaw could be anywhere by now.

"James Morris Fenamore," Cole said softly. "Where you at?"

A short time later, he thought he could hear the distant sound of singing and laughter. He looked over at Venters for confirmation. Venters nodded. He had heard it, too. Someone was down there, but who? Was it Fenamore, Jack Dill, or both?

Sometime later, a man stepped from behind the cabin and strolled through the trees. Before Cole could get a good look at him, the man had vanished behind a rise in the land.

He looked over at Venters who was still looking through his field glasses. The deputy looked up at Cole. "Was that Fenamore?"

Cole shrugged. "I didn't get a good look. Could have been that Dill fella."

A short time later, the muffled sound of a pick striking stone rang out on the air. This went on for a few minutes followed by hours of silence. Maybe Lundy and Dill were partners?

Cole and the deputy watched from their vantage point until dark, but the man never showed himself again. Cole decided to scan the darkness one last time before heading back to camp. As he did so, he saw the flickering glow of a lantern moving toward the cabin then reaching it. The lantern glowed from inside for a moment then went out. Whoever it was had gone to bed.

With tired eyes, Cole and the deputy gathered their horses and headed back to camp. Descending into the canyon proved more difficult in the dark, but after a few stumbles and close calls, the horses reached the bottom safely.

Cole resurrected the fire from a few seething embers then added more wood. He crawled into the shelter and went to bed. The deputy was already inside, asleep, and snoring.

The next morning, well before daybreak, he and Deputy Venters once again made the climb out of the canyon and found themselves perched on an overlook about one hundred yards closer from where they had been the day before. The new position would offer a much better view of the cabin come first light.

When the sun broke over the peaks, Cole could see a roan and a black tied back in among the trees. Behind the horses, inside a nearby corral, was two black mules and Otto's two mules. Lundy was here all right and so was Dill.

A tapping noise emanated from back inside the claim for some time until it finally stopped around noon. Moments later, a large man wearing a black felt hat and an old denim jacket over a dirty pair of overalls stepped out of the mine. He stood there for a moment with his hand shading his eyes against the sun.

"That's Lundy," Cole said. "That's Fenamore."

"We gonna go get 'em?" the deputy whispered.

"Not just yet," Cole said. "I think we ought to wait for the marshal."

Lundy looked around as he walked. At one time he looked in their direction then looked away. Seconds later he was inside the safety of the cabin. There was no sign of Dill.

Cole and the deputy watched the cabin for the remainder of the day, but no one showed outside again. That evening, back in camp, Cole built up the fire for warmth, ate some salt pork and biscuits, and turned in for the night. He found it hard to sleep.

"What you thinkin' about, Cole?" Venters said. "You been real quiet today."

"I was just doing a little thinking about how all my life I've wanted to find the man that murdered my family and now I have. And here of all places. I still don't know about the fate of my sister yet. Maybe Lundy, Fenamore, knows where she's buried. I've been thinking, too, about all the people Fenamore's stepped on or killed over the years. There's a lot of broken lives with Lundy's boot prints on them, including mine."

Venters nodded. "My ol' daddy used to always say, 'It ain't the size or the fanciness of a man's boots that counts, it's what he does when he puts them on.' I believe that was his way of sayin' that every man has choices and choices have consequences."

"True words," Cole said. "We'll all be judged someday by the tracks we leave behind." Cole lay on his back until he heard Venters snoring then closed his eyes and drifted off to sleep.

As the two slept, the smoke from the fire lifted from the canyon and drifted with the night breeze in the direction of Dill's cabin where it threatened to reveal their secret.

Surrounded

Inside the Dill cabin, James Morris Fenamore sat at the table, deep in thought. He took a cigar from a dusty box on the shelf behind him and struck a match alight on the tabletop. After lighting the cigar and shaking out the match, he took a long draw on the cigar then let out a cloud of smoke. He took a drink of whiskey from his flask, then put the cigar back in his mouth. Takin' Dill's claim had been easy. Lundy looked over at Jack Dill, bound and tied. After tricking Dill into being his partner, ambushing him had been a cinch.

Robbin' and killin' folks had always come easy ever since twenty years ago when he had robbed and murdered a family in Missouri along the Black Dog trail. It served 'em right for travelin' alone and unarmed, he mused. A few days later he had been arrested in Kansas for stealin' chickens and held in jail overnight. The sheriff had suspected him of the murders over in Missouri a few days before and questioned him but let him go for lack of evidence.

Fenamore leaned back and enjoyed his cigar. Dill had the place pretty well stocked. There were jars marked flour, cornmeal, oil, and black beans. Against the far wall was a crate of sprouted potatoes and another of onions. A few rusty pots hung near the fireplace, and a stack of books sat on a shelf.

He took one of the books and brought it back to the table. There were no words on the cover, so he opened it up to where it was marked with a black crow feather. Some words had been underlined on one of the pages, so he read the marked words out loud. "Be sure thy sins shall find thee out," it read.

Lundy stopped reading and closed the book. It was the Bible. A book he hadn't read since his Granny Fenamore had died when he was a boy. He could barely remember how she looked or the sound of her voice, but he remembered her religious ways. Granny Fenamore had been a prayin', God-fearin', Bible-readin' woman. She had raised him to the age of eight before the cholera got her. She was the only one who ever loved him.

Lundy took another drink of whiskey and looked over at Jack Dill as he sat slumped over, tied to a sturdy support beam that held up a portion of the roof. The old man was still breathin', but after the beatin' he had taken, he wouldn't be stirrin' for quite some time.

So far Dill had refused to tell him where he kept his cash money he had got from sellin' several bags of gold. But he would. He would.

Lundy tried to get the words, "Be sure thy sins shall find thee out," out of his head. A burst of wind blew open the shutter. As he went to shut it, a great horned owl began to call eerily from its perch on a spruce limb. "Hoo…, Hoo,…, Huh-huh-huh-hoo…" Its voice was low and haunting and held a tone of condemnation. Lundy shook his fist at the bird watching him now with an evil eye. The owl was a bad sign.

"What do you want?" Lundy growled. "Leave me alone." He closed the shutter and sat back down. He took another drink. Maybe the bird was trying to tell him something. Being on the run most of his life had caused him to often feel as though he was being watched. He felt that way now.

After hiding the German's gold, he had met up with Dill at the Cave Saloon and talked him into bringing him here as his partner. So here he was in Dill's cabin with Dill's gold, just the way he planned it; easy as pie.

Lundy took another drink and wiggled his big toes which were sticking out of holes in each sock. The sight of his bare toes wiggling made him laugh. He rested his feet on the large rug that stretched across the floor beside the table. The rug was dusty with many bald patches from wear, and it covered a trap door that led to a crawl space under the cabin.

The great horned owl persisted. Lundy pulled on his boots and stepped outside. "What do you want?" he hollered.

Fenamore sniffed at the air thinking he could smell smoke from someone's campfire. He decided to go take a look around.

The owl pitched from its perch and flew uphill in the direction of the overlook where Cole and Deputy Venters had been hiding. Mordecai followed the owl, muttering to himself as he climbed the steep slope. When he reached the ledge of the overlook, he sat down to catch his breath.

Once again, he smelled smoke. He got up and drew his large knife and began to walk into the wind in the direction of Cole's camp. After walking only a few more feet, he stopped to sit down again and catch his breath. He was in no shape to be climbing in this thin air. The wind up here was stiff and much colder.

A pack of wolves began to howl beyond the clearing. He reasoned to himself that it was possible the smoke he had smelled earlier had come from Dill's own chimney. And then, he was concerned about the wolves.

The thought of a warm fire, more whiskey and a soft bed beckoned him to return to the cabin. He sheathed his knife and walked back down the hill, mumbling as he went. Minutes later, he was back inside and soon asleep.

On the third morning, Cole and Deputy Venters moved to a vantage point much closer to the cabin. Cole laid on his belly for most of the morning. It was near noon when Lundy finally showed himself. He hurried towards the mine with his rifle in his left hand and a pail in the other.

Soon Lundy was inside the mine. It was midafternoon before he finally came back outside. He looked around, then hurried back to the cabin.

Cole wondered why Lundy seemed so spooked. Did he suspect he was being watched? If so, why?

Deputy Venters whispered over to Cole. "Wasn't that Fenamore?"

Cole nodded. "That was him alright."

"What do we do now?" the deputy questioned.

"I'm thinkin' on it," Cole said. "I figured for the marshal to be here by now. Let's give him a little more time before we move in."

Marshal Lindsey and his deputies made their way up Grouse Creek. They picked their way along following Cole and Venters' tracks until they came to a wide bench. From there they followed the tracks until they came to the rim of a small hidden canyon.

"It appears they went down there," Lindsey said.

The marshal and his deputies descended the steep terrain and found Cole's camp and lean-to shelter at the bottom. After looking around and finding no one, they left the canyon. Upon reaching the rim, they followed tracks north until they reached the place where Comanche and Venters' bay horse stood picketed.

By now the wind had kicked up again. Comanche greeted the sight of the marshal with a whimper and a bob of his head. Bret Lindsay dismounted and handed the bridle reins of his horse over to Dirk Ross.

"You fellas stay put here. I want to see if I can spot Cole."

The marshal crawled to the edge of the overlook and peered through his field glasses, scanning the terrain from left to right. Some two hundred feet below him, he saw Cole lying prone, facing east.

Lindsey trained his field glasses in the direction Cole was facing and noticed a cabin among the trees. Cole was watching the Dill cabin. Not far to his right lay Venters. "They're down below, boys," the sheriff said. "They're watchin' the cabin."

Marshal Lindsey observed the situation further. He noticed a draw that would lead him to within twenty feet of Cole's position. If he was careful, he could make it without being seen.

"You two stay here for now until I motion for you to come. I'm goin' down to Cole," he told Dick and Dirk Ross.

The marshal dropped off into the draw and followed it out of sight until he reached a boulder he had used as a reference earlier. Looking around the boulder, he spotted Cole to his right.

"Cole," he called out softly.

Cole turned and looked his way. It was the marshal. "Come on over," Cole said. "Be careful about it."

The marshal quick crawled over to Cole and settled in beside him. "Howdy, Cole. Is that Fenamore down there?"

Cole nodded. "He's down there alright. He's holed up in that cabin. I was waitin' for you before I made a move on him."

"Have you seen any sign of Dill?"

"No, we ain't seen hide nor hair of Dill yet."

The marshal frowned, "You reckon Fenamore's done killed Dill?"

Cole shrugged. "Hard to say for sure, but I'd say odds are Dill's stiffer than a pickle."

"Yeah, I suppose you're right."

Venters crawled over and joined them. "Is Dirk and Dick with you, Marshal?"

"Yes, they're up on the overlook waitin' for my signal."

Cole checked his rifle and his pistol. "I think we should surround the cabin and give Lundy a chance to come peaceable."

"You think he'll come peaceable?" the marshal said.

"No, I figure he'll go out with a fight, but maybe Dill is still alive. If he is, we may be able to get him back safe." The marshal nodded then turned and signaled to his deputies to come down the draw. Five minutes later, everyone was together on the same overlook.

Cole pointed with his rifle down toward some boulders outside of the cabin. "If we can get down there to them boulders, we'll be sittin' pretty good," he said. "I'll go first. You all cover me. Once I get down, I'll send for you."

"Be careful, Cole," the marshal said.

Cole nodded then headed down the mountain using the cover as best he could. Before he could reach the safety of the boulders, a shot rang out from the cabin and kicked up dirt next to him. He hot footed it on down the mountain, finally reaching the boulder safely.

Cole and the deputies returned fire on the cabin as Marshal Lindsey charged down the hillside amidst a spray of bullets. He dove behind a boulder about thirty paces from Cole's position.

"Just like old times, ain't it, Cole?" Lindsay hollered. Cole and the marshal continued to provide cover fire as all three deputies spread out and made it safely down the hillside.

Mordecai Lundy crawled over to another shooting port in a lower log of the cabin wall and continued to fire on the deputies' positions. Cole and the others returned a barrage of gunfire toward the cabin until the shooting stopped from within.

After taking a moment to reload, the marshal called out. "Fenamore, this is U.S. Marshal Bret Lindsey. We know you're in there. Hold your fire. We've got the cabin surrounded. If Jack Dill is in there with you, you better send him out right now." There was no answer for quite some time.

"Don't make us come in there," the marshal hollered. "Send out Dill, and we'll talk."

"Ain't no one comin' out just yet," came Lundy's reply from within. "If you let me go, I'll give you Jack Dill."

"We want to see proof Dill's still alive," the marshal hollered. "We want to see him."

Lundy walked over and kicked Jack Dill in the side. "Tell me where the money is, and I'll let you go."

Dill moaned and raised his head. "You can have it. There's a trap door under the rug. Under the floor is a crawl space. That's where you'll find a wooden box where I keep my cash money."

"You ain't lyin' to me is ya, Jack? Cause if ya are, I'll gut ya good."

"No, I'd rather live. I want to see my boy again down in Cortez."

Lundy cut the ropes that bound Dill's hands and ankles and lifted him to his feet then pushed him toward the door. "You try anything, and I'll shoot you in the back."

Dill opened the door slowly and stood in the doorway. Lundy stood out of sight. "This suit ya, Marshal?" Lundy called out.

"Let him go!" the marshal demanded.

"I can't do that just yet. I need him until I get what I want."

"What do you want?"

"I want you to give me a head start ta gettin' outta here."

The marshal looked at Cole who shook his head. "No, the agreement is you give us Dill, then we'll go from there. One way or the other, you're comin' back with us. Either ridin' upright or draped over a saddle. It's your call."

"I reckon I'll take my chances," Fenamore said, shoving Dill forward. He slammed the door behind and latched it shut. Jack Dill hurried for cover and joined the marshal.

"You alright?" the marshal asked.

"I'm alive. That's a might far better than I thought I'd be."

Lundy pried open a crate marked dynamite and grabbed several sticks. He lit one and tossed it out the window. His throw fell short, and the big boulder Cole was hiding behind took most of the blast.

Lundy lit another stick and threw it harder this time. When it landed at Cole's feet, Cole quickly snatched it up and threw it back through the cabin window. The explosion blew off a portion of the roof, filling the air with burning debris and smoke.

The blast knocked Lundy unconscious and tipped over a kerosene lamp that had been burning on the table. The burning fuel ran slowly along the uneven floor toward the crate of dynamite.

Lundy woke up disoriented and choking for air. He lifted the bear rug and dropped through the trap door in the floor to the crawl space below. Finding the money box, he took out the cash and stuffed it in his pocket, then crawled out the back of the cabin. He stumbled forward through a thick veil of smoke as he made his way to his horse. Black smoke was now billowing from the windows and doorway as flames began to engulf the entire cabin.

"The cabin's on fire," Cole hollered. "If there's more dynamite, the whole place is gonna blow. Let's get away from here."

As the men scrambled up the hill, the cabin exploded, sending pieces of flaming debris high into the air. The blast knocked all six men to the ground. Another explosion followed as the dynamite continued to ignite. Black smoke filled the air making it almost impossible to see.

"Look," the marshal yelled. "The forest is catchin' fire. It's goin' up like a tinder box. We've got to get to higher ground."

The men climbed on up the hill to the overlook, arriving out of breath. The air was now thick with the smell of burning spruce.

Cole took his field glasses and scanned the smoke and the flames below. To his disbelief, he caught a glimpse of Lundy on his black horse riding off into the fire.

"Lundy's alive, and he's gettin' away," Cole hollered. "I'm goin' after him." He pulled his bandana up over his face, mounted Comanche and headed back down the hill.

"Don't go down there, Cole," Lindsay yelled after him. "You'll die in that inferno."

Cole and Comanche charged on down the mountain into the smoke and flames. Within seconds, he disappeared into the thick, hot veil of smoke, out of sight.

Hot Pursuit

On his way to pursue Lundy, Cole hurried to the corral, lassoed the gate latch and pulled open the gate. Within seconds, all the mules were free as well as Dill's roan.

"Go on now, get," he said, shooing them with a wave of his arms. He turned his horse and headed into the flames. By now the dry woods were catching fire all around him, as it spread with the wind from treetop to treetop.

Given a full rein, Comanche leaped over burning logs and scraped under low hanging limbs, in hot pursuit. When Cole finally caught sight of Lundy ahead of him, he took a shot with his pistol. Lundy veered left and began to follow a gorge that cut down the mountainside. From it flowed the makings of Wolf Creek.

The flames closed in around Cole reaching at him like desperate hands that threatened to swallow him and Comanche up whole. Ahead he could still see Lundy and the black leaping through shrouds of smoke like an apparition.

Comanche seemed almost to fly as he leapt deadfalls and rocks in pursuit. Comanche was starting to gain ground on Lundy's black horse. Cole fired at Lundy again as the black leaped a deadfall and sailed on down the mountain.

Four seconds later, Comanche sailed over the same deadfall and raced onward, down the steep mountain. Cole prayed for deliverance as the mountain was becoming much steeper with each stride of his horse.

Up ahead, he began to hear horrific screams and noticed that Lundy's clothes had caught fire. The man appeared to be completely enveloped in flames as he flailed his arms wildly.

Almost instantly and without warning, Lundy and the black dropped from sight like a falling rock. Comanche followed onward just behind.

Suddenly Cole found himself thrust into a wide-open expanse of blue sky. At that moment, he went over the edge where Wolf Creek plunged one hundred feet into Wolf Lake in a raging torrent of mist and foam. His stomach leaped as he watched the surface of the water quickly rising to meet him and prepared himself for the cold blast.

Lundy, still on fire, hit the surface of the lake first, with a loud splash. A couple of seconds later, Comanche hit the water followed by Cole who hit, boots first, quickly disappearing under an array of icy bubbles. The sudden impact, followed by the cold grip of the water, caused him to lose his breath.

The air bursting from his chest was immediately replaced with an icy flood that filled his mouth and lungs. Cole clawed his way to the surface and gasped for air. As he turned around, he noticed Lundy swimming quickly toward him with his bowie knife clasped in his right hand. His face and body were badly burned.

Cole reached for his own knife, but before he could grab it, Lundy leapt on him. Cole caught the killer's wrist as Lundy tried to plunge the knife downward toward his body. The force of Lundy's weight took them both under the cold water where they struggled for control of the knife. When they came to the surface again, Cole struck Lundy in the face causing him to drop his knife.

Lundy grabbed him around the neck with both hands and held him under. Cole fought to break free but could not. As he was about to lose consciousness, he reached down to his side and drew his own knife. He stabbed Lundy in the belly causing him to release his grip. Cole wrapped an arm around Lundy's neck and held him firmly above the water

"My name is Cole Harden," he said between breaths. "Twenty years ago, you robbed and murdered my family in Missouri. I found them dead, and my sister was gone. What did you do with my sister?"

"I killed her and left her to the coyotes," Lundy gasped. He began to flail his arms and curse wildly as he tried to free himself from Cole's grip.

A short time later, Cole felt the man's body relax in his arms. He had gotten an answer, though it had not at all been what he had wanted to hear. Any hope that he once had of his sister being alive was now gone, and this broke his heart.

Cole let Lundy sink toward the bottom of the lake. The man's wild, long hair floated about him like seaweed as he sunk into the amber depths, his eyes open, staring upward. It was the end of the road for James Morris Fenamore and his murderous ways. Cole swam to the edge of the lake and collapsed on the bank, exhausted.

Comanche had swum to the far shore and now came around to be at Cole's side. The horse put his velvet soft nose up to Cole's face and blew a breath of warm air across his cheek. He gave a soft whimper as if to ask his master if he was okay, but Cole didn't respond.

A blue haze hung like mist over the mountains as the fire below continued to burn. Marshal Lindsey, Jack Dill, and the three deputies rested safely on higher ground with their bandanas pulled over their faces to protect them from the smoke. As they looked back down the mountain toward Wolf Lake, they saw a mile of smoke and flames. It was a terrible sight, and somewhere in its midst was Cole.

Bret Lindsey shook his head. "I can't believe Cole went down there after that killer. I've seen him get in a lot of tough scrapes and live, but this time is different. If it was anyone else, I'd say let's pack up and go home, but since it's Cole, we better camp up here tonight and go look for him in the morning. Maybe we'll see a miracle."

The marshal turned to Dick Ross. "Ross, I think Mr. Dill here is in no shape to travel alone. He should get off the mountain and see the Doc at South Fork. Fetch his mules and take them with you."

"I'd be obliged to ya if you'd help see me down," Dill said. "Thank ya kindly."

"We best get goin' then," Ross said.

"God-speed, Dick," the marshal said. "Mr. Dill, I'm glad to see you safe."

"Yes, sir," Dill nodded. "I hope your friend gets that no-good scoundrel."

The marshal grinned like a cat lickin' up a puddle of spilt cream. "You can be sure; Cole always gets his man."

When Cole awoke it was late in the evening, and the temperature was dropping to near freezing. He had bad burns in places. His clothes were still wet, and he had breathed a dangerous amount of smoke into his lungs.

A burning log nearby gave off some warmth, so he moved over next to it and tried to sleep. Sleep, however, was hard to come by because of the painful burns to his skin. What little sleep he managed was fitful and nightmarish.

Sometime in the night, he saw a large shape moving toward him from along the lake shore. It was Mordecai Lundy, and he was stumbling forward, dripping wet and holding his large knife. His face and body were badly burned.

The killer soon stood over him. "You shoulda' known I ain't killable," he said. He gripped his knife with both hands and plunged it downward at Cole's chest.

At that instant, Cole sat up with a gasp, his heart hammering in his chest. He was sweating and had a high fever from his burns. He felt his chest. It was fine. He looked around. Lundy was nowhere to be seen. He had been dreaming.

"Don't worry, boy," Cole said to his horse who stood over him whimpering. "It was just a bad dream. I'll be okay."

The waterfall splashed loudly across the lake, and all around him, tree trunks glowed and popped and smoked. Cole drank some water then tried to go back to sleep.

At daybreak, a horse nickered loudly from on top of the cliff above the waterfall. Comanche answered back with a loud whinny that shook Cole wide awake. He sat up and looked around. It was morning.

Bret Lindsey and his deputies sat their horses atop the tall cliff looking down at him. "I can't believe you're still alive, Cole. It's a miracle," the marshal hollered. "Are you okay?"

"Near as I can tell," Cole hollered back.

"We saw the fire swallow you whole, Cole." The marshal was puzzled. "How in tarnation did you get down there anyway?"

"I wouldn't recommend coming down the way I did."

"How did you come down?"

"At the waterfall."

The marshal looked at Venters. "Did he just say he went over at the waterfall?" Venters nodded.

"You're pullin' my leg, Harden," the marshal hollered. "How'd you get down there?"

"Right over the top. First Lundy and the black and then me and Comanche."

The marshal shook his head. "You must be the luckiest man alive." He pointed to the far side of the lake. "I see a black horse floating along the far bank, but I still don't see Fenamore."

"He's dead at the bottom of the lake," Cole hollered back.

"I can see plum to the bottom, and I don't see Fenamore's body nowhere."

"Come on down," Cole hollered. "There should be a game trail along the side of that drainage."

The marshal and the deputies found the trail and made their way down to him. "Goodness, Cole, you're a sight."

"I have a few burns is all. I'll be fine. There's some magpies fussin' over yonder," Cole said. He drew his pistol and proceeded to check it out. He found a few drops of dried blood on the rocks near a twisted pine. There were red stained drag marks leading off into the brush. Cole followed the blood into the thicket a short way until he spied Fenamore's body lying behind a bush. He cautiously moved closer. A look of relief settled on his face.

"Here he is. Dead as a rock."

The others hurried over to take a look. "That's Fenamore all right," the marshal said. He scratched his head. "I still can't figure out how he got out of that cabin all ablaze like that."

Cole shrugged, "The lake either, for that matter. I guess it don't make no difference now, though."

"No, I reckon not."

Cole searched the pockets of Lundy's overalls finding a wad of wet cash he assumed had belonged to Jack Dill. In the right chest pocket, he found two more items. The first was a round buckeye nut; the second was a folded piece of partially burnt paper. It, too, was wet.

He carefully extracted the paper and unfolded it. As he began to read it, he couldn't believe his eyes.

"Bret, you're not gonna believe this."

"What is it, Cole?"

"It's a map Lundy drew of where he hid Otto's gold, and you can still read it."

Marshal Lindsey was stunned. "You don't say."

Cole nodded with a grin. "Let's fetch Otto's mules and go get his gold back."

"What do we do about Fenamore?" Venters asked.

The marshal leaned and spat. "You fellas take him down and leave his body in the jail at South Fork so he can be photographed and identified proper. Cole and I will go fetch up Otto's gold and head on back to Platoro."

With the map Lundy had drawn, it didn't take long for Cole and Marshal Lindsey to recover Otto's gold from the hollow of a large cottonwood tree along Piedra Creek where Lundy had hidden it. After loading the gold, they headed for Platoro with Otto's mules in tow. Two days later, they arrived safely back at Platoro camp where the men welcomed their safe return.

Shortly after bidding his friend Bret Lindsey goodbye, Cole made his way to the Golden Egg claim to surprise Otto and Heidi with their mules and gold. When the couple saw their mules, they were filled with joy.

"You found our mules," Otto said. Heidi clapped her hands together. "It's an answer to our prayers!"

PLATORO THE SUMMER RANGE

"I was able to recover your gold, too." Cole lifted a bag and showed them.

"The gold, too?" Otto said.

"Yes, sir, nearly every bit of it."

Heidi raised her hands in the air and began to cry with relief. "Thank you, Lord Jesus," she said.

Otto wiped his brow. "We sacrificed and worked so hard for it. I thought for sure we would never see it or the mules again. Now we can buy our farm in the San Luis Valley."

Cole watched as Otto touched the bag of gold. "That much gold will go a long way toward helping you folks purchase a sizable piece of land," Cole said.

Heidi joined Otto's side. "Thank you, Cole. Otto and I are much obliged to you for all you have done for us. I think the Lord must have sent you to be our guardian angel this summer."

Otto stroked one of the mules gently behind the ear. "Heidi and I have been talking of going down the mountain with you when you take the herd, if it would be agreeable with you. We don't think we could spend another winter up here alone."

"That would be fine. It will be another four weeks or so before we'll be ready to leave the high country. We'll gather the herd from up above Platoro and bring them down to the meadows here. We'll also pull everything off of Red and Mammoth and the Saddle Creek. You may have cattle on your front porch again for a spell," he chuckled.

"Oh, that would be comfortin' to have the cattle around," Heidi said. "They'll keep us company."

"When we get down to the San Luis Valley, maybe we could be neighbors," Otto said.

Cole smiled. "I'd like that just fine."

He climbed back up in the saddle and sat his horse. "I best be gettin' back to the herd. I'll check in on you folks from time to time. Otto, you're welcome to ride herd with us anytime, and you both are welcome to join us around the campfire, too." Cole said. "We tell stories and read from the Bible and a book called *Ben-Hur*. We do a little singin', also. And come the seventh of October, we're fixin' to have a potluck for those who haven't left the high country yet. We hope to leave ourselves, after breakfast on the eighth, if the weather holds."

"We would like that," Heidi said. "I'll bring a pie, and Otto could bring his fiddle."

"What became of the man who stole our gold?" Otto asked.

"I'm afraid he's in hell," Cole said. Otto nodded in understanding.

"You folks keep an eye out for grizzly. Ben and Jake said one broke into Bill Shawcroft's cabin up the Saddle Creek two nights ago and killed him. They found him yesterday while bringin' down cows from the Saddle Creek bowl."

"That's only four miles from here," Heidi said. "I thought the bear was long gone."

"Yes, ma'am. I don't mean to worry you folks, but I seen fresh grizzly tracks down river just this morning. The berry crop is poor this year. The bears are out lookin' for food before they den up. It would be best to keep your meat hanging somewhere away from the house, too."

Otto nodded, "We'll be careful."

Cole tipped his hat. "It was good to see you folks again. Take care now." The Kulmans waved goodbye as he rode out of sight.

Otto put up the mules and unloaded the gold. When he had finished, he took a pail from a nail on the side of the cabin. "I'd like to celebrate our good fortune with a fresh raspberry pie tonight. I saw a patch of berries last week that should be ripe about now, and I want to pick them before the critters get to them. Would you like to come along?"

"I would like that, but I think this time I'll stay and finish the laundry while the weather is so nice for drying."

"Okay, then I should be back in an hour or so."

Heidi smiled. "Be careful. You should take the rifle with you. That bear could be around here."

"That is why I want you to keep the rifle here. Keep it with you even when you do the laundry."

"I will," Heidi nodded.

Otto gave his wife a kiss, then walked the river down around the bend and out of sight, whistling as he went.

The Return of Silver Top

Heidi went back to the house and fetched the rifle, some bullets, and a basket of laundry. She sat the laundry down, then took five bullets from the pocket of her dress and fed them one by one into the rifle, then chambered a round. She leaned the gun against a tree by the clothesline and began to scrub Otto's trousers over a washboard with a bar of lye soap. As she worked, she sang in German a cheerful song from her youth. Singing had always helped to take her mind off worrisome things, and it did so now.

When she finished Otto's trousers, she pinned them to the clothesline. As she hung out her extra dress, she began to get the feeling she was being watched. Heidi stopped and looked around a moment then went back to scrubbing and singing until she finished another arm load of linen. After wringing out each sheet and garment, she hung them on the clothesline, pinning each article neatly.

Heidi hung the last sheet and watched it furl gently in the breeze. She turned to go back to the cabin, and as she ducked under the clothesline, she stopped and screamed. There between her and the cabin was a grizzly. It was likely the same grizzly that had killed Bill Shawcroft up the Saddle Creek, she reasoned.

Now the sow bear stood just a dozen steps away, snapping her jaws while long strings of drool hung from her mouth. Her eyes appeared as black pits within yellow bloodshot circles. The bear opened her mouth and roared, revealing a cluster of sharp teeth.

Heidi screamed with all her might once again. Her gun was not within reach, and the bear was walking closer. "Jesus, help me," she screamed, as she ducked back behind the clothesline and the flapping sheets.

The sow grizzly let out another roar then charged. The angry bear became confused amidst the sheets and clothesline in which she now found herself entangled. She swiped and tore at the line, dragging it to the ground with her.

Heidi ran and snatched up the rifle just as the bear came for her once again. In her haste, the first two shots missed. The third shot hit the animal hard and turned its charge. The grizzly ran off into the trees, bleeding as it went.

Heidi shook all over. She dropped the rifle and brought her hands to her face, weeping. She leaned back against an aspen tree and sunk slowly to the ground; her face buried in her lap.

Suddenly she heard something coming up fast behind her, and she was once again gripped with fear. She turned to see Otto running as fast as his legs could carry him.

"Heidi!...,Heidi!...," he called until he reached her side, out of breath. Otto embraced her and held her tight as he observed the scattered clothes and the blood upon the ground. "It was that grizzly, wasn't it," he said.

Heidi nodded, sobbing. "Yes." She retreated deeper into his embrace.

"Are you okay?" he said.

"No." She shook her head. "I was so sure I was going to die."

Otto continued to console his wife. "It's going to be all right," he said, still struggling to catch his breath. "Let's get into the house where it's safe."

Otto helped Heidi to the cabin. Once inside, he bolted the door behind them, and the two collapsed onto the bed, exhausted. Suddenly, there was a loud thud against the door and then another. It could only mean one thing. Silver Top was back!

PLATORO THE SUMMER RANGE

Upriver a ways, Cole got word that Ol' Rebel had gone missing. Ol' Rebel's stubborn streak had once again gotten him lost or possibly in trouble. Cole had an idea where the troublesome steer might be. A short while later, he found the ornery devil in a small narrow canyon about a half mile below Platoro. He was alone, belly deep in grass, at the base of Mammoth Mountain.

Cole lassoed Ol' Rebel by his sweeping horns and pulled him along to the meadow's edge and shooed him off with a slap of his lariat on the steer's haunches. It was the second time this week the steer had gone off on his own.

On his way back, Cole passed through the meadow riding by the grave of little Eva, the dance hall girl who had been mauled by the grizzly earlier in the summer. Someone in the little mining community had made a wooden headstone and put a rail fence around it to keep the cattle away.

Continuing along the tree line of Mammoth Mountain, he came upon a good stand of raspberries that were just ripe for the picking. Cole swung down from Comanche and half hitched the horse by the bridle reins to an aspen. He leaned his gun, barrel up, against a spruce, and began to fill his bandana with the dark red berries. He couldn't help but eat some as he picked. The berries were sweet and would make for a fine pie or cobbler.

While he picked, Cole thought of Abby. Sometimes he wished he could just look up and see her standing there amongst the wildflowers she loved so much and take her in his arms and hold her tight.

He sat down a moment to rest against the big spruce and laid his rifle across his lap. The sun cast a soothing warmth upon his shoulders and caused the pine needle bedding around him to give off a pleasant aroma.

Cole tilted his hat down over his eyes and folded his arms. He smiled and closed his eyes as he continued to think of Abby. She so loved the mountains. She especially loved painting some grand vista or the numerous wildflowers that bloomed along the mountain meadows. The paintings he had seen of hers looked as real as any photograph.

Cole's breathing slowed as the sun relaxed his muscles, and his head began to droop until his chin rested against his chest. As his mind wandered with pleasant thoughts, he noticed a colorful patch of wildflowers growing within arm's reach beside him and picked a handful of them.

"Hello, Cole," came Abby's soft voice.

Cole lifted his gaze toward the sunlight. To his delight, Abby stood before him holding the reins of her horse. "Abby, is that you?" he said. "What are you doing here?"

"I missed you," Abby said. "I wanted to surprise you."

Cole walked over to Abby and held her in his arms. "I missed you, too, Abby. These flowers are for you," Cole said, holding them out.

With a smile, she took them and smelled them. "Thank you, Cole. They're beautiful."

"I brought my paints. It's such a beautiful day I thought I might sit here with you a little while and paint."

Cole set up Abby's painting easel for her as she sat on a log nearby. She took out her brushes and paint and placed them at her side then began to paint the aspen glade that lay before her and the mountain peaks that rose beyond. Cole watched her intently as the breeze lightly tossed her long flowing hair.

"I'm glad you're here," Cole said. "I missed you."

Abby smiled and gave a brief glance toward him. "I missed you, too."

Cole continued to watch as Abby dabbed carefully with her brushes into various colors and placed them carefully on her canvas. The two of them quietly enjoyed the pleasant afternoon. After a time, Abby stopped painting, put down her brush and looked at Cole.

"Remember the dream I told you that I had about you? The one where I saw something stalking you?"

"Yes," Cole said, "I remember."

"Well, I had that dream again last night, but this time I could see what it was, and it frightened me."

"What was it?" Cole said.

"It was a grizzly. I came to warn you to be careful, Cole. My dreams have a way of coming true."

Just then Abby stood and pointed. "It's behind you. Look behind you," she screamed.

Cole jerked, raised his head and pushed his hat upward as the sun shone brightly in his eyes. His heart beat rapidly in his chest. Comanche stood silently nearby, watching him curiously. Cole looked about now, clutching his gun in his hands. Abby was nowhere to be seen. He had been dreaming.

He didn't know what to make of his dream and Abigale's warning. It had seemed so real. Cole wondered how long he had been napping as he gathered up what berries he had picked earlier. Judging by the position of the sun, he hadn't been asleep long. He placed the bandana full of berries in his poke and seated his rifle in its scabbard then began to tighten the cinch on his saddle.

Comanche's ears swiveled, and he gave out a nervous whimper. The paint turned its head and looked back up the game trail behind them and began to dance and pull against the reins.

Cole turned around to see a grizzly walking down the trail directly toward him. He recognized the bear as the same sow grizzly that had rushed Bob London and likely the same one that killed Hiram and Little Eva on the Fourth of July; probably old man Shawcroft, too; the bear they called Silver Top.

The hair on the bear's face, neck, and shoulders was matted and glistened with bright red blood that dripped from a fresh wound. The instant the sow saw Cole, she let out an angry roar and charged. Cole pulled his rifle from the scabbard and began to fire as fast as he could shuck the lever. The bear took a bullet between the eyes and dropped instantly just a few feet away, where she now lay, still as a stone, with her head lolled over a log, her mouth slightly agape. Cole watched for her chest to rise, and when it didn't, he cautiously walked over to her. The one eye that looked up was pale and cast over and didn't blink when he touched it with the barrel of his rifle. Silver Top, the killer grizzly that had terrorized the Platoro region all summer, was finally dead.

Cole thought of Otto and Heidi. It stood to reason that the bear had been wounded and had come from the direction of the Kulman's cabin. He took Comanche by the bridle reins and climbed into the saddle as the horse danced nervously in a state of panic.

Cole headed for the Kulman's cabin, praying all the while. As he neared the yard, he noticed the scattered laundry and the strung-out clothesline, then a handful of spent rifle casings on the ground. A trail of blood led toward the house.

Upon reaching the cabin, his worst fears were confirmed. The door was ajar and splintered with deep furrowed claw marks. There was also a swath of wet blood smeared across the threshold of the door frame along with a woman's shoe.

"Otto? Heidi?" he hollered. There was no answer.

"Otto? Heidi?" he called much louder. There was still no answer. He stepped inside and called once more.

"We are okay," Otto's assuring voice came from the loft. He came down the stairs holding his rifle. "A grizzly tried to attack Heidi. We thought it was gone, but it came back and tried to break into the house. I shot at it through the door, and it left again."

"You don't have to worry anymore," Cole said. "I killed the bear a moment ago upriver. It came upon me while I was pickin' berries."

Heidi came down the stairs, the palm of her right hand resting flat against her chest. "Cole, you are our guardian angel," she said.

"Ma'am," Cole said. "I'm glad you folks are okay. I was worried about you."

Otto put his hand on Cole's shoulder. "We thank you, Cole. You are a good friend."

Cole smiled. "I'll check in on you tomorrow." He walked to the door and stopped there a moment to observe the claw marks once again. "My, my," he said, shaking his head as he walked out the door.

"We'll look for you tomorrow for dinner," Heidi said.

"I'll be here." Cole swung up on his horse and tipped his hat. "I'll see you folks tomorrow." He rode to the river and took it west and out of sight. He went back to the bear and skinned it, including the claws, and boned out all the meat, also saving the large portion of greasy fat that lined the bear's back and belly.

Cole made a trip up the Middle Fork with a good portion of meat and fat as a gift for the Ute. As he approached the waterfall, he called out a greeting in Ute. After a time, a man and a woman stood before him, uphill among the spruce. Cole pointed to the loaded paniers behind him. The Ute couple approached cautiously as he unloaded the precious meat and fat they so desperately needed. The man and the woman wore clothes woven of rabbit and elk skin. They nodded in thanks as he tipped his hat and rode away.

The next day Titus sought out Cole to talk to him. "Howdy, Cole. I been wantin' to talk to you about somethin' that's been weighin' on me."

Cole stopped his horse beside the cowboy. "What is it, Titus?"

Titus looked down, then away, then back at Cole. "I took somethin' didn't belong to me a while back, and now it's too late to give it back," he looked down again. "I found a money pouch of gold hidden up by Big Lake that belonged to that dance hall girl, Eva; the girl that died this summer. The pouch had her name stitched on it." Cole sat his horse quietly, listening to the young cowboy.

"I thought maybe somebody had left it for good and forgot about it, but then I met Eva at the saloon a couple days later. I didn't tell her I had took it. Now she's dead, and I can't make it good."

Cole nodded his head in thought. "Someone said she was from over to Creede. She might have relatives there that could use the money."

Titus' eyes lit up, and he nodded. "I know some folks that live over to Creede. I can write them and see if they know of her relatives."

"That would be a good start, and it would be the right thing to do."

"Is that what you would do, Cole?"

"It is."

Titus turned his horse and held his hand out. "Thanks, Cole. I'm glad you're here with us."

With the arrival of September, a true feeling of peace had settled upon the mountains. Shiloh Tremble was now in jail, the killer grizzly that had terrorized the Platoro region all summer was now dead, and Mordecai Lundy and his gang were no more.

As far as Cole was concerned, there was no better month to be in the mountains. The air seemed fresher, the sky, bluer, and the autumn colors were becoming more vibrant by the day. The bothersome flies and insects that had tortured the cattle earlier in the summer had now all disappeared with the colder frosts.

Each clear day and frosty night that passed caused the aspen to take on more color. Wild strawberries and choked cherries now ripened along sunny southern slopes, and the wood ferns had turned yellow on the hillsides.

With September also came the rutting of the bull elk. Every morning and evening the mating calls of the Wapiti echoed from the hillsides as they beckoned to potential mates. Some nights, they bugled all night long while the cow elk of the herd answered with sharp piercing whines or mews.

Many a September day Cole spent riding through golden aspen glades rounding up the cattle. He and the men tightened the herd daily as they searched for strays. When they found them, they brought them to the meadows below Platoro.

The cattle were anxious and seemed to sense the coming snows. A dozen Golden Willow beef had been sold to miners who planned to stay the long harsh winter.

The last days of September brought a dramatic release of the remaining aspen leaves. With each gust of wind, hundreds of the golden colored leaves would leap from the treetops, riding the air currents downward. It was as if God Himself was reaching into a bag of gold coins and tossing them to earth.

Some leaves made it all the way to the ground, while others sprinkled softly upon the dark green boughs of the spruce causing them to look like money trees adorned with gold coins.

"Look at the money trees," Garth said, observing the golden colored leaves upon the spruce. "I wish it really were gold coins on those trees. I'd fill my pockets full and my poke and I'd load the wagons full until they couldn't hold no more. I'd be a rich man."

"You already are a rich man, Garth, just for the sight of it all," Cole reminded. "The way I see it, any man with his lungs full of this clean air and a good pair of eyes to see all this beautiful creation is a rich man. That's the real gold."

With the arrival of October, though most of the leaves had dropped and the hillsides were stark and bare, the woods still held a magnificent beauty. The wind blew cold off the once naked peaks now handsomely clothed in a gown of white snow. Below, the air embraced a crisp chill.

Nearly all the folks and most of the elk, deer, and other critters had now left the summer range to seek out the lower elevations where the land was warm and still held herbage and vegetation. It would only be a matter of days before the first big snows came to blanket Platoro in a winter cloak, leaving it still and abandoned and pristine. The rabbits and the grouse were now dressed in their white coats as God had planned it for them, and what few leaves that still clung to the aspen were brittle and had turned a pumpkin orange in color.

By the 7th of October, Cole and the men had gathered all the cattle to the meadows below Platoro and were ready to make the trip home. The longhorns were vocal with the anticipation of going home. Some had already begun to head down the mountain on their own, following the course of the river as they went.

Otto and Heidi had all their belongings packed and tarped in their wagon so as to be ready should there be a sudden departure. Heidi had enjoyed watching and listening for the sea of cattle gathered outside her cabin window. She would miss these mountains, too. Most of all, she and Otto would miss baby Uriah as they remembered his life and the little grave that marked his short time here on earth.

It was now time for both man and beast to leave the summer range behind and drift to the lower, warmer climate of the San Luis Valley. The men were ready and so was Cole. He would miss these mountains, but he would be back again someday. At the moment, it was Abby that filled his mind and thoughts. He would see her soon.

With all the cattle accounted for and the wagons loaded and tarped, it was decided that the outfit would pull out the following morning.

At noon, the men gathered at camp where Paulie and Stump had been cooking a Thanksgiving style meal of grouse dumplins, bear roast, mashed tators, biscuits, beans, and mountain raspberry cobbler. Otto and Heidi brought venison stew and some sugar cookies and pie. After prayer and a time of giving thanks to God, everyone dug in and ate their fill.

That evening, with full stomachs, everyone was in good spirits. Cole had promised to finish reading out loud the last chapter of *Ben-Hur*. He fetched the book and opened it to where it was last marked and began to read out loud:

"The light in the eyes went out; slowly the crowned head sank upon the laboring breast. Ben-Hur thought the struggle over; but the fainting soul recollected itself, so that he and those around him caught the other and last words, spoken in a low voice, as if to one listening close by: 'Father, into thy hands I commend my spirit.'

A tremor shook the tortured body; there was a scream of fiercest anguish, and the mission and the earthly life were over at once. The heart, with all its love, was broken; for that, O reader, the man died!"

Cole stopped reading, visibly shaken by such a reminder of the great love Jesus gave for us all.

"Is there more?" Luke said.

Cole nodded and continued to read until the words finally ran out on the last page. He closed the book and looked up. The men were silent for a time as if touched in their spirits.

"That was a good book," Ben said.

"Yes, sir, it surely was," Bob agreed.

As darkness settled in, it began to snow hard. Cole and the men went to sleep early and hoped the snow would not be too deep come morning. For now, it fell slant ways upon them and piled up as it drifted and clung to the land.

The Home Coming

On the morning of October, the 8th, Cole awoke to eight inches of powdery snow and a bright sun. His breath smoked in pale wisps that hung in the cold air. The approaching dark clouds in the distance promised more snow to come.

As Cole and Stump fixed their last mountain breakfast, and Paulie readied the mules, the rest of the men still lay asleep under a blanket of white, powdery snow.

Cole was amused at the sight of the mounds of bodies buried under the snow. He watched as, one by one, each of the cowboys began to sit up, breaking through the white powder that covered them, like plants emerging from the soil in the springtime.

The older men sat up first followed by the younger ones. Each began to look around in awe at the glistening white landscape dotted with small clusters of brittle orange-colored aspen leaves that still clung stubbornly to a few of the trees.

The cattle milled around, bawling loudly, eager to leave; their backs frosted with ice. The heat from their bodies rose like steam as the sun touched their frozen hides. Moses and Samson hung around camp, close by.

Griz Montoya rubbed his eyes and yawned. "I heard the wolves howling again last night. Their voices moan of the heavy snows to come."

Titus Martin and Garth Benoit both burst out laughing at Griz' proclamation and could hardly stop to breath. "Wolves, my foot," Garth said. "I don't know how you could have heard anything last night the way you were snorin'." Everyone laughed, including Griz himself. Today he had awakened in good humor because today they would be headed home.

"I see the lead oxen are ready to go. They're calling us sleepy heads for sleepin' so late," Griz said, before yawning once more. Moses, Samson, and Trail Boss stood impatiently nearby, ready to lead the herd off the mountain.

The men soon gathered around with their cups of steaming coffee awaiting a hearty breakfast of fried potatoes and biscuits topped with lard gravy.

At breakfast time, Cole addressed the men. His eyes met with each of theirs. "I've been proud to ride with you men. I consider you all my friends. You worked hard for the brand and showed integrity. We faced some real dangers and found out what we were made of.

We mapped out new stock driveways and found steady sources of water. We learned how to best run cattle in these mountains. Some met the Lord and got to know Him as their Savior. We shared hardships, but we shared pleasant times as well. This is what God made us for."

When he finished speaking Griz walked forward. "I made this necklace from the claws of the grizzly you killed. I give it to you for leading us." He handed the necklace to Cole. "It will help you remember the summer."

Cole admired the bear claws. "Thanks, Griz," he said, putting on the necklace. The men nodded with approval.

Bob London stepped forward and also addressed the men. There was a look of sentiment and reverence in his eyes. Like Cole, there was an almost religious appreciation he held in his heart for this magnificent land they were about to leave behind.

"First, I'd like to say, Cole, that you're lookin' more and more like Griz everyday with all them claws around your neck," he chuckled. Cole laughed, too.

Bob turned to the men. "Take a good look around, fellers. There's no place like this Platoro country. It's some of God's greatest testament.

I'm proud of every one of you. McKnight will be, too, when he hears of how you all worked for the brand. I know he'd be especially proud of Cole, too, for leadin' us. We've lost very few livestock, and the cattle are as fat as longhorns can be."

Bob gestured toward the snow-covered landscape. "It may seem like the dead of winter up here, but when we get down off the mountain, it will be warm and feel like autumn again. Once we get all the cattle home and in the main pastures, you all will be paid then cut loose for a week." There was a loud cheer from the men.

London turned to Cole. "Cole, you started out this here adventure with a prayer. Would you lead us in another before we head down the mountain?" Cole removed his hat and bowed his head. The men did likewise.

"Father, we thank Thee for the opportunity to work for the brand in these mountains. We ask Thee for Thy mercies as we travel home. We thank Thee for the chow we are about to eat and for Thy Son, Jesus. We thank Thee also for Thy love and for Thy beautiful creation. We pray in Jesus' holy name, amen."

"Amen," came a collective reply.

"Everybody eat up," Stump said.

One by one everyone filled their tins with the delicious food. Cole and Bob filled their plates last and ate quickly with an eye toward an increasingly angry sky. Large flakes of snow were once again falling from a dark cloud above.

"Cole, it looks like we've got company," Paulie said, pointing upriver.

Cole looked up to see a small band of Ute Indians. There were three men, four women, and a handful of children. Two of the women were being led on poor looking ponies. The half dozen or so children followed along behind on foot.

Cole, Bob and Griz rode over to meet them. Cole gestured and said "hello" to the older man leading the first pony. The old man nodded back in recognition. There was very little emotion on his face as he approached.

"We leave mountain with you," he said, in very broken English. His eyes were filled with sadness as were the eyes of the others.

"Winter come early, stay long." The man gestured toward the snow and the dark clouds above. Cole nodded in understanding. The old Indian walked over and touched Cole's necklace and felt the claws. He nodded out of respect.

"Mama-kwa," he said, which Cole recognized as the Ute name for bear.

Cole looked at Bob. "Bob, we owe these people safe passage down the mountain and food in their bellies."

Mr. London nodded. "You're right. We'll figure it out at the bottom of the mountain. It's alright by me if you're wantin' to take 'em with us."

Cole turned to the man. "I give you my word. You will have safe travel with us."

The old Ute nodded. "Towaoc," he said. He and his people had been watching the cowboys from the cover of the woods all summer and had seen their integrity and honest work in the saddle.

A little girl about six or seven smiled at Cole. "Bith Ahatini," she said.

Cole looked at Griz for the translation. "She calls you 'the dreamer'."

Cole remembered the fitful night he had spent at Three Forks after eating the poisonous mushrooms and how he had heard those same words spoken before. He chuckled and nodded at the little girl in understanding.

A little boy about the same age as the girl clutched a carving of a bear in his left hand. He walked up and handed it to Cole. "Mama-kwa," he said. Cole took it and held it with appreciation as the old man spoke, this time in Ute, while Griz translated.

"He says it's a small gift for the meat you gave them. They call you the Bear Killer." The old man continued to talk. "He says the children are especially sad to be leaving the high country. They hold the bear to be sacred. There are good bears and bad bears. You killed the bad bear. The good bear, the big one, is their protector and friend."

"Come, have some food before the trip," Cole urged them. He motioned for them to follow.

Cole, Bob and Griz rode back to camp. The Ute followed at a distance. Cole took up what was left of the food and brought it to the Indians who ate it gratefully.

The men quickly figured out what was going on. If they had any problem with the new arrangement, they didn't let on.

After the wagons were inspected and ready to roll, Cole took his hand and swept his saddle clean of snow and mounted up. After a moment of reflection, he raised his hand and shouted, "Let's go home, men."

PLATORO THE SUMMER RANGE

The cowboys gave some whoops and whistles, then fell into their positions with the herd. The cattle were anxious to leave the snow behind and soon fell into long lines which stretched out along the wagon road.

Cole looked back at the mountains and the glistening snow covered landscape hoping to lock the grandeur of it in his memory forever. As he rode along, memories from the summer flashed like pictures in his mind's eye. He recalled bringing up the cattle, the flash flood, evenings around the campfire, and the bright starry nights; the views from Conejos Peak, baptisms at the river, the Independence Day celebrations, and much more.

As they traveled on down the wagon road, the snow began to disappear behind them. That night they made camp at the South Fork and by nightfall on the following day, they made Elk Creek.

On the third day, the wind blew hard from all directions causing the cattle to become skittish and stubborn, but by night fall, they had pushed the herd as far as Fox Creek. They made camp there, keeping the cattle up against the hillside.

The band of Ute huddled together about a hundred yards away next to a fire, cooking some roots and bulbs they had gathered along the trail. Cole took them some meat and some potatoes and bid them good night. The Ute were grateful for the food and said so through smiles and nods.

The cowboys filled their bellies and sat around the fire reliving the adventures of the summer. They got very little sleep as they anticipated getting back home to see their sweethearts, families, and wives.

Cole rode watch during the night, and come morning, noticed that Ol' Rebel had once again wandered off. At sunup, he left the herd and went to look for the missing steer. He found the animal's tracks and followed them back upriver about six miles. The tracks continued, and he had to make a decision.

Cole remembered the story Jesus told about the shepherd who left his ninety-nine sheep to go look for the one that wandered off. He decided to ride one more mile before turning back. At Sheep Creek, he saw where the track of a wolf entered the trail and then another and another. A half mile later, he found Ol' Rebel. Rather, what was left of him. The wolves had fed and gone, their tracks leading off into the spruce. Cole was sullen in his heart. He had done all he could to give the steer safe passage, but Ol' Rebel had gone his own way one too many times.

Cole reined Comanche around and rode back down the trail at a good pace hoping to get back to the rest of the herd soon. Before long he would have the others through the entrance gate and safely within the fold of the Golden Willow.

After getting word of the men's imminent return, those at the Golden Willow waited with great anticipation. Abby couldn't wait to see Cole again. Although she had gotten three letters from him over the summer, she missed the sound of his voice, his gentle touch, and the way he looked at her.

During her prayer time this morning, she sat down at her favorite spot along the river and watched it flow by. The sun was shining down through the pines causing the water to sparkle. Abby unlaced her shoes and dipped her bare feet in the cold river for a moment as she prayed. When she opened her eyes, she saw a golden aspen leaf floating on the water against the bank.

She picked it up and held it in the palm of her hand. She remembered what Cole had said in his letters about letting the aspen leaves remind her that he was thinking of her and that when the golden leaves started falling, they would be home soon after.

Abby dried it off with the hem of her dress and placed the heart-shaped leaf in her Bible and closed it up tight for safekeeping. Cole would be home soon, and the thought of him holding her in his strong arms again gave her a warmth in her heart. She smiled at the thought, then headed back to the ranch to help get ready for the homecoming.

The men and the cattle got an early start. The Ute were not far behind Otto and Heidi who were following up the drag just far enough back to avoid all the dust.

Paulie and Stump led the way, driving the wagon teams. The cattle were strung out behind them a mile and a half with the lead steers, Samson and Moses, in the front of the herd. Trail Boss soon joined them at the front, this time making the trip without her calf, Peaches. It wouldn't be long now before they would all be home.

Back home at Las Mesitas at the Golden Willow, young Brian and Lindle rode to the top of the mesa to watch for the return of the herd. It was about noon when the cattle came into view of the mesa. A lifting of dust in the air preceded their arrival.

"I think I hear them," Brian said, tilting his head as he listened.

"I can see them! I can see them!" he said, pointing.

"Praise the Lord," Lindle said, admiring the sight. He put his hand on Brian's shoulder.

"Let's ride down and welcome them home, pardner."

An hour later, Paulie and Stump pulled into the ranch yard first. "Whoa," Paulie hollered, bringing his wagon to a stop. "Boy, am I glad to see this place again. It was colder than the innards of a block of ice when we left three days ago."

"How did the mules do?" Lindle asked.

"They traveled real good goin' up and comin' down both. They did everything asked of 'em."

Paulie got down from the wagon and stretched his legs. Just then Stump pulled up with his team and chuckwagon still in fine shape. "Hello, Boss," he said. "It's good to see you again."

By this time everyone, including Seth Callahan, had gathered to welcome the men home. It was a blessed sight to see Seth sitting on the porch wavin' to everyone.

Cole and Bob headed the lead cattle toward the open corral gate and continued to bring in the rest of the herd.

"Howdy, Cole," Brian hollered from his perch on the top rail of the gate. "Howdy, Uncle Bob. Welcome back."

As Cole rode into the ranch yard, he looked for Abby, who was there waiting. The sight of her comforting smile was so refreshing it nearly took his breath away.

"Welcome home, Cole," Abby waved. "I missed you." Her eyes gleamed from below the parting of her long hair which cascaded over her shoulders.

"I missed you, too," he smiled. "It's been quite a summer. I can't wait to tell you all about it."

When he got closer, he reached into his hat and pulled out a flower which he handed to her as he rode by. "See you in a bit," he said with a smile. Cole rode off to prod an ornery steer that was reluctant to go through the gate.

The large herd of cattle kept coming as more of the men arrived with them, hollering and whistling and swinging their lariats to prod the bawling beasts onward. Cole and Bob directed the process until all the cattle and men had arrived safely through the gate and into the fold.

Otto and Heidi Kulman pulled up in their wagon followed by the small band of Ute who huddled under a grove of cottonwoods. Cole rode over to show them a good place to camp where they could draw water.

When all the cattle were penned and accounted for and the wagons unloaded, Cole stripped the gear from his horse and let him roll. He then went over to say hello. Abby waited for him on the front porch. She was wearing a white dress adorned with little blue flowers. She was smiling. Somehow, she looked different, even prettier than he remembered.

Cole walked up to the porch and dusted himself off. As he approached Abby, he removed his hat out of respect. "You look even more beautiful than I remembered, Abby," he said with a smile. He took her in his arms and held her. "I've been aching to do this for a long time."

"Me, too," Abby smiled.

PLATORO THE SUMMER RANGE

Presently, Lindle and Charlotte came over and joined them on the porch. "It's good to see you, Cole," Lindle said, reaching to shake his hand. "The cattle look fat and well cared for. It's good to have you all home safe."

Miss Charlotte smiled warmly. "I hope you'll join us for supper tonight, Cole. We can't wait to hear about the summer."

"Yes, ma'am. I'd like that."

Bob London came over and shook hands with the McKnights. "It's good to see you folks again."

"Welcome back, Uncle Bob. I'm glad you're home," Abby said. She gave her uncle a big hug.

"It's good to see you, too, Abby. You look fresh as a daisy, and Brian's sprouted like a weed at a waterhole."

"Welcome back, Bob," Lindle said. "I see we have some Indian guests. I'm pleased to see it, too."

"Cole took them in. They were awful needy."

Lindle looked at Cole. "What are your plans for them?"

"They have decided to leave the mountains. I promised them safe travel and a place to stay for the time being. I'll take care of the situation so it's not a burden to anyone."

"I'm sure we can arrange something, Cole. Until then, they are welcome to stay here as long as needed. All winter, if they like."

Cole nodded. "I better get Comanche brushed down and fed so I can get cleaned up for supper."

As he looked about, the air was warm, and the cottonwoods were a mix of green and gold. The oak brush on the rocky hillsides had turned a crimson red and the sage a golden yellow. He took in a deep breath of the sweet, sappy fragrance of willow and cottonwood that he loved so much along with the smell of the yellow colored sage that mingled with it.

After feeding and tending to Comanche, he went to his bunkhouse and heated up a pail of hot water. Cole grabbed a bar of lye soap and scrubbed off a week's worth of dirt. After his bath, he shaved and slicked back his hair. He put on his best clothes and polished his boots then laid down to rest.

Later that evening, Abby knocked on the door. "Cole, it's Abby. Are you awake?"

Cole sat up in bed. "Yes, I'm awake." he said, "I'll be right out." Presently he stepped outside on the little porch where she waited for him.

"Hello, Abby."

"Hello, Cole. I came to let you know that supper will be ready soon. Uncle Bob won't be joining us tonight. He and Aunt Beth had other plans. I was wondering if you wanted to come early and visit before we eat. We all can't wait to see you."

"I'd love to. Just let me grab my boots and my hat."

Presently, he met Abby back outside. He took her hand and walked with her across the grounds toward the house.

"I missed you every day, Abby."

"I missed you, too, Cole. It was a long summer without you."

The two walked to the house where Cole opened the door for Abby, out of respect, and followed her inside. He was greeted by the wonderful smell of a pot roast cooking. It was a comfort to be back home indeed.

Unexpected News

Cole sat in the parlor visiting with Lindle while the ladies finished up with the meal preparations. When the table was set, the men joined the ladies in the kitchen. After the prayer, everyone sat down to a wonderful meal of tender pot roast with carrots, mashed potatoes and gravy, green beans, fried cabbage, creamed peas, and warm fresh baked rolls topped with fresh churned butter and jam. It was a celebration feast indeed.

After the fine meal, dessert was brought out. Cole was given an extra big slice of apple pie on a fancy crystal dish.

"I remember you mentioned apple pie was your favorite," Abby said.

Cole nodded, "I don't believe the prodigal son himself was given a better welcome home feast." Everyone laughed, remembering the Bible story reference. He took a bite of the pie. It was delicious. He smiled while he chewed, as Abby's eyes rested upon him.

After the dishes were put away, Lindle suggested that everyone retire to the parlor to relax and visit. Everyone sat and listened with great interest as Cole regaled the stories of the summer. It was a time of laughter and much amusement as he made light of some of the circumstances they experienced. At other times, they held their breaths in quiet suspense as he told of the dangers he and the men had faced.

Brian sat on the floor with legs crossed and chin propped on his fists, his eyes resting on Cole as he listened intently. Cole showed Brian a scar from when the cougar attacked him. He also let the boy hold his bear claw necklace as he told of the killer grizzly.

As the stories wound down, the mood in the room took on a more thoughtful nature. Abby got up from her seat beside Cole and went over to the piano. "I want to play a song that I wrote for you this summer," she said.

Abby played and sang a beautiful serenade that touched his heart. Her voice sounded like an angel to him as he listened to her sing the words she wrote.

"That was wonderful, Abby. It was real nice," he said, clapping, as she smiled and bowed.

Cole looked about the room at all the gentle faces. "I feel humbled by your hospitality. It's been a real special time."

Abby stood up from the piano. "We have one more surprise for you, Cole."

She walked over to the oak bureau and picked up a letter. Her hands trembled as she handed it to him. "It's for you."

Cole took the envelope and examined it. He didn't recognize the name or address on the front. "Says it's from a Mr. and Mrs. Luke Conroy of Saint Louis, Missouri. I wonder what this could be?"

"Open it," Abby said, smiling. "Please read it out loud," she urged.

Cole looked puzzled as he unfolded the letter. He began to read it out loud:

"Dear Cole David." He stopped reading abruptly and looked up. "No one has called me that for years." He began to read again.

"Dear Cole David, I can't tell you the joy that filled my heart when I found out you were alive! When the McKnights contacted me by letter, I couldn't believe it. All these years I believed you to be dead. Now God has given you back to me."

Cole's heart was racing as he continued to read on. "It's me, your sister, Lauren Rose! I am alive and well, and I have so much to tell you."

Cole choked back a lump of emotion and stopped reading. He took a deep breath and let it out slowly. Abby and Charlotte were holding each other and already sniffling and dabbing their eyes with their handkerchiefs. Lindle blew his nose. He took off his glasses and dabbed at his eyes as well.

Cole tried again to clear the lump in his throat. His hands trembled as he continued.

"You don't have to read it out loud if you don't want to," Abby said.

Cole shook his head. "No, it's okay." He cleared his throat and did his best to read on out loud.

"I can imagine how you must have felt all these years assuming I was dead because until now, I thought the same of you. While that terrible man was killing Papa and Mamma and John Andrew, I hid in the back of the wagon. I had been sleeping when I heard voices and then screams and gun shots. I peeked through the slit in the canvas and got a good look at the man that killed them.

I hid under the mattress and crawled down through the floor of the wagon. Remember that old rotten board Papa always complained about but never got around to fixing? God had a purpose for that old board the whole time.

I kicked it out and squeezed down through the narrow hole in the floor of the wagon. I tore my dress and was cut up badly, but I got away and hid in a briar bush. I crawled as far back into the stickers as I could. I got cut up by the briars, too, but I believe the thorns kept that man from looking too hard for me there. When I was sure the man was gone, I went back to the wagon and saw Ma and Pa and John Andrew dead. I didn't see you, but I just assumed you were dead as well.

All this time I have never been able to forget that man's terrible face. A few years ago, our family's case was reopened, and I was able to provide a detailed sketch of the man's face from my memory. The constable said that the drawing looked just like a man that had been suspected for a number of other murders. The man's name was Fenamore, I believe."

Cole stopped reading for a moment as he remembered back to that terrible scene. He remembered hearing the shots then finding his family dead. He remembered finding the bloody piece of Lauren Rose's dress. He also remembered laying for hours in the dirt, crying out to God, his eyes dripping with tears, his lips quivering uncontrollably over a long string of spittle.

If only he had not taken the family's only rifle and gone off to hunt rabbits for their supper, his family might all still be alive. That had been his reasoning at the time. Now he was awakened from the terrible memory by Abby's gentle touch and soft voice. "You don't have to finish it now if you don't want to."

"No, no, I'm fine," he said. "I'm glad you are all here with me."

Cole continued to read. "After finding everyone the way they were, I was terrified. When I heard another horse coming, I ran and ran until I fainted away. Looking back now, I realize that horse I heard coming may have been yours.

I ran and walked for another two days. I was so tired and thirsty I wanted to die. A family traveling back to their home in Saint Louis found me along the road and took me in and cared for me. They said I was badly in need of water when they found me and unable to speak for weeks from the trauma.

The man was a doctor, and he knew just what to do for me. They took me back to their home and raised me as if I was one of their own children, Cole. They cared for me and loved me like angels. Remember how Mamma always said God had angels looking out for each of us? It's true.

I have been living in Saint Louis all this time. I am sorry you never knew this. I married a man who is wonderful to me. His name is Luke. He is a doctor. You would approve of him and like him very much, I'm sure.

We have three lovely children; a boy and two girls. Their names are Cole, Rachel, and Elizabeth. They have just now learned they have an uncle, and it excites them so. You have a family again, Cole. We love you and can't wait to see you. I bet you are tall and strong like Papa was. You always looked so much like him, even as a boy.

I thank God for the McKnights. They spent the summer trying to see if I might be alive. Imagine my surprise when one day I see an advertisement in the Saint Louis paper asking about me.

It's a miracle, Cole. Count it as nothing less. God cares about us all. Please write back as soon as you can. I look forward to hearing from you and catching up on your life.

Love always, your sister, Lauren Rose Conroy"

By now everyone in the room was sobbing. Cole sat speechless for a moment; his mind full of questions? "How did you find my sister?"

"We wrote to a lot of big city newspapers just in case your sister was still alive," Abby said. "It seemed like a long shot in the dark finding her, but we wanted to try. We were surprised to hear back so soon. We wrote back right away and received this second letter last week," Abby said.

"I hope you don't mind us getting involved, but it was something I wanted to do for you ever since you told me you didn't have any family."

"I can't thank you all enough," Cole said, folding the letter.

That night he spent some time in prayer thanking God for the many answers he now had for a lifetime of questions. He lay listening to the distant murmur of the river as he asked God for forgiveness for his anger and doubt, then went to sleep, at peace.

On Friday, the week following, Cole went to speak to Lindle and Charlotte in private concerning his feelings for Abby. "I know your daughter is a grown woman, but I feel it proper to ask for your blessing first," Cole said. "I would like to ask her to marry me."

"Charlotte and I have great respect for you, Cole. We have prayed for this day since the first time we met you. You have our blessing. I know you will take good care of our daughter. She's a wonderful woman."

After his conversation with Lindle and Charlotte, Cole found Abby playing the piano in the parlor. He knocked on the door. Abby stopped playing and turned around.

"Come in, Cole," she said with a smile.

Cole entered the room with his hat in his hand. "It's a beautiful afternoon. I wondered if you would like to take a walk?"

"I would love to. Let's walk up to the mesa and watch the sunset. The view from up there is so wonderful."

He and Abby walked up the rocky trail that led to the top of the mesa. "You know, you made quite a difference this summer," Abby said.

"How do you figure that?"

Abby wove her arm through his as they walked. "Well, for starters, you've made a good impression on Brian. He looks up to you. You're all he talked about this summer. 'When's Cole coming back? I wonder what Cole's doing today?'"

Cole nodded and smiled. "I think a lot of Brian, too."

"Daddy says he noticed a big difference in the boys since you got back. He says you made men out of them.

Another way you've made a difference is in the matter of Graham Lassiter. Daddy says we could have had a range war with Lassiter, but thanks to you, he's in jail in Denver along with most of his men."

Cole nodded. "The Valley will be a real peaceful place to live with them gone. I've got enough money saved to buy my own ranch. I plan to start lookin' for a spread soon here in the San Luis Valley."

Abby smiled. "You know, Graham Lassiter's spread is for sale, and it borders Daddy's ranch to the west. Word is they're dividing it into two parcels. Daddy says your friends, Otto and Heidi Kulman are planning to buy the north half. You could buy the south half. We could be neighbors."

"I'd like to ride over and look at it soon, and I'd like you to come with me," Cole said. He took Abby's hand and led her up the narrow trail to the top of the mesa. The two sat side by side on a large rock and enjoyed the view. The sinking sun cast an orange glow upon their faces.

Abby kept her arm woven through his as she leaned against his side. "You know while you were gone, I came up here and sat on this very rock and tried to guess which of those mountains you were on. If I could see it, somehow it seemed like I was sharing it with you. After your first letter I often sat outside and pretended I was with you sharing the night sky together."

Cole watched Abby as the breeze played with her long hair. "Have I ever told you how beautiful you are?"

Abby sighed. "More than once, but I never tire of hearing it."

"You are beautiful in every way."

Abby looked deep into his eyes. "When I'm with you, I feel safe and content. I had that with Keith, but I never dreamed I would feel like I do again."

Cole smiled. "When I'm with you, it takes my breath away. I feel something I haven't felt in such a long time: I feel whole and complete. I've had a lot of time to think this summer about what I want out of life and about my future. I can't see it without you in it. I've spoken to your father and mother about how I feel, and they gave me their blessing, so now I have something to ask you."

Abby took a deep breath as Cole removed his hat and got down on one knee in front of her. She put her hand to her mouth as she realized the reality of the moment. Her body trembled as her eyes welled with tears of joy.

"Abby, I want you to be the mother of my children, to share the rest of our lives together, come what may. I want to spend the rest of my life pleasing you, and I want to be the father to Brian that he needs. I want to be your husband, Abby. Will you marry me?"

"Oh, Cole, the answer is yes. I will marry you. I would love nothing more than to be your wife." Abby threw her arms around his neck, and the two held each other in a tight embrace for some time, lost in the moment.

Abby wiped tears of joy from her eyes. "I've been praying for a man like you to come along. Someone who loves God like you do. Someone who would love me and Brian and help him grow in the Lord and as a man."

Cole smiled warmly and wiped the tears from her smiling face. "I've been prayin' a lot, too, for someone like you. After all these years of ridin' the trails, I'm sure I'm where I'm supposed to be. Bein' with you feels like what's been missing is finally filled. I feel like I'm finally home here with you."

"It's was quite a summer, wasn't it, Cole?" Abby mused.

"Yes, it was." He held the woman he loved in his strong arms and felt her retreat deeper into his embrace.

Abby squeezed his arm and smiled. "We can get married in the spring, and we can send for your sister and her family and the Reverend can perform the wedding at the church. Afterwards, we can have a feast and music. It will be wonderful."

Cole leaned over and closed Abby's soft lips with his own. He felt her form relax in his embrace once again. Still wrapped in his strong arms, Abby turned her face toward the setting sun and smiled. "Welcome home, Cole Harden," she whispered. "Welcome home."

Steps to Salvation

Is your life empty and unfulfilled? Did you know that you can be saved from your sins? The only way to be at peace with God and have a fulfilled life is through salvation in Jesus Christ.

Recognize Your Sin

"All have sinned and come short of the glory of God." (Romans 3:23)

"If we say that we have not sinned, we make [God] a liar, and his word is not in us." (I John 1:10)

Repent and Believe

"Repent ye therefore, and be converted, that your sins may be blotted out, when the times of refreshing shall come from the presence of the Lord." (Acts 3:19)

"That if thou shalt confess with thy mouth the Lord Jesus, and shalt believe in thine heart that God hath raised him from the dead, thou shalt be saved. For with the heart man believeth unto righteousness; and with the mouth confession is made unto salvation." (Romans 10:9,10)

"He that believeth and is baptized shall be saved; but he that believeth not shall be damned." (Mark 16:16)

Follow and Serve Christ

"My sheep hear my voice, and I know them, and they follow me: and I give unto them eternal life." (John 10:27,28)

"Seek ye first the kingdom of God and his righteousness." (Matthew 6:33)

"Let us hold fast the profession of our faith without wavering." (Hebrews 10:23)

"Be thou faithful unto death, and I will give thee a crown of life. He that overcometh shall not be hurt of the second death." (Revelation 2:10,11)

Bibliography

Dobie, Frank J. (1981). *The Longhorns*. University of Texas Press.
Haley, Evetts J. (1949). *Charles Goodnight-Cowman and Plainsman*. University of Oklahoma Press.
Gwynne, S. C. (2010). *Empire of the Summer Moon*. Scribner.
Sides, Hampton. *Blood and Thunder*.
Chrisman, Harry E. (1998). *Lost Trails of the Cimarron*. University of Oklahoma Press.
Ambrose, Stephen E. (1996). *Undaunted Courage*. Simon & Schuster.
Moulton, Candy (2001). *Everyday Life Among the American Indians 1800 to 1900*. Writers Digest Books.
Moulton, Candy (1999). *Everyday Life in the Wild West 1840-1900*. Writers Digest Books.
Ludwig, Wayne (2018). *The Old Chisum Trail – From Cow Path to Tourist Stop*. Texas A & M University Press.
Peterson, David (2009). *Ghost Grizzlies – Does the Great Bear Still Haunt Colorado?* Raven's Eye Press.
Pettit, Jan (2018). *Utes – The Mountain People*. Johnson Books.
Ross, Dick (1997). *Lakes and Trails of the Conejos*.
Feitz, Leland (1969). *Platoro Colorado – A Quick History*.
Feitz, Leland (1998). *Conejos County – A Quick History*.
Kershaw, MacKinnon, Pojar (1998). *Plants of the Rocky Mountains*. Lone Pine Publishing.
Evenson, Vera, Stucky (1997). *Mushrooms of Colorado*.
Wallace, Lew (1880, 2015). *Ben-Hur*. Harper.
Buckley, T. R. Cowboy *Songs and Poetry*.

About the Author

After studying creative writing at Missouri Southern State University, the author moved to Platoro, Colorado where he gained firsthand knowledge of cowboy culture by driving cattle with local cowboys in the mountains around his home. With more than twenty years of careful research, the author gives the reader a vivid and authentic window into the past in this historical, inspirational thriller.

The author's hobbies include hunting, kayaking and nature photography as well as helping with a ministry his brother started called Peterson Outdoors Ministries which provides faith-based outdoor retreats and adventures for active military and wounded veterans and their families.